MODERN DIVINATION

ISA AGAJANIAN

MODERN DIVINATION

First published 2025 by Tor
an imprint of Pan Macmillan
The Smithson, 6 Briset Street, London EC1M 5NR
EU representative: Macmillan Publishers Ireland Ltd, 1st Floor,
The Liffey Trust Centre, 117–126 Sheriff Street Upper,
Dublin 1, D01 YC43
Associated companies throughout the world
www.panmacmillan.com

ISBN 978-1-0350-4998-1 HB
ISBN 978-1-0350-4999-8 TPB

1 3 5 7 9 8 6 4 2

A CIP catalogue record for this book is available from the British Library.

Typeset by Palimpsest Book Production Ltd, Falkirk, Stirlingshire
Printed and bound by CPI Group (UK) Ltd, Croydon, CR0 4YY

For Wendy. I know you would have been so proud of me.

PROLOGUE

Her own face lasted longer in the public eye. It was plain, unassuming and, most importantly, it was easy to forget.

It still took effort to maintain this shape, admittedly less than for a full-body transformation. Her edges weren't normally this clean, but rather faded like residual colour on a dirty paintbrush. Her eyes were brown, but not nearly this bright. Under this spell, her appearance still boasted some semblance of life, even if the reality was much grimmer.

Leona Sum was dying. Slowly. Unforgiving to the eyes.

A young woman with dark ringlet curls entered the bathroom behind her, flashing a cordial smile to Leona's reflection in the mirror before disappearing into a stall. She reeked of power, of gods-gifted magic. *A goldmine,* she thought. Of what brand, Leona could only discover by trading one spell for another – this mask for a moment of facing her true form.

Leona's fingers curled around the edges of the sink. Her mask slipped undetected. The colour in her skin faded to ash. Her unglamoured body had wasted to paper skin and brittle bones during her pursuits of change. She couldn't stand to face herself in the mirror, so she cast her gaze to the sink.

She didn't need to see the other woman to find out what

magic she possessed. This spell spread like a sound wave, emanating from the epicentre of her body, until it could needle out the truth. What kind of magic was the girl hiding? Was it anything useful? Anything that could save her?

She'd given up trying to prevent her looming death. The end was inevitable, after all, and she was in no position to challenge fate. But Leona knew this was not where she was supposed to be when judgement day came. She would be the rising sun of a new generation of witches, at the helm of a new order. She would die a saint. A martyr. She would not die without having first changed the world. And for that, she needed to live.

If the magic in her own body wouldn't sustain her long enough, she'd have to get creative.

The toilet flushed. Leona killed the spell like the embers of tobacco beneath her foot.

'Did you hear that too? That whistling?' the girl asked. She started the tap at the sink beside Leona, scrubbing her hands raw.

Leona laughed, settling back into her new skin. 'I thought I was just imagining it.'

'Oh no,' the girl said. 'I would have assumed it was you, but it didn't sound like anything humanly possible.'

Leona watched the girl flick her hands dry. Whistling? Over the years, she'd developed her own catalogue of magical responses to the spell, each one a tell for the gift a witch possessed. Whistling was new, not something she could trace back to a magical gift she'd encountered before. It could be good. Promising. Interesting, at the very least.

'I *love* your shoes, by the way,' Leona said.

The girl paused beside the hand dryer, shifted her weight onto her other hip and smiled. 'I'm so glad you said that. I couldn't tell if they were too clunky for the outfit tonight.'

Small talk could get you far. Small talk could make great waves in the grand scheme of things. The girl was comfortable here in this conversation. She could afford to keep her friends waiting. Leona had seen the group of supposed uni students positioned sparsely around a large booth before she came in. Blithe smiles, vodka-flushed faces. The scent of magic had been clear: of the group, one body possessed blessed blood.

'Are you a student?' Leona asked.

Her last sourcing in Edinburgh had been messy, which drove her back to England, and then *here* to Cambridge, which she hadn't touched yet. She could only assume the girl beside her belonged to one of the many colleges. If Leona had known it would be this easy to spot a witch, she wouldn't have wasted so much time.

The girl nodded. 'Medieval studies, actually. Are you?'

'I wish,' Leona said. 'I think I'm past my prime for uni.'

In truth, Leona was only thirty-three, but her affliction aged her decades. What the girl could see of Leona Sum made her dismiss the comment entirely. 'Hardly. We don't all get into academia the same way. There are plenty of folks in my programme that took their time getting here. It's not about age. It's about how you want to spend the time you have left. I'm keen on spending it studiously.'

Perhaps, if Leona had more of it, she would have agreed. She couldn't remember the last time she'd wanted to do anything other than survive.

Still, she gave a wistful sigh. 'I've thought about it.'

'Are you here with anyone?'

'Stood up, actually.' A shameless lie. 'I was supposed to meet someone, but . . .'

'You're welcome to join us if you want a drink. I'm Margarita,' the girl said with a small tilt of her head. 'I swear we are all proper adults with good conversational skills.'

'I wouldn't want to impose.'

'What's a worse imposition than being stood up? I should head back outside now, but if you change your mind, I'm at a booth near the centre. If not, it was nice talking to you. I needed that compliment.' The witch, Margarita, wiggled her shoe before turning on her heel. 'See you around.'

Leona checked the time on her mobile as the door swung shut. Her husband would be irate with her if he knew. If they could still stand to look at each other while sharing the same bed. The late hour was nothing to him, but being *here,* doing *this,* defied each and every one of his wishes. She'd have to lie. Again. He was always much harder to lie to.

A new face looked back at her in the mirror's reflection. Leona didn't fuss with the details on this one; it was a different enough visage from the former that Margarita wouldn't bat an eye once it passed her. She left the loo, ordered herself a drink at the bar, and turned her sights to the little TV screen hanging behind the counter.

'Crazy, isn't it?' said one of the other students behind her. 'I can't imagine any of the stolen pieces are worth much.'

'You don't think anyone on the dark web wants some old bones?' asked another.

'Maybe,' Margarita said. 'Seems like a lot of unnecessary work for bones though. I imagine they're simpler to source than through museum theft.'

The barman slid Leona a drink. The news broadcast above her head paired tasteful, close-up shots of forensic evidence collecting with a slow cycle of missing artefacts from the National Museum of Scotland's collection against a white backdrop. The glass felt heavy in Leona's hand as she tilted it back.

'What about the coins?' someone asked.

'What about them? They're rusted as hell.'

'*Someone* would want that. Someone would probably pay big money for a piece like that.'

'Maybe,' Margarita repeated wearily. 'I think we should order a round.'

'On you?'

'If the table pleases,' she said, to which they all jeered in agreement.

Leona heard her squeeze out of the booth. With her magic – her *body* – weakening by the day, would Leona's shape hold? If the girl got too close, would she see through the different shape of Leona's eyes or the slope of her nose like the illusion of a two-way mirror? If no one had seen the mask slipping yet, they would soon. This was probably her last chance at sourcing a gift that could fix her.

Margarita's hand grazed Leona's bicep by accident as she leaned over the crowded countertop to order. 'Sorry. Excuse me.'

Leona shifted her stool aside, feigning disinterest in the girl, and returned her attention to the news.

At the National Museum of Scotland, authorities were still cleaning up her work. Their current count of vacancies in their collection was still off by half a dozen. They made no mention of the iron collar she'd taken or the cursing bone residing in her bag.

Even stranger, they didn't mention the blood. She hadn't meant to leave it there; she just hadn't had the time to clean it all up before dawn.

Not that she wanted them to find it. Rather, the negligence of humans astounded her more and more every day.

In any case, Leona Sum had cleaned up better than she thought.

PART ONE

CHAPTER ONE

The colour of magic was gold. Glittering, fluid, and uncommonly bright as of late.

Aurelia kneaded her eyelids, trying to break the blinding, gilded wall resurrecting itself behind her eyes. The annotated pages of her study material lay flat before her, lit by streaks of early morning light, yet Aurelia could hardly read them, and every word had since lost its meaning.

Her housemate, Ryan, cleared their throat from the doorframe of Aurelia's bedroom. 'Did you get *any* sleep last night?'

Twisting in her seat, Aurelia offered a conspiratorial arch of her eyebrow. Years of cohabitation with countless sleepless nights strung between the pair meant that Ryan wouldn't have to ask twice. They knew better than to question, to tease, to tell Aurelia Schwartz that her habits, no matter how ingrained they were into her daily routine, were unsustainable.

Nothing would change, just as nothing *had* changed. But that only served to further a miserable point: Aurelia's magic was faltering for a reason she couldn't place.

'How were drinks last night?' she asked. 'Anyone miss me?'

'*I* missed you terribly,' Ryan answered, accepting an open

invitation to curl up on the twin bed beside Aurelia's desk. 'Though, I can't speak for the others.'

'Damn.'

Aurelia made herself as attentive as possible for her housemate's recollection of the previous night, though her stomach was roiling with a hunger she'd been neglecting for hours, her vision teasing sinewy threads of gold at its edges. Ryan's lethargy was palpable; Aurelia's was no simpler to mask. For once, it worked in her favour. One of the few odd benefits of her inhuman state was her exceptional management of alcohol, which fielded plenty of jealousy from her housemate when they were stumbling home from the pub on her arm or throwing up their last meal in the bathroom. Ryan didn't realize, and could never discover, that alcohol had no effect on her, or that every time they'd been drunk together, Aurelia was *lying*.

'It was nothing special,' Ryan said, sighing like a sad dog. They removed the beanie that was practically fused to their shaggy, yellow bleach job long enough to rake a hand through their hair before swiftly replacing it. 'We talked. We drank. We said goodbye about ten times before anyone actually left. Only difference was I wobbled home alone.'

Aurelia shut the book in front of her, the tabletop mirror's reflection taunting her from across the cover. 'I was busy.'

'Yeah,' Ryan lamented, '*so* busy. I'd like to think I'm more enjoyable to spend time with than . . . What's that you're reading?' Squinting at the title through their rectangular glasses, Ryan conceded with a shake of their head. 'I'm losing to *Homer the Theologian* for God's sake. Next, you're going to tell me you don't want to live with me any more.'

Aurelia scoffed and scraped the remnants of mauve lipstick away from her mouth with a bitten fingernail. 'And make you look for a new housemate? I wouldn't do that to you.'

'Because you love me more than Homer?'

Ryan could ignore the evidence of fatigue on her face, but Aurelia couldn't stop her gaze from wandering to the blood vessels in the corners of her eyes or the colour caught in her chapped lips. Aggravated roadways of red in all the wrong places. She wished she could excuse it with a hangover, but there was no facet of being a witch that wasn't a double-edged sword.

Aurelia's fingers clamped around the ticklish spot on Ryan's knee and squeezed. 'Mhmm. More importantly, I wouldn't do that to myself. I think Frederick's going to raise our rent soon.'

'Figures. You know, Lawrence was there last night. Bet *he* missed you.'

'What makes you say that?'

'Weren't you seeing him?'

Aurelia let herself snort. 'You're really funny, Ry.'

'I wasn't being funny. He's got a nice nose. Like an ancient Greek sculpture. Charming too.'

None of that was untrue about Aurelia's university colleague. Lawrence Kressler was soft-spoken, tender enough to sink teeth into. Too kind to have been afforded the messy break-up Aurelia made from him. His hair was the colour of walnuts, always soft between Aurelia's fingers. His smile came with a refrain, a nervous curve starting on one side of his mouth before the other. That smile was the second thing she'd loved about him. The first was that he'd smiled at her at all. He was decent in a way that many of her peers hadn't been. She'd long since fallen behind socially, and no one else had been kind enough to meet her where she was.

Realistically, Aurelia knew she had no room in her life for variables like him, for decent boys that needed to be assured they were more than decent, boys with doe eyes and soft hands that searched for love instead of short-sighted flings. He'd tell her he didn't have to do serious, but she never trusted those words. It was a lie when he'd said it. When other men and some other women had said it. Having said it before, pretending that it was the truth, Aurelia knew that Lawrence's heart was more delicate than hers. It demanded things she couldn't give, even if he was too kind to ask for them aloud.

She wished often, with the soft and wanting, too-human piece of herself, that she had more to give. Ryan knew that better than anyone, so they added nothing, sensing the sore spot they'd inadvertently prodded.

Aurelia pushed the chair back from underneath the desk. 'I'm going to make us some tea.'

'Thank you.'

'Because I *do* love you more than Homer,' she said. That part was never a lie. Ryan's mouth tipped into a grin beneath the severe tug of their hat past their nose, none the wiser that anything Aurelia could say to them might be untrue.

It was hard not to let such earnest looks of adoration eat at her like a burning candle; the secrecy of her mere existence spawned a welling guilt inside of her. She felt her housemate's needling affection follow her down the steps of their shared house to the tiny kitchen, staring her in the face through the open drawer of her tea supplies. It had taken years for her collection of teas to grow this large, but each box, jar and loose tea bag encroached into precious drawer space that used to belong solely to Ryan, and every charmed cup of tea she made for them was a payment more costly than anything they could have imagined.

As a green witch, assembling an efficient tonic came as naturally to Aurelia Schwartz as breathing, but the sensation of a working spell – a vital difference between herself and her beloved, human housemate – gave her no satisfaction today. Her fingers hovered restlessly over the jars of loose-leaf blends and various herbs. Seconds passed, and she swallowed hard. It should've been simple. She shouldn't have had to speak the words aloud to source her herbs or imbue her blend with something stronger than botanicals, because true magic was born of blood and intention. Those spells that were born of mere thought, that took more effort to stop than to release, were the easiest to forgive. She let them slip in secret like a held breath.

But a spell as simple as this should not have resisted her. She could feel her magic pressing on the inside of her skull, her vision pulsating with brightness.

And gold everywhere her mind wandered.

She flexed her fingers impatiently, then cracked her knuckles one by one. She didn't *need* magic to make tea. No hangover tonic was worth a bruised ego first thing in the morning. She plucked an unmarked sachet of lavender and chamomile, placed the kettle on the stove, and searched for a task to distract herself while the water boiled.

The house had at least one faulty fixture at any given time; Aurelia had lived with Ryan for almost four years now and tested a number of magical fixes for all of them. None were particularly taxing or intricate. It was all common magic: a foundational toolkit of spells – or intentions – that any witch could access. Common magic required little energy from the spellcaster and made maintaining the creaky, narrow house in Cambridge significantly less costly.

Which Aurelia and Ryan needed direly. Ryan had been renting the house at an unbeatably low price from a friend of their parents' whose patience was wearing thinner with every house key they lost. Aurelia could afford the rent split with consistent waitressing or tutoring, but only until their landlord, Frederick, decided to evict them, and that possibility was becoming more likely every day.

The persistent leak of the sink faucet was evidence that Aurelia's most recent charm had worn off. She jiggled the neck of the faucet, frowning.

From upstairs, Ryan asked, 'Have you eaten yet?'

She couldn't remember the last thing she'd eaten. At the mere suggestion of food, her gut turned in anticipation. 'What do you want?'

'Some toast, maybe.'

'And jam?'

'If you're feeling generous.'

Aurelia nodded to herself, relieved. She couldn't sabotage toast in any way that really mattered. She needed something to focus on. Even sleepless, her mind was abuzz with worry. If she could not commit herself to a single thought, she'd flit through all of them restlessly until she was worn down and utterly useless. And there were big things waiting for her at the end of this week, *promising* things that required all her vigilance to make use of. If she couldn't keep her magic in line, she would make sure every other facet of her life was precisely where it needed to be.

Except for their bread, the lonely, hardened end of which dangled limply at the bottom of its plastic wrap. Aurelia glanced at the time flashing over the stove, then moved to pour Ryan's cup of tea instead. The window to her left faced an empty street, but she could hear the whispers of a conversation slowly nearing. She drew the blinds shut, turned toward the cup, and mouthed the words to a simple incantation: *I wake the body, the soul, the mind.*

If it worked, she felt no relief from it. Aurelia brought it upstairs, setting it down on the corner of her desk to cool. 'Come to Tesco with me. We're out of bread.'

'But it's so bright.'

'Please? I have to meet with Dr Carney in a few hours.'

'Again?' Ryan wiped their glasses on the hem of their sweatshirt so that Aurelia could see their eyes narrowing back at her. Aurelia's supervisor had seen more of her lately than Ryan did, assigning her small, unofficial jobs like cataloguing the scores on his undergraduate papers or switching out the cartridges in his pens. Dr Carney was old and lonely. His hands were stiff with arthritis, and Aurelia could sit quietly, humouring his long-winded, mumbled musings on the new journal publications he was reviewing.

It wasn't the worst way to spend an extra hour each week. If it meant she could be 'astute' and 'dedicated' in any letter of recommendation he wrote for her, Aurelia would nod and hum until she'd made herself his favourite disciple. If she played her cards right, she could stretch his word into a prosperous future for herself in academia.

'Fine. I'll go by myself, then. I'll be quick,' Aurelia assured them. 'I'm booked solid with tutoring sessions until the end of term and a faculty dinner at the end of the week. Bread's the only thing I have time for right now.'

'So, I lost to bread, then,' Ryan lamented. 'That's even worse than Homer.'

But it was always *time* that seemed to be the issue for Aurelia Schwartz. It moved too quickly to catch hold of and enjoy. It spurned her advances like an unrequited love. She was constantly out of it, or with too much of it dispersed between periods of sporadic busyness – in all cases, she was left wholly unsatisfied.

She fixed her curls in front of the little mirror, defining the most obedient dark strands with a pinch of her fingers. She grabbed a jacket from the foot of her bed, then her sturdy tote bag from the frame. Leaning against the door-frame, she wiggled her feet into her worn leather Chelsea boots and commanded, '*Drink*. Before it's cold.'

'What would I do without you?'

She straightened her back, deceptively proud as if she was not perpetually guilt-stricken over things that were out of her control. The truth was that Ryan Jena would not love her so much if they knew what she was, and that forced Aurelia to become something worse than a witch: a liar. But what Ryan didn't know couldn't hurt them, so Aurelia answered, also truthfully. 'You would miss me terribly.'

*

Like most things in the natural world, the definition of 'witch' had evolved from one form to the next. The tools that made a modern spellcaster could be bottled and sold, priced like produce at a farmers' market or a carnival prize. Every other bookstore from her home state of Washington, USA to Cambridgeshire, England had a niche dedicated to the spiritual practitioner, prescribing meditation and green eating as magic for the lost soul. As with the word 'witch', so did magic take on new meanings.

There was a fine line between the realm of humankind and the realm of the mythical, and Aurelia Schwartz trod it like a tightrope over two high-rises. It corded around her bones, the difference rooted deep within her nervous system, colouring her blood a darker shade of red. It was most poignant on days like these, where the late autumn leaves had all been squashed into piles of mulch along the stone sidewalks of Cambridge, ushering in the frigid temperatures of winter. The sound of rustling branches was as integral to her survival as her heartbeat, thrumming in time with her pulse. Pausing briefly on her walk to Tesco, she bent to pluck an unbroken leaf from the ground, then pocketed it.

For a witch with the gift of green magic like her, energy was a deliberate choice. Cambridge was flowering and replete with vegetation, and life could be siphoned from the deep inhales of any scenic route. She absorbed some energy from the petals on which she stomped – a spell being as simple and undetectable as tearing a leaf or a weed from between cobblestones to pin to her bedroom wall.

If she felt brave enough, she could speak the words aloud:

Fulfil me. But that would forever be the extent of her spell-casting. She only performed spells that were necessary to keep her magic functioning and finely tuned like an instrument, and she refrained from all the frivolous casts that could indict her.

Anything more than the bare minimum was a risk she didn't dare to take.

Not that green magic was inherently dangerous. It was one of the more benign gifts among witches. Gifts gave a witch the secret language of more specialized intentions – some strange, some deadly. Some, like Aurelia's, could make feasts blossom, fill bellies with fresh fruits and well-rounded potatoes.

With words unspoken, she made things grow. She only needed to know the right ones.

Still, even the most harmless spells felt dishonest when they were failing.

Aurelia didn't know when it began, but she remembered the first time she'd been afraid of it. Two weeks previously, in mismatched levels of inebriation, she and Ryan had been walking home from a gathering not unlike the one she had missed last night. Their street was vacant, save for a few chittering birds collecting tourist litter off the ground. Some more silent ones watched from above, nimbly dodging the spikes on apartment rooftops.

She remembered thinking to herself that the local birds were *too watchful for their own good.* Just before her boot caught on a crooked cobblestone and sent her stumbling. A spell burst free from Aurelia's outstretched hand to keep her from kissing the rain-slicked road. She hovered above the ground in shock, silently cursing the birds for their distraction, scrambling to her feet before Ryan noticed anything amiss. A trail of gold dust settled between the stones in her wake – a signature in the shape of her hands. It was the colour of magic, the residue of spellcasting. It could have been a beautiful thing if it wasn't so damning.

Had it been only an hour earlier in the evening, an accidental outburst like that would have been met by the disbelieving stares of other university students or the inebriated, half-shut gazes of people stumbling out of pubs – any of whom could have called attention to the peculiarity.

Of course, she was more than a peculiarity. More than a trick of the light or an inconsistency. More than a mirage or a liquor-fuelled vision. But being just that in the eyes of a human was all she could hope for. With any luck, they'd blink, and she'd vanish.

She took a different route to Tesco so as not to pass the scene of her slip-up. Paired with the uncertainty of the morning, Aurelia didn't know if she could stand to return to that street. She'd been avoiding it like the plague and stepping on cobblestones as rarely as possible.

Her turning stomach sabotaged her beeline toward the bread. She reached into a refrigerator and turned a pre-packed, hard-boiled egg over in her hand, skimming for an expiration date.

'Fancy seeing you here.'

That voice had her grimacing within mere seconds. She recognized it immediately, her fingers digging relentlessly into the soft egg. They'd had enough overlapping classes over the years to recognize the sound of each other's footsteps, to know the face behind the words written on all their assignments.

Theodore Ingram. It was almost impressive how immediately he made her recoil.

'Oh. *You.*'

Her nose wrinkled involuntarily – he was like a foul smell she couldn't clear from her sinuses. He was a tall, pale boy with deep auburn hair and small features that were perpetually turned up in smugness. Seeing his face so often across lecture halls, through library shelves, trained into a mask of arrogant determination, had cursed her with the urge to touch her finger to his brow and push him hard like a sticky button.

His eyebrows now knitted together in irritation like he was trying to banish a ringing from his ears, but it wouldn't subside . . .

Like she was an itch he couldn't get rid of.

'Don't look so pleased to see me,' he said, bearing a shopping basket full of assorted produce like armour to defend against her vitriol. His unbuttoned tailored coat swayed at his knees, making him a shapeless shroud of black wool and misery.

'I try not to,' she said, stuffing the egg back in its refrigerator slot. 'I'm just surprised, you know. I didn't think you'd have time to leave your house with all those grant applications you've been submitting.'

Ingram smiled shrewdly. 'Have you been following my work, Schwartz?'

'No,' she rushed, teeth gritting as the clear door shut heavily. 'It's just impossible to ignore that the Venn diagram of our applications is a circle.'

'There's no point in being jealous,' said Ingram, which was

already more than he usually said to her on any given day. Aurelia bit her tongue as she moved to her intended aisle to pick at the plastic wrappers of bread loaves until she found one she wanted. He was exceptionally skilled at uncovering her hidden insecurities, but she didn't need to start laying them bare for him any time soon. 'I know you got one of the field-work awards recently. What do you plan on doing with it?'

'Don't you have something to do today? Elsewhere?' As Aurelia scanned her item at the self-checkout, Ingram began unloading his basket of produce at the station adjacent to hers.

'Since you asked.' He had a habit of speaking in fragmented sentences, as if every word was a white-hot iron in his throat. 'Might go home and read. Nice day to relax.'

She pictured him in a house by himself, plush slippers by the door, and heirloom furnishings scattered about a sitting room. The kind of comfort and elegance Aurelia could only dream of seemed like nothing, like the bare minimum, when she was picturing him there. His presence constituted a finer way of living. She was torn between resenting people like him and wanting to be one. How she ached to be so cavalier – to belong to his group of posh socialites just to know what the view was like from so high up.

Pity she hadn't figured it out yet. Three years in opposition with the same group of peers should have been more than enough time to decide she didn't care for most of them. She discovered second hand how intimate they all were with one another – unearthed the sensitive promises they made and ruined like relics of a bygone era. She gathered that, for a collective whose common trait was wealth and abundance, they built their allegiance on the things they *didn't* have. Love, attention, *trust.* They all spoke in debts and currency. Of time that was wasted and patience spent.

And she was certainly well aware of the comments they made to undermine her work.

Before Aurelia had befriended Lawrence Kressler, she'd overheard him in conversation with the taller, dark-haired boy in the library. Aurelia's name in Lawrence's mouth was like a sweet candy as he bolstered her latest work on medieval occultism like it was his own to be proud of. Ingram had spoken, it seemed, just to tear her down – the beginning of a pattern that'd run for years. The inception of a never-ending cycle.

'She's a novelty,' Ingram had said, thinking they were alone. 'Nothing more than some American fad that Carney's dieting on.'

For days afterward, Aurelia replayed that moment in her mind, wishing she had never heard it. But she did. It was then that she realized some words flowed from him like honey and silk, but he was keener on the type that would sting.

Aurelia dragged them to the forefront of her mind whenever her thoughts veered into idealism.

'I heard Tricia's doing something tonight,' Ingram added in what was obviously an afterthought while Aurelia twisted her fingers into the loose plastic.

'Tricia Werner from class?' she asked.

A touch of bemusement etched itself into his features at the thought of knowing something she didn't, and she wished she could crush that look beneath her foot. 'Another *study group,*' he said.

Tricia's study groups were known among the history students to be more akin to dinner parties than study groups – the kind Aurelia often saw in movies where everyone wore turtlenecks and loafers and smoked cigarettes while draped over the couch. In her mind, the weight of old money lined the pockets of each attendee and shrouded their faces in silk. There was something *hip* and elite about being there. Maybe it was the fact that Aurelia never got invited.

'I wouldn't know,' Aurelia said, allowing the edge in her voice to creep through. She hated giving him the satisfaction of being a scab on her mind, hated that one of many things he had to be so good at was knowing her faults. Every conversation was infused with something devilish and superior, like he knew well how easily he could wield her discomfort like a weapon.

He always looked like that, though. Like he was in on a secret that no one else knew and hung it over their heads like dread.

'Are you going?' she asked.

Ingram shrugged. 'Not my thing.'

'Then why did you ask?'

'Curiosity.'

'Super.' With a squeak of her boots on the tile, Aurelia took her bread and left the checkout station and—

Whiplash. Perhaps it was the immediacy of the turn. She kneaded the inner corners of her eyebrows and shut her eyes for a moment against the gloom outside. Nothing seemed to help. A shimmering gold spark ricocheted between every wall in her mind, dizzying her even further. The whisper of an enchantment: *Let me out. Let me out.*

'And one more thing.' Ingram brushed past her with a gentle clearing of his throat. She adjusted to the light, the dark shape of his coat like wings behind his body. She didn't want to think of the birds any more, wanted to leave them in that regrettable, unrepeatable moment. Her body demanded relief. It forced her to exert a tendril of the power that was overwhelming her bloodstream. It had been asking for permission for weeks, but she'd had little time to answer it. In a moment of weakness, it let itself in – poured itself out.

'It's slippery out there,' Aurelia heard Ingram say, fuzzy like a thought lost to time. 'Be safe.'

The sounds of pedestrian traffic around her reduced to a solitary whistle in which only her pulse remained. Loud and clear. Like it was a prisoner within her ribcage. Her heart was pounding, her neck craning beneath the weight of her teeming head.

Ingram didn't know what he was talking about. He couldn't have known about the fall that was weighing so heavily on her. But the ground beneath her boots was not slippery at all; it was rough and spongy, darkened by the constant patter of rain, but not slippery. There was something missing from his words, and figuring out what that was would drive her insane.

Taking herself home was an ordeal. She didn't pause to right her breathing. She stumbled more than once, her hip knocking into the brick pillars of the fences she clung to for stability. By the time she'd reached her front door, the pinpoint of her vision had all but collapsed in on itself like a star, and her fingers were fumbling over the keychain in her coat pocket.

'That was quick,' Ryan remarked, poking their head out of the kitchen doorway. 'Are you OK?'

Aurelia shook her head, dropped both her keys and her bread. 'I think I'm going to be sick.'

Ryan threaded their arm around her shoulders, catching her just before her knees buckled in. 'Rory, what happened?'

Nothing. And that was the truth. Though Ingram's comment had roused her paranoia, she was caving under the culmination of a dozen small magical failures and the guilt of a lifetime. She habitually spread herself so thin that cracks would form that allowed mistakes through. It wasn't so much a question of *why* as much as *when* her magic decided its limits.

Ryan helped her tug the bright orange puffer coat down her arms and followed her to the bathroom, all their reassurances softer than a whisper, so that Aurelia could answer at any point. Her teeth ground tightly together – partly from the physical pain that flooded her head and partly from the fact that she could not tell Ryan *why*.

'You're OK,' Ryan whispered, soothing a hand down her back. 'I've got you.'

Sometimes it hurt, being loved so much, knowing she could never realize the same kind of affection herself. How could she when half her nature went unknown? When she would only ever be half of herself in their presence?

This was the part of witchcraft Aurelia had never made peace with: conjuring white lies to save face with those she loved. Because she was a *witch*. And they were *human*. Love transcended time and death, but rarely did it thrive among creatures like her. The prospect of it had been nothing more than a shared delusion in which she pulled the wool over someone else's eyes, and they trusted her enough to walk blindly.

'I don't deserve you, Ry,' she whispered.

They scoffed and forced a smile that only made Aurelia's heart lurch. 'Don't be stupid.'

The colour of magic was gold, yes; but sometimes, it came up murky, with the acidic taste of panic and a half-digested lunch. Aurelia hadn't eaten anything in hours, but as the pain amassed to agony, she doubled over on the bathroom floor and vomited.

CHAPTER TWO

After the events of the past week, seeing their housemate weakened by something she could not explain to them, Ryan's attention became frivolous. They followed Aurelia everywhere, constantly questioning if her forehead felt clammy or her stomach was upset.

The faculty dinner seemed to make Ryan uneasy. It was the one place they could not go, the one place where Aurelia, who'd quickly grown irritable about her housemate's constant fussing, could choose to turn off her phone and ignore them.

She'd thought that having Ryan around while she got ready would quell some of their worry. They both slipped into familiar positions, with Aurelia in front of a warping standing mirror and Ryan dawdling on the bed behind her. Perhaps, if Ryan saw how steady she was on her feet, they'd stop hovering.

It had become a ritual for them over the years to dress each other up like dolls.

Aurelia had never made a conscious decision to slight nice things, but constant frugality and all her sister's hand-me-downs made a personal sense of style tertiary to the factors of need and cost until she'd moved abroad for uni. Perhaps, if her sister Annette had favoured skirts and dress shoes, Aurelia might have come to Cambridge with a more intimate knowledge of herself; but she came clothed in the shadow of a family who had only ever been like shadow to begin with. It had swathed her in her sister's boxy athletic jackets and skin-tight yoga pants, clothing that had a purpose, sure. Just not the kind Aurelia cared for.

Thankfully, Ryan Jena had come with an identity to shed too; and, to their American housemate's delight, a much keener eye for fashion.

Aurelia held an emerald silk slip dress to her body by the hanger. 'You think I could get away with this again?'

'You're going to freeze.'

'I'll have a sweater on underneath my gown,' Aurelia noted.

Ryan's chest lifted slowly and fell with an audible huff. Aurelia tried not to notice, but Ryan pressed on anyway.

'You don't have to go tonight, you know.'

'This is big for me, Ry. I don't want to miss it.'

'What's the worst that happens if you don't go? It happens every year, doesn't it? You should tuck into bed for the night with some soup and a candle or something.'

With every comment they made, she'd bitten back a grumble. This was supposed to be a chance at relishing in her successes as much as it was to create opportunity for more. One of the few occasions in which she could plant the seed of her name into the minds of respected research historians. Ryan would not be allowed to know the true reason behind her sudden hot spells and nausea.

Truthfully, she didn't entirely know either.

Her power had been insistent against the cage of her

skeleton, causing it to quiver and jolt unexpectedly. Aurelia continued taking familiar routes for all her errands, stopping at landmarks of foliage that she'd always counted on to grant her some relief and sustenance, but they were no longer sufficient.

So, it wasn't completely her fault. But it had become much more apparent to her how much of her life had been a lie to her best friend. That thought was enough to keep her tossing and turning a little later into the night.

'We could watch a movie,' Ryan offered meagrely.

Aurelia lowered her head and gave the hanger a half-hearted wiggle.

'Promise you'll text me if you need anything.'

'*Yes*,' she conceded. 'Can you just . . . Tell me if this looks OK? Please? I've worn it so many times that I think even the fellows will know it's the only nice thing I own.'

The squared neckline draped from delicate straps of the same colour across her shoulders, and the bottom hem glided over her calves when she walked. It *was* a nice dress, and its wear shouldn't have made it any less elegant. But it was old, and she could feel it in every step. She'd gotten it at an antique shop back home, and while its age had been the appeal for her initially, it never once felt new to her.

After a considerate silence, Ryan responded, 'Of course. It's hot, but not *too* hot. Like the person everyone wants to bring to their company office parties.'

'Perfect,' Aurelia muttered to herself, taking in her reflection in the mirror. Her dark curls were almost long enough to graze the tops of her shoulders and barely long enough to fasten behind her head in a pathetic, doggish ponytail. She pulled the top half of it up with her fist to visualize it and shivered, barer without it around her neck.

Her murky brown eyes and olive-toned cheeks had a newfound sullenness to them that caught her off guard. Every day, she sat in front of a tabletop mirror and layered the same shade of lipstick over her honeydew ChapStick, but she hadn't noticed the formation of dark shadows in her skin until now.

Maybe everyone else would see it too. If they kept a tally of every night she lost to studying and graphed it beside her old, starred papers and her rewarded grant work, she might have felt less embarrassed of the bags beneath her eyes or the hollowness beneath her cheekbones. But no one else really cared about Aurelia Schwartz. That was fine, of course. She didn't think much about anyone else if she didn't have to; so why now? She wasn't there for student body recognition, and certainly not for anything other than her work.

Still, it mattered a great deal to her that she'd be a poor figure in that gown of emerald silk – that she'd worn it a dozen different times, and somehow it didn't look like it belonged to her at all. It mattered to her that she'd moved to Cambridge years ago with the bare minimum and hadn't since owned enough to make her bedroom feel lived in.

Try as she might to deny it, she held on tightly to so many things that did not matter. Of all the godforsaken weights she carried, the worst were those she kept just to ignore.

*

She didn't know what to expect from the faculty dinner and King's College. Dr Carney had given her the dress code – formal, gowns required – and a note of encouragement via email, but the last formal event she'd been to was as an undergrad, when having a job outside of classes was prohibited and she'd had more time for things that warranted beautiful dresses.

From what she did know, there were a handful of other PhD candidates that had been invited. She assumed, having herself been invited by Dr Carney, that they were meant to be displayed like tokens of achievement by the older, tenured professors and alumni. Aurelia didn't mind it as much as she probably should have. She arrived, nails needling into one another, to find her folded name badge on a table with those of a mix of seasoned and burgeoning historians, and the sight filled with an unspeakable amount of pride. For that, she could play a part gracefully, mingle frivolously, and employ that charming tilt of her head that people seemed to find so trustworthy. By the end of the night, no one – at least, no one that truly mattered – would be able to deny how much she belonged here.

She had arrived precisely on time, shivering beneath her gown, and a little damp from the rain that snuck beneath her umbrella. Most of the others were still trickling in, and she meandered around the dining hall, searching for a familiar face with the folded card wedged between her fingers. She traced the font, committing the crisp swoop of her middle initial to memory. When she got home, Aurelia would pin it to her wall like an award beside the various leaves and gifted drawings from Ryan.

Chances to socialize with researchers from other colleges didn't come as often for her as they'd done for others in her programme. So many of them had been propped up by generational wealth or their pre-existing nepotism to get to where she'd wanted to be; and where she found herself scrambling, *clawing* with all she could muster, others could often wind up on whims.

None of them tried to hide it either, which Aurelia used to think of as admirable. But that was when she first came to Cambridge, and academia was still rosy and simple enough to touch. Since then, she'd mastered Latin and laboured through Greek, yet she still couldn't comprehend her former classmates' language of contempt. They were a watchful flock of birds, one pearl-white wing extended over each of them, and she was a creature less dazzling. Like roadkill no one wanted to look at.

Aurelia felt a tap on her shoulder, and then, 'Hello, stranger.'

Margarita Palermo was a rare exception. Another international student who studied at Caius whom Aurelia had met by chance after squandering any and all social relevance among her peers at Pembroke. Meeting Marga had felt like an olive branch from the universe amidst the endless ego torment. She was smart, uncommonly beautiful, and exceptionally kind. It was a kindness that Aurelia took for granted. They didn't talk much these days.

Seeing Marga brought an instant smile to Aurelia's face. She turned, embraced her, and mumbled a silent, cordial apology for standing her up at the pub. Marga's hair smelled like jasmine tea. Her curls were tighter and more even than Aurelia's, though just as dark. A bold red, unbothered grin laid Aurelia's apology to rest. 'I get it,' Marga said. 'But now that I'm seeing you, it's been too long. Come sit with me.'

Another student sat at their table that she didn't recognize – likely from another college. He was a non-intimidating boy with shaggy hair who appeared much younger than Marga and her, though make up tended to do that. Aurelia had opted for her usual shade of mauve lipstick, which aged her enough to look like she could be a seasoned scholar, paired with a cherubic blush, which emphasized that she still possessed the kind of youth reserved for prodigies.

Marga asked, 'If I fall asleep, will you kick me underneath the table to wake me?'

'I can be nicer than that.'

'You, nice? There's no one else I would've asked to wake me like that, but I know you'll get the job done.'

Marga's knees pointed toward Aurelia, her weight balanced in the seat on the side of her hips. 'I'm glad you're here,' she said. 'I don't know what I would have done with myself for an hour if I'd been by myself.'

'What about your supervisor?'

'She's sick,' Marga said with a beleaguered sigh. 'Besides, it's different than having a friend here, especially when it's one I have so much to catch up on with. Tell me about what you're working on.'

So, Aurelia did, folding and unfolding her name card within her fingers, while the faculty members trickling in continued their chatter around her. The question quickly swept her away, and Marga, despite her earnest listening, interrupted Aurelia before the table filled.

'Hold on.' Her gaze swept across Aurelia's hairline, and she leaned forward, lifting her fingers apprehensively to the mass of curls pinned away behind her ear. 'I promise I'm listening. You just have . . .' The fleshy heel of her palm brushed Aurelia's cheek as her fingers plucked a green stem from within Aurelia's hair. 'A leaf? No, a flower? It's absolutely charming, but I should take it out before everyone else gets in.'

Inspecting the stem in her pinched fingers, Marga didn't notice the vivid shade of red Aurelia's cheeks had assumed. If she did, she said nothing, sparing Aurelia the embarrassment of explaining the heat in her face or the sudden, starved clench of her jaw.

Nor did she comment on the tension between Aurelia's scalp and what had been uprooted from it. To Aurelia's relief, the stem simply appeared to stick in her curls.

'It's a dandelion,' she said, before Marga tucked it into her napkin.

'Well, now it's gone. You can keep going if you want.'

She smiled, mingled, spent her words like currency and ate her food primly. Her voice rang confidently, holding its own among the scholars. They absorbed the explanation of her work with full investment; she felt for the first time that she would not have to bend to fit the mould, at least not as much as she had already done.

If this was a glimpse into what lay ahead for her, Aurelia was satisfied with it – irrevocably and shamelessly satisfied.

The last empty seats filled; she spotted Dr Carney several seats away, who greeted her mid-sentence with a wave before approaching. He must have been in his late seventies. The hair that remained on the back of his freckled head was white with age, and the crow's feet around his eyes were carved deeply from decades of laughter and grimaces. He wore thick, round spectacles with a prescription strong enough to enlarge his eyes to the size of tablespoons atop a bulbous nose. He was as tall as Aurelia, with just as much weight to him as a step-stool. She suspected she could lift him onto her back and carry him without any hesitance or strain – and that he might allow it if she asked.

She stood, escaping the bubble of conversation at the table to speak to him. Clasping her hands between his, Dr Carney whispered, 'Are you ready for the evening? I'm so glad you decided to join us.'

She nodded once, quickly.

'I shared your most recent research paper with a few of my colleagues from the other colleges. They're very interested in meeting you.'

She raised an eyebrow, as if the praise was unprecedented. As if it didn't vindicate her efforts and terrify her simultaneously.

'They had wonderful things to say. For you *and* for me. It may come as a surprise that I was once heralded as a patron for the next generation of Pembroke medievalists. I can't help it – it gets to my head. I wanted to share my gratitude with you. I owe much of that to students like you, Miss Schwartz. I am *old*,' he explained. 'No one expects me to produce the same results as I did twenty years ago, and I fear my time is running short. The faculty believe I should have retired long ago.'

Had Dr Carney not been so easy to read, Aurelia would have agreed. There was something to be said about a man who could hardly grade his own assignments at the head of a programme full of new adults that needed grace and sensitivity. He was older than most of the professors she'd seen at Pembroke, but he was also, for the most part, more lenient. He'd seen and learned enough to know what made successful academics and what broke them. That he could see something shining in her made it easier for Aurelia to make it through everything else life threw at her. She wanted to make him proud, to prove him right, to show that a prodigal medievalist from the States was capable of leaving a lasting mark in her field.

After the meal, which consisted of French onion soup, followed by braised lamb shank with a medley of fresh vegetables, and a slice of lemon meringue pie, Dr Carney began to introduce her to his aforementioned colleagues. She shook the hand of an older professor – not older than Dr Carney though, who moved into another conversation as soon as they'd become acquainted.

'You must be Miss Schwartz,' the man said, introducing himself as Felix DiBroggio, PhD. 'I'm very curious to know how your studies at Cambridge are treating you. You see, I read some of your undergrad thesis on occult symbolism in early medieval religious texts. It's impressive work for a student.'

'I'm flattered,' Aurelia answered, grinning ear to ear at the old man's praise.

She normally hated compliments followed by the phrase 'for a student,' but the professor seemed to show enough of a profound interest to quash that thought; it didn't bother her enough to dwell on it.

He was taller than Dr Carney and wore a brown and green tweed tie beneath his formal robes, with silvery grey hair combed back to expose his receding hairline. Aurelia glanced back to Marga with her jet-black curls and smooth brown skin, wondering if she would have felt this unafraid without her there at the table.

But the sight of her was not comforting, and she found Margarita Palermo's face consumed with worry, her fingertips consumed with the task of tearing her cuticles to pieces.

DiBroggio offered Aurelia another comment of praise; but in the same way she was distracted by Marga, Marga was distracted by something else – her gaze faraway, so far that Aurelia couldn't follow it to find the origin of her concern. She wanted to see it. She wanted to kill it. She wanted to clutch Marga's hands within hers the way her father had when she was young and chewing her nails down to the nubs.

The professor prattled on obliviously, although it was for the best that he didn't realize that she had lost all interest in his words. In her periphery, Marga's hand flew to her head. Aurelia's stomach lurched simultaneously. She hoped it was nothing more than undercooked lamb.

'Anyway, I was just noting to Victor that the output coming from his students is beyond the likes of most. Do you find yourself *challenged* by his supervision?'

She used his conversation as a device to pull herself back to the present. The question was loaded enough that she could almost ignore her vision blackening at the edges.

'I do,' she answered, growing indifferent to the conversation. 'He asks an unanswerable question, and I strive to answer it.'

The man smiled, the corners of his eyes filling with creases upon creases.

A plate fell to the ground where Marga should have been sitting, and when Aurelia's attention flew to the seat, she found it empty.

'Is everything all right?' DiBroggio asked.

'Oh. Yes, sorry.'

'This room,' the professor chuckled. 'It carries a strong echo.'

It was impossible to shake. Aurelia's head was throbbing again, her vision pulsing with colour. Blue. Black. *Gold* . . .

'Where was I? Yes. *Victor*. He has fostered a great number of burgeoning minds. I'm sure you've met Mister Ingram, yes?'

Then, DiBroggio turned and gestured to Theodore Ingram, who couldn't have been a more unwelcome sight.

She couldn't help the rate at which the smile dropped from her face. The professor may not have seen it, but she and Ingram were never a comfortable pair.

Even here, given the chance to prove herself to the fellows with her brightest smile, she was haunted by his mere presence.

'Hello, Schwartz.'

He shifted uncomfortably in his gown, similarly haunted by her.

Without acknowledging him, she told DiBroggio, 'We know each other.'

'Ah, *excellent!* I was in the middle of telling Miss Schwartz that the work coming from Victor's students is incredible. I'm sure you must see the benefit of working under him as well.'

She grimaced. From the encouraging nod that Ingram gave, she didn't think he cared. In fact, he might have considered it a hefty boost to his already bloated ego.

'I'm very grateful for his instruction,' Ingram replied. Maybe he, too, understood that Carney's career was on treacherous ground.

'He's done marvellously, then,' Felix DiBroggio said. 'I'd say that no medieval studies professor has brought up brighter students than he has. The next few years will be so promising for you – I've no doubt. I look forward to seeing more from you. Hopefully, in one of *my* seminars.'

Aurelia's smile had dimmed. Theodore Ingram met her eyes, lips pulled tightly into a grimace of his own, and she turned her gaze to the floor.

'Thank you, sir,' she said. 'Your well-wishes mean a lot.'

'They're well deserved,' DiBroggio replied. 'I must finish making my rounds here, but I'll leave you two talking. I hope our paths cross soon, Miss Schwartz.'

'So do I.'

The old professor left with a flourish of his gown, and Aurelia shook her head at the debris he'd left in front of her.

'I didn't realize you were invited,' she said, injecting venom into every word – wanting it to sting.

'Likewise. Imagine my surprise to see you here. Weaselling into the fellows' good graces.'

She winced at the implication of his words. 'Imagine that.'

Ingram plucked her name card from the table and twirled it in his fingers neatly. 'Say, what does the J stand for?'

'Does it matter? Look, I don't know why you're surprised – I'm Carney's best student. If anything, I question the validity of your invitation.'

'Simmer down.' He teased her as if they were friends, but the reality that they were *not* friends only made it seem cruel.

He turned his nose up to the ceiling, and she suspected that he wouldn't grant her the common decency of looking her in the eyes when he spoke. Aurelia noticed the clench in his jaw from where she stood, and reckoned they were still too close for comfort.

Of course, she thought, she'd never been threatening. She'd never been more than a novelty to him.

He began, 'You and I have always weighed a fairly even scale academically, but you must not be very bright if you can't see that every professor has favourites. Ours seems to have a propensity for you.'

'I'm honestly impressed by how efficient you are at ruining my evenings.'

He cut her a stern glare. He was never a worthy match in the game of intimidation. His viciousness lay in his words, not his eyes. They were olive green and warm even when the rest of him was colourless and cruel – a weakness that he kept guarded from her at all costs. His gaze travelled lower, and where there ought to have been cruelty, there was . . . something else.

He recognized her dress. She had never wished so much that it was new.

Then he spoke, hardly convincing. 'Would it kill you to spare me one pleasant conversation? Preferably one where you don't look like you're about to eat me alive?'

She scanned the arrangement of tables to find Marga again, but they were all in disarray on account of the feast. She presumed her friend had headed for the ladies' room and made a mental note to check on her as soon as she could extricate herself from her current conversation.

Her vision was still hazy.

Black. Grey. Gold again. She thought of Ryan and their overwhelming concern. The empty promises of good health.

Her arms folded across her chest.

'What threat do I pose to you by being here?' Ingram asked.

If his question was genuine, she might have been flustered by it; but he sounded facetious as always, and that was a much easier hand to read.

'You know, Ingram,' she said, 'I wanted to have this one thing to myself.'

His expression soured. He leaned into the space between them like a ship coming into bay.

'And you *have* it. Let me make this very clear to you, Schwartz: I am not taking anything away from you.'

'Then what makes it so hard for you to accept the fact that I've earned this spot? Try all you want to coddle your pride, but I'm here for a good reason, and I deserve to be here just as much as you.'

If not more, she thought. Yet, doubt encased her in its cold cocoon. He was capable of causing that whenever she'd started to believe that nothing could touch her.

He sucked his gums, his dark brows furrowed over inquisitive eyes. She longed to be out of that stupid dress, under the covers of her bed and hidden from all those academics for the rest of her years at Cambridge.

'You adorn yourself in pity, Schwartz. And you overestimate how much I think about you.'

Ingram couldn't match her forwardness. When she kept his gaze, he couldn't hold it. He scanned the room, paying her fury no mind, twisting fingers in an open wound. 'I think you enjoy wallowing,' he continued. 'As if constant bitterness is all that gives your accomplishments any credibility. Be honest with yourself, Schwartz. Do you relish it? Because all you've ever given to me are grievances. And all your . . .'

She rarely caught him at a loss for the right words. He was a medievalist, above anything, but he was intimate with languages in a way she'd always envied, and he could turn them inside out, wring them for all their barest elements.

When, at last, he settled on, 'Dissatisfaction,' the word felt more monumental than ever, and totally catastrophic.

Aurelia knew herself well enough to know that she held her grudges like her final breaths, that this was true, and how much she loathed this ingrained pettiness within her. She knew herself well enough not to open her mouth and give him another loose lie – but who the hell was he to think *he* knew her so well?

She searched for Dr Carney in the crowd and couldn't find him. Then Marga, to no avail. This wouldn't be the first time Aurelia left without niceties, but she yearned for a scapegoat. For something *else* besides her fragile pride to steal her away from the argument, so that she could say she'd been the bigger person.

She drew a deep breath to thaw the ice forming in her chest, and her lungs filled with the scent of an expensive cologne. He could have picked this one up on a whim. He might have collected dozens, all as undoubtedly expensive as this one, the way she collected leaves and postcards and placards with her name. She thought of her shared bathroom cabinet in

Vancouver, Washington, holding her sister's singular fragrance bottle – the way Annette had wept and screamed when Aurelia had accidentally broken it trying to reach it on the top shelf. It had been a gift. One that Aurelia could not afford to replace.

She promised her sister that she'd try to, but by the time Aurelia was old enough to work, that perfume had gone out of production. Maybe Annette had forgotten. They'd grown enough by now to let things like that fade into insignificance, but being close to Ingram made her feel like she was sixteen again, crying at the edge of her bed because she couldn't fix the thing she had broken.

He never failed to remind her of all the ways she was inadequate, with or without words.

It was a nice scent though, not like the strawberry and mint her sister had treasured, but just as subtle. She leaned into it, brushing against his shoulder while he stood unmoving before her. Rolling onto her toes, her voice fell to a whisper. To a curious listener, they might have looked like lovers in a hushed exchange of secrets, of promises. They were close enough – and he didn't flinch.

But it was a promise as much as it was a threat. 'Go to *hell*, Ingram.'

Adrenaline pulsed through her body, and every heartbeat reverberated through her ears with the smash of a gong. And her head . . .

God, her head.

She waved him off, turned on her heels, and slipped through the crowded hall as gingerly as she could, abandoning the event for a breath of fresh air. The pain was debilitating. It had claws that sought to gouge out her eyes from within her skull. If anything could have salvaged the evening, it would have been the pride she felt from seeing Ingram's bewildered expression as she left with the final word, but whatever it was that had been agonizing her – and likely, it was also the reason Marga had disappeared – had seemingly taken hold of him too.

She wove through the hallways, ducked through two sets of heavy doors and crept out into the night. Marga, who was nowhere to be seen, would have to forgive her for sending a last-minute apology text after the fact. *You know how insufferable men are,* Aurelia typed in her mind, only to be met with the words in gold. Forbidden, unwelcome gold.

The wind pushed through her hair and sent a smattering of goosebumps up the length of her arms. She wrapped her gown tightly around her chest, guarding herself against the near-freezing temperature of the Cambridge autumn. If her housemate discovered she was subjecting herself to it, it would destroy the last shred of patience they were clinging to. There was only so much stubbornness one could take before they finally snapped.

Aurelia didn't care. Not for the cold weather or her housemate's potential lecturing. Certainly not for Theodore Ingram.

When she'd left, he'd seemed almost . . . *unbothered* by her words. Significantly more unbothered than she was by his. He had the contemptible capability of making her anxiety spike by simply entering the room. It was the way that he held his head just a little too high and refrained from her gaze that infuriated her. That she was jealous of his lackadaisical mannerisms and the ease with which he floated by in his studies. Maybe it was the way his trousers were always unwrinkled and how his coats always fitted him well, like he could afford to have them made to his measurements. He knew excess so well that even his ego had grown much too big for him; and it branched out to her and reeked of rottenness.

At least she could blame the headache on him. As if it would ease the pain.

She bent over the edge of the otherwise freshly manicured lawn and plucked the first dandelion of the season. She pressed it between her palms, letting the petals of it twirl within her hands and tickle her. It was barely magic – just a desperate and meaningless act of destruction – but it was all she could manage at that point to give herself a boost.

The dandelion recoiled and shrivelled in her hands. Such a small thing could not restore the fullness to her cheeks or the youth to her eyes, but it was something. Even the most insignificant act of picking and pressing flowers could feed her when she was at her wits' end.

'We need to talk.'

Ingram appeared at the top of the steps behind her, hands stuffed into his pockets. She crunched the weed in her fist, and it simmered to ash.

'There is nothing I'd rather do less. What don't you understand about that?'

He stepped down to her level, which offered her no advantage, given that he was considerably taller than her. With anyone else, she might have been threatened by the proximity of anger, but he was nothing like that. She suspected his hands were uncalloused and his skin too sensitive to have ever acted on rage before.

'Listen,' he spat. 'I'm not sure what I ever did to make you hate me so much, but I'm sick of the way you blame *me* for your fragile insecurity.'

Her jaw shifted. 'Do you ever ask yourself why it matters to you so much that I'm here, Ingram? Why are you so bothered that I received the same invitation you did?'

'And I could ask you the same thing, Schwartz. God, you're dense.'

'Yeah, *I'm* dense,' she scoffed, turning her back to him. The rough brown dandelion crumbs slipped from her hand, and she squashed them into the step with the ball of her foot. '*You* thought it was a good idea to follow me out here for a chat, because you can't leave well enough alone.'

'And *you* assume I have your worst interest in mind every time I have to see you.'

If it was meant to elicit sympathy for his argument, it did the opposite. He didn't think as critically before he spoke as she did, didn't juxtapose his intentions and his words on two different planes in his mind. He didn't beat them to death and wring them for their true worth. He'd let slip how he regarded her as a chore, something taken care of through elimination. Implying that he was perfectly content without seeing her another day in his life.

Although that option was frankly more appealing to her than whatever *this* was.

His eyes drifted to the small stain left on the floor from the crushed dandelion.

'You know, I always suspected you had something unnatural tucked up your sleeve,' he muttered.

'And what would that be? You wouldn't go so far as to insinuate I'm sleeping with the old man, would you? Or are you just *that* delusional?'

He pointed his gaze back to her, unabashedly confused. 'Not like that.'

Her eyes narrowed, but her vision began to fade, and the fatigue in her muscles didn't help to recover it. Her sight blurred around the edges.

'You don't know what you're talking about. You make pathetic excuses to undermine my work, Ingram. I'm not some novelty that disappears once you're tired of me, you know.'

'What did you say?'

'I'm saying that, *maybe* I just don't like you. Maybe I'm tired of seeing you have everything I want.'

He stopped behind her, lost. At some point, her train of thought sped up enough that he became unable to follow. There were few things she would sacrifice her patience for, and she didn't feel like making him one of them.

'Don't act so oblivious. I heard you say it. To Lawrence. As if that's the worst thing you ever said to me to put me down, make me feel small. As if you don't constantly demean my work simply because *I* wrote it.'

His lip curled, and she mirrored him – trading him one confident stance for another. She forced herself to look him straight in the eyes, to match the inquisition of his gaze with one equally as ferocious. From here, she witnessed the clench of his jaw and the eventual faltering of his stare. *If only it were so easy*, she thought, *to be wounded by someone you don't respect.* He couldn't have been so caught up in her opinion of him that she could shuck him off with something equal to a petty taunt.

Yet she could see the shift in his stern features, the resignation settling in. It didn't make sense. It should have sated her anger.

'Don't pretend you know me,' he said. 'Don't act like you know a damn thing about what I want.'

Of course, she *didn't* know – but it was what she wanted that he always seemed to have. Pride, unyielding confidence, charisma . . . An inner circle that would do more than just tolerate her.

Sniffling in the cold, Aurelia mumbled, 'It doesn't matter.'

'Maybe not to you. But it matters a great deal to me. So long as you treat me like I'm a nuisance, I don't stop wondering what I did to deserve it. You're a bitter person, Schwartz. You're sad, and I feel sorry for you.'

Ingram turned back toward the stairs and left her with his icy resolution. 'You wanted to be done. So, we're done. Have a good night.'

'Excuse me?'

He ignored her and cleared his throat for emphasis.

'Come back here!'

'I thought there was nothing you wanted *less* than to talk to me. Make up your mind, Schwartz.'

Upon opening her mouth to chastise him again, a wave of nausea penetrated her stomach. She threw her hand to the stone doorway for support, but it did little to help when her vision went so black that she could no longer see where to step.

Aurelia doubled over with an audible gasp and felt Ingram's hand around her elbow. Her heartbeat was deafening in her ears. His voice beneath it was muffled and thin. 'What's going on with you?'

'It must have been the food . . . And you . . . *Dick.*'

'It can't be,' he said, unsteady himself. 'I haven't eaten.'

Food poisoning didn't feel like this, but she had nothing else to point to. Her senses were fading into numbness, and her knees gave out beneath her.

Her magic began to beat her from within, thrashing against her body until she released it. It seeped through her skin with such a blistering heat that it made her wonder if this was what being set aflame felt like. A spark of gold broke through the blackness of her diminishing sight, and she pleaded, *Not now. Not with him.*

As the world around her reduced to a blur of colour and motion, that radiance of gold surpassed the shape of her body and enveloped Theodore Ingram too.

She swallowed, recoiling from his hand to rip the glow from his body. Without him there, her weight toppled against the doorway.

She began to count in an attempt to ground herself.

Three things she could see: the carved detail of the stone, the mark of aggravation etched into Ingram's brow, and the golden shimmer that extended from her figure to his.

Two things she could hear: her own pulse knocking against the inside of her skull and another strained groan from Ingram's mouth.

She couldn't remember what the next sensation was

supposed to be. It was a trick Ryan had taught her the first time her anxiety had swelled into pure panic, and since then, she'd succeeded at catching herself before she could reach that breaking point.

Before she could touch something, Ingram sputtered, 'Jesus, do you smell that?'

Aurelia inhaled, chasing whatever scent he had caught in the air that so visibly repulsed him; but there was nothing. The night became a little clearer as the gold aura around her body granted her sight past the steps and onto the college lawn.

It was covered in dandelions. Some of them were still rising from the drenched soil, even as she willed them to stop. She couldn't conjure up any plausible excuse in all the memory of her old teachings that would justify this betrayal of power, but the shimmer tied the growing flowers to her magic. It was her fault. Her fault.

'Shit,' she whispered. 'Shit, shit, *shit*.'

At the first rush of clarity, Aurelia bounded down the steps to rip the weeds from the ground. Her gaze shot briefly to Ingram, but his gaze was wholly attentive to her.

She didn't care.

What was another reason to find her unsettling when it was only *him?*

They were still sprouting, reaching up to grab her hands as she severed them from their resting place. She muddied her dress as she kneeled down to reach as many as possible. On her knees, in the mulch, she must have looked deranged. Where she expected to find bewilderment on his face, she found complete indifference.

He was clearly preoccupied by the phantom scent she had never tracked; his nose wrinkled in disgust. His expression was so focused and narrow-minded that it was almost trance-like. She shook it from the forefront of her mind and kept pulling, uttering words into the ground. Maybe, if she said it aloud, the earth would pity her. Maybe it would listen.

'Hey,' he said quietly.

She shook her head.

'Something's wrong,' he added. He didn't seem to care much that her dress was now covered in spots and her nails caked in dirt. Whatever it was existed apart from her, and that puzzled her enough to pause her weed-pulling and gawk at him.

'You need to leave,' he said. '*Now.*'

It was her turn to be oblivious. She pushed herself upright with considerable effort. Ingram lurched toward her as if to help, but stilled at the sound of communal shock that came from the direction of the dining hall.

'What are you talking about?'

'God damn it, Schwartz. Something is wrong, and you need to *leave!*'

He flung open the doors at the top of the steps and disappeared inside. Aurelia mustered all her urgency to follow him, but her mind was so weakened by the multitude of sour happenings and dulled sensations that she reached the inner door to the hall seconds after he did.

Inside, the lights went out.

The faculty dinner attendees clamoured for the open doorway. Instinctively, Aurelia reached for Ingram in the shadow – the only person she could trust to be on the other end of the darkness – and she closed her hand around his wrist. A chorus of shouts erupted from within the hall, and the weight of other bodies began to crush hers, pushing her back into the doorway.

At once, she heard Ingram cry out for air as if something was strangling him. She gripped his wrist with a pressure that would certainly bruise. 'I'm right here.'

'I know,' he rushed. 'Me too.'

Adrenaline coursed through her, joined by something electric she could only hope was not magic.

'I think someone is dead,' Ingram said gravely. His words, in spite of their hushed tone, became an echo within the remaining crowd, one that grew and stoked their frenzy into a wildfire.

Aurelia's mouth fell open in protest – it didn't make sense. His words, her dandelions, this night . . . She didn't know if anything was real at this point; it was all happening in a blur of black and blue behind her eyes. Her grip on reality was giving out. What had settled inside her gut was pure terror.

'Why would you say—'

'God,' Ingram gasped. 'Leave! Get out of here right now!'

She didn't know why he said it, why he didn't flinch when she'd buried herself in the flooded earth despite those same brown-tinged fingers being twisted around his wrist. She couldn't see the other fear that clawed at him or find the scent that seemed to suffocate him. All she knew with certainty was how it felt to be herded in the darkness, like cattle moved toward euthanasia. And that, in pitch-black nothingness, attached to her by an unyielding iron grip, he said that *someone was dead.*

A blood-curdling shriek rang out from the centre of the hall, just as someone restored the lights.

Finally, she thought to run but froze instead. She felt each heartbeat in her fingertips, against her skull. The shifting, sweaty bodies of those around her forced Ingram's hand to slip; and then he was gone before she could call for him again and ask why he was not coming with her. They forced her through the bottleneck of the door, none willing to look back from where they'd come. Did they know? Had they heard?

Aurelia looked before the crowd overtook her, through a pinhole of haze and darkness, and for a second, she could see the blood spilling across the floor. The gleam of metal. A woman's body – pierced through the chest with a broad, silver sword.

Marga's body.

CHAPTER THREE

Aurelia couldn't count on her hands how many times she'd been visited by prophetic dreams in her lifetime. Half of them came from that week.

Since the medievalists' dinner at King's, several things upset the perfect balance of Aurelia's life.

First, all colleges and faculties in Cambridge closed their doors two weeks earlier than scheduled, with the winter holidays just around the corner. With the closure came the exodus of students from their college accommodation. Aurelia had planned to spend a few weeks in Cardiff with her friend, Chloe Alvinson, for the holidays, but Chloe was immediately summoned home by her parents once news of the closure reached them.

Aurelia couldn't lie to herself and say it didn't hurt to be an afterthought. Ryan had left just a day before, on a four-hour train ride to Liverpool to be with their family.

'I would have stayed if you'd told me,' they'd sent amidst a series of infuriated text messages from their housemate.

Except Aurelia didn't want them to stay – not at that point. She had even considered keeping the fact from Ryan altogether. When the last of her prayers were crushed underneath Chloe

Alvinson's heels, she couldn't stand to think about her housemate's overbearing doting. It didn't take long to miss them again, and even sooner did Aurelia start wondering if it was *cruel* that she would be so averse to the love of her best friend when she most needed something to lean on.

In a moment of weakness, she called Lawrence Kressler again. Fortunately for them both, it went straight to voicemail.

In her state of shock came the second thing: a recurring nightmare of her old friend's bloody body impaled by the silver sword. In it, she *was* Marga, their bodies melting into one unified form as she drifted into unconsciousness. The lights of the event hall diminished into blackness. Aurelia – or Marga – reached out for a body to cling to where she knew other people should have stood, but her hands felt nothing, slipping through forms like ghosts.

But they were there. Their voices were unintelligible, more alike to the hisses of snakes and low growls of beasts than accented English. Marga clung to sounds that were words only a few seconds previously, when the lights were still on.

It was only radio static. Then, nothing at all.

In the darkness before her, the features of a face would appear vaguely, different every night. Marga would call out to it for guidance, like a god, to be her beacon of light and safety. To Marga, its responses made sense, but to Aurelia, the voice was a jumble of hums and mismatched syllables.

A dissonant forging of Marga's voice and her own would scream, 'You can't take it from me! I never wanted this!'

Then came the sword, plunged deep into her sternum, and Aurelia woke with a heartbeat she felt in her fingertips, a cold sweat slicking over her body, and a rawness in her throat that could have only come from screaming bloody murder.

On those nights, she had no one to call. No housemate whose door she could knock on for comfort, no friend whose visit she could anticipate the following morning. She'd vastly overestimated the hour at which people awakened in this city.

Her fingers would float toward the centre of her chest where the sword had been lodged. She traipsed them over the skin as if it were scarred, before assuring herself it had only been a dream.

No dream had ever felt so real.

From the onslaught of sleepless nights came a wave of exhaustion that no amount of tea could salvage. Where enchanted juniper and bay concoctions should have succeeded, they failed too.

Her frequent hopes and pleas went unheard. If magic could not alleviate her terrors, nothing would; and the gods did not wait around for the cries of desperate witches.

Third came the peculiar influx of winged creatures at her windows. Normally, Aurelia would not have thought twice about a pigeon on the ledge of her upstairs window, but there were always two or three perched at a time, cawing in conversation. When she walked to the corner store or past Heffers Bookshop, the batting wings of ducks absent from their rivers followed her. They watched her with the dialled-in focus of a hunter or a big cat, not in their usual distracted manner of begging for crumbs and avoiding a collision. She had never felt like prey to a bird before this week.

But the crows . . .

They gathered around her with hunger in their beady eyes. Waiting to eat. Wanting to devour.

She took a seat at her desk, placing her cup of tea on a wooden coaster while she skimmed through the pages of her grimoire. Her phone read eleven forty-five. No messages or missed calls. Outside, the rain collided with her window. Aurelia lit one of the scented candles on her desk. It wasn't the kind made for ritual magic, but it was not a spell she hoped to conjure.

It gave her comfort if nothing else, and having shadows dance behind her made the room feel just a little less lonely. Tomorrow would mark two weeks since she witnessed her friend's impaled body lying in the crowded dining hall of King's College. Michaelmas term should have been ending now. Everyone she knew was already gone.

It was a cruel awakening to her isolation. When crisis hit, her friends had homes to return to, families who would ask if they were all right, communities to lean on for support.

Aurelia had none of those things – at least, not within reach. To return to the country and state she would have called home was an option she didn't have; and she sat discomforted with the fact that neither her family nor her friends would be of any comfort to her if she had them in her grasp.

But the new-found privacy had given her a rare, unprecedented opportunity. She'd never been able to open her grimoire without fearing her housemate would round the corner of the staircase at any given second and find her. Typically, she avoided casting verbal spells in her room – the walls had always been thin enough to draw attention to small noises. She'd been relegated to all the undetectable forms of magic that stirred the energy in her blood. She kept her room cluttered with plants, pinned those perfect leaves to her bedroom walls with an egregious number of clear thumb tacks; and when she needed a lift, she would seek out the brownest plants and mend their withering leaves.

Historically, Aurelia hadn't needed more than that to keep her abilities harnessed and her powers efficient. She'd been following the same scenic routes, had mended the same browning petals and nourished her magic like a well-oiled machine.

Tonight, in her grimoire, she searched for a forgotten passage on levitation, hoping that she'd merely misplaced an answer to her burning questions. Her restless nights had been occupied by many things, including a shameful recollection of her slip-up on the cobblestone streets of Cambridge several weeks ago. It was, perhaps, one of the smaller things weighing on her, but it also seemed easier to get rid of.

Much to her dismay, she only found a passage on small object levitation. A common spell, not to be confused with flying, which was a gift.

She closed the heavy leather cover over her grimoire and leaned back in her chair. Witches weren't born with more than one gift. Some could handle water with the force of a solid weapon. Others spoke to the dead. Her gift was her gods-given green thumb. While any capable witch could will their houseplants to grow a little faster, she could command anything that grew in the soil with precision.

But her tutor once told her that the principles of magic could not be transfixed in stone. The smartest thing any witch could do was accept that their magic would betray them eventually.

Her arms folded over her chest, slender fingers curled into the thick rib knit of her taupe sweater, forcing a pill to form as she refrained from lifting her hands to her teeth to chew on her nail beds. It had been dark outside for hours now, but she checked the time again. Her phone was absent of messages, the cobblestones below void of people in conversation.

The candle did not cast a comforting shadow behind her.

A flash of crimson and ink barrelled into her window, and she leapt from her chair with such a jolt that it crashed behind her. Her heartbeat skipped as streaks of red washed down the glass. *Blood.*

A bird fell to the pavement below, bleating from the impact beneath her window. She rushed down the stairs, knocking the legs of her chair aside clumsily. 'Shit, shit, shit.'

A crow twitched and writhed outside her front door, laid in the exact centre of her doorstep as if it had been carried there in the teeth of a dog and dropped as a gift. It was nearly as bloody, and its wings were snapped in several places, delicate white bones protruding from its inky feathers. Its beak was crushed in, and those black, beady eyes were covered up with its own torn flesh.

She clutched her neck, easing the knot of bile that formed in her throat. Lowering to her knees, Aurelia stared, dumbfounded, at the winged creature. It had been damaged and broken beyond what a simple crash warranted, as if the bird had been violated by something with claws and teeth and *power* before it had even set flight and travelled to her window.

It twitched. From its cracked beak came a final, guttural cry that branded into her mind . . .

Then it died.

Every breath tasted like iron. She pivoted toward a stash of rags beneath her kitchen sink, doling out silent assuagements to herself so that she wouldn't cry. The carcass had to be moved.

She'd have to touch it and feel the way its skeleton shattered in her hands when she lifted it from the doorstep and disposed of it. The premonitory sensation it conjured up in her mind made her unsteady on her feet. She would have to wrap it up and toss it through the door of the bin next to where it had taken its last breath – a crude and unfit burial for a creature so regal.

God, was she lonely.

After she moved the body, she buried her head in the palms of her hands and wept, for she had tucked away all the hurt she sustained with little complaint, and every poor hand that she was dealt had piled on top of one another until she found herself too far gone to fold. She missed Ryan. She missed the steady routine of normalcy. She wanted to go home, even if it couldn't fix anything, because it would have been a predictable misery, a necessary numbness.

But no one was there to console her, just as no one could watch her flipping through her grimoire. No one to witness the glow that circled her fingers from a spell she couldn't remember casting. She pulled herself together and boiled water for tea. Chamomile to calm.

The streetlight went out as midnight came, and she slid solemnly under the covers to chase an hour or two of restless sleep.

Theodore Ingram's name flashed across her phone.

She considered him inevitable, like bad weather in England, but it was all too easy to forget his contact was ever there.

They'd worked together on a project once as undergrads before her presence became a sour and spoiled thing in the hearts of her peers. Even then, he was unusually cold to her . . . Not particularly unkind, but impressively aloof. It wasn't easy to ignore him in person, but her phone held no messages or calls from him from all the years they'd studied together. She found no other trace of him besides his initials in a grey circle, unembellished and formal. It was always *Ingram* to her, and rarely Theodore, because nicknames were reserved for the people she liked, and he was assuredly not one of them. The best days in undergrad were those where he sat in his seat for lectures and said nothing during discussions, where she didn't have to hear his pretentious, overreaching opinions on material, or see him fiddling with his pen.

But he was calling her, and she couldn't help her curiosity after what had transpired at King's College. She picked up her phone before he could be sent to voicemail. 'What do you want, Ingram?'

There was a shaky sigh on the other side. 'Wasn't sure you'd answer.'

'Surprise, surprise.'

'Where are you right now?' he asked. There was an unevenness in his words that didn't seem right, like he was out of breath, or trying not to be heard.

'I'm in bed,' Aurelia said, pulling the blanket up to her chin. 'I'm trying to get some sleep – being kept awake by unlikely callers.'

'You know what I mean, Schwartz.'

She had no clue, of course, but he'd piqued her interest.

'Are you still in Cambridge?'

She sighed, turning her face against her pillow completely.

'Hello? Are you with me?'

'God, Ingram. So many questions. *Yes*. I'm here.'

There was a pause on his end, long enough that she considered calling his name to see if the call had dropped.

In a graver, more serious tone, he asked, 'Are you alone?'

The last thing she wanted was for Theodore Ingram to know she'd been abandoned for the holidays. Something about being alone now embarrassed her in a way that hadn't been embarrassing before. She had stayed here plenty of times for the holidays, but only now did she have no other option, left with her night terrors and her *birds*. Only now was she plagued with the graphic memory of witnessing her friend's death.

'I'm alone,' she confessed. Shame crept in as much as she tried to bar it out. 'I'm also very exhausted and confused, so I'd like to know what you're calling me for.'

'Hmm.'

He made that sound a lot, always considering her answers more than necessary, as if he could piece together three things when she was only giving him the answer for one. Somehow, he caught the roughness in her words that made it clear she'd been crying.

He could be scarily perceptive sometimes.

'I don't mean to interrupt,' he said. 'Something's come up though, and I just . . .'

Alone in her bedroom, the silence was kinder, now a distant feeling that couldn't swallow her whole. She allowed it this time, lingering in it until he made up his mind and spoke again.

'I just needed to make sure you're all right.'

Sincerity was a flat note in his voice. Aurelia sniffed back the remnants of her tears. 'I'm all right, Ingram. Just tired. Can't stop thinking about Marga,' she said. A criminal understatement. She'd have killed for a night of uninterrupted sleep.

'I need your help, Schwartz. Do you think you could manage another hour?'

'I don't know.'

'I swear it's important.'

She rubbed her eyes with a hard, bony knuckle. 'It's pretty late, Ingram.'

He said her name again – her *first* this time, not her last – and all of this newness was waking her up a little. She felt a new kind of gravity tying her to the earth.

'I'm not asking you to pretend that we're on decent terms, but I need you to understand that I wouldn't be calling you if it wasn't terribly important. Can you trust me on that?'

Trust him . . . Had he ever been a trustworthy person? Or had his attitude been so abhorrent that she had no need to ask herself? How could she have decided his trustworthiness if not by giving him a secret to keep – something valuable that was not worth losing?

In the end, she let her desperation decide for her; that, although she detested him and his ego, he had no reason to lie to her. If anything, he was the most brutally honest person she knew. So honest that she hated him for it.

She typed her address out in a message for him, catching a glimpse of the time. Then, faintly, the ding of the notification on his phone.

'I can be over in ten,' he said. 'Promise me you'll stay put.'

'It's twelve-thirty in the evening. Where else am I going to go?'

'I mean it, Schwartz. No jokes.'

She hadn't meant to be funny. 'Since when are you so insistent on being in my company, Ingram? Late-night visits, asking me to promise you things.' She threw his name back with a false cynicism, like it was bait. Instead of reeling him in, it pushed him farther. Slowly, antagonizing in its precision, a silence formed between their words that prickled and roused every bump on her skin.

Something tapped on her window, and she half expected to see the mauled bird looking back at her through the glass with its crushed-in skull. All she could see was night, sprawling like a breath over the city.

'Since it occurred to me you might be in danger,' Ingram said. His voice came and went, impermanent as a ghost.

CHAPTER FOUR

He'd waited until she'd opened the front door to shake the rain from his umbrella and close it. That short walk through the gate and past the garden left his hair wet and scraggly, dampened enough to match the dark colour of his garments. They met each other with a similarly displeased expression; hers had been festering while his was anticipatory. His deep-set eyes were far too lost in thought to take in the severity of her anger, but he braced himself for it anyway, brushing past her to escape the rain and into her house.

'What the hell is your problem?' Aurelia asked.

'Not even seconds through your door, and you're already upset with me. Fucking *Christ*.' He grumbled something unintelligibly, his fingers curling around the length of his sopping umbrella. The sound of the lock clicking into place startled something in his body into waking.

Aurelia pressed her back against the door, folding her arms over her chest with a grimace. 'You can't just say something like that and hang up.'

'Well, I had to get here. And I'm here now, aren't I? Besides,' Ingram said, running a pale, red-knuckled hand through his hair to push it back into place, 'this isn't something we should be discussing over the phone.'

He looked so out of place against the cheap collection of decor in her house that he seemed more like an intruder than a guest.

'Go on then,' said Aurelia. 'I was nearly asleep when you called.'

Instead, Ingram took his time assessing the room around him, skimming every furniture crevice and dark corner, turning to peer out the front window again before he opened his mouth to speak. He often tested her patience in small ways like that – glances that extended for too long where there should have been words. He propped his umbrella up in a shadowy corner of her hallway, and Aurelia caught the small quiver in his hand.

Behind that gesture was enough fear to taste.

Impatiently, she stepped into the adjacent kitchen and drew the window shut. She felt his relief just as palpably as his paranoia, dissolving on her tongue like sugar. 'Better?' she asked.

Ingram nodded, and she watched his Adam's apple work with strain over the high, black turtleneck of his sweater.

'That night at King's,' he started. 'Before it all went to complete *shit*, you started tearing up the front lawn.'

'I can explain,' she cut in.

'Oh, can you?'

Why she had offered an explanation was beyond her; nothing came out. As she ran her tongue along her gums, devising tens of ridiculous excuses she could make to quell him, the walls of her mouth began to taste like sandpaper.

'There were dandelions.'

His eyes narrowed, and he raised his chin, so that he looked down on her more than he already needed to.

'No. There weren't.'

'Of course, there were. They bloom early in the winter, then—'

'*No*, Schwartz.'

'What are you debating, Ingram? I saw them. I *grabbed* them. I pulled them up in fistfuls while you were groaning about some phantom odour—'

'And *you* looked at me like I was crazy—'

'Because you are,' Aurelia said, restless for him to skip to the part that would warrant his untimely arrival. She started down the narrow hallway beneath the staircase and into the living room where Ryan usually slept. Ingram followed at her heels, his black coat brushing the backs of his calves with each step. 'Have you come all this way to share a diagnosis with me? Admit to me that you're a sociopath? Or a narcissist?'

Or explain how you knew about Marga's death before we could see it?

At present, the thought of Marga was the only thing that kept her from decomposing into rage. He'd known more than he'd let on about Marga's death, but there was a hesitation in his movements that she'd never seen before; if she wasn't careful with her tone, he might tuck the answer to all her questions back in his pocket and leave.

He raised his hands in front of him to form a vague indication of the visual in his mind – but as they inevitably shook, the lines were lost, blurred beyond recognition. No jokes, he'd said.

Trust me.

'Before our altercation I overheard Marga say to one of the fellows from Caius that she was hearing a whistle in the crowd. I saw him shake his head when asked about it, but it was obvious that despite this "no", it persisted. She stumbled and fell like it was so loud that it destabilized her. I couldn't hear it, and neither did the others around her. Just as you saw something I didn't, and the odour I smelled was strong enough to be right in front of my face; but no one else looked bothered. *No one.*'

The pull of slumber thrummed against Aurelia's eyelids with every beat of her pulse. The adrenaline in her veins burned just as strongly in opposition with it, but it only made her dizzy.

'There were no dandelions, Schwartz. I've no doubt that you saw them, but what you had in your hands was not that.'

'You're not making any sense,' Aurelia told him, collapsing into the couch. They were all disconnected fragments of information. Numbers out of order.

Again, Ingram followed, perching himself on the armrest opposite her. 'Think about it: three of us experienced something that wasn't perceivable to anyone else. I think . . . we were meant to be having different reactions to the same dog whistle. I knew it. You knew it. I saw the golden shimmer on your skin as clear as daylight, and I suspect that we would have seen the same one around Marga had we been in the room with her.'

Her breath hitched in her throat, forcing up the familiar taste of iron in her mouth.

Theodore Ingram had seen gold too. He hadn't gawked at her as if she were abnormal. She should have known something to be amiss when he pulled the meaning of it from something other than a dream or hallucination.

His voice dropped to a guarded whisper. 'You see it now, Schwartz.'

And though it wasn't a question, she nodded. Not all of those fragments had a place, but they might soon – after the disbelief faded.

'I don't think it was an accident that we responded the way we did,' Ingram said. 'These past few nights, I've been waking up with night terrors, and every night it's been the same thing. There's darkness. The sword. A *face*. Maybe I'm going mad, but it seems too significant to overlook.'

Even if his words were half-gibberish, there was some horrifying, unrealized truth behind them. They'd seen the same things and, possibly, the same faces. Between the two of them, they were bound to figure out what they were seeing.

His green eyes searched for understanding with a quiet desperation.

'I *know* you see it,' he muttered. 'You *must* see it.'

Aurelia sighed. *I don't want to see it any more.*

'I've . . . been having them too,' she said, tearing more skin from her cuticles. 'But it was a traumatic experience. To expect me to forget something like that is . . . I don't know. I haven't been able to force the image out of my head. I can't pretend like everything is all right when it's not. I just witnessed the murder of my friend, Ingram; and as unlikely as it was, some part of me believed I would be next.'

'I know,' he said softly, in what could have been an attempt at comfort if she didn't know better. If they were friends, he might have held out his hand for her, given her fingers a squeeze for reassurance. She might have led him through her hallway and embraced him like she did when Ryan Jena had hard days.

But Theodore Ingram was not her friend. She knew it by the way he sought her out just to keep his distance, quickened his pace so she couldn't maintain it. His gait was slightly uneven, a millisecond of difference between the fall of his left foot and his right. She never asked about it, didn't even know if anyone else noticed, but it was more pronounced when he rushed. It mattered to him, for some reason, that she'd never forget how little he wanted to be around her. She kept a trove in her mind of all his snide comments, the musings on his own academic research that always seemed to mention hers. Rarely did he regard her unless he could rival her or say her name without a bitter remark tacked to the end of it . . .

So, comfort was hardly the first thing he thought of when it came to her. If anything, it was a blessing that he didn't want to argue the validity of her trauma.

His eyes were circled with darker flesh than the rest of his face, the same way hers were. The sullenness made his face a little kinder. 'So did I. I suspect our self-preservation stems from something different, though. I think it would have been one of us at the end of that sword if she hadn't gone first. You see,' Ingram slowed deliberately, 'Margarita Palermo was a witch. Just like *you*.'

'I don't know what you mean,' Aurelia lied, before a spark of energy scattered through the muscles in her hands. To let another spell slip through would only damn her further – *if* there was any hope left in dissuading him from the truth.

He paused to pick apart her bewildered expression, then

gave an exasperated sigh, as if the truth was only a mild inconvenience instead of something that threatened her survival. Her twenty-three years might have been eleven or fifteen without that same perpetual state of defensiveness.

'You don't have to act so surprised, Schwartz. I know we don't see eye to eye, but there's no point in denying it to me. Only witches glow like you do.'

'What's it to you?' she spat. 'What are *you* exactly?'

Ingram's gaze fell to his hands as they folded around each other.

'Are *you* a witch?'

He opened his mouth to respond but stopped himself once again. She could compile every instance of his open-and-closed lips in her head until he looked like a fish, sucking in its flaked food.

Aurelia's heartbeat was in her throat, in her ears, pounding against her temples.

'It's *complicated*,' Ingram decided, which meant nothing and everything at the same time.

Aurelia rose from the couch with her fingers still curled into its arm. 'How long have you known?'

'A while.'

Her nose wrinkled in disgust. Through her clenched jaw, she breathed out, 'Have you told anyone?'

Ingram scoffed. *The bastard scoffed.* As if it was that simple, and she was merely oblivious to it.

'Why would I want to do that?' He pinned her with a narrowed, accusatory gaze. 'D'you think anyone would believe me?'

A quick survey of his face told her he was genuine – or at least genuine enough. His eyes darted from the obscured window to his hands, folded neatly on his knees.

'And Marga,' she said, trailing off in consideration.

He hummed in affirmation. 'I think someone came to Cambridge in search of a witch to kill.'

Aurelia's mind swam with questions. She began with, 'How . . .' but could not for her life decide how to finish.

How did you figure me out?

How can you be so sure that witch lives were at stake?

And if they are, what happens to me?

Ingram stared, brow furrowed in anticipation of her question. But it didn't come.

'It's a pattern,' he said. 'They are . . . making rounds.'

He'd taken the conversation somewhere else, some place she couldn't recognize. The silence strung between them leaked with his growing impatience.

'You think this has to do with what happened in Oxford?' Aurelia asked.

He nodded. 'And Glasgow.'

'Edinburgh?'

'London, too.'

Places that had all been touched by vandalism and scandal as of late. Museums with missing artefacts, government institutions with ruined access systems. Now, universities where students left their rooms for promises of opportunity and networking and died before they could return.

She'd only found out recently through an online post that she didn't finish reading. Between applications and essay tutoring, she'd lost sight of current events. She was almost certain that she would still find the article open in a tab on her phone.

'How did you draw that theory? I didn't see that anyone else had died from those incidents. Maybe this is an exception . . . Maybe the worst is over.'

Shame came to her delayed. It felt so wrong to talk about the worst, like it was as harmless as losing the lead role in a school play or being unfairly grounded by a parent when, in reality, it was the murder of a friend that had occurred before their very eyes. Nowadays, she'd say anything to remind herself that it could have been her – and that it *wasn't.*

Anything to sleep at night.

'The vandalism is just a cover for them,' he explained. 'It's not their primary goal. A body was found at the British Museum in London—'

'And it was—'

'Inhuman,' he finished. 'But it wasn't reported on, which is enough cause for question about whether or not the other cities incurred more damage than they let on. I suspect every one of them has had at least one witch murder.'

Aurelia swallowed the knot in her throat as much as she could, but only a fraction of the strain subsided. Between this and the dead bird on her doorstep, she wouldn't be able to digest her last meal properly.

'How'd *you* figure it out, then?'

He took in a full, patient breath. 'I have . . . friends in high places. But that's beside the point. Artefacts were stolen from the British Museum. I haven't been able to discern their logic for the items they took, but there were chalices, world currencies, ceremonial tools, and – as you can assume – *weapons.* Mostly small items, easily concealed within the pockets of a large coat or a duffle bag.'

He demonstrated by fluffing out the bottom of his own coat. 'They dipped their hands into every bubbling pot with the intention of stirring, and they were somehow capable enough to make out with all those treasures undiscovered. It's . . . honestly impressive.'

A shudder ran down the length of her spine – something Ingram took note of with a sobering expression.

'Do you think they'll come back to Cambridge?' Aurelia asked.

He nodded plainly. 'Can't be certain that they ever left.'

'You think they're still here?'

Another nod. Almost considerately, he said, 'You should get out of here for a while, Schwartz. I figured you'd be gone for the holidays anyway.'

She shrugged, tightening the circle of her arms around herself to ease the ache in the pit of her stomach.

'What about your room-mate? Can't you give them a call?'

'Ryan has already gone home.'

'Hmm.'

The pressure in her stomach flew upwards. Aurelia rushed to the kitchen sink to vomit. It burned as it climbed up her throat. Her fingers gathered all the loose, looping strands that fell in front of her face, shielding them from whatever waste might not totally escape her.

The last thing she needed was for Ingram to hear her

pained, terrified retching down the drain, but he followed her, startled by the suddenness of her gait. His hand touched down lightly on the back of her shoulder. Her first instinct was to recoil, but she didn't want to add to the task of cleaning spittle from her floors after all of this.

'Let me just—'

'I'm *fine*, Ingram.'

She shoved the sleeves of her sweater up to her elbows and wiped her mouth with her wrist, turning to him with a pointed glare as he left her.

After a moment, her grim expression failed, and with it went the steely facade that Ingram used to pretend he didn't care. That he had better things to do and more interesting people to talk to.

'You all right?'

She sniffed, but she might as well have shaken her head, because he accepted it like an obvious 'no'.

Concern was new, and it had no place on the grid that floated in her mind. Whether his display of decency was a change for the better or a temporary conciliation in dire circumstances, it wasn't something she wanted. She wanted him to dispel the caution from his features, to spout another crude sentiment at her. For normalcy's sake.

If that was the only thing that she could maintain among all the supposed constants that had already let her down, she wanted to hold fast to it.

Somehow, he knew it. It made sense to assume that he had some magic of his own that allowed him to see its golden mark at King's, but there was something else behind those words – *it's complicated* – that made her doubtful. Whether he knew the extent of her magic or the ways she used it every day, she hadn't kept her secret well enough.

It had come crashing down around her – rubble and ruin and defeat.

Why couldn't it have been someone else?

'Look, Schwartz—'

'Can you go?'

His head cocked to the side ever so slightly. 'Do you honestly want me to?'

She spat the residue from her mouth into the sink and washed it down the drain. She prayed he couldn't smell it from the doorway.

'I don't know,' she said. Hours lost to nightmares and crying over dead birds had left her eyes dry and itchy. 'I'm terrified. I can't leave Cambridge. I can't afford a ticket to the States this late . . .'

Stopping to clear her throat, Aurelia concluded with a quiver in her voice. 'No one here has ever known about my magic before.'

'I doubt anyone else will,' he assured her. 'Unless they know what they're looking for.'

'And *you* do?'

The words escaped from her like a curse, but he remained unflinching.

'You know, I could just leave, Schwartz. If you despise me so much, I'm sure you can manage perfectly well without me. Maybe I'm wrong, and you'll be safe and sound staying where you are in Cambridge. Or maybe I'll hear about you in the papers next week – a few pages away from Palermo's obituary . . . I should have known you'd be too stubborn for your own good.'

The counter's edge dug into her back. Everything was cold in her house without Ryan, and somehow Ingram's presence made it even colder.

With a deep, regulating breath, she reminded herself: he couldn't possibly know what was good for her. Only a few nights ago, she was locked into a brutal rally of insults with him on the steps of King's College, and now he was in her flat, trying to soothe her. Within that time, he'd done nothing to atone for the things he'd said to her, nor had she done anything to warrant a change of heart from him.

But there he was, in his tailored trousers and expensive cologne, telling her that a lifetime of secrecy was all for nought. Trying to show her kindness as she sought to obscure her fear. If he'd truly discovered her secret, he could have easily spoiled it. It would have been simpler to hold it against her than to help her.

Dredging up every ounce of dignity she had within her, she admitted, 'It's hard for me to believe that you're looking out for me. And I'm . . . *sorry,* I guess.'

Ingram shrugged, batting her sincerity away like smoke with a flippant hand. 'Just forget it.'

'You *were* though,' she muttered. 'You came to help me, and I'm not even your friend.'

'You know, Schwartz, up until that night at King's, I thought we could be friends. Certainly, not the best of them, but something more than tolerable. I never realized how much it pained you to be just *that.*'

'It's stupid,' she said. 'I've always held grudges.'

He lowered his gaze. 'Still, I can't say I'm proud of what I said. Or that I believe it. To be fair, I hadn't remembered saying it until you shouted it back in my face. Honest to God.'

Where was the upturned chin or the crooked, devious grin he always taunted her with? Was it shame that poisoned his features?

His posture looked all wrong to Aurelia, as if Ingram himself couldn't properly convey the meaning behind his words. His face held no solution either. His brow softened, his lips parted with the continuation of his clumsy apology. She thought he might dance around the word 'sorry' all night if it meant he didn't actually have to say it.

That was another twist in the wound.

She recognized the note in his features as humiliation.

Her own features twisted into a scowl. Petite and unassuming women like her had taught themselves to seem vicious for centuries. She had to be mean, ruthless, to get anywhere.

Don't look at me like that. Don't make me feel sorry.

Slowly, he spoke again. 'I saw you the other night. I think you were walking home – it was late.'

She turned to rest her elbows on the countertop, hanging her head in her hands to shield her pooling eyes from his view. Against her fingertips, her pulse was jarring and irregular.

There it was again . . . The excess of power that tapped at her glass figure like a bird asking to be set free, lest she shatter into a million irreparable shards. Too much for one small body to contain. It was alive and unrelenting, fighting all the restraints she'd forced upon it over the years.

Had it been Ingram that roused it? It only made sense. The quick trip to Tesco that left her queasy and disoriented, and then at King's College . . . Now, here, in the vacancy of her living room.

You've seen me, she thought. *You, of all people. You see me still.*

Why hadn't she felt it before?

'Is that how you knew?' she asked. Ingram shook his head – which somehow made it even worse.

He repeated, 'I've known for a while.'

Her fingers curled around the edge of the countertop, tethering her to her wits.

'I leave Cambridge tomorrow morning for the holidays,' Ingram explained. 'It's a small place where I stay, only a few hours away from here, but there's an extra room . . . If you need it, it's there. We can stay out of each other's way. I'm more than capable of keeping to myself, but you'll be safe there. Will you think about it?'

'Why are you doing this?' It dawned on her that the hollowness in her gut was really a substance. A mass of resentment instead of an absence. Maybe it was fear or shame – she didn't totally know. Aurelia had grown up under the watchful eye of witches, and never had they elicited a response like this.

It's complicated, he'd said. *How so?*

Ingram turned, denoting an end to their conversation with his lips pursed tightly. 'You need an option, and I have one. It wouldn't feel right to leave after all this. Despite your *attitude,*' he said, 'I can't bring myself to believe you deserve it.'

They hovered in uncertainty, him analysing her in a way that chilled her to her core.

It had to be magic. At least, the miserable, damning facet of magic that had been draining her for the past several weeks.

Aurelia almost laughed, recognizing for the first time since he arrived the sardonic person that she knew him to be. But in the familiarly snide tone of his, she found a twisted sort of comfort. The ringing in her ears had subsided to a distant hiss, like wind through a leafy fern or sand in an hourglass. Ingram leaned back in a subtle *contrapposto* – back to pride, back to himself. Maybe he, too, felt the shift in the atmosphere, being whatever he was . . . *Complicated.*

The word fitted him clumsily, unlike *difficult,* which clung to him in all the right places.

'Tomorrow morning, huh?'

'Ten fifteen from the train station.'

After everything she said to hurt him, to scald him as a rogue firecracker might, she would have to believe his intentions were sound and that he did, in fact, have her best interest at heart. It felt like throwing herself off a cliff without seeing what lay at the bottom. Only knowing that she'd have a long fall to figure it out.

'I . . . I don't know.'

He sighed. 'Just think about it. Besides . . . I want to put an end to whatever this is. As much as I'd like to, I can't do that on my own.'

Ingram turned to fetch his umbrella from the nook by the front door while she fastened her attention on his words, looping them over and over again until they meant nothing.

He seized her attention back with a shake of his heavy black coat. He was slender, but it moved with a weight that made him look solid and made of steel. 'You'll text me, right? You have my number now.'

She'd always had it. She can't imagine that he'd forgotten, given the way her presence seemed to taunt him.

She sniffed back the last of the mucous in her nostrils, and somehow, he found a response in that too.

'Even if you decline,' said Ingram. 'Promise me I'll hear from you tomorrow.'

'You will.' The confidence in her voice came from someone who hadn't just thrown up the contents of her stomach a few minutes before. Someone who was not afraid to sleep as soon as she was alone.

With a flourish befitting the version of Theodore Ingram she'd always known – *and despised* – he opened his umbrella and left into the dark.

CHAPTER FIVE

He didn't recognize the voice that carried him into this dream.

It was a woman's voice behind him – smooth and husky, the origin of her accent unfamiliar to him. Spilling from her mouth was a nursery rhyme, though he couldn't understand the language. It was almost French . . . He deciphered remnants of vocabulary from her speech the way one puzzled over a familiar scent.

But if it was, he should have been able to understand it.

Looking down at them, he saw his hands were small and tanned, unlike the ones that belonged to his corporeal form. He hunched over a chopping board in the kitchen with a sharp-ened knife in one hand and a moist bunch of mistletoe in the other. The counter only reached his stomach, pressing through the thin fabric of a faded marching band T-shirt.

Layered over the woman's song was an onslaught of rotating thoughts and white noise, and though the response of their shared unconscious wasn't as clear and developed, Teddy quickly knew that it was the voice of Aurelia Schwartz.

But she was only a teenager here. She was thinking about how she had owned those tennis shoes for years – since she'd turned twelve – but still hadn't outgrown them; and every few seconds, the stringy remnants of a herb she cut fell from the board onto them, littering the floor around her in a natural confetti.

She came back to this scene every evening that felt particularly troublesome, when nightmares and dark visions lurked in the corners, waiting to infest her sleeping body. It served as sanctuary. A guarded tomb beneath the palace of her mind.

He wondered if it was a memory.

The woman behind her asked with the extension of a dark, stout finger, 'This one?'

Teddy responded, moving without agency of his own. 'Mistletoe . . . for opening locks and sealed passages. For stopping nightmares.'

'Excellent,' the woman said. 'Cut the next one.'

He shovelled the chopped herbs into a glass jar with the edge of the knife. Aurelia moved, and so did he, his hand a shade darker and not his own. His lips felt the movement, but her voice came through.

The woman placed a second bunch of herbs on the chopping board. 'Fir prevents nightmares too,' Aurelia offered.

'You remembered. Very good. This one next.'

Aurelia accepted the newest proffered stalks without attending to the fir, turning them thrice in her hands, observing the branches and flowering. She'd never seen this one before, and the odour seized her hard.

Of course, Teddy hadn't seen it either. Herbology was a discipline he could have been taught, but his knowledge would never amount to hers, no matter how many hours more he might have spent on studying it. The gifts of witches would always surpass the capabilities of common magic, and he was predisposed to a different gift, much to his chagrin.

The rancid odour jogged a memory though.

The stalk was warm and heavy, like the warm ligament of a human body. Aurelia brought the branch to her nose and inhaled the scent deeply, letting it overtake her respiratory system with foulness. Like rotting flesh. Like death.

He knew that well. Too well, and too recently.

'It's disgusting,' Aurelia said.

The woman chuckled, and Teddy wanted to put a face to the sound, but Aurelia wouldn't turn to look at her.

'It's hawthorn,' said the woman, 'from the tree of Cardea, goddess of the hinge. Hang it above your bed or in your door. She will keep the bad spirits at bay.'

'I don't like it. I don't see why we need it.'

'Hopefully, you won't,' the woman started, 'but you ought to familiarize yourself with it. Never forsake preparedness. Breathe in again . . . Remember it.'

It had a repugnant scent, but Teddy couldn't object as she raised it up to her face for a second inspection.

'Breathe, *ma lumière*. So that you always carry it with you.'

'It's awful.'

'Magic – spellcraft – is not a light thing. It's heavy in every sense.'

The woman's warm hand fell onto Aurelia's shoulder, and Aurelia lifted the stalk to her nose until the leaves brushed it.

A deep breath.

The woman whispered something in her ear – *Teddy's* ear – and the tangle of her words made his blood run cold.

There were cracks in the walls of Aurelia Schwartz's haven, and through them crept the terror. He couldn't speak or startle her awake before the pain seized them in this shared subconscious state. There was the sword, plunged deep into her sternum.

Teddy woke, grasping for his own chest.

Lighting the lamp beside his bed, he caught the soft cooing of a pigeon outside his window. He drew back the curtain to meet its inquisitive gaze.

'Convenient.'

It stared, but there wasn't much else it could do for him other than stare and listen. Their conversations were always one-sided.

'Tell her I'll have company. I'm sure you'll be there before I am.'

The creature flapped its wings in response.

'Don't look at me like that. I'm tired. It hurts.'

Without as much as a quiet coo, it tilted its head with another question.

'Go on,' Teddy said. 'I have nothing else.'

The bird seemed to take offence at his shortness, bleating angrily until he came closer to silence it. 'Shoo.'

Reluctantly it fled from his window. He would never hear their goodbyes before they left to deliver their messages, but in his mind, they were cordial. They saluted with the naivete of boyhood – children pretending to be soldiers. Birds pretending to be boys. What was he, in the end, except a man pretending to be good?

PART TWO

CHAPTER SIX

She arrived at the station promptly at ten, a brown, canvas duffle bag hoisted over one shoulder and a tumbler full of tea cradled in her hands. She scanned the changing names of cities on the screen above her head, recognizing most only by name and reputation – only a few through personal experience. Though, recognition wouldn't have helped her either. Ingram hadn't told her where they were headed.

He also hadn't arrived yet. Outside, the rain fell steadily over the streets of Cambridge, and Aurelia sipped from her mug, eyebrows raised as she anticipated his strut through the automatic doors of the station. The restless tapping of her foot marked the passage of time quicker than the tick of the clock that hovered over the centre of the room.

With two minutes to spare, he appeared as a dark and shrouded figure against the pale grey of the sky. His wool coat swung as he threaded deftly through the crowd, layered over a deep navy-blue turtleneck and black trousers. With his dark leather boots, woollen gloves and a hickory-coloured mop of hair, the only contrast to his facade was the pale pink face that shone. On it was the oft-worn expression that formed whenever he was subjected to her company – a tight-lipped, furrow-browed, and inhospitable glower.

'You're on time,' said Ingram.

She shrugged her response, adjusting the duffle bag's strap on her shoulder. 'You sound surprised. I'm punctual.'

She followed him through the barriers to the platform and asked, 'Where are we going?'

'To visit someone. Gemma Eakley.'

'Am I supposed to know that name?'

The train whirred to a standstill in front of them. He boarded in front of her, selecting the emptiest train carriage he could find. The blackness of his coat rose like a great, unsurpassable wall over her, and as he lugged his own duffle bag onto the rack above their heads, the darkness flared out around her like a fortress.

'She's family,' he answered.

Aurelia collapsed into her seat, followed down by his unrelenting stare.

She was used to his abrupt responses – sentences that were never fully formed and resembled beat poetry more than human conversation. Before last night, she could not recall a single interaction between the two of them that hadn't erupted into hostility or come close to it. She imagined he was gentler to their colleagues, that he knew how to speak with them in that particular way that had been inaccessible to her, but if she thought about it for more than a few seconds – and she did while she waited to see if anyone else entered the carriage – she couldn't recall witnessing it. If she had, it'd been years since. The clearest memory she had was of him and Lawrence, propped against a wall by their shoulders beside each other, talking about her.

Ingram took her duffle bag from beside her legs and hoisted it over their heads to store away beside his. He sat across from her, one leg crooked over the other, with a book in his hand, a pen between his teeth and a pair of earbuds fastened in. The writing utensil hung lazily in his mouth while he thumbed through the book's pages.

I should talk to him, she thought, but she didn't know how. She wasn't sure what to say or what *not* to say – if there were topics off-limits to the cynical twenty-three-year-old. With difficulty, she forced herself to swallow down her pride, following the trail of his earbuds to the phone in his coat pocket before resolving to break the silence.

'Have you had coffee?'

'What?' His face remained stern in the stupefaction of interrupted silence.

'Do you need coffee? I usually need some kind of caffeination in the mornings.'

He took in her position, perfectly upright and attentive, swaddled in her heavy college sweatshirt and coat, somehow managing a delightful demeanour in the face of their circumstances.

Aurelia raised her stainless steel tumbler. 'You could have some of my tea. I don't mind sharing.'

Which was a lie, but it was an effort toward the right direction – whichever direction that might be.

'Green?' he asked.

'Earl Grey with lavender, sugar and a dash of milk.' She waited with her mug outstretched to him until he accepted it.

She would have given anything to be sharing tea with Ryan now, to be in the company of someone who valued her commitment to making the perfect hot drink.

She and Ingram were old enough to know that the offering was shallow. She'd been so dedicated to their constant bickering that every outreach of goodwill felt like a farce. Over the tilt of the tumbler, he studied her, sipping slowly as if assessing for the taste of poison.

He might always find himself asking if she was kind to him out of want or out of obligation. For the first time, that thought made her feel something other than smug, but she couldn't place it.

Ingram wiped his thumb across his bottom lip to catch a drop of moisture. 'It's good.'

Her nose wrinkled. 'You think so?'

His response was a deep hum that came from the back of his throat, his signature of sorts. She could recognize him blind by the simple sound of his hum. It was the kind of sound that escaped after inhaling the scent of a fresh-cooked meal, or of someone who struggled to hide their confusion when taught an advanced mathematical concept. It was also the sound of uncertainty that came when a person didn't truly believe whatever was being said to them.

Really, it was all the same coming from him.

'Can't stand green tea,' he said. 'The bitterness of it . . . It's no fun.'

'I don't know that I'd leave it up to *you* to decide what's fun,' she responded. His lips turned up ever so slightly at the corners as if he hid a secret behind his teeth.

'That's fair.'

She forced herself steady, hoping it would draw more from him, and that by consequence the guilt in her gut would dissipate; but to her chagrin, it festered. To be genuine was an exhausting thing.

Ingram slouched in his seat. 'You should get comfortable. We have a while.'

Comfort hardly seemed attainable, but she wasn't aware of how tense she appeared to him until now. She folded her arms across her chest, unfolding them again within seconds. He observed her body language with the astuteness of a big cat before it struck.

'What's it like where we're headed?'

'What do you want to know?'

Aurelia's mouth twisted in spite of herself. She was uncertain of how to talk with him in a way that wasn't small talk. She had a feeling that, much like herself, he wouldn't enjoy trivial conversation, even if they'd been friends.

'Who is Gemma?'

He frowned.

'Loaded question,' he said. 'Leave it at "family". But if you expect her to be anything like me, you'll be sorely mistaken. We're very different people. You'll be properly on the mark if you look in the other direction.'

'Maybe she'll like me, then,' Aurelia said.

'She'd probably *love* you.'

Those words were laced with resentment. The last thing Aurelia wanted was to have him make a first impression in her stead. Gemma must have known she was coming. Certainly, the woman would have questions regarding the last-minute guest who would be staying with them.

Despite Ingram's assurance that Gemma would not be anything like him – which, in Aurelia's mind, meant snide and contemptuous – she could not shake the pre-existing notion that his family would be all dark clouds and misery; and that was vaguely amusing.

Ingram buried his nose into his book again, contented without her disruption. It was easy for him to end a conversation with silence, but that was only another thing that made Aurelia Schwartz writhe in her seat. She could spin quick conversations into lectures that lasted hours if she wasn't careful – her lips moving fast enough to accommodate the ideas that flickered at light speed in her mind. She had to keep talking. Otherwise, she might lose ideas to the chasm of her memory like a grain of salt in the Atlantic. It was one of the few habits of hers that made her feel younger than her years, one that she was grateful to have put an end to.

Not that twenty-three was old at all. But it was an odd stage of life, where people suddenly expected her to *know* things that she'd been too young to learn before. Where mannerisms were meant to be shed like garments that no longer fit, but throwing them out seemed wasteful. It took years of living on her own to learn how to keep the chatter confined to her head, to sedate her mouth for the sake of disappearing.

When it came to magic, it was always better to be distracted than out of control.

'What are you listening to?' Aurelia asked.

He removed an earbud and handed it to her, barely shifting his attention from the open book in his lap. She had to lean further to accept it – which might have been a metaphor for her attempts to gain his amiability had she not been half-assing every kind word that came from her mouth. Still, it was more than Ingram cared to do. If all her efforts led to a dead end, at least she could say that she knew what to expect . . . Knowledge would suffice where control dampened.

She tuned into what she discovered was French new wave.

He peered up at her to gauge her expression, sheltering a grin from her view, his green irises hidden by the curve of his lashes. Only at his bemusement did Aurelia realize how her own features were contorted. She returned his earbud with a sigh.

At least he's self-aware.

'How can you focus on anything you're reading with *that* in your ears?'

'Easily,' he replied. 'I'll admit it's not the most calming thing in my playlists, but I'm used to it.'

'Does Gemma play a lot of French music around the house or something?'

Aurelia noted the subtle shift in his posture a second later, letting the half-smile droop from her face. She'd struck a nerve, somehow.

But which one?

She wasn't intending to use it against him, but it'd be useful to know. Theodore Ingram knew more about her than she did about *him*. The simple awareness of her magical nature was enough to make her hesitate.

She needed leverage, an upper hand. A safe in which to guard the only fragment of control she still possessed.

With a lowered voice, she ventured, 'I've heard about your family.'

'Have you?' Ingram asked with blatant scepticism.

'I'm told you're disgustingly rich.'

His gaze solidified against hers with the efficacy of a flicked switch. His jaw flexed, yet he said nothing – in his defence or to his detriment.

'I've been told plenty of things,' she continued. 'Maybe you should tell me them yourself . . . In the spirit of honesty, y'know.'

'You pry,' he drawled.

'I'm curious,' Aurelia explained. 'Can you blame me for wondering who the person in front of me is when I'm supposed to be staying under their roof? Maybe I should know these things, Ingram, so I don't walk into your home without knowing about your parents or what they expect of me. If they're as wealthy as I'm told, I'm sure I'd make a shitty first impression. Then again, maybe that's how you want them to see me. Maybe you want to see me crash and burn.'

He was less inclined to hide the tension in his face now. He gazed out at the rolling hills that passed without giving her an answer. Aurelia felt it coming, though. The twinge of guilt she harboured over corralling him like a timid sheep soiled the aftertaste of tea in her mouth.

'You won't get to meet my parents,' he said. 'Don't expect to see them.'

Even softer, she pressed onward. 'Which of them gave you your magic?'

'*Don't*, Schwartz.'

'Why not?' Aurelia surveyed the carriage once more. She knew it was empty before, otherwise she wouldn't have risked referring to their magic aloud. He might have seen her as something reckless and unpredictable – not because she *was*, but because he hadn't been allowed to catch another glimpse into her over-processed mind.

Knowing about her magic was more than enough.

'We're the only ones left, Ingram.'

'You think privacy is all I'm concerned for?' he scoffed, leaning back into his seat defiantly. If his shields were ever lowered, they'd since been fortified – taller, thicker this time. 'You think you can implicate magic in our conversation like another pawn in your little game, but you're mistaken, Schwartz. I'm not discussing it with you.'

'*You* invited *me*. You said I could help you figure out whatever this is. We both know that you wouldn't have offered me a place to stay out of the goodness of your heart, and, despite what you said to me at King's College, I *am* smart enough to deduce that you have some stake in this. Don't intend to know what my motives are, Ingram. I was only wrong to assume that you'd want to bury the hatchet and make amends along the way.'

'You want to make amends?' Ingram asked.

Did she? The sentiment had escaped her unbidden. She shrunk inwards, calculating a potential forfeiting of their petty rivalry before answering, 'I don't know. Don't you?'

She had never seen him dumbstruck before, nor had she

realized that his jaw could go slack – that the defined edge she knew so well was only the product of a sour expression. It might have been endearing if it wasn't so goddam *frustrating*.

With a considerate breath, he admitted, 'Honestly, I'm predisposed to steer clear of you altogether. I'm not naive enough to believe that we can forget all the unkind things we've said to one another.'

'I never said anything about forgetting,' Aurelia told him, lowering her gaze to her lap. 'I forget a lot of things, but I've never forgotten what you said in all the time we've known each other. I wish it were that easy.'

'Then what is it you want, Schwartz?'

She shook her head, wishing she knew. Every desire that came to mind was unattainable – so what point was there in sharing it, other than to admit to him that her aspirations were sometimes bigger than her capabilities? To grant him access to a softer, wistful side of her that even Aurelia couldn't stand?

To rattle her own protective cage?

She raised her hand to her face and massaged the strain from her jaw. 'I'm figuring it out.'

Ingram nodded, punctuating the end of their conversation with a clearing of his throat. He reverted to his previous position, poised against the window of the train with the open book propped up in the negative space between his crossed legs.

He flipped to another page with ease; she couldn't decide whether it was real or not.

'Let me know when you do.'

*

They spent the rest of their ride in silence – two and a half hours in total from when they'd first departed Cambridge Station. The weather was a violent rapture as Aurelia stepped onto the platform, re-adjusting the wide strap of her duffle bag over her shoulder.

Eyeing her lopsided figure, Ingram assured her, 'I'll get a cab.'

'How far are we going?' Aurelia asked. She didn't mind walking in the rain. It would save a few pounds not to pay the fare – and the fact that Ingram felt compelled to call a cab could only mean that their walk would be arduous.

Or that he underestimated her ability to brave a little cold weather. The predatory howl of the wind seeped through her jeans, up the sleeves of both her jacket and the sweatshirt beneath it to kiss her skin. She'd packed a pair of gloves in her bag but hadn't expected to need them yet, and so they were buried beneath all the other garments and toiletries, out of reach.

As he tapped at his phone screen, she stole a glimpse at the puzzled expression on his face from a new angle. His coat sleeve brushed her arm. They weren't often subjected to closeness like this, and she half expected him to jump at her touch.

'This is the closest station our train will take us to, but it's not where we're supposed to be,' he said. Sheltered beneath the canopy outside, he offered her a vague estimation of the setting with his hands. 'Where we'll be staying is the most remote part of an already-desolate town that sits on the outskirts of this city. It's worth noting that this station is also the least populated stop along the train's route.'

'I assume the departures are busier than the arrivals . . . I've never been on a train so empty.'

'How often do you get out of Cambridge, Schwartz?'

His travel and hers were incomparable, and he must have known that. 'Not often. I have other things to do.'

Ingram gave an impatient sigh. 'Townsend Hill is an insignificant place. It's not a place you choose to go if you have any other option.'

But I'll be safe there? she thought.

A smaller, weaker voice in her mind was still asking, *Safe from what?*

Ingram never answered her question on the train. He had evaded several of her questions since last night. She hadn't held her defences when he accused her of being a witch, despite the fear of discovery that drained her skin of its warmth, but he still hadn't admitted how he knew – or *what* he was . . .

Her stomach churned. Had to be hunger.

Aurelia's vision flickered for a moment as she weighed the consequences of making a mistake like this.

'Here,' said Ingram, circling his fingers around the strap of her bag. 'Let me.'

'It's not that heavy,' she said. Her grimoire was the heaviest thing in there and the last thing she wanted to relinquish to him.

'You're straining,' he argued. 'You look as if a slight breeze might topple you over.'

'Shut up, Ingram.'

'Suit yourself.'

Ingram read the number plate of a blocky, green car as it

came to a stop at the kerb. They swiftly stowed their bags beneath their boots, piling into the small vehicle. In the narrow reflection of the rear-view mirror, a red-faced man in his forties asked, 'Townsend, yeah?'

'Yes,' Ingram said plainly as he attempted to configure his long legs over his duffle bag. Following the first flutter of amusement at his discomforted, spidery limbs, Aurelia grasped a seam and yanked the bag closer to hers, creating a gap to house his legs.

'Thanks.'

'Don't mention it.'

The scent of tobacco stained the car's interior. The exhaust sputtered. The man asked, 'Odd spot for a getaway, yeah?'

Ingram sucked his gums impatiently. 'Sure.'

'Some odd folks too. You know anyone up there?'

Neither phrase seemed like something Ingram wanted to expand upon.

'Excuse me,' said Aurelia. 'How far is the drive?'

The man laughed. A keychain dangled from the vehicle's ignition. The word 'Papa' was etched into a leather tag, followed by a smiley face. 'Couple o' minutes, but it's all gravel roads and mud after this. You pack your wellies?'

Aurelia had clung to the same pair of weather-treated leather boots since she first moved to this country, and they'd collected more than their four years of wear in the form of scuffs and creases.

'Bottom of the hill should be perfect,' Ingram interjected. 'Thanks.'

Oblivious to – or in spite of – the blunt arrogance in the

posh student's command, Papa cleared his throat with a boom and began to monologue. 'My brother once saw a psychic in Townsend. The missus dragged him by the ear for some *spiritual counselling.* I try not to go there myself. I'm not one for characters.'

Ingram touched his temple to the glass with an exasperated sigh.

'What did they say?' Aurelia asked, picking the rough edges of her fingernails.

'Well, my brother wasn't too happy. The visit caused a big fight between him and his wife. The woman said he'd been unfaithful. I can't really blame her for being angry, but a week later, she'd gone and filed for divorce. Now I'm stuck with 'im.'

'I meant the psychic,' Aurelia said.

At her side, Ingram shifted in his seat, massaging a strain in his calf as the car passed a family walking home from a Sunday morning mass. 'Ah,' Papa said. 'A load of rubbish. You can't go on making assumptions like that for total strangers. It was spineless. No sense of shame, that woman. My brother never cheated on anyone. But you can't blame a man for looking, can you?'

'What ever happened to the quiet drivers?' Ingram mused.

Aurelia meant to snap, but the driver simply laughed it off. 'It's all right. My honour's intact.'

Ingram had nothing else to add. Aurelia forced herself to bite her tongue, too.

He'd touched a nerve, and she was desperate to find it. In whatever unspoken disagreement that had festered during those brief minutes, Ingram's cool absent-mindedness told her he considered himself above it all, that it mattered little to him what either of them thought.

Papa continued, 'I never believed in psychics. In my opinion, it's all bullshit. If you've come for some counselling of your own, go to therapy. Don't waste your money on psychics. 'Specially not the ones here. They're good for swindling and spinning tales. Not much else.'

The last of Papa's words faded into the low chatter of the radio. Her face grew clammy with an anxiety that would endure through the last of their drive.

Ingram avoided looking at her and Papa. He kept his focus on the empty gravel road that branched from the city's limit, but she knew in the familiar knit of his brow that he was thinking of something else.

Beyond the flat, blue-green fields, hills rolled, blanketed in the same shade of forest green. They rose through the blue fog, clawing past its wintry breath with hands of twisted tree bramble. The wind blew fiercely and hummed around the car, rustling the tall stalks at their sides.

Townsend hovered in the distance. The vague descriptors she'd been given thus far conjured no precise image; but with it in her sights now, those words were perfect.

The car jostled less as they moved from gravel to cobblestone, the road hardly suitable for motor vehicles. *Maybe a horse-drawn carriage,* she thought. *Two men with wheelbarrows.*

It was charming . . . And *quiet.* All of it confined to less than a square mile, its streets lined with flowers and overgrowth, not even wide enough for two cars to pass. As the cab crept toward the hill, eyes stared back, seeing her clearly through the glass.

Behind the shabby windows of storefronts or in the apartments that sat atop them, curtains parted and made way for curious eyes to meet her. Faces with wrinkles carved deep and plentiful that looked nothing like hers were watching, the people holding cloth bags beneath their elbows. Some whispered to each other, as if she could hear them through the cage of the car, which meant their words were the kind that could betray them.

Aurelia bristled in her seat, eager to be rid of the car. That must've been it – the car. They couldn't have been common here.

Tall, crooked buildings leaned over them in shades of green, brown and muddy beige. Watchful eyes aside, she didn't understand Ingram's aversion to this place. It was quaint, cute.

Papa was quick to depart at the opposite boundary of the town. Aurelia didn't blame him. Ingram's stand-offishness thickened the air of any room until it was impossible to breathe.

A breeze crept eagerly underneath her layers again, as if it had been waiting for her to crawl back into its clutches. She tucked her hands into her pockets and huffed into the high collar of her coat, warming her face with her own breath before the frost could absorb it.

Ingram sniffled beside her, watching as she fixed the strap of her bag again. She forced the disdain from her face and smoothed the wrinkle that formed on the bridge of her nose. *Don't help me. Don't even think about it.*

Not that his quiet attention felt better. Even the way he cleared his throat was detestable.

'Up the hill,' he said finally. 'See it?'

'Of course I can.'

He rolled his eyes. 'Don't sound so pleased with yourself. It's imperceptible to humans.' The steep slope of the hill began where the cobblestones ended, standing tallest in the regiment of rolling hills. A faint glow emanated from a cottage at the top, calling like a siren through the thick cover.

'Hurry,' Ingram said, treading ahead. 'Before the rain starts again.'

Aurelia grumbled, straining to match his pace as her boots sunk into the mulch. Her breath clouded in front of her. The tall grass brushed her thighs as they advanced and hissed against the bottom edge of her coat with the tips of dew-coated tendrils.

'I won't offer to carry your bag again if it injures your confidence, but you can ask, and I might say yes.'

'I can handle it, Ingram.'

A self-assured grin crawled over his face. Their trek didn't tire him the way she wished it would.

'That was weird, you know.'

'What was?' asked Ingram.

'That ride. Your behaviour. I mean, I'm glad to know I'm not the only person who incurs your wrath, but . . . That might've been the most uncomfortable six minutes of my life.'

He made an elegant snort. 'You make up enough wrath for the both of us. I'm hardly rude.'

'*That* was rude,' Aurelia huffed. 'Not even entertaining. I always thought people like you were taught manners and etiquette, but I can see no one ever taught you the importance of social awareness.'

With a wide-eyed, incredulous stare, he asked, 'People like me?' His expression was wild, bemused. Ire twisted around her gut like a vice.

'You know . . . Spoiled rotten. Fed your formula with a silver spoon. In need of nothing . . . I can go on if it doesn't click,' she said. She could have blamed her intense redness on the fervent wind that propelled itself up the slope of the hill, but that would've been a lie. 'Maybe you'll never have to *ask* for anything in your life, but politeness goes a long way. I shouldn't have to be the first person to tell you that.'

'You've been awfully invested in my finances lately, Schwartz.'

Aurelia scowled. '*That's* your takeaway?'

'Merely an observation,' he answered, walking a few paces ahead.

'Because you paid for my ticket, you ass,' she mumbled to herself. And because he *insisted* on it. The last thing she wanted was for him to make debts for her to repay. It sickened her that he had money to waste on someone who refused to give him the time of day while buying her own housemate a coffee involved hastily checking her bank account.

Of course, she was invested. The scale was forever tipped in his favour.

'Look,' she began with a sigh. 'I appreciate the offer to stay and for getting me here in one piece, but I can't help wondering if I've made the wrong choice in coming.'

'We're not even there, Schwartz.'

'And that's *bad*.'

Ingram stopped. Assuming he was waiting for her to catch

up, she closed the gap, but he remained immovable and unyielding like another tree rooted in the green wave.

Her back straightened proudly, but she was shivering, compliant to the wind like a blade of grass.

'I can guarantee you haven't made a mistake.'

'And why is that? Ever since I agreed to come here, all I've done is think the opposite.'

He shrugged, attempting to mask the uncertainty in his own posture, but the pieces didn't all converge with even seams, like an image made from two different puzzles. He resumed his strut past her.

'You enjoy pissing me off, don't you?' she asked.

'You'd like to believe that, wouldn't you?' The dense floor of grass soaked the hems of his trousers, but he didn't seem nearly as bothered by the weather as she was. 'Look at yourself, Schwartz. You've been nothing but uncivil to me since we met. I told you that I regret all those things I said in the past, and I meant it. I *do*. But I've also moved on, and you've had more than enough time to do the same.'

'But—'

'It's been years. *Years* of you regarding me with vitriol while I convinced myself that you weren't all that I made you out to be. Not that I needed to do that . . . I could have managed fine without having you around to breathe down my neck, but I knew it was unfair. Almost as unfair as you holding this grievance against me for years while I was none the wiser to when it started.'

'I didn't like you enough to give you that satisfaction.'

'Yet you have the energy to expend hating me. At some

point, the blame is all yours, Schwartz. We could have reconciled years ago if you weren't so *fucking stubborn*.'

Aurelia's throat closed, walls engorged as he passed her on the hill once again.

'Didn't I tell you I was sorry?' she asked.

Ingram gave a mirthless laugh. 'Sure. But you didn't mean it.'

'That's not fair. You're assuming things.'

He hummed, regarding her with a cool condescension that reduced her to childishness. She maintained a steady pace behind him even if it strained her, trudging. There was no way to *trudge* without embodying buried adolescent rage.

'What is it going to take for you to see that I'm trying?' she asked.

Ingram shook his head. 'Why bother? We don't need to enjoy each other. You'll sooner tire yourself trying to enjoy my company.'

'But you fight me all the same. Why am I here, then?' Aurelia asked. 'So you can tell me how much I *hurt your feelings?*'

She could offer him something rare, like humiliation. And all it took was a word. '*Please*, Ingram.' A word and a name – a cast for the broken leg. 'Don't make me ask again.'

He was almost as rigid as she was, but she felt a little smaller, meek under his self-assured stance. He scoured for a distraction in the distant copse of trees at the bottom of the hill. 'At this point, I don't know,' said Ingram. 'Maybe pity.'

Aurelia's fists curled in her pockets. 'I hate that we can't be civil with each other. What do I have to do for you to take me seriously? Beg? We won't last more than a day under this roof with so much resentment lingering between us.'

'That *would* be miserable . . .'

He walked on, leaving her to quicken at his heels.

'*Fine*,' she spat. 'I am jealous of you. You and your stupid fucking clothes and your decent fucking marks. Is that what you want? Because I hate knowing that I work so hard to succeed in my studies while you have it so *easy*.'

'Do you think having first-class work at Pembroke was something I did on a whim? You think it's *easy* for me to win grants? That my theses write themselves while I'm off gallivanting with reckless abandon?'

'But it's always easi*er*, isn't it? It always has been and always will be for you. That's the problem. You can look down at me from your cosy little palace of privilege and undermine me, because I'm not as sociable and my daddy didn't load my pockets up with money before he sent me off to my parent-financed flat and let me live off my generational wealth. You consistently belittle me, but you completely ignore what I'm capable of. And that's what pisses me off most about you. That I can't be above this. Even if you regret what you said, I'll harbour those words in my heart until the day I die, because you're probably the only person I'd want in my corner as far as our work goes, and I didn't think you respected me.'

'That's where you're wrong, Schwartz,' he said. 'You're so reluctant to be wrong for once that you'd rather believe me irredeemable.'

'I know,' Aurelia said, shrinking into herself. 'But you always loved to tell me when I was wrong and . . . And I don't know. Maybe I'm angrier at you for that than I should be. Maybe I let it cloud my judgement when you'd already moved on . . . I think, for once, I'd like to know how it feels to be as assured as you.'

Silence grew between them, and then a crack – the soft line of his grin against his steel exterior.

'Look at yourself, Schwartz. You're *assured* enough to believe that I am assured about anything when there is so much that confounds me.'

Relief tore through her. She brought up her hand to massage the muscle beneath the strap on her shoulder.

'I was wrong,' she said. 'You knew that . . . But I know your mistakes just as well. We could benefit each other, Ingram. As much as it pains you to admit it, having me in your corner – and having you in mine – would be an academic failsafe. Think about it. We're the best researchers in our programme, yet we can't even endure a faculty dinner without squabbling. We're punishing ourselves twice over. And I'll be as miserable as I need to be if it means we stop doing that. I'm sorry. I'm fucking *sorry*.' Her hand quivered as it raked through her hair. 'We don't have to be friends if that isn't what you want, but I don't want you to hate me any more.'

She swallowed the knot in her throat. That had to be enough. Seconds passed before Ingram spoke again, each exponentially more dreadful than the last, but she would wait until he budged, pushing at the immovable object until it gave – just a little.

Besides, Aurelia had exhausted everything that she had left to say to him. Words without filter were honest, but they were also messy and raw, scraped off her like plaque from her teeth. She'd given him more of her shame than she'd intended to, and he could see right through all the empty spaces left in its wake.

If he didn't forgive her then, what other dignity would she have left? She'd be miles from where she started – not quite back at the beginning but buried underground.

He shifted beneath the weight of his own bag and extended a gloved hand to her. She accepted it, meeting him approximately in the middle before the tight line of his lips shattered.

'Truce,' said Ingram.

A weight plummeted from her shoulders with the soft squeeze of his hand.

'Truce.'

'I'll take your word for it.'

It sounded vaguely like a threat, like he didn't truly believe the naked sincerity she'd laid bare for him.

But they crossed the final distance toward the little house, and he didn't ask for more.

That had to be enough.

CHAPTER SEVEN

'So, is Gemma your aunt or something?'

At the top of the stairs, poised to knock, Ingram stopped short at the question.

He whispered, concealing his answer from whatever powers lurked within the walls of the house. 'Do you mind if we don't get into that?'

Aurelia shrugged. He rapped his knuckles on the worn, wooden door. The scent of something earthy and sweet wafted through the gaps by the hinges. She was salivating, famished and completely parched. The long walk through flooded soil had drained her. Her stomach lurched as she succumbed to the mere thought of a meal.

'That smells heavenly.'

'It's potato stew. Tastes about as heavenly as you'd expect. Gem cooks with the hand of God.'

As she dug her heels into the dirt, Ingram turned to her from atop the steps with a comforting half-smile that didn't sit quite right on his face. 'You'll love Gemma's cooking. She's basically a recluse all the way out here, but on special occasions, she'll send a dish to some of the neighbours at the bottom of the hill – and they all love her for it. I've never met a person who didn't love Gemma.'

'So, everyone *here* can see this place?'

He paused, reflecting on the implication that he lived – or *stayed*, as he so aptly insisted – in a town full of witches.

'Gem always explained it as a . . .' The crease reappeared between his brows, in which she found a relief from the alarm that his smile rang in her. 'A *selective* ward. Those that she permits to see the house will see it. She doesn't raise the ward for witches like herself, but she's pickier with humans. Inherently distrustful of the lot. Most look up at the hill and see nothing at all. And if, for some reason, they venture here, they're struck with an imposing desire to turn back.'

He turned to the closed door and pressed his ear to it before knocking again. She stiffened with each beat.

Never before had Aurelia knowingly sought another witch. Doing so would have thrust her into the predicament of revealing her own nature, and frankly, she found the idea to be nothing short of catastrophic.

She wiped her nose with her sleeve and asked, 'Which are you?'

'An infrequent resident.'

And an insufferable liar, she thought.

Metal clanged beneath running water, and a hoarse British curse came through from the other side.

Aurelia wasn't entirely sure what she'd expected Gemma to look like, given the way Ingram guarded every piece of information she asked of him. She'd never admit how often his upbringing piqued her curiosity, but her mind flew from the criminal to distantly royal. Always fantastic, likely untrue.

In appearance, the woman in the doorway could have looked like him once – but years of unbridled laughter had carved marks in her skin, and sunlight amassed as freckles on her pink face. Some people were readable. Gemma opened her home wide to them like the covers of a book, but he'd never been accommodating – not in the slightest.

Gemma was taller than Aurelia, with more muscle corded around her bones than the rigid college student shivering below her steps. Twisted around her fist was a rag caked in stew, steaming in the cold. Framing her sun-kissed skin were tufts of black hair that fell from a fat bun hanging at her neck, sprouting strands of silvery hair. The crow's-foot wrinkles gathered beside her green eyes were formed by the kind of joy that normally only came with unblemished youth.

And though her eyes were the same warm shade as Ingram's and her kinked hair was still dark like his where it hadn't yet turned silver, she wasn't akin to him in any other way. The exuberant smile that tugged at her chapped lips was entirely something else.

'Gem,' he said plainly.

'You came early,' the woman stated, standing on tip-toe to wrap a firm, stocky arm around his neck. His bag fell as he squeezed her with a reciprocal intensity, and she swayed him side to side, moving the much taller man the way rough waters tip a boat. He beamed back, neck craning from her pull.

Aurelia had never seen him alight like this.

Unversed in this spectacle of affection, Aurelia threw her

gaze into the grass and spotted a child's toy on the ground beside the front steps – a filthy, knitted unicorn plushy that was probably white or cream-coloured at some point but was now an unsavoury grey-brown. Ingram hadn't mentioned a child, had he?

'I wasn't sure if you'd make it this year,' Gemma said, pressing a kiss to the side of his face.

'I tried to send word,' he said. With his hands on the sides of her shoulders, he pulled away. 'Would have been nice to *call* for a change, but I caught one of your boys to relay the message.'

'What message?'

'Last-minute complication.'

Aurelia shot him a scornful glare. 'You didn't tell her I was coming?'

He shrugged, which only exacerbated her disdain further. He lifted his bag and passed through to set it somewhere inside the cottage.

The woman openly inspected her.

'I'm Aurelia,' she offered. 'I'm so sorry, I thought he would have told you.'

The woman waved Ingram away like a petulant bug before meeting her with a warm, leather-skinned hand.

'Ah,' said the woman. 'He never tells us anything. I'm always happy to see new faces. Come inside. Bloody cold out there.'

A spread of weathered oracle cards lay face up on a coffee table at the front, and just past it was a kitchen wherein the countertop was covered with the peel of fresh vegetables, and spice bottles. Aurelia smelled paprika. Bay leaves. *Cinnamon.* Her tongue wetted in a doggish way. Gemma's potato stew was already her favourite, the cottage brimming over with the scent of autumn and warmth; and a memory of youth recurred in Aurelia's mind . . .

Of warm summer afternoons spent preparing the usable bits of herbs from their stalks, harvested in rain-drenched springs spent trekking through the mulch . . . Gabrielle would cook with them or make her tie their unbroken stalks for use later.

Beside the front door, a wrought-iron rail guarded a downward-spiralling staircase. A line of three doors bracketed one side of a hallway next to the kitchen, and two bracketed the other. The cottage was cluttered in a way that *homes* usually were. Composed of beloved things. There was hardly a sufficient amount of space to *stay out of each other's way*, as Ingram had promised.

But with all the handmade quilts that littered the room, the tea sets and magical tools that rested openly on dark wooden desks, and the scent of seasoned home cooking, the house enveloped her in an intimate embrace that she couldn't help sinking into. The cottage invoked a hazy and bittersweet nostalgia for something else she once knew.

Gabrielle. What Aurelia would give to be there again . . . her tutor's home on the border of Oregon and Washington, drawing sunlight in through faded, sunflower-printed curtains. A buried whisper of long-forgotten magic traced the path of veins behind Aurelia's eyes, and she forced it away.

From the kitchen, Ingram asked Gemma, 'Why are you so keen on living without a cell phone? We *are* in the twenty-first century, you know. It wouldn't hurt to have one for emergencies.'

'What emergencies do we have up here? A stray dog in the garden, maybe!'

He groaned, grabbing the ladle from beside the pot of stew, already poised to fill a bowl and make himself at home. 'Wouldn't it have been nice to anticipate company rather than have it arrive unannounced?'

Aurelia scoured the floor for a crack in the wood that would distract her, hiding little as redness marked her face in shame.

'Easy now,' said Gemma.

Ingram hummed, spooning the stew into a crudely tossed and glazed piece of pottery. 'Heard you were taking new clients. I had the most hideous drive up here from someone whose family you gave some "spiritual counselling" to.'

'I had to,' Gemma responded. 'Money's tight, darling.'

'You should have called me.'

'Out of the question. Besides, that woman has a right to know she's married to a snivelling *cunt*.'

'*Was* married,' Ingram corrected. 'They're divorcing.'

'Oh! Good for her.'

Aurelia shifted, dispersing the pressure from the balls of her feet to her heels. The floorboard creaked, reminding Ingram of her presence. The comfortable smile crumpled on his face. It was all too easy for him to forget that she was there.

Maybe that's a good thing.

Swatting him out of the kitchen, Gemma exclaimed, 'Stop it! I haven't even made Lou's bowl! She'll be furious if you eat without her.'

Ingram sipped from it. 'Where is she?'

'Down in the basement.' Gemma pointed to the staircase

with her ladle. 'You can fetch her for me if you'd like. Aurelia darling, do you need a separate room or . . .'

Her cheeks burned even hotter. 'Oh, we're not—'

'She can stay in my room,' Ingram interjected, cutting her a disinterested glance before she could open her mouth to protest. 'I'll be sleeping in the basement.'

After placing her duffle bag in the last room in the hallway – a tidy spare with a few miscellaneous books on the back shelves and a blinking digital clock – Ingram beckoned Aurelia to follow him downstairs.

'Who's Lou?' she whispered as they descended the spiral staircase.

'Louisa. Gem's kid,' he said shortly.

She'd never been good with children, although in all fairness, she'd never tried to be; but she reckoned one was manageable. One wouldn't make her hightail back to Cambridge.

Below ground, Aurelia heard a shuffling of papers and saw a young girl with mushroom-brown hair leap to her feet and exclaim, 'Teddy, Teddy! Where've you been?'

She ran to him but stopped just short of a hug, which surprised no one other than Aurelia. Ingram crouched down to her level, held out his hand, and she slapped it hard.

'You monster,' he said. 'That one hurt.'

'Did it really?' she asked excitedly.

'Yeah, totally.'

She must have been six or seven with hair that hung pin

straight, save for the limp curls formed at the tips brushing her shoulders. She hadn't asked about Aurelia yet, though it didn't faze her much. She wouldn't know what to say. Aurelia often resorted to silence when faced with the task of entertaining kids.

Finally, Louisa asked, 'Who are *you?*'

'She's a *friend,* silly bug,' Ingram said. 'Her name is Aurelia. Try not to tear her apart, all right.'

With a huff, the girl said, 'I wasn't gonna.'

Aurelia waved from where she stood, leaning against the rail of the spiral staircase for support. Ingram paid her no mind, despite the fact that calling her a 'friend' made her mind swirl with unease. The details of their new-found camaraderie were unnecessary for anyone other than the two of them, but hearing him reduce it to a simple thing like friendship triggered a nervous ringing in her ears, an alarm blaring.

To see the person with whom she had argued and agonized overusing childish nicknames and smiling with his teeth overwhelmed her. It struck a feeling she couldn't quite place, tinged with shame and confusion and *affection.* None of which was truly comprehensible after such a long day of travel.

She was riddled with exhaustion, yearning for the full-sized mattress and pillow that sat just over her head. A stranger's bed never felt so attractive to her.

No, not a stranger, she thought. *Ingram's* bed.

Louisa explained to him that her mother was teaching her cursive, or 'joined-up writing', and he teased her about whether she'd write to him at school. The young girl rocked back and forth on the balls of her feet with giddiness as Ingram caught every word without fail.

Aurelia tapped his shoulder, spoiling their tender reunion. Ingram turned to look up at her with wondrous, wide eyes, revealing the expanse of his unguarded expression. Whatever she meant to say faded from the foreground of her thought, lost in that raging sea. The muscles in his face weren't taut. There was no glower, no gravity. She'd never seen him so comfortable. So unbothered.

'I think I'm going to head upstairs,' she said softly. He nodded, then turned away – probably remembering. He wasn't allowed to be that comfortable with her.

'Are you staying for dinner?' Louisa asked.

His voice softened. 'She's staying through New Year, Lou. Maybe a little longer.'

Aurelia nodded. 'I hope that's OK with you.'

The young girl shrugged, her features contorted in innocent disgust. '*I* think that's fine. But *I* don't make the rules.'

Aurelia forced a feeble smile and mouthed the word *great* before Ingram and Louisa resumed their conversation. To watch them any longer felt like an intrusion. The girl retrieved her writing practice sheets and displayed them to him with pride. He met her precisely where she was, with care and undivided attention, a feat he'd never been capable of with Aurelia Schwartz, which made her heart drop to the pit of her stomach.

Without another word, she slipped upstairs and tucked herself into the bed. Sleep fought her and lost.

*

It was almost eight in the evening when she finally rose again, groggy and disconcerted, fingers over her chest to ensure that the sword wasn't truly there. She'd fallen asleep in her jeans. The red indentations from the stiff denim on her hips peered out as she stretched her legs. A minute passed as she recollected her surroundings. Shadow cast blue over everything, from the wardrobe to the walls and the soft white sheets kicked down around her legs. All she discerned with certainty were the blinking zeros of a digital clock that had to be reset.

This was normally Ingram's room, but it held no trace of him at a glance. If she were to open the white armoire, she'd find a few of his coats and some knitted sweaters made by Gemma rolled up on the top shelf; and if she flipped through the pages of the twenty-something books that sat askew on the dusty shelves behind her, she might find his handwriting in the margins. The smell of the evening's stew slipped beneath the closed door, reminding her that beyond this room was a house that felt fully lived in and personalized. However, in her first waking moments, the window beside her showed only a black evening sky and a field of nothingness beyond it; and the room, with its lack of photographs and number of dusty surfaces, offered no comfort to her. The noise of the television in the basement seeped through the cracks in the floorboards with a seductive taunt. An assortment of muffled laughs sifted through the wood just after.

Up here, she was alone. Not enough. Too much.

Her cell phone had no service here on the hill, not that it would change anything. Had her family even known about the attacks around the country? It had to be world news by now – so why hadn't anyone called to check on her?

As those distant voices swirled like smoke beneath her pillow, she considered all of Ingram's warnings from her flat. The face from her dream moved behind her eyelids, shimmering and transparent, never truly there.

She thought of Marga. Not with the sword in her chest but as she'd been before. Brilliant, compassionate, beautiful.

Aurelia yearned to be back in Cambridge. She yearned for an alternate history in which Theodore Ingram had never called to tell her things were wrong, as if living in blissful ignorance of the danger that might be following her was better than taking this preventative measure. She wouldn't have had to question whether all the trouble of appeasing him was worth something – she'd be left with some semblance of dignity, knowing she had the chance to deny him.

Too much change in so little time. All her efforts to hold fast to normalcy were crushed beneath their feet in a twenty-four-hour span. She felt a cavernous ache being spooned from her gut.

Save for a folded note slipped beneath her door, she wouldn't have had to face any of the others that night.

Left you a bowl of stew on the kitchen counter. The one with bumblebees, not the butterflies.

If you need anything, I'm just downstairs. Don't hesitate to ask.

– T

CHAPTER EIGHT

Although she was certainly able to avoid Ingram, Aurelia wasn't sure she could help the anthropological curiosity of seeing him in his natural habitat. He had assured her they could easily cohabit without being involved with one another, but the reality of sharing a small house with other people was to share the noise. What the isolated house lacked in outside traffic, the quartet made up for with chatter; and no one had left since they'd first arrived.

Louisa was the chattiest, as children tended to be. Through the closed door of the spare bedroom, Louisa's voice was akin to a scuttling mouse. Gemma's voice was robust and confident, like a stage actor.

As for Ingram, he did exactly as he promised and stayed out of her way. He was disappointingly reliable and made the least noise out of everyone.

She found him outside with Louisa in the morning, bundled in his black raincoat while the young girl brought him bugs like offerings. Aurelia placed them squarely through a window beside the coffee table while she accepted morning tea from Gemma.

'Are you all right, darling?' the woman asked, spilling a few drops as she poured from a floral pot. 'You look a bit . . .'

Aurelia frowned. She felt more well-rested than usual. Her nightmare had spared her from a reprise after she woke in the night, and she'd fallen asleep soon after. When she surveyed her reflection in the frilly bathroom mirror, she found every feature in its correct position, including the stray hairs that never seemed to prefer any direction. They were the result of her last haircut with Ryan – bangs that soon grew too long to lie flat over her forehead but didn't stay tucked inside any of her hairpins.

Gemma chose a small cup from her cabinet and offered it to Aurelia.

'I don't mean to pry,' said Gemma. 'I only mean that you seem a little stressed.'

Aurelia shrugged, sipping the contents of her teacup in careful assessment. 'That's just my face,' she said. 'I'm always stressed. I don't know if I've ever been relaxed a day in my life.'

'Truly?' Gemma asked.

'Oh yeah,' Aurelia replied.

Louisa's laugh permeated the walls, drawing Aurelia's gaze out the front window again. Ingram was ruffling the girl's hair, mussing up her loose ponytails for a laugh. She shoved him by the hip. He smiled, barely budging.

So, he has feelings, Aurelia thought.

And another expression besides that one he always gave to her. Aurelia wasn't enamoured with the idea of frolicking in the rain with Ingram, but it enticed her to some degree, if only to give her something to do. To someone else, he wasn't the worst company to keep. To Louisa, his arrival was a lavishly wrapped gift.

Gemma stopped Aurelia as she slipped her feet into her boots, offering her an insulated flask of tea.

'Will you take this out for me, darling? Give this to Teddy.'

'Oh. Of course.'

'Excellent. There should be enough for two if you want more . . .'

Shielding herself from the cruel bite in the air, Aurelia trudged through the softened dirt to reach them. She opened her mouth to call his name, but a thought flashed through her mind before she could speak.

Teddy. An ill-fitting nickname for someone as rigid and sharp as Theodore Ingram, who pierced through the silvery backdrop like a spirit cloaked in black. It was *cute*.

It wasn't something she'd call him.

'Ingram,' she yelled. The boy nodded in a wordless salutation; hands buried in his coat pockets. 'Gemma made you some tea.'

'What's in it?' His long fingers unscrewed the cap with a feather-light deftness, and he inhaled the scent thoughtfully.

'Cacao and mint. And the usual additives,' Aurelia said. She pulled her hood over her head and stuffed her hands into her own pockets, leaving only her face exposed to the icy winds.

His brow quirked. 'Hmm.'

'It's not a green tea,' she added.

Ingram's eyes met with hers, studying her. She rocked onto her heels and searched for Louisa in the grass, trying to lose sight of his inquisitive, prying gaze.

'Thanks,' he offered calmly, and sipped the hot beverage with caution.

'Can I ask you something?'

Ingram's chin perked up in a questioning nod, so she

persisted. 'I take it that Gemma's not your mother, and by the look of that bedroom, this isn't really where you live.'

He nodded again, urging her on wordlessly; but she was embarrassed to say it aloud . . . Maybe that's how it was supposed to feel to discover – not like ravishing, but a careful fumbling in the dark.

'I know your parents are—'

'Well-off?'

The frankness of his interjection silenced her. What else could he have said? He could not deny the wealth he'd come from, and surely he knew how everyone else saw him – looking up from beneath the dark woollen wings of his expensive coats. He was an ink blot from which one could divine no other shape than that of success.

So, he didn't try to. Still, the answer was worth more than a second's hasty reply.

'I stay here sometimes,' Ingram began. 'My parents and I don't get along much. If I'm not at uni, I'm with Gem.'

'Holidays included?'

He nodded, sipping again.

'That's rough,' Aurelia said, bracing against a gust of wind.

'Hmm.'

She made a conscious effort to hold fast to her position as the breeze attempted to push her into him. The wind sent her hair flurrying away from her face and neck, and it seemed to annoy Ingram that she took more time to push it back into place this time. She hunched her shoulders, bracing against the cold, wishing she'd packed a scarf.

She still hadn't unearthed her gloves from the floor of her bag.

'Why?' she asked.

Ingram narrowed his attention on Louisa, who was bounding down the hill to investigate for more bugs. Aurelia followed suit, watching at his side like they were two sentries at the gates of a palace.

'It's simple,' he said. 'They expect something I can't give them. And their time is too precious to waste. Our disdain is mutual. They have as many issues with me as I do with me.'

'Can't imagine why anyone would have an issue with you.'

He almost smiled. She wondered what it would look like; it had to be something different from the smile he gave Gemma and Louisa.

'They have reasons,' he said, cool and unbothered by her curiosity – perhaps because he deflected her questions so skilfully. 'None that really matter considering I don't live with them any more. We steer clear of each other. I put my head down, do my work, and as long as I behave myself, they've no need to visit. Everyone wins.'

'So, where *do* you usually spend your time?'

Ingram rolled his eyes, but his irritation didn't reach his tilted lips. 'You have too many questions.'

'I've been told,' Aurelia said, shifting back and forth on the balls of her feet. 'You say that like they're uncommon.'

'They're unnecessary.'

'Are they? You seem to know a lot more than what you'll tell me. I don't know what you want or why we're here. Hell, I don't even know where this place is. Townsend is just another name on a map I don't know.'

'That's the point of it all, Schwartz. I come here to disappear. Not to socialize.'

'So, this is your Walden.'

It wasn't a question, but he shook his head in answer. 'It's a sanctuary. Not a retreat.'

'But it's still not where you live,' Aurelia noted. 'You evade all my questions as if answering them would make you any worse in my eyes, but you forget that you're already pretty bad. We were never on good terms, were we?'

Crinkles formed in the corners of his eyes. 'I suppose we aren't. I have a place in Cam, about six minutes from yours by taxi. Aside from this little excursion, I spend most of my year there.'

'Any flatmates? I've been living with the same one for years now.'

'No.' The word escaped quicker than he'd intended based on the way his body tensed. Subsequently, he softened – just enough to meet her gaze for a moment and ask for pardoning. 'I prefer it that way.'

Louisa rose to her feet – a tiny, impish figure beneath the tall grass – and came bounding over to the two students with her latest discovery. 'Teddy, look! I found a fat cricket!'

'Let's see it, then,' he called.

When the girl reached them, she unfurled her hands to reveal the insect perched in her palm with a surprising ease. A few of her mushroom curls tumbled loose from the two elastics holding the bunches dangling from the nape of her neck. Out of breath, she added, 'I found it by the path.'

'Impressive,' Ingram murmured, nodding in approval. 'Find me another.'

With a subtle flex of her palm, the bug leapt from Louisa's hand, and she retreated to her former excavation point.

'Did you need something, Schwartz?'

She sighed. 'Something to do.'

'This isn't really the place for doing things.'

'Well, what do *you* do when you come here?'

He scratched the back of his neck. 'Mostly, I go over curriculum with Lou. Tutoring and such. Lou's homeschooled, you see.' Then, betrayed by a note of cynicism, he added, 'She's sheltered.'

'And after that?'

He shrugged, casting them into another wordless end. Aurelia's toes were freezing through her boots as she idled next to him. She forced some sensation back into them with a stiff curl. 'It's nice out.'

'Not really.'

She shifted again, kick-starting some much-needed blood circulation. 'At least it isn't raining.'

'You're awfully pleasant today,' Ingram remarked bitterly.

'I'm sure it's of little importance to *you*, but last night was the first in weeks that I didn't wake up trembling in fear, thinking someone was trying to kill me. So, yeah. I'm feeling pretty ace today.'

Ingram twisted to meet her gaze. Standing next to him, shoulder to shoulder as they'd been outside the train station, was strangely intimate. She stepped aside, flooded by the cold that his body was holding off. He opened his mouth to say something equally flippant and presumptuous, but he stopped short again, almost puzzled. The open-mouthed fish craving for something to eat.

'It's kind of funny, actually,' she began. 'In my dream, I was in this room. It was pitch black, and there was a closed door with light on the other side. I knew, somehow, that the door wouldn't budge if I tried to open it, which made me panic. Not that I'd ever been afraid of the dark or anything. But the panic itself was different from what I'd started feeling over Marga. It felt . . . normal. Forgettable. There was enough of me that knew it would all be gone once I woke up. You know how it goes.'

Ingram's brow furrowed as all the pieces of his disguise began to settle back into place. 'Not sure I do.'

'Whatever. Point is that it was an odd dream, but not that nightmare I've been having since King's. I think my housemate might've been there too, but I couldn't see them. They were opening the door and—'

The jarring caw of a large crow tore her from her recollection.

'*Shit.*'

'Hmm?'

The crow rummaging at her feet thrusted its beak at something in the grass – probably Louisa's cricket.

'Nothing,' Aurelia replied. 'Just these birds. Maybe I'm crazy, but I feel like they're following me sometimes.'

'Just crows?' Ingram asked.

'Mostly. It sounds so stupid when I say it out loud.'

'It doesn't.'

The bird left as quickly as it came, the force of its wingbeat sharp enough to throw a loose strand of her hair awry. She tucked it back behind her ear, wrestling to subdue the sudden pounding of her heartbeat. No common bird should unnerve her that much, but the gravity in Ingram's voice *did*. Four little words from his mouth steeped in consequence: 'Just crows?' 'It doesn't.'

He was watching her fix her hair, following the line of her fingertips behind her ear and down the length of her neck. She barely caught it, but the sudden fixation of his gaze touched her with a warmth that broke through the wind.

Ingram uncapped his flask then and took another confident swig. 'Maybe you should ask Gemma about it.'

'What would she know?'

'A great deal,' he said. 'If I were you, I'd ask.'

Aurelia nodded, the rain forming heavier droplets on her face with each second. The wind pitched again, sending a shiver through her raincoat.

'We'll be inside in a minute,' Ingram told her as if she should already be turning to leave, straightening his shoulders against the breeze. She thought of digging her heels into the mulch and rooting in place just to get on his nerves, but it was simply too cold to be worth it.

As her back turned to him, he added, 'Thank you. For the tea.'

She nodded, tucking her hands back into her pockets, wishing she still had something to hold onto.

Gemma kept herself commendably occupied within the wards of her house, which was both awe-inspiring and dread-inducing to Aurelia Schwartz. She approached the kitchen counter again, caught in the watchful periphery of the woman's gaze.

'I also have a tea collection at my house,' Aurelia said.

'Oh, really?'

'I brought my favourite blend with me in case I can't live without it. You can try some if you want.'

Gemma smiled. 'That'd be lovely . . . So, you don't know how long you'll be staying?'

'I have no idea. I don't entirely know *why* I'm here.'

'I'm sure you'll figure it out soon enough.'

Before Aurelia could raise a question of her own, Gemma continued. 'Funny girl doesn't know that magic is unusual, since I'm all she's got, and now she expects everyone to have it.' Outside the window, Louisa reappeared at Ingram's side with a new critter in her hands. 'Once when she was still at school, she conjured up a hoard of bumblebees on a boy that called her a name. Children are relentless. I'm sure you remember it much more clearly than I do. She doesn't get out much any more now that I homeschool her. New faces are always very exciting.'

Yes, Aurelia remembered being eleven, sitting on the field's edge at recess while other children formed makeshift kickball teams. She'd tear dandelions from a patch and split their leaves before regrowing them. A cycle of divine growth and primitive destruction.

Louisa was only seven, Aurelia learned. She'd had no more than a year or two of time in school to become an abnormality, before it was too much for them to handle.

'So soon,' Aurelia muttered. Gemma only sighed, as if it was inevitable.

'I hoped I wouldn't have to, but circumstances change. Hardships tend to strike at once. I'll enrol her again eventually, but this is nice – what we have now. She has a chance to study the limits of her magic without the prying eyes of other kids. And occasionally, another witch arrives at our doorstep, just like you.'

'So, he told you.'

It sounded like a question – she'd offered it tentatively, with space to be denied. The discovery had already worn off from the first time Aurelia stepped into the cottage, but hearing Gemma confirm it was something else – relief or understanding.

She was among witches, *friends*. There were walls erected around her that would need more to pry open, but others could still be brought down.

'Oh no, darling,' Gemma responded. 'The swans did.'

'Do your swans speak English?'

'Of course not.' Gemma smiled as she wiped the spout dry. 'The birds tell me many things though, and a swan told me just three months ago that a magical gardener would arrive in my hour of need. When Teddy showed up with you, all of my crops had been rummaged through by some rodents in the night. I could only assume you'd be arriving soon to fix them.'

Ingram's words clicked into place. 'You're an augur,' Aurelia said.

Gemma nodded, blowing into her teacup. Augurs were an old kind of diviner that read from the flight patterns of birds to interpret the future. Diviners were rare in these days of dwindling magic users, which Aurelia never understood. If one could foresee the downfall of the witch race, could they not have prevented themselves from disappearing with it? Was it such an inevitability that no one fought to endure it?

The woman returned the emptied teapot to the counter with a clink. 'By the gods' graces, I've been allowed friends that reach the heavens. I'm fortunate for them. They spin me tales of all the places I'll never get to see.'

'In their entrails?' asked Aurelia. 'You see that much?'

Gemma paused. 'Or I could just ask them. It's a bit more polite than cleaving them open.'

'I thought—'

'The practice of divination through entrails is archaic, but it works. I don't fault you for the confusion.'

Picking at her nails again, Aurelia asked, 'Could you tell me what it means to be followed by birds?'

The augur raised her peppered brows. 'What sort?'

'They're crows,' Aurelia explained. 'I think. They might be ravens for all I know. Whatever they are – they've been knocking at my windows and following me around for over a week now.'

'Just a week?'

Aurelia nodded, unable to gauge through Gemma's expression if that was better – if it made a difference to have them follow her through life or stake their claim midway through. In any case, she was a claimed thing, like a flattened badger to be torn from its bones.

'It feels like an omen. What does it mean?'

The older woman closed her eyes, tucking her chin into her chest with a silencing finality that drew Aurelia closer. Through the tight lines of Gemma's eyelids spilled a colour that wasn't there before, and Aurelia lost track of her question, trailing off stupidly – tellingly. It'd been so long since she'd last witnessed a witch using their magic. Her sudden silence made it dismally obvious that she'd decided to stare.

'An omen, you think?' Gemma Eakley's voice was still distant when she opened her eyes. The warm green of her eyes had yet to settle into its rightful place, although her irises were littered with leftover flecks of gold.

'I think so.'

'And you presume that it's a bad one?'

'I'm not familiar with the idea of good omens,' Aurelia answered, 'and I never believed crows to be a welcome sight.'

'Ah, but that's where you're wrong, darling.' Gemma circled around the counter, clearing the last of the stars from her eyes to reconvene with another one of her chores. 'You see, no creature is ever purely malignant. That's a misconception spread by inexperienced non-diviners. To interpret three crows in the sky as a mark of death is irresponsible divination, but that's what the wives' tales are born from. The birds carry messages, you see . . . I only know them because I can speak to them.'

Aurelia should have known it wouldn't be as simple as pulling a card and having a solution. If it *was*, diviners would be less important. Perhaps she should've been awestruck in the presence of one – and she might have been if every thought hadn't been travelling through her mind with the dizzying slowness of tar.

Thankfully, Gemma didn't patronize her, and so Aurelia resisted the urge to draw into herself in embarrassment.

'Some birds *are* delegated the task of relaying certain messages, and it's common for crows to be the bearers of bad news. Unwelcome arrivals. Harbingers of death . . .' Gemma trailed off, nearly losing herself to another glittering haze. She grounded herself, gripping the counter's edge. 'But it would be unfair to assume the worst from anyone.'

The pointedness of Gemma's conclusion made Aurelia wonder if she was still referring to the birds. The woman's friendly, chapped smile tugged proudly on her freckled face. Somehow, it was wrong. The curve, the intention. Aurelia didn't know if it was more than a bit of social awkwardness.

She stood from the counter. 'Well, thank you, Gemma.'

They'd answered nothing, but Aurelia suspected that the original question was already lost to Gemma Eakley. 'Of course, darling. Any time.'

'I'd be happy to look at your garden sometime too.'

'My . . .' Gemma blinked slowly, cocking her head in the mechanical manner of pigeons. Then, with a clap of her hands and a reprise of her grin, she exclaimed, 'Yes! My garden. Fetch me whenever you would like.'

Which Aurelia knew to mean, not now.

Another time.

She closed herself inside the bedroom again, opened all of Ingram's drawers and cabinets, and began a search of her own.

The nocturnal machine in her head spurred to life.

She'd never been patient. Dedication made her a dependable student, but stubbornness made her an innovative one. It irked her to have a problem set before her in which no one would let her search for an answer.

The problems only seemed to be piling up. There were questions of the nature of this house, of its need for wards, and its elusive occupants. Where did Gemma's peculiar aversion to sharing her premonition come from? There was, of course, the unsolvable puzzle of *Ingram*, who had told Aurelia to ask about the birds while undoubtedly feeding Gemma reasons to say nothing to her about them.

Aurelia had too many questions about him to consider them in anything other than bite-sized pieces. If she wasn't already overwhelmed, breaking his stubborn wall would certainly end her.

He was downstairs now, *doing God knows what.* He moved quietly, like grief or fog. Aurelia climbed onto the bed, reaching over the headboard to the bare shelf of books behind it. She chose the most tattered one, a bright yellow beast from the Hardy Boys series. The handwriting he'd scarred its pages with was sloppier, and the notes were disorganized, but it was fascinating to find his annotations in something so old. She could only imagine how young Ingram had been when he began marking it; the last time she'd seen a Hardy Boys book was in her elementary school library, and she hadn't been annotating her books back then. She envisioned the pen clicking between his teeth while they'd idled on the train and wondered if the ink had been blue or black. What had he been reading then? She couldn't remember the name of it, but she remembered the pale creases embedded in the spine and the fact that he'd closed it without a bookmark.

A wrinkled photograph in the pages of the Hardy Boys book forced it open. Aurelia plucked it from the folds, shutting the book's covers with a small clap. She was doubtful that he'd be coming back to it any time soon.

Two boys stared back at her, washed out by the radiant summer behind them. She could tell that the boy on the right was Ingram. The auburn strands in his hair were more pronounced in the photograph, and the boy on the left had a delicate hand woven through them, casting them over Ingram's face.

Both wore an untarnished expression of glee. Ingram's soccer jersey and the other boy's sweater shared the same school emblem; the latter leaned into Ingram with an arm around his shoulders, mouth close to his face – as if in the aftermath of, or lead-in to, a kiss.

Ingram was younger here, of course, but Aurelia suspected he could still smile like that if he tried. When he smiled at Gemma and her daughter, it was a close match, but Aurelia had never seen one like this – not until now.

She returned the photograph to the book. Fatigue was ruining her.

Surrendering to the pull of exhaustion, she perched on the edge of the bed and flipped lazily through the other books of his that were within arm's reach.

Besides, she had questions, more questions than either Ingram or Gemma could answer in so few hours. Questions that ranged from his parents and this cottage to the discovery of her magic – all that he'd previously deflected with razor-like precision. He was both an iron cage and all the things held captive within, but she knew the colour of witchcraft and how it shimmered through cracks like light.

And now, she knew how it felt to lose her grip on it.

Only one thing she was certain of: that Theodore Ingram

had answers hidden somewhere behind his inky black veil of secrecy, and she would open him up to find them, piece by piece, even if it meant pulling him apart.

She heard a soft knock at the door before Gemma called her name. Aurelia sat up in her bed, closing the book she'd spent the past hour skimming through, on which Ingram's navy-blue handwriting in the margins had bled into the cover in the form of fingerprints. It could have been one of Gemma's books that he'd taken upon himself to vandalize. He could be the kind of person to take more than half of something if given the chance to share.

'Come in,' Aurelia answered.

Poking her head through the opened door, the woman asked, 'Aren't you joining us for dinner? It should be ready in just a minute.'

'Oh. I didn't realize I was–'

'Invited? Of course, you are. I'd be a terrible host if I didn't extend the offer.'

Aurelia bristled. She hadn't meant to undermine the woman's kindness, but Ingram's words – 'we can stay out of each other's way' – were a sentiment she'd taken to heart. So far, he had done precisely that, and she felt she should do the same, lest he decide to revoke his feigned complacency with her. After all, she'd been the one to propose an end to their squabbling; even if he'd agreed, that didn't mean he was entirely on board with it.

But this wasn't his house. It was Gemma Eakley's. So, she

kicked the duvet off her legs, meeting the older woman sheepishly at the door.

'Thank you, Gemma. I'll be right out.'

'Take your time, darling. If you'd prefer to stay here for—'

'Oh, no,' Aurelia hurried, slipping on a cosier pair of socks. 'I only meant to not overextend my welcome.'

The woman scoffed. 'Nonsense. You're more than welcome to the house in any way you'd like.'

'That's very kind of you.'

'No person who comes to this house arrives by accident,' said Gemma. 'And I trust Teddy's judgement enough to believe that you have no ill-intentions.'

Down the hallway, Louisa was organizing makeshift place settings at the small coffee table. It was hardly big enough for three people to gather at, let alone four. Perhaps Ingram's avoidant dance would encourage him to dine out.

Behind the extended countertop, Gemma bent over the oven and pulled from it a circular white dish brimming with a perfectly browned crust. It filled the cottage with the warm scent of meat and vegetables.

'That smells incredible, Gemma.'

The oven door shut with a flick of the woman's ankle, and Gemma flashed a full, toothy smile. 'I'm not a proud person, but I can't deny that I am the best cook I know.'

Aurelia felt something brush against her shirt, and she turned, expecting to find Louisa Eakley with her napkins but came face to face with Ingram's chest instead.

'Logical fallacy, Gem. You only know six people in the world and half of them are in this room.' He rested his forearms on the counter beside Aurelia, too close for comfort. He must have ignored the heavy blush that coated her face, because it was hardly *un*noticeable.

'But *you* would say it,' Gemma explained as she served ample helpings into individual dishes. 'So would Lou. Aurelia darling, try this and tell me how it tastes to you. Careful now. It's still hot.'

The woman handed her a crooked ceramic dish, ornamented with crudely painted caterpillars.

'I made that one,' Louisa said from the table. She'd arranged all four place settings and ensured a symmetry between them all, but the table was still as small as ever.

'I love it,' Aurelia said, stabbing her fork into the crust. 'I used a bowl with bumblebees on it last night. Did you make that one too?'

Louisa nodded, a smile growing on her face. Above her, Aurelia noted the hint of a smile flickering on Ingram's face, quick and elusive as if passed under the shadow of candlelight. There was a lack of space between his shoulder and hers, and he glanced down, eyeing her as if she was a riddle to solve. She refocused her attention on the shepherd's pie in her bowl. She wasn't sure that she wanted to be solved – figured out. If he was a closed book, it was only right to become one too. Driving her fork into a soft shred of lamb, she took a bite. It burned her.

'Still hot?' Gemma asked.

Aurelia nodded, lips half-parted to suck in a cooling breath. Ingram chuckled, and Gemma's eyes darted between the two of them. 'You know, darling, you must be very special if Teddy brought you home to meet us.'

The lamb scalded a path down her throat as Aurelia downed it completely to speak. 'We aren't like that. Not at all. If anything, he's the reason I didn't think I would be invited to dinner.'

She regretted the words as soon as they left her mouth, nearly as much as she regretted stuffing hot shepherd's pie into it. She braced herself for the harsh correction Ingram would make to cover up his tracks; this time, she would have deserved it.

It never came.

In the fraction of a second that Aurelia caught sight of his expression, she found something that resembled genuine hurt. With another flicker of light, the expression was gone. The silverware in Louisa's hand clanged behind them.

'So, you've gone and made her feel unwelcome,' Gemma said, swatting Ingram's arm. 'I should have known you'd be such a twat without me breathing down the back of your neck.'

He rolled his eyes, and whispered close to Aurelia's ear, 'You're *trouble*, Schwartz.'

But he'd put up with her for years, harbouring enough wretched sentiments to warrant something much meaner. Was it sad to think of this as progress – that she hadn't even noticed him come in? That his presence felt, upon first impression, unencumbering enough to miss the familiar, uneven sound of his footsteps, or that his eyes softened enough to add, *Maybe I'm used to your trouble.*

Gemma raised her eyebrows and asked, 'Tell me, darling, does he forget his manners at university?'

Aurelia stabbed at her shepherd's pie and answered, 'He is probably the most mannerless person I've ever had the misfortune of meeting.'

There was a knowing glint in Gemma Eakley's eyes as she smiled and dried her hands on a dishrag. She then looked to Theodore Ingram and commanded, 'Eat.'

They clustered around the table, their dishware covering every inch of its bare wooden surface. With Louisa on her left and Ingram to her right, Aurelia felt the girl kick out her small foot and hit his leg repeatedly in a game of footsie. The seven-year-old was winning, not that Aurelia could chart the strategy of winning a game like that. Gemma shook her head at Louisa's incessant giggling and chided, 'Demons, both of you. Clean your bowl before it gets cold.'

For a moment, the players surrendered to the game maker's rules, and the table went still, save for Louisa's run-over laughter. It was the kind of innocent laughter that bubbled over its limit and went on long after the joke was finished. Ingram made a face at the girl across the table, and she pulled her features together in a ferocious scowl. On a whim, Aurelia brushed Louisa's leg with her own to further the game.

'Mummy said *stop it!*'

'I did,' said Ingram.

'Liar!'

He scoffed and shook his head. 'The trust I have is in mine innocence.'

Aurelia's nose wrinkled at the phrase. She recognized it from something – a poem, maybe – and based on the way Ingram's eyes met hers before Gemma derailed the conversation again, he'd wanted her to.

I'm trying. Desperately, she thought.

She'd have to get used to this sort of comradery; the constant vigilance required to understand Ingram's jokes. She tried again and again to place the phrase as she poked through the last of her dinner.

After they'd eaten, Ingram helped Gemma wash the dishes, scrubbing while she dried and tucked them into their usual resting places. Gemma set an old jazz record on a turntable in the basement, and the sound of brass and crooning wafted up through the spiral staircase to serenade them.

'Do you want to see my joined-up writing?' Louisa asked, already holding her practice pages out for Aurelia to examine. Settling on the couch beside her, Aurelia took them, following the curves of the cursive script long enough to satisfy the young girl with a falsified critique.

'Marvellous,' Aurelia said.

'Do you know joined-up writing? Mummy has been teaching me.'

Aurelia nodded, handing the pages back to Louisa for safekeeping. 'I do.'

'Will you write me something?'

'What do you want me to write?'

Louisa shrugged, examining her work with pride. 'I dunno. Whatever you want. I'm not so good at reading it yet.'

From a side table, Aurelia found an uncapped pen and half-used notebook, scribbled something down with the pad resting on her thigh, and offered it up for Louisa's scrutiny.

'What does it say?'

In the kitchen, Ingram peered over his shoulder at the two girls sitting on the couch, his gaze lingering long enough for Aurelia to catch it – to affirm it was real this time.

'It says "Louisa Eakley is a great ceramicist."'

'What's that?'

Gemma swatted Ingram's shoulder again, rushing him for a cleaned dish.

'Someone who sculpts things out of ceramic,' Aurelia explained. 'Like bowls and vases.'

Louisa took the page and placed it at the top of her pile. 'I didn't make the bumblebee bowl. I just painted it.'

'Should I write you something else?'

The girl sighed, disappointed. Children were unknowable. 'No. This is OK.'

After clearing the kitchen of its mess, Gemma followed her daughter into the basement. By now, the record had ceased, whirring into silence before Gemma would replace it with the old box television. She invited Aurelia, but there was a weariness in Ingram's eyes that said it'd be better for her not to come – that he'd rather not have anyone lingering in the room where he was meant to sleep for the next few weeks.

'Next time,' Aurelia told them. 'I'm pretty tired.'

Ingram smiled. Without taunt. There was even some gratitude in the shallow etches in his cheeks. After Gemma disappeared down the steps, Aurelia smiled back at him.

He ran a pale hand through his hair and muttered, 'Sorry about Lou. She can be a bit hard to deal with sometimes.'

'She's a kid,' Aurelia said. 'I expect a certain amount of difficulty from them. I think I'll hold up.'

He knocked his wrist against the iron railing of the staircase as he thought. 'Well, thank you. Truly.'

'Of course.' She flinched, tearing too deep into her cuticle. She folded her arms around herself, tucking her hands away to prevent further mutilation.

'You're all right?' he asked. His voice was unusually soft and careful.

'Oh . . . yeah.' When he frowned, Aurelia added, 'Why? Are you?'

Ingram stood rigid like a stalk of vegetation bent by the wind but not yet broken off, nodding passively, but she knew better. Something troubled him; she knew because it was often *her* that troubled him. He stepped toward her timidly. His hand rose between their faces, the path toward her face made obvious.

'What are you—'

'Just checking.' He touched the back of his wrist to her forehead, his lips pursed tight, brow pulled tighter.

Aurelia sucked in a sharp breath and protested, 'You don't need to look after me, Ingram.'

'So *keen* on keeping me at arm's length that you'd let yourself burn to death,' he muttered. He grazed her cheek with his thumb, then wiped his hand on his shirt as if he could rid her residue from his hands. 'You're running a fever.'

She thought of Ryan, holding her hair over the toilet. Ryan sitting on the edge of her bed while she picked something out to wear for the King's College dinner. Ryan wanting to take care of her.

'I swear I'm OK,' Aurelia said. 'I just . . .'

A jolt of energy shuddered through her fingers with an

answer of its own. Ingram caught the spark of gold that encircled her fingertips before she could stop it.

She rushed, 'My magic hasn't been cooperative lately. It must show a bit more today.'

'*Cooperative . . .*'

'Acting on its own accord,' Aurelia said. 'I was told that this could happen if I let it overwhelm me.'

'Does that happen often?'

She felt the wall's edge dig into her spine, and she gave a half-hearted shrug.

'Only when I don't use it for a while. If I can't release it, it accumulates. And if it becomes too much, it bursts out. I have my ways of keeping it regulated, but they all seem to be failing.'

He raised his brow. Wrong question.

'Magic evolves the same way that we do,' she explained. 'My tutor always said that the only thing any witch should expect of their magic is that it would eventually betray them.'

'Morbid,' he said.

'Somewhat.'

'Does it worry you – that yours does?'

'I'll be OK,' she assured him. 'Will you?'

He nodded, saying nothing more. He couldn't deter her this time . . . Some matters were worth hiding more than others, but if she could know one, no matter how inconsequential, it'd pry the door open for another.

'Can I ask you something?'

Ingram tilted up his chin inquisitively, and it amazed her that through such an insignificant gesture, the air felt less sweltering and thick.

'Go on,' he said.

'That thing you said at the table. I know it, don't I?'

'I said a lot of things.'

'When I pinned you for playing footsie. You said something about innocence.'

'Ah.' Ingram sucked his gums. 'So, it *was* you. I knew there was something foul afoot.'

She saw the words written on his features plainly, a memory falling into place. *You see it now, Schwartz*. Words written on a page that she'd read years ago in a class they'd had together, before she'd turned her head toward medieval studies, and abandoned the vague subject of English literature.

It was an inconsequential thing, Shakespeare's words and their origin, but it was worth all of a shared glance over a crowded dinner table, composing a secret that only *they* were in on – something small and unimportant that they alone would understand. An inside joke, albeit one that Aurelia had to think a little too hard about. In that way, it was sacred. It eased her mind to be something other than the object of his puzzlement – to be someone who *shared* in a secret with him rather than fought for one.

She wrinkled her nose again. 'Though she be but little, she is fierce.'

Ingram smiled. It was the only confirmation she'd receive from him. He rapped his knuckles on the railing this time, moving toward the distant sound of the television.

'Goodnight, Schwartz.'

Aurelia scraped her fingernails down her cheek, unnerved at how unfinished she felt with a word like that. 'Goodnight' was a tender thing, but it was also final, and she had more to say, didn't she? She moved to catch him before he disappeared down the staircase, but he opened his mouth first, halting on the steps. She waited impatiently for a word that never came.

'I'll see you tomorrow,' she told him instead.

He swallowed, parted his lips, and said, as if confiding in a new secret, 'OK. Sure.'

CHAPTER NINE

'What's the closest spot for Wi-Fi?' Aurelia said the following day.

Ingram spat his toothpaste into the sink.

'Good morning to you too. You'll have to go into town for that. Gem has no internet.'

'Really?' Aurelia moved aside to let him pass through.

'Yes. Aside from a decent fridge and that box television downstairs, she refuses to keep any modern technology in the house. I keep telling her she needs a phone for emergencies. Stubborn as a mule, that one is. Dunno how I keep ending up with the stubborn ones.'

He hadn't yet changed out of his pyjamas, which left him baring more of his arms than she'd ever seen from him. She couldn't remember a time she'd seen him in anything other than a turtleneck. He didn't seem like someone who existed in the summer.

He turned to face her, two steps down the basement staircase, with a loose grip on the handrail above him. Aurelia spoke first, curiosity expelled from her features. 'Ever ask yourself if *you're* the problem?'

He smiled, 'All the time.'

She followed him into the basement. They were alone in the cottage now – Gemma was huffing at an uprooted crop in her garden while Louisa kept busy with her toys in the grass. Ingram unzipped his duffle bag atop the couch. A crocheted afghan covered the length of it, with bed pillows pushed into the corner of the L-shape. It didn't seem long enough to fit all of him – not comfortably. Aurelia almost felt guilty for taking up space in his room. *Almost.*

'Can you take me into town, then?' she asked.

Ingram sighed. 'If you'd let me get changed, I was planning to leave in a few minutes.' He gestured inexactly to a pile of clothes set aside on the coffee table.

'I guess I'll—'

He tugged the grey T-shirt over his head, half-turned from the step where she stood with her hand tight around the rail of the staircase. She was blinking too much, too flustered, suddenly aware of the pink freckles on the side of his torso.

'You'll what?' Ingram raised an eyebrow, squaring toward her. He was too comfortable being shirtless, and Aurelia – not comfortable enough to look away. She'd seen bodies like his countless times before, hadn't she?

She averted her gaze, pallor betraying her, and she set her mouth into a grimace. 'I'll wait upstairs.'

He nodded, becoming equally flustered as she was. She relaxed her grip around the rail and sped up to the ground floor, singed by the heat of his eyes on her back.

*

Ingram shut the door behind him and called out to Gemma. 'We're heading into town for a bit.'

The stout woman rose from the garden soil, a lonely head above the grass. 'Would you mind taking Lou with you? She's already dressed.'

The girl stood, slathered in soil from Gemma's garden. She drove a trowel into the dirt, pushing a fine strand of fallen hair from her forehead to reveal more dark smudges of dirt across her cheek.

Ingram cleared his throat. 'You want to come to Petro's?'

She nodded and discarded her trowel quickly by the front steps.

'Wait,' Gemma said, leaving the front door open as she hurried inside to fetch something. A towel, Aurelia assumed, or something to wipe the streak of dirt from Louisa's face. Instead, Gemma returned with a hairpin, summoned her daughter with a curl of her finger, and pushed it into the front of her hair. 'You can't forget this,'

'Sure, she can,' Ingram said. 'We're just going to Petro's.'

'As a precaution,' Gemma offered.

'It's unnecessary.' His jaw set sternly. He curled his fingers around Louisa's shoulder and gave it a soft, protective squeeze.

Aurelia cleared her throat, placing herself between them. 'Can we go? I'm starving.'

Gemma lowered her head and said, 'Yes. Yes, of course. Have fun.'

The three began their descent into Townsend, quiet and dutiful like foot soldiers marching toward enemy lines. Only when Gemma slipped out of view did Aurelia ask Ingram, 'What's with the hairpin?'

'It's how Gem keeps track of her. She watches over Lou like a hawk. Borders on invasive. I can't bear to think of what it'll be like for Lou when she's older.'

'Why does Louisa need to be tracked?'

Louisa raced ahead, cutting a few insignificant minutes from the journey. Ingram's gaze roved through the brush, his hands buried deep in the pockets of his coat. The high neck of it guarded her from seeing the layers beneath it, but Aurelia was willing to bet it was another turtleneck. She'd speculated sometimes, when lecturers were going on long-winded tangents, if Ingram was hiding a web of tattoos or a grisly scar. When summer settled in and their interactions became, as a result of the academic schedule, less frequent, she'd pictured him asleep in a coffin, hands crossed over his chest, hiding from the sun like a vampire.

'She doesn't,' Ingram answered after a minute of unresponsiveness. 'Gem's so bloody paranoid that she makes Lou wear it every time she crosses the wards. I thought she had stopped using it by now. There are other ways to keep track of your children. All it does is give Lou reason to be afraid.'

'Did something happen?' Paranoia like that didn't usually arise from nothing. She looked at the girl trotting quietly ahead, thin braids swinging behind her.

The question jabbed at something Ingram had been hiding, still buried too deep for Aurelia to see. Even he could not deny the involuntary twist of his features. 'It's nothing of consequence to Lou. The last thing she needs to learn right now is that the world is out to get her. Preferably, she doesn't have to learn that at all.'

Aurelia swallowed, stiff and shivering. With the young girl out of earshot, she told him, 'I talked to Gem yesterday.'

'About the crows?'

'Birds, generally. She said she knew I would come here.'

He sucked his gums and threw his shoulders back in a stretch. 'Did she now?'

It sounded like an accusation, but Aurelia couldn't tell for whom.

'Is that why you invited me?'

'Course not. If I'd known we would have a reason to resort to this, I wouldn't have left my house for weeks.'

'So, you didn't know anything would happen at King's College?'

'No,' he insisted. A shiver darted up Aurelia's spine as Ingram's line of sight landed on her. 'But I want to know why it did. I want to prevent it from happening again.'

'You seemed fairly convinced that this is where I need to be. You never told me why.'

'I *did* tell you, Schwartz. I think you'd be in danger there.'

She bit her tongue. It was still too vague. Ingram knew this too and, deciding to spare her the mental gymnastics required to unfold his responses, he added, 'Consider it a goodwill outreach. An olive branch. If no one else knows about your magic, who do you call when something goes amiss with it?'

'Usually, I keep a pretty tight leash on it.'

'Well.' A grin threatened to split apart his stony mask of deliberation. 'Looks like it slipped.'

They cut their steps short down the steep slope of the hill. In the pockets of her puffer coat, her hands reached for each other, effectively tightening the coat around her torso. Her cheeks dampened with the first trickle of rain.

'You never told me how you knew Gemma.'

'You know, you're awfully nosy sometimes, Schwartz.' He'd tried to sound light-hearted but failed. She lost the intent somewhere in the middle, between mischief and jest. Two different songs playing simultaneously.

'Be frank with me for once, will you?' She stopped in her tracks, and he hung his head, stopping too.

'How much do you want to know, Schwartz?' His words were doused in contempt. 'You asked me the other day if she is my aunt, and she's not. She took me in when I was sixteen because I had shit parents of my own. If they weren't angry with me for some reason or another, they were absent; and *absent* is putting it nicely. Does it matter so much to you how we met? We're taking care of you.'

He sighed, his words muddying together. He cast his gaze far beyond the boundary of Townsend Hill, and she caught the flex of his hand at his side.

'We take care of each other,' Ingram said. 'Gemma has done more for me than my own mother ever could. So, when I tell you she's the kindest person you'll ever meet, that's because it's true. God knows I've given her more than enough reason to hold me for ransom.'

Louisa waved them on from the bottom of the hill where the grass met cobblestone, but Ingram's posture remained stiff.

His unease was harrowing enough to taint the air with an unbreathable tension.

'Let's go,' he said. She resumed her stride, biting her tongue, but there lacked a resolution to his bitterness. She couldn't let it fester.

Softly, she asked, 'Were you a very bad teenager?'

A small but genuine smile cracked through his hardened exterior. 'Aren't we all bad teenagers?'

'So, you were.' Aurelia tucked her hands beneath her arms for warmth. 'My dad'll tell you I was a horrible teen, but I wasn't.'

'I can imagine – since you turned out so bloody rotten.'

'You're wrong though,' she answered. 'It's just you I'm rotten with.' The wind accosted her again and sent another shiver down the length of her spine, through her jacket, her sweater and shirt. She tucked her nose into the high orange collar, desperately seeking warmth. Even with all her layers, it was excruciatingly cold. Ingram's shoulder brushed hers as they walked, and she prayed that he would stay there, that she could come up with an excuse to be close to him, if just to keep her limbs from solidifying and breaking off.

'So sure of yourself,' he said.

She mumbled a response into her high collar. 'Why wouldn't I be? I'm actually pretty cool when I'm not thinking of pushing you down this hill.'

'As if you could.'

They halted simultaneously, eyes fixing to the other's like magnets. Ingram became distinctly aware of the space balancing between them; Aurelia lurched toward him, and he stumbled back, narrowly evading the feeble force of her hand.

'*Ha*,' she said, drily.

His lips pursed, and she knew Ingram saw her then as she saw him in her house – an intruder, someone without a measure for trust. She watched him soften, walked beside him as they crossed the boundary of the hill, and laid her questions to rest.

Louisa urged Ingram into a closet-sized art gallery whose window displays promised painted scenes of sunflowers and warmer days. He told Aurelia to run ahead, gesturing to a quaint cafe down the road, the sign for which drooped cheerlessly from excess rainwater.

'What do you want?' she asked, hoping he would let her repay some of the debt she owed him, or make right on the trouble she'd assumed.

Louisa tugged his arm again, and Ingram said, 'Don't worry about it. I don't trust you with my order.' Which was either an elaborate cover for his generosity or an insult to her memory retention, because he walked in moments later and ordered a plain chai latte.

The bulbs strung above Aurelia's head were dingy and scraped. The aroma of fresh-baked scones settled on the back of her tongue, and she felt her stomach lurch with hunger. She'd chosen a table in the back before her two companions arrived, but the cafe remained empty except for them. While Louisa scoured the poster-covered walls of Petro's cafe, the fresh-eyed young barista behind the front counter took his order with a wistful expression. Through the small formalities of food service, Aurelia could tell the barista was flirting – and she was *good* at it. Even if Ingram was oblivious to it, Aurelia was not. She saw the shift in the barista's body language between her order and his: the subtle lean, the asymmetry of her stance. Thinking of those tried-and-true tricks she'd used before being used on *Ingram*, who was as staunch as he was self-important, made her want to laugh. He was half-distracted by Louisa Eakley anyway. He'd asked her a question, 'Lou darling, what do you want?' But she'd been too busy reading something on the wall to know.

A middle-aged man with a bald head and an apron brought a cup and saucer to her table, and she thanked him. She noted the smile beneath his thick tawny moustache. He brought his hands to his hips and asked, 'Where are you heading?'

'Heading?' Aurelia nose wrinkled.

'People don't usually stay in Townsend,' he said. 'For the most part, they stop for a night and carry on.'

'I'll be here a while,' Aurelia said.

'Ah. My mistake, then. *Welcome.*'

Ingram hung his coat on the chair opposite hers, and the man left them with a quick 'good morning'. Louisa trailed behind Ingram with a spring in her step, the fresh-faced barista's gaze following shortly after. Ingram paid her no mind and unearthed his laptop from the bag he was carrying.

'Checking the news,' Ingram explained casually, as if she'd asked to know what drink he ordered instead.

'For Cambridge?'

Ingram nodded, donning a familiarly studious expression. She hid a small grin in the face of her cup as she sipped, sorely missing something to study, even if it was a dire threat. The barista who took Ingram's order brought it to him in a paper cup. He mouthed his thanks, bringing it to his lips before he could notice the digits scrawled on the side. Seeing Aurelia there, the barista seemed to hope he didn't notice them either.

Aurelia took the screen of his laptop in her hands and turned it toward herself. Ingram kept his protest to himself. He slung his arm over the back of her chair, ghosting around her shoulders as he placed his paper cup beside hers, phone number faced away.

A quick search fell short of anything useful. Maybe that was for the better.

'Hmm.' Ingram nodded, disappointed. She nodded back, relieved. 'You keep looking at my drink, Schwartz.'

'Wondering what you ordered that was so difficult to admit to me,' she said, typing something else into the search bar. 'My coffee's bitter. Hey, you have a number on yours.'

He leaned back in his chair, arm still perched on the back of hers, and granted the barista a quick look over Louisa's head.

'She's cute,' Aurelia said.

'Think so?'

'Sure. Do you?'

Ingram tilted the screen more evenly between them, evading the question. He cleared his throat, which drew her attention to the pink in his face he'd done a poor job of hiding. 'You can have some of my drink if you want. Can I have a taste of yours?'

She handed him the cup of too-bitter coffee. Ingram slid his fingers through the loop, brought it to his mouth, and made her painfully aware of the redness of his lips – how they looked perpetually bitten and cherry-sweet. She twirled his paper cup to read the swirly digits of the barista's phone number and the punctuation of a small heart.

'I should have warned you,' Ingram said, wiping his lip. 'That's four pounds down the drain.'

'Yeah,' she muttered, absent-minded. 'D'you think this is something?'

She left the cup in its place and scanned the article he'd tapped into. It was a grungy online guerrilla publication with articles penned under pseudonyms and intermittent protest documentation. This one possessed few details from the event at King's College, but as they scrolled, they were met with a low-quality photograph. A dormitory bedroom, deconstructed, belongings thrashed. The horizontal blinds guarding the photographer from night were bent into unruly shapes.

It was Marga's room.

Ingram's hand glided over hers, and he said nothing of it as he zoomed into the image and locked onto a piece of evidence that the room belonged to Margarita Palermo. He seemed to know simply from the pattern of her bed sheets, which reminded Aurelia that she had no clue how close they'd been before. She often thought of herself and Ingram as being two ends of a spectrum with everyone else falling somewhere between. It was difficult to imagine being close to anyone who was also close to Ingram.

In retrospect, she'd never given Marga the chance to be close; feeling guilty over that seemed to impress her own importance in Marga's life – like she was a reward Marga had wanted to reap – which riddled her with guilt all over again.

She wanted to vomit. Her skin was sweltering from the unease. 'So, they came back.'

'Or they never left,' Ingram said gravely. He turned to meet her gaze and realized just how close they were – close enough that one could catch a glimpse of the other person's cherry-red mouth.

Neither option was comforting. There was no benefit in being right over something so trivial. There was danger at their heels, at their university, near her home.

'What's that?' Louisa closed her book, but Ingram closed the screen of his laptop quicker.

'College things. Nothing exciting.'

The young girl pouted. 'You're lying. Why can't I know? Aurelia will tell me.'

Ingram lifted it from the table then and tucked it beneath his arm for safekeeping. 'She won't be doing anything like that. Trust me, darling, it's no fun.'

He ruffled her hair, the absence of his arm around Aurelia's chair leaving a shiver in its place. Louisa fought on until a slice of cinnamon cake was delivered to their table, and Ingram let her take a bite.

Over the table, Aurelia watched them, studied that veil of secrecy he carried on himself and how it cast over the young girl's eyes. Sure, Louisa didn't need to know. The purpose of coming was to leave that behind, to watch the devastation happen from a distance.

But he was so good at lying. At hiding. Being charming instead of honest.

Aurelia looked into those warm green eyes and saw something truly dangerous. Something *new.*

The morning rain began to slap against the window of Petro's cafe. Ingram filed his laptop away again and spoke nothing of their discovery to her for as long as Louisa was there.

CHAPTER TEN

They'd passed a bookshop at the edge of town, only a couple storefronts from the hill. Aurelia wasn't the type to overlook a bookshop, but it was spectacularly unassuming. Faded brown windows were framed by a faded brown brick exterior, bowed slightly under the weight of generations – like the rest of the little town, blossoming somewhere it shouldn't have been.

She found it, though. Ingram had cupped his hands over his brow as he squinted through the darkened glass to see inside.

'Is he in there?' asked Louisa.

Ingram shook his head. 'He should've been by now. Maybe tomorrow.'

'Who?' Aurelia asked.

'Family friend,' said Ingram, in a manner which did not imply friendliness. 'The name's Alaric.' His sharp-syllabled articulation dragged her back to their conversation in her house. He'd wanted her to remember, to draw paths back to the beginning, when she'd been hell-bent on forgetting every second of it. *This* was his friend in high places.

She should have known that inside jokes were only the gateway to deeper ventures.

'Alaric,' she mused, rolling the second syllable on her tongue like a breath mint.

'Yes,' said Ingram. 'The one and only. Come on, then. We'll try him again tomorrow.' He started briskly toward the curtain of grass at the beginning of the hill. Aurelia hurried after him, toes damp within her boots from the puddling rain.

'I'm tired,' Louisa whined. 'Will you carry me?'

The girl clung to his hip, hopeful. Ingram petted her hair and answered, 'Lou darling, you have to walk a bit first.'

Ingram had a different accent than Gemma, but he pronounced that word the same way she did, and just as softly – 'darling'. Tacked it onto Louisa's name as if it were incomplete without it. Aurelia never witnessed Ingram's kindness when it was unstained by resentment or driven by an ulterior motive, but the pure, unadulterated kind was all he had for Louisa Eakley. Aurelia hadn't yet acclimated to the tenderness that came when he spoke to her.

'The whole way?' Louisa asked.

'Only a bit. Aurelia and I have something to talk about.'

Aurelia wasn't used to that either, being called by her first name – especially not from someone who only ever used her last.

The girl trudged ahead, forcing through a wall of grass nearly as tall as her. Within seconds, the sea of green had swallowed her whole, save for the sound of rustling.

Still, he said nothing, and they climbed until there was nothing but them and empty space needing to be filled. Aurelia said, 'It's weird, y'know. You calling me that.'

'Your name?'

Aurelia bayed against the sharp wind. Close to him, it couldn't reach her. Close to him, she was a little warmer too. 'No one ever calls me that,' she explained. 'Not even my father.'

'Does he call you something heinous like muffin? Or cupcake?'

'No,' she said, rolling her eyes. 'At King's, you asked me what the J stood for. It's Jean. He calls me Rory Jean.'

'*Rory Jean?*'

'Yep.'

She could tell he was trying not to smile. He took his bottom lip into his teeth and bit hard, only the corners giving him away. He said it again, trying it on for size like a garment, or like taking a sip of communion wine. Tasting her name the way she'd done just moments ago for the stranger.

Savouring it.

Her eyes lost focus in the brush. 'Sometimes he calls me pumpkin, though. But everyone else calls me Rory. You're the only person I know who doesn't.'

'Why is that?'

Her attention reconvened on his profile. She'd looked at him nearly every day during lectures or by chance on the greens, and never before had she been so addled by his face. He'd been predictably miserable thus far, and so proud that every expression he wore was made of some arrogance; but today, of all days, he was lighter. As she traced the line of his cheekbones – down the tip of his nose and the angle of his jaw – against the roving grasses of Townsend Hill, she discovered his silhouette to be much different here. Maybe it came with a change of scenery or the comfort of home, but she'd never seen him smile so much.

'I don't know,' she admitted. 'Never really thought about it.'

Truthfully, she always called him Ingram because he always called her Schwartz, and at some point, it became inessential to remember which one of them started it – only that they could both say it in so many ways. Disgusted, dissatisfied, wedged between much louder (and less eloquent) words.

'So, you'd let me?' he asked.

'Let you what?'

'Call you Rory. What else would I mean?'

Sometimes, it almost seemed like he could belong here, as gusts of wind tousled his neat hair and iced his cheeks. In Cambridge, she'd seen him often torturing his hair to neatness, but here, he didn't mind as much. With a lock of it grazing his forehead, Aurelia thought of the boy in the photograph smiling back at her in his school soccer jersey. Wondering if he could ever become that person again. Certainly, age must have granted him good things – time didn't only make a home for strife – but she had never seen them. He hid them away, fortified by his misery.

Finally, she answered, 'I don't care. Call me whatever you want.'

'Of course, *pumpkin*.'

She grimaced. 'I'm guessing that's not what you wanted to talk to me about.'

'Not quite,' said Ingram. 'Before I met you at the station, Alaric gave me a tip-off about the sword. It's been in the secure possession of the university, soon to be en route to London for investigation. Eventually, it was supposed to be returned to the British Museum. It's missing again.'

'Someone's clearing their evidence.'

'I imagine they pillaged Palermo's room that night, too.'

'That's fast work,' Aurelia said, making no effort to mask her scepticism. The interconnected colleges of Cambridge could all be reached with a walk, but that was only after a culprit escaped from one without being caught.

Then again, they'd done it before.

'Does anyone else have access to your flat?' she asked.

'No,' he replied. 'You overestimate my tolerance for company.'

'Oh, I don't know. You're such a *pleasant* host to me. I had to ask.'

'What are you thinking, Schwartz?'

'Well, they came to Pembroke. They knew how to find Marga's room. Maybe they knew how to find our homes too.'

'That's an awfully ambitious spree,' Ingram responded, scratching his neck above the high collar. 'I'd have to go back and see for myself. Unless you have someone you can call.'

She had a number of people that knew where to find her flat, but few that she would delegate that task to. Mostly they were ex-flings, bridges she'd burned before they could ever be reached.

'What about Lawrence?' Ingram asked.

Aurelia would have scoffed if she didn't catch the ire in his friend's name. Those rare glimpses of tenderness, of vulnerability, were like bruises she could press. Perhaps Lawrence and Ingram weren't as close as they'd seemed. Or were they closer, like Ingram had been with Marga, in ways Aurelia had always chosen to ignore?

She withheld her kneejerk reaction to correct him. 'No one except my housemate has access. Unless they've made copies of our key without telling me.'

Louisa squealed. Ingram snapped his head around to find her in the thick brush, tensed again for the sake of running to her.

Gemma waved from the doorstep cheerily. Once he saw her, the relief returned. There was a man by her side, a tartan cap on his head and a thick brown beard beneath it. Louisa lumbered through the grass with her arms outstretched to embrace him. He lifted her into a hug with an aged groan.

Aurelia asked, 'Is that your friend?'

Ingram shook his head. 'That's Martin. It's rare we get any mail up here, but when we do, it goes to his house, and he brings it up the hill for us.'

'Teddy darling, I think you've got something!' Gemma yelled from the doorstep.

'Damn it.'

'What?' Aurelia frowned.

He scratched his neck again, a gesture she'd long since added to her growing list of his tells.

'If *I* have mail, it means that someone couldn't wait until I was back in Cam to involve me in something.'

'Your parents?'

He nodded curtly, visibly irked by the ease with which she remembered them. She wished she knew why he sought to rid himself of them – what reason he had to *run*.

She touched his arm and slowed him until he could face her. 'Do they call you that too?'

'Not sure what you mean.'

'Teddy,' she said. Just two syllables, as easy to pronounce as 'Theo', but delivered with care. It meant something to him. She didn't want that meaning, the weight of a chosen name, to get lost in her clumsy American drawl. 'I've never heard anyone call you that before Gemma. Is that what they call you?'

He opened his mouth to say something else, but he turned away as he spoke, and she heard none of it.

'Where is it?'

'On the counter, darling,' Gemma said with a vague gesture.

Aurelia watched as Gemma tucked a strand of her daughter's hair behind her ear, muttered something about her unkempt hair, and brushed the lint from her coat. There was love in her words and the lint within her fingers. Louisa complained. Loved children hardly knew how lucky they were until they were grown.

It was because Aurelia Schwartz had never had a mother that moments like those seemed so intimate and sacred to her. And because she'd never had a mother, she was left to want from afar, to make a spectacle of mothers and daughters that were undeserving of her wandering gaze.

She tugged off her boots and said nothing, but a dull ache settled in her chest, just low enough that she could write it off as hunger. After all, even *good* coffee was a bad meal replacement.

'Does Martin know who sent this?' Ingram asked.

'Isn't there a name?'

'None,' he said. 'Why did you say this was for me, Gem?'

'Martin told me it was. Don't you want to open it?'

He nodded, wearing his old, tight-lipped look of introspection. The weight of the envelope bent around his fingertips. He slid his pinkie underneath the fold, and Aurelia heard a dull clink of metal against wood.

She kneeled to collect the coin-sized object that tumbled from it, then two more. 'Don't bother moving or anything.'

'Wasn't planning on it.'

From the look and weight of the objects in her hands, she suspected they were, in fact, pure gold. If they were coins, it wasn't a currency she was familiar with. The faces of the first two were engraved with different shapes, but the third . . .

It was the heaviest, smooth and mirror-like. Aurelia raised it to her eyes, searching for a defining mark just as Ingram cast the letter away as eagerly as a simmering coal.

'Gemma,' he said.

'Yes, darling?'

'Did Martin say anything else about this?'

She shook her head, flustered by his demand.

'Nothing about the delivery?'

Aurelia stood and redirected her attention to the other two tokens.

The first was roughly the size of a US dollar coin, ringed in delicately carved foliage. Sediment gathered in the etches, but to her trained eye, it was undoubtedly lavender. Certain plants could not disguise themselves as easily as others, not physically interchangeable the way that buckthorn plants and cherries were.

The second was a rune. She recognized it as the Younger Futhark rune Algiz. She'd written about these runes in a dissertation several terms ago – 'The Emphasis of Medieval Europe in Modern Occultism' – but she'd first encountered them under the instruction of Gabrielle. Her tutor explained that, like many forms of divination, its meaning could be changed by merely inverting it.

Algiz was life. Inverted, with a name of Yr, it was the antithesis – death.

The third was still a puzzle. She turned it over like a lenticular print, hiding answers in its other angles.

'Stop touching those,' Ingram said.

He came toward her again, and she lifted her hand to his stomach to preserve the distance between. 'These are artefacts,' she whispered.

'And they have your fingerprints all over them now,' he said, removing her hand from his stomach to observe the glittering tokens from her side.

'They already have someone's fingerprints on them,' she said.

Of course, Aurelia knew it wasn't the same. She'd learned enough about artefact preservation to know that she shouldn't be touching these without gloves – if at all. She handed them to Ingram anyway, ruining them with his skin too as she grabbed for the discarded letter.

Through all her lethargy and fatigue, she analysed every angular stroke of black ink and light smear voraciously. It was the largest and lightest of the envelope's contents, but it may have very well been the most important. She flattened its crisp edges with reverence.

You made it so hard to find you. I will blame your doubt on our rocky start; even I can admit we got off on the wrong foot.

I am a reasonable witch, pleading for your help. Let me tell you what I came to King's for. Perhaps, if you knew the truth about your friend, about our deal, you might even be inclined to join me.

Whether or not you allow me to persuade you, take this as a warning. I wear many faces, but you each wear only one, and I have already seen them. Yours is the magic I covet. The trails you've left behind are unmistakable. Brighter even, because they burn in opposition with one another. The rot in the roots. The cycle of life . . .

You must already know how invaluable the sum of your magic is. I will not waste time telling you. Instead, consider the enclosed artefacts. They're worth a great deal to the British Museum; and are a small sacrifice of mine to invite you closer. Come to me, and we can end this game before it starts. Leave the pursuit to me, and I will follow them to you relentlessly.

My condolences on the loss of your friend. She let me chase.

Leona

A knot rose into Aurelia's throat. Somehow, she'd been able to absorb the threat with distance and objectivity until now, until reading the final sentences, seeing 'your friend' penned by the supposed hand that had killed her. Only then did it manifest itself as real.

She read it over again, stumbling on the collectiveness of it: two trails to follow instead of one, twisted in opposition, alight like a flare.

'Rot in the root,' Aurelia murmured, swiping her thumb over the ink.

'Careful—'

A hidden enchantment in the ink searched the pad of her thumb, and she too cast the letter away. Ingram's hand lowered to his side, caught in the shy act of touching hers to inspect the burn. Aurelia's fingers curled into a fist near her stomach. 'What does she mean by that?'

He shook his head. 'Nothing. It's not important.'

'It seems pretty important.'

'It's not the point, Schwartz. The point is—'

'Why can't you just tell me?' Aurelia made herself impossible to miss, though Ingram tried desperately to avoid her. 'I know what the point is. This person – this *witch* who killed our friend is willing to do anything to find us, and you can't even tell me why.'

Gemma gasped. The contents of the letter struck Aurelia with such tunnel vision that she'd already forgotten the woman was there.

'You didn't tell her?' asked Gemma.

'Tell me what?'

Ingram shut his eyes, finding no space in the room that either Aurelia or Gemma hadn't filled. 'Stay out of this, Gem.'

'If she's the only one here that will give me an answer, I want to hear everything she has to say.'

'Don't involve her in this, Schwartz. My family isn't

something I can spare if this goes awry. The less they know, the better, and that goes both ways.'

Gemma stepped closer to him, berating him with a cold, vicious stare. Slowly, she uttered, 'What haven't you been telling me? You *know* that isn't true – you are *always* my concern. We're responsible for each other. More than you will ever realize.'

'I know, Gem, but—'

'Then you'll know that you are my problem too. I expect your trouble, Teddy Ingram, but I will *not* be made ignorant of it; nor will I allow you to do this to someone under my roof. She has a right to know.'

'A right to know *what?* That I'm dormant? That I have magic I'll never use? It doesn't matter! What's the point of this, Gem, besides pushing me? You and I have always kept each other safe, and that's exactly what I'm doing.'

'You know bloody well that's not true either.'

Ingram bristled, sulking away from the woman's approach. He looked at Aurelia, then to the floor, and finally to Gemma again, confining his voice to a whisper. 'I'm so tired of this, Gem. Do you think the guilt doesn't follow me everywhere I go? You think being in this house is easy?'

Still, Aurelia could hear it. Ingram's shoulders slumped, defeated by the resolution that he had nowhere to go that she couldn't reach him. Asking Gemma to spare him wasn't something he could hide, but it must have been large enough, heavy enough, that it was worth asking in front of Aurelia.

'Yet, *you* can leave,' Gemma said. 'Teddy darling, this has never been the same for us. You're too old not to realize this.'

That affectionate suffix on his name rang hollow. He drew back as if it'd struck him in the chest.

'This was a mistake,' he mumbled and shook his head. He picked up the wallet and keys he'd placed on the coffee table minutes previously, and before Aurelia could object, he said with more confidence, 'We shouldn't have come.'

'Oh, come on now,' Gemma crooned, just as Aurelia rushed, 'What the hell are you doing?'

'Nothing,' Ingram said.

With an unbridled air of exhaustion, Gemma said, 'Is leaving really preferable to the alternative?'

'I thought you'd be relieved, Gem. Isn't this what you've always wanted? No more reminders of your precious boy. I should think you'd be rejoicing at the fact that I'm leaving.'

The augur did little more than allow her fingers to twitch, and an open kitchen cabinet behind her slammed shut. Ingram flinched. A wild look flared to life behind his eyes, a momentary righteousness that Aurelia knew would pass and leave in its wake only shame and loathing. He gathered up his few belongings again. The door swung open, untouched, to see him out.

Aurelia hurried after him. 'You can't just *leave*, Ingram.'

'Why can't I? Give me a break, Schwartz. You're a big girl. You can handle yourself here for a while, can't you?'

'Because I'm *talking* to you. All I've wanted was to *talk* to you, like two normal fucking people, and all you do is push me away. What the hell is your problem?'

The downpour was beginning outside, and Ingram paused to consider it. Aurelia thought she could reach him then, suspended in his hesitation, but he shook his head and said, 'You think I'm a coward, don't you? *She* has thought me cowardly my whole life. And after being told so many times of what I'm supposed to be, at some point, I will become it. Be glad, Schwartz. Maybe you were right about me. Now, if you could just step aside . . .'

Ingram decided that braving the rain was preferable to her. She raced after him down the steps, accosted by it.

'Why can't you just tell me?' she pleaded.

'Because it doesn't matter! Do you know what it's like to constantly be reminded of something you wish you could forget? You're pressing me for answers that I wish weren't true! And they don't *have* to be true – not if we ignore them.'

Behind them, Gemma was standing in the doorway, still in her socks with her arms folded across her chest. Aurelia raced to close the gap between his wide stride and hers, and she reached for his wrist, tugging him back. Ingram wriggled his hand free. She thought he'd set off running again – that she'd lost him already – but he waited. She was coming up short. She didn't know how to speak to him in a way that wasn't angry. It seemed like every kindness thus far had been torn apart by his sharp cynicism.

'*Leona* doesn't know what she's talking about,' he said. 'There's nothing she can get out of me.'

It left her stuck, her mind grasping for the right words. By then, he'd adopted a pitying expression, which she hated just as much.

'Please,' Aurelia said. 'I'm trying to understand, Ingram, but I need you to throw me a fucking bone here.'

He looked to Gemma for seconds that felt like minutes under the weather's assault.

'Look at me,' Aurelia told him. She saw that momentary flash of hope in his eyes, less like a flicker of candlelight and more like lightning at the height of a storm. 'Look at where I am. Where you asked me to be. I know you never wanted this to happen. I can't blame you for not liking me – if you never learn to like me, I know I could live with it. But you asked me to *trust* you, Ingram . . . And against my better judgement, I *did*. I still want to. I need you to prove me wrong right now and tell me the truth. Isn't it more cowardly to run? Time after time, you spurn my questions. If you're tired of hiding, I'm tired of being hidden from.'

Within arm's reach, he was still as far away as ever, frightfully immaterial. She thought she could reach out to the place where he stood and run her fingers through air.

Her heart was thunderous while she wondered whose turn it was to speak, whether it was *waiting* or *speaking* that she'd have to labour through. She felt that labour in the palms of her hands. All of her was furious – her mind, her body, and the reactive magic within them that was failing her more every day. She tucked her fists beneath her arms, but there was energy speeding into them. It raged up through her wrists, around her torso, and flooded her head, ravenous and consuming like an inferno.

Ingram curled his fingers softly around her elbow. 'Go inside, Schwartz.'

She shook her head. 'You have to let me try first.'

He scowled; but she was grateful for his hand then, which

was still circling her arm. A harrowing dizziness marred the edges of her vision. The ground lurched beneath her. She stumbled, fighting to retain a gift that only wanted to be expelled.

'Stop doing that,' Ingram said.

She wasn't doing anything – not intentionally. She was trying to *stop* whatever was happening, to tuck her hands so far beneath her arms that they'd reach back into herself.

The grass blew wilder. Ingram swallowed, a note of fear in his eyes.

'Breathe,' he pleaded. 'You need to calm down. You have to make it stop.'

'I can't!'

The ground beneath her feet shifted again, and she lost her footing. This time, Ingram pulled her hard against him. Half-dazed, she saw the result of her involuntary expulsion of magic sprout in the spot where she'd been standing. The culmination of her gift had split the earth, and from her place erupted the gnarled, twisted branches of a tree, amassing over them like an impermeable wall.

Ingram seized her wrist, unyielding as she fought to tug it back; but branch after branch stretched from the tree's moving trunk, reaching for the house and the slope of the hill. Worst of all, it reached toward the town. Where were the wards around Gemma's cottage? The tree would break them soon, if it hadn't already; and the secrecy that Gemma Eakley had tried so hard to preserve would be butchered.

Gold sparked around her hands violently, striking her skin like hot oil. Ingram cursed to himself and drew his hand away, scalded by it.

'I'm sorry,' she rushed, but it was nothing beneath the sound of tree bark splintering upward into claws.

Then, the earth seemed to settle. Horror splintered through the trained stoicism of his face, but mostly, she saw indignation. Shame pooled in her gut. Her body had expunged its magical excess, but at what cost?

She pulled herself away, shivering like a dog. 'I'll fix it,' she insisted. 'I swear, I can—'

Her hands shook as she brought them over her eyes. Magic was supposed to be something she owned, not something that owned her. She had raised it and pruned it like a temperamental plant when it was carnivorous and hungry for her flesh.

'*Go inside*, Schwartz,' Ingram commanded. 'You've done enough.'

The branches ceased to stretch and writhe. Aurelia's heart dropped. She'd tried for years to make herself impenetrable to him, but it never worked; and now his ire lit a flame on the suture that held her together.

In a rush to defend herself, she said, 'Y'know, if you would have told me from the start, all of this would be—'

'You wouldn't have understood it.' With a tense hand, he forced the wet, sinewy hair from his forehead. 'Maybe you already think I'm a bad person, but I promise you I can be so much worse. Gemma knows it. I know it. But you . . . Your magic,' he uttered spitefully, 'is the kind that makes things grow. It fills the world with life. You're allowed to make mistakes like this. To be reckless. You don't even know how lucky you are, Schwartz, to be unafraid of destruction; but you are so goddam lucky. You're going to walk inside and pour yourself another cup of tea, reinvigorated by this little act of release, and I'll be out here cleaning up this mess. My magic is the kind that ruins,' said Ingram. His eyes were alight with frenzy, his voice uneven, syllables crooked. '*My* magic is the kind that kills. And if I'm not careful, every living thing in my vicinity will suffer for it. Every blade of grass, every person in this town, this blasted tree. Tell me what good comes of magic like mine, Schwartz. Look me in the eyes and tell me what that is.'

She shook her head and wiped the rain from her face with an equally damp sleeve.

'*Nothing*,' he hissed. 'I have spent all my life reaping the consequences of *one mistake*. It's a hellish way to live.'

That was the word for witches like him, whose heels were followed by ruin. Witches who destroyed the living as easily as they reduced towns to their frames.

Reapers.

She didn't hear about them much any more.

'I'm inevitably going to be the one who fixes this too. There isn't much else I'm good for here. Common magic never came easy for me. But if all I am good for is destroying the evidence of your mistakes, then I will be good at that. I've spent so many years trying to be good for *something*, and I'm going to make myself fucking perfect.'

Her palms twitched, but there was nothing left inside her to slither out unbidden.

Softly, Ingram asked, 'Gemma hasn't told you about her son yet, has she? His name was Kenny. And he was my . . . my best friend.'

It made sense then. That sort of anguish could only be discovered through suffering from it.

'Did you . . .'

'Kill him? I may as well have. It was my magic that ended his life. I'm the reason he's gone, and Gemma knows that; so, it makes no difference to me. I have debts to repay. A responsibility to be powerless and docile.'

She thought of the other boy in the photograph, with his arm around Ingram's shoulder and his lips so near to Ingram's face. The smile on Ingram's face from being kissed or having been kissed seconds earlier. The strain in his voice that smothered the word *friend*, as if he'd been forced to don it reluctantly when he'd meant something else.

Something deeper. That, Aurelia would have understood; but it was less about her than it was about Gemma. About trusting Aurelia enough not to brandish that longing like a weapon against him in front of someone it would hurt even more.

Given their sordid past, she couldn't blame him. Out of all the things she'd been sorry for, this was the worst. She wished he'd given her the chance. She wished, the same way she'd wished to be someone Marga could have confided in, that Ingram would have told her, so she could say that they were not so different.

'I wish you'd stop keeping secrets from me,' she told him.

He looked down at her, seeing nothing, seeing clearly through her. She clung to the last shred of her strength, hidden with all her shame and desperation. It was the smallest part now, diminished by the pity growing in her heart.

Swallowing her pride, she said, 'We're in this together, you know. Whether you like it or not, this issue concerns us both. No matter how much you try to deny the magic that runs through your blood, it's still there. And the fact that Leona wants it so badly means it's still relevant. You can't avoid it for ever.'

'Maybe for you. You've never had blood on your hands. Go inside,' he said sharply. He'd found something else to look at. Anything but her.

'And what will you do?'

'Fix this.'

She bit her tongue, thinking of her sister's broken perfume bottle, of an age she wanted to outgrow. 'Don't say that. I'm *sorry*. I said I'm sorry.'

He waved her away and commanded again. 'We'll be lucky if your little outburst doesn't cost us our safety. Go inside, Schwartz. One of us has to clean up the mess you've made.'

Her face burned with humiliation. Had it been a mistake to demand an answer? Was it such a bad thing for him to be known?

Perhaps it would have been wise to answer him with caution, but Aurelia Schwartz didn't yield to men who gave her orders. Not even pitiful ones that wielded the hand of death. Be it hard-headedness or perseverance, she'd wanted to be there. She wanted to make it work. There was more at stake than their hospitality, and they hadn't yet discovered what it was. She'd be damned if she let someone like him take it from her under her nose.

So, she gritted her teeth and swallowed the curse she'd

wanted to give him instead, leaving his last words without punctuation. She turned up her chin and disappeared behind the mass of branches, into the cottage – away from him.

CHAPTER ELEVEN

He didn't return for dinner that night. For all that Aurelia knew, Ingram hadn't stepped foot in the cottage after he sent her away.

While they gathered around the table, Gemma made no mention of the argument, and for the sake of Louisa's cheerful attitude, Aurelia wouldn't be the one to bring him up. She added little to their conversation, feeling out of place at the table with his family. After all, she had no qualms with Gemma Eakley – just the person who'd known her son.

She helped dry the just-washed dishes, although Gemma insisted she leave the cleaning to her. The woman scrubbed the plates of their strawberry sauce streaks loudly. Chores were her outlet. She created them eagerly.

Was it worry that Gemma sought to ignore? Or the bitterness that she'd opened her home to someone as insistent as Aurelia Schwartz, and it had been compromised?

Aurelia tried to apologize, sliding a plate into the cupboard above her head.

'Don't give me that,' Gemma answered. 'What's done is done. I might have done the same in your shoes.'

The weight of her guilt lessened atop Aurelia's shoulders. She tried her luck. 'Has he always been this difficult?'

Gemma nodded. 'Absolutely. He's probably at the pub now, trying to drink himself to death.'

'Could he do that?' She couldn't recount the number of bottles she'd emptied in her attempt to shove her own sorrows out. It was certainly more than what any bartender would allow.

'Not easily,' Gemma responded with a sigh. 'Gods know he tries. He has an affinity for *wallowing*.'

Louisa reappeared from her bedroom with the colouring books and utensils she'd gone to retrieve and raced down the steps toward the basement ahead of her mother.

Ingram's words echoed through her mind, strung together in the handwriting she'd seen in all his books' margins.

I think you enjoy wallowing. Do you relish it?

'So, he does this often?' Aurelia asked.

'Often enough.'

'Do you think it's worth it to go after him and apologize?'

Gemma shrugged, slinking back against the edge of the countertop. The lines beside her lips were more pronounced now, the crease in her brow equal in depth to the one that usually marked Ingram's face. Something else was gnawing at her.

'That's up to you, darling. I'm not too worried about him. He'll come around after he's had his fill of misery. If anything, I worry about you making it home safely in the dark.'

Aurelia gathered from the bow of the woman's head that she worried for Theodore Ingram more than she cared to let on. How did Gemma Eakley manage a person like him? Aurelia would have sooner cleansed herself of his essence than harbour him like a fugitive.

Unprompted, Gemma's voice dropped to a whisper. 'I know he told you about Kenny. You mustn't tell Lou. I know it seems strange that I keep him from her, but I promise I have my reasons. Don't think that I am a bad mother. He is as much my child as she is.'

Aurelia shook her head. 'You don't need to explain yourself to me.'

The woman opened her arms, and Aurelia sunk into her embrace without question. Being held by Gemma was the closest Aurelia had been to Gabrielle again. She was warm, and every inch of her exuded comfort. The careful brush of her stocky hand in Aurelia's hair made her heart ache.

How long had it been since Aurelia held another witch this closely? Years, if ever. Years since Gabrielle. Tucked away at the top of Townsend Hill, she wasn't afraid of being sought by the humans who might recognize the conglomeration of their magic and misuse it.

Years since she'd felt safe enough to let her magic slip through the cracks. If only it hadn't formed in the most condemning way. If only being held like this didn't leave an aftertaste of guilt in her mouth – she didn't need to be taken care of. Comfort was too much to ask for from a woman whose wounds had been reopened so recently from her hands.

Gemma stepped back, occupying herself with another needless chore. 'I am . . . so glad that you're here.'

Aurelia was becoming soft, which did no one any good. 'I'm going out to find him,' she said.

Gemma smoothed her hands over her printed blouse and assured her, 'My light will stay on for you. In case you need it.'

'You don't think he'll come with me?'

Gemma smiled softly. 'It is easy to lose your way here. Even with a friend.'

She pulled on her raincoat and left the cottage. By then, Gemma had joined her daughter in front of the box television in the basement while the young girl scratched at her colouring book. Aurelia made herself presentable enough to look like she belonged at a pub.

She broke up the distant songs of hooting owls and yowling cats with the crunch of her heavy boots through the grass, brushing through something dark and silky.

Where the tree had pierced the ground, there now laid a trail of ash and debris. Most of it had already blown away in the winds, but a thin, fragile layer remained fastened to the dewy grass as a reminder and a warning. She wondered as she walked what it had looked like as Ingram decimated the tree. Had it combusted violently, *burning* into the ash that clung to her wet boots? Or had it merely dissolved like mist?

He only said that his magic could destroy, but to what extent? He hadn't meant to take Kenny Eakley's life, but what harm would he do if he'd wanted to?

She always had questions. One conjured up a dozen others until she was swimming in them. It took a scholar's brain to drive itself so brutally into ignorance. That was the relentlessness academia had demanded from her – to seek answers to questions that may not warrant them at all.

With the steady beat of her boots underneath her, she

thought of Marga Palermo's ransacked room, the shape of the blinds and the cuts in her bedspread. Aurelia slipped her cell phone from her pocket, braving the weather with her bare hands to turn it on and check for service. Nothing.

What was she looking for? A text from Ryan? From Ingram? Maybe enough connection to search for the image of Marga's dormitory and stare at it until it looked less like someone's bedroom and more like a crime scene.

Her father must have tried to reach her by now. She'd inherited her sense of reservedness from him, but Hanukkah always made him particularly sentimental; and this was the second year he had spent it without her.

Walking through the silent town, she couldn't help but circle back to something Gemma said about her son. The boy in the photograph, fifteen years old with Gemma's dark hair and green eyes. His features were vague in the blackness behind her eyelids, but they existed . . . There was colour to it.

It looked a bit like Theodore Ingram. Sure, he was now arrogant and miserable, but Gemma had found the resemblance, a freckle or stray hair that both boys shared. He was the closest thing to Kenny that she could cling to until – at some point – it was only Theodore Ingram.

Until nothing of her son remained.

He is as much my child as she is. The present tense of her words bestowed Kenny Eakley a life. Maybe he *was* still alive to her through Ingram.

It was early enough in the night that she wasn't the only moth moving toward the light of the city outside Townsend. Aurelia kept her head down and her ungloved hands buried in the pits of her pockets while she and her nameless counterparts completed their voyage in silence. She kept her posture rigid, trying to look taller, more intimidating, but the others in the grass didn't so much as glance in her direction. A shadow was a shadow, even if it was small and took her shape.

She thought of the man at Petro's too, the pleasant expression of surprise to hear that she was no mere passer-by. Who were the others? They must have been visitors, or travellers, using Townsend as a resting place for whatever more inspiring destination they'd end up in later. Better a tourist than a conqueror, she thought. Not another witch who would cast the town into upheaval.

She couldn't imagine anyone stayed there for ever.

It reeked of booze. This pub sat at the edge of the city where they'd first arrived and was pungent enough to smell from the pavement outside. As the door swung shut behind her, a sporting event on the television above the bar made a fragmented crowd erupt into jeers. She scoured the room for Ingram and found him quickly, sitting at the far end of the bar in conversation with a girl. She saw their bottles clink together behind the sea of roving faces.

An inebriated man to her left made a comment about her ass that made her wish she could get drunk. She'd seen her housemate succumb to that urge before: drinking to forget, to drown. Aurelia had nursed enough of their hangovers to know the reality was miserable; but it must have been nice, she thought, for a person to dilute themselves so easily. To lose whatever twisted happenstance that addled them to the influence of a bottle and purge it the next day.

She'd gone about compartmentalizing differently. Rather than rid herself of things, they would amass in her mind and speak over one another. It was so loud. All the time.

Aurelia 'pardoned' and 'sorried' her way through the crowd, the puffs of her coat making her a large obstacle to avoid. At the opposite end of the bar, she flagged down the nearest bartender. He was younger than the others – her age, it seemed. Collegiate, bearing a pleasant-mannered smile, too wide-eyed to *not* give her a free drink for promises of kissing in the back alleyway.

Sex. Carnal pleasures. Indulging the cravings of her body was the most efficient way to silence her mind. She didn't have to think while she was fucking – or getting fucked. Trouble only came after the fact, when someone asked her, 'What now?'

Can I stay?

Can I see you again?

'What are you drinking tonight?' the bartender asked. Flirting with bartenders promised no commitment. He turned up his chin as he spoke, tossing back a short lock of honey-brown curls, which was loosened so strategically to induce the urge in some unsuspecting patron to reach over the counter and brush it back.

'Not sure.' She had to strain to be heard over the cacophony. 'Do you have any ciders?'

'Just this one,' he said, unearthing a bottle. She mouthed an approval, and as he uncapped it, he said, 'An *American* girl. What brings you all the way out here?'

'Searching for something that'll put me in danger,' she said coyly.

He grinned, blissfully unaware of what trouble she had the capability of putting him in. 'What's your name?'

'Rory,' she said.

He gave her his hand over the counter, which she took gently and held a second longer than necessary. 'I'm Simon,' he said. 'I hope we're treating you well here. Can't say you've picked the right town to be in, though.'

'I'm certainly happy I came,' she told him.

At the other end of the bar, the girl across from Ingram laughed at something he'd said (which Aurelia thought couldn't be *that* funny. He was *never* funny.) His returned laughter was uninhibited in a way that she'd never heard before, and there was enough comfort established between the two that the girl felt emboldened enough to touch her hand to his knee and lean in to him.

It was almost unnerving how quickly Ingram's eyes found Aurelia's, over all the clamour and drunken exultations. He still wore the dazzling stain of his laughter as he looked at her, but she knew then that he was faking it. Faking something. She didn't know yet what it was, but there was a detachment in his demeanour.

She ignored the swell of relief in her chest and faced Simon again, sipping from her bottle.

'Good?' he asked.

'Sufficient,' she said with a smile.

Simon smiled back, and said, 'It's on me tonight.'

He was *pretty*, with smooth tanned skin and a small

dimple at the bottom of his chin. Certainly, he'd done this dance with plenty of girls across the counter, maybe even tonight. Aurelia didn't care. On another night, she might have toyed with the straw of a cocktail she'd later ask him to share or struck up a conversation built entirely out of sweet nothings; but she was here for someone else tonight. And that *someone else* was now doing everything in his power to lose sight of her.

'Thank you, Simon,' she said, with an infinitesimal crinkle of her eyes. 'I'll see you around.'

Aurelia sauntered toward Theodore Ingram and his currently faceless counterpart. She'd been turned away from Aurelia Schwartz this entire time, but from the back, Aurelia saw the lob of short, dark hair that looked a bit like hers – only straighter.

Aurelia pressed through the last of the crowd, bottle in hand to flank them, and said, 'Ingram. We need to talk.'

He groaned, pressing the bridge of his nose between his thumb and forefinger. 'Can't it wait, Schwartz?'

On his barstool, he was a smidge shorter than her, and she filed away her flutter of satisfaction to expound upon later. 'I don't see why it should. Sorry to interrupt you both, but I suspect I'm not spoiling anything.'

'Just a little,' he mumbled.

The girl's eyes were brown, too, warmer than Aurelia's, and significantly less fatigued. Aurelia would have chosen a darker shade of lipstick, but the similarities were jarring. She fought back an unwarranted pang of jealousy. She wasn't drunk. Nor was he. Although she understood, as he hid his face in the slow drag of his hands, that he was pretending to be at least mildly tipsy. 'Sorry, who are you?' the girl asked.

'A *friend*,' Ingram said sharply. Aurelia winced at the word, a small shift in her expression that didn't go unnoticed by her doppelganger.

'You two aren't—'

Aurelia forced herself to laugh. 'God, no. I actually despise him. I'll grab a seat. Is here all right?'

'*Christ*,' Ingram muttered.

The girl bristled. Aurelia leaned closer to her, catching her off guard with a whisper in her ear. 'For the record,' she said, 'he snores like an elephant. Open mouth, drool and all. I wouldn't touch him with a hazmat suit – it's horrible.'

The girl downed the last of her drink and said, 'I should go. It's getting late. Excuse me.'

After a moment of bumbling, Ingram's head still down without objection to the stunt, Aurelia stole her doppelganger's place on the stool and said, 'What's your secret? You're such a good fool for such pretty girls.'

'What do you want, Schwartz?'

'What are you doing here, Ingram?'

He raised his bottle.

'No games,' she said.

'I'm drinking. Lying. Not flirting with barmen to get free drinks.'

She scowled and brought the floor of her bottle to the countertop more aggressively than intended. Ingram smiled to himself, scraping his hand down the back of his neck as he folded over the counter. She'd seen iterations of that smile before, the one that was barely there, hidden in the corners of his mouth; but it was still new to her. Something had softened in the hollows of his cheeks and smoothed the crease in his brow.

It made her realize how tightly wound she seemed in juxtaposition.

She breathed deeply, holding fast to her bottle for a different kind of support. 'Honest answer?'

Ingram looked her squarely in the eyes and told her, 'Trying to self-sabotage with something other than memories of my dead best friend.'

They sat in silence, measuring time through the few clear words in everyone else's conversations. Finally, Aurelia said, 'Sounds like fun. Can I?'

Ingram gave her his bottle, and she took it. She sniffed. It was foul.

She raised the bottle to her lips to discover it tasted even fouler. 'That's disgusting.'

'It's strong.'

'What difference would it make when you'd still need ten of them? Why have it if not to enjoy it?'

He shrugged and held out his hand for her bottle, which she relinquished without protest. He sucked the moisture of it from his lip, breathing in the fragrance of it. 'She'd have liked me better if I wasn't sober,' he admitted.

She clinked his swapped bottle with hers and said, 'That makes two of us. *Drink.*'

His eyes bore into her as he drank, and she stomached more of his rancid beverage for camaraderie's sake.

'You wanted to talk?' Ingram leaned back against the wall that bracketed the bar top.

'I did.'

'Did that change? You're awfully taciturn for someone who walked in here with so much conviction.'

She shrugged. 'Haven't figured out where to start.'

I'm sorry.

I'm pissed off that you strung me along.

I may not have hated you then, but I do now, and I don't even know why. But I get it – why you did what you did.

She wanted to be angry with him – she *did* – but determined as she was, she couldn't blame him. She might have done the same thing in his shoes. He was like her in so many ways that they might've wound up here regardless of what things they omitted to one another: spiralling headfirst into their eventual decomposition.

Beneath his wealth and hubris, there was a mirror image of herself. Everything she had become, be it wild, messy or tenacious, stared back at her in the shapes of his face.

The morbid thought entered her mind that she could end up like Kenny if she got too close to him – that Ingram would swallow up her identity and replace it with his own if she let him. She wouldn't know better. They'd been twisted around each other for so long that the difference wouldn't show.

Not until it was too late.

Aurelia cleared her throat and tucked a curl behind her ear that then tumbled back down stubbornly. Ingram eyed her surreptitiously until she spoke. 'How'd it happen?'

He glanced around the crowded room and breathed deeply

amidst the privacy of noise. 'Slowly,' he told her. 'We were fifteen when it happened. He and I had been inseparable since we'd met in year seven. He knew I was a witch from the moment he saw me, but he was the first witch I had ever known, so I'd only thought he was a bit odd. He was odd in plenty of ways, though. That's what I liked about him. That, and the fact that he was kind. Boys of that age haven't had the chance to decide if kindness is important to them, but he did. And he chose to be kind to me.

'It was . . . a hard thing for anyone to witness, let alone someone who'd just turned fifteen. As much as I loved his oddities, they made up the pyre for the other boys in our class to burn him. They were horrible to him. They'd been horrible for so long. The signs were all there. I should have looked closer. Been a better friend,' Ingram said, trailing off sadly. Aurelia swallowed the mass of sorrow in her throat.

'He killed himself?'

'With my magic.' He cleared his throat, fidgeting with his drink, which was still *her* drink. The better-tasting drink. 'He always felt too much. It was so admirable of him, really, to have that much consideration for others, but they had none for him. None. I think about what he might be like if he'd had the chance to grow up. You would have loved him, Schwartz. I hadn't known much love during those formative years of my life, being brought up the way I was. Now, I don't know if he'd be proud of the person I am today. Then again, I don't think I would be this person if he hadn't died. It spoiled everything, losing him. He was my confidant. It's painful knowing how much you've lost, and I'd lost the only person in my life who really knew me. *Jesus,*' he whispered, then took another drink.

'I didn't hurt him. I would've never hurt him. But in the end, it was still my fault,' Ingram said, wiping his mouth in a hurry as if he knew the extra seconds would stop him from sharing. 'Gemma won't say it out loud, but I know she believes it. She keeps quiet for Lou's sake – for the sake of preserving this haven she made after he died.'

'She loves you, though. I know she does. I see it in the way she talks to you.'

'Because I remind her of him.'

Mulling it over, Aurelia didn't know why it was such a bad thing to him. How long must two people know each other before they become a pale imitation of the other? She wondered how much of Teddy Ingram was made up of Kenny Eakley. Were they so similar that Gemma could use him to fill the empty shoes of her son? That Ingram would bend to fit the mould of his friend seemed unlikely, but she'd never known that version of himself he spoke of – the one that wasn't tough and bitter like unripe fruit.

'Maybe,' she said softly. '*Drink.*'

They drank, staring each other down over the tilt of their bottles. She replaced hers on the ring of condensation she'd left, where a crust had formed from countless other bottle placements before her time.

'Do you think it's so bad,' she asked, 'that Gemma sees her son in you?'

'No,' he answered, but it was unconvincing. 'It's not like I'm innocent in it either. She's the closest thing to a mother that I've ever had.'

'Besides your own?'

'Celia Ingram is not my mother,' Ingram said flatly. 'Nor does she want to be. It's a damn shame she's so committed to my dad to stay despite his cheating, but not committed enough to care about the kid he got saddled with.'

'Didn't think you'd be the "riddled with mommy issues" type.'

He smiled more easily this time. 'Suppose not.'

'If it counts for anything,' Aurelia noted, 'I never had a chance at that. I never knew my mother either. And my dad was never keen on remarrying, so wicked stepmothers were out of the question.'

'Is she alive?' asked Ingram.

'I think so. My dad doesn't like to talk about her. You hear a lot about absent fathers but little about absent mothers – there's supposed to be a maternal bond, y'know. She'd had my sister two years before me. And I know I wasn't an accident. No one tells me, though – why she left after me – and I still don't know where she went. You carry someone inside you for the better part of a year, letting them eat from you and wring you dry, and then you *vanish*.'

'Sounds like mommy issues to me, Schwartz.'

'You'd think so, but I don't think I ever had to be alone the same way you were. I had this *tutor* named Gabrielle. She was this French-Haitian witch that used to practise in my mom's coven. Taught me everything I knew about my magic. Loved jazz and costume jewellery. Didn't really love my father. He was good to us,' Aurelia explained. 'If we were fully human, he might have been the best father around; but we *weren't*. He doesn't want to be a witch, and I get the distinct feeling that he hates magic.'

'Can't fault him for that. Some kinds of magic shouldn't be realized.'

Aurelia lowered her head silently, knowing that wasn't the case for her father. He was a green witch like her. She'd always felt lucky to inherit his gift. Gifts weren't passed down so completely from parent to child, but she'd been so proud to be a branch on her father's tree. Sometimes it felt like he'd broken her off to evade infestation.

'You know how it goes, then,' Ingram said. 'To lean on someone else for parenthood.'

She shook her head, still gripping her bottle to ground herself. 'Gabrielle made it clear that she wasn't my mother, even if I spent the better half of my life under her instruction. Sometimes, I wished she was – just so I could know what it felt like.'

'It feels *good*,' he said simply. 'As long as you can delude yourself. You should have no problem with that.'

Aurelia glared, finding his eyes in the dim light of the pub. They looked grey and soft under the harsh yellow glow; and as she studied him, with his cheeks flushed with heat and his hair slightly askew on his forehead, he looked like the kind of person she'd have gone home with. Which was ironic, really, considering she was already there. He was annoyingly perfect. She hated him a bit for that, but mostly, she hated how there were fewer things to hate about him every day.

Finally, he'd given her what she wanted, an answer. *Honesty*, albeit reluctant. He'd answered her question but offered more too – spilling himself open for her inspection. Perhaps that was his way of apology, doing right on what she'd asked just before it was too late.

'*Really* wish I could've been drunk for that,' he said, with a quiet, disjointed laugh.

Aurelia pointed to his bottle. 'We could pretend. *Drink*.'

After another gulp, he teased bitterly, 'What happened to your righteousness, Schwartz? Is my honesty not what you've been championing all along?'

'I think I've had enough of your honesty for one day.'

'I propose we lie to each other for the rest of the night. To maintain equilibrium.'

'You would,' Aurelia muttered. Omission and silence made up his language, but it wasn't hers. She didn't harbour the heavy kind of secrets that Theodore Ingram seemed to always keep in his pockets, ready to pull him underwater with the first opportune current.

At least, she didn't have any that involved him.

'What happened to her?' asked Ingram.

'My mother?'

'Gabrielle,' he said.

Aurelia wished she knew. 'Never found out. I'm not sure if I will. When I was preparing to apply to universities, I lost track of everything else that wasn't my schoolwork. That's when I last saw her. I'd been more infrequent with my visits, and she rarely asked *me* to come. At some point, after I'd moved here, I realized that our last visit might *truly* have been our last. It was so easy for her to disappear. I'm told that she moved,' Aurelia explained. 'My dad doesn't keep in touch with her, and my sister didn't care to learn about her magic either, so she never sought her out.'

'Do you think she'd know where your mother is?'

She sighed. 'Sometimes, I think . . . I think it was harder for Gabrielle to lose my mother than it was for me. She didn't know. Or maybe she just never wanted to say. I was the last thing that tethered her to our family; and once I was gone, she had no reason to stick around. *I* want to be drunk for this.'

'Club of the motherless,' Ingram said.

'Cheers.' She lifted her bottle again.

'I'm out,' he said. 'I'll get you another one, Schwartz.' He caught Simon's attention, which wasn't difficult now that Aurelia had made herself privy to his curious gaze. With little to say, the bartender uncapped another bottle and handed it to Aurelia.

'And the boys from school,' she said. 'What happened to them after Kenny died?'

'They're probably in very respectable universities now,' Ingram mumbled. 'Doing averagely in their classes. I gave them plenty of grief when he was still around. After him . . . I'd simply given up by then. Boys are ruthless at that age, but I was only ever ruthless for him. I always suspected that Gemma didn't like the idea of us together, but there was nothing I could do about that. When it came to classmates, I couldn't have cared less what they thought of me. I was fairly discreet with my bisexuality, but they all knew. Made a lot of problems for Celia. Getting into constant fights meant a lot of calls to my parents. She would have brought the iron fist of Catholicism down on my head for fancying boys.'

'Boys never get better,' she countered. 'I had to harden myself at a young age; they don't get to me much any more.'

'I can't imagine that anyone gets to you,' Ingram told her. 'You look as if you'd rather eat someone whole than let them inside.'

Sourly, she said, 'That's the goal.'

'I always liked that about you, though,' he said. 'Your ferocity.'

She searched his face for a sliver of that breakable person she thought he might've been, yearning to introduce it to the similar, barely-there part of herself.

It was still there, she thought. She'd repressed it well, but it was still just a heart inside of her, covered up by flesh and bone, penetrable and soft. If she didn't feel herself bruising, it was because she'd acclimated to it, not that those bruises weren't there.

'Sounds more like fear than fondness to me,' she told him.

'Whatever you prefer. Do we drink?'

She raised the bottle to her lips and drained it.

Final orders passed with several bottles in their wake. His deep auburn hair flattened against the wall as he threw his head back and laughed. Aurelia's cheeks were aching, too, rather from resisting her own laughter. She tilted her head into her hand as she leaned against the counter, and he caught sight of the cricket match rerun playing above their heads.

'I used to play, you know.'

'Cricket?' she asked.

He frowned. 'Is that what's on? I meant football. Or *soccer*,' he drawled, mimicking her accent.

'It's *cricket* they're playing. Don't tell me you're actually tipsy. I'll be green with envy.'

He rubbed his eyes with his knuckles. 'Been a long day. Just tired. Do you want to get out of here?'

It seemed like a cruel joke that the last person who'd said those words to her was Lawrence Kressler, with his lips pressed against her hair in the darkness of a movie theatre. He'd wrapped an arm around her, tugged her a little closer to whisper in her ear, and she had been more than happy to oblige.

If they had a wager for which of them could say it best, Ingram would have lost without a shadow of a doubt. She had the niggling suspicion from the glassiness in his eyes that she might've had to carry him into Townsend and up the hill. *How anyone could believe he was intimidating*, she thought. People witnessed that devilish grin and cried wolf, but he was nothing more to her than a wet dog with sharp teeth.

And still, a pain in the ass to deal with miles away from where their beds were. Aurelia made a note to chastise him for his lack of foresight, but at present, she couldn't bring herself to be angry with him. To his credit, he'd given her more than what she came for with little provocation and paid for the rest of her drinks too.

They began the journey back to Townsend in the dark. It was almost midnight when they started their ascent of the hill. To her delight, he didn't need to lean on her, but she could tell he was tired from the slowness of his steps – she didn't need to rush to keep to his pace.

Mostly, it was silent. They'd said enough, *shared* enough. Occasionally, he would offer her something else, another precious piece of unsolicited information like, 'Gemma used to call me Theo like everyone else. She only started calling me Teddy after *he* died. I think it's because the names were so similar.'

He seemed the truest version of himself when he was there in Townsend. Now, against the backdrop of night, he nearly disappeared, a dark figure against the dark brush. How many other people could say they were as tightly interwoven with Theodore Ingram as she was? If anyone knew him so well?

'I have to ask you something,' she said.

He bared that devilish smile to her. 'Haven't you asked me enough tonight?'

'It's about what happened at King's College.'

'Something important, then. Go on.'

The crunch of grass beneath their boots was distracting her. She itched as it grazed her waist through the winter layers that covered her from head to toe.

'How did you know about Marga?'

He stopped, half a step ahead of her. 'What do you mean?'

She'd kept it vague, hoping he would answer more than one of the many questions she had about Marga Palermo, but she'd meant it when she said she'd had enough for one night. She was tired of questioning, of being uncertain, and having to dwell.

So, just one.

'How did you know when she was murdered?'

It became so quiet on the hill that Aurelia thought he was holding his breath.

'I could . . . *feel* it,' he said. 'As if one of the bulbs in a string of lights had gone out.'

'And that string – were we on it too?'

He paused again. She cleared her throat to spite the chill in the air and risked freezing her right hand to bring it up from her pocket and pick her nails again.

Nodding, he said, 'We were.'

Her other questions could wait until morning.

He didn't move. His eyes narrowed at her, lingering on the angles of her face. Her skin prickled with the sensation of being watched. Of being *seen*.

'By the way, thanks for that,' he said.

'For what? Ruining your fun back there?'

Ingram ran a hand through his tousled hair, smoothing it. 'Debauchery isn't nearly as fun as I make it out to be. If we *are* being honest with each other, she was a bit dull.'

'You must've seen something in her.'

He shrugged, turning toward the light of the Townsend Hill cottage, a beacon for their arrival. It silhouetted him in a hazy glow. 'She was *pretty*,' he said. 'And I needed a distraction.'

Aurelia tried to ignore how much that girl looked like her as she resumed her stride up the hill, tugging at his coat sleeve to pull him along. 'I'm sorry, y'know. For what I said earlier.'

'I know,' said Ingram. 'But I meant what I said now.'

'That she was dull? That's rude. Sounds like she dodged a bullet.'

A bemused smile broke through his stony facade, and she wished she could tuck it into her pocket like one of her perfect, unbreakable leaves.

'That I'm thankful you came. You are interesting company.'

She tore her eyes free from the redness of his lips and the rosiness of his cheeks before they could ensnare her.

'Although I don't know why you decided to be so nice to me, Schwartz. It's a little unnerving.'

'I'm hardly nice. It's probably just cabin fever. Being stuck in this little house in the middle of nowhere with you.'

He raised an eyebrow. 'You think that's what this is?'

Of course not. But she had to wonder if she'd lost her mind with how little it took to make her blush when they spoke to one another now, and she wouldn't give him the satisfaction of knowing that.

Not now. Not *ever*. There were more worthwhile things to devote her time to.

She shook her head. 'No. Not really.'

'I don't suppose I could make you understand how much trouble we've made by sticking together like this.'

'I already understand. It's too bad – I like it here.'

'So stubborn,' he said. 'I bet your skull's at least an inch thick.'

'Don't you ever wonder how I've bested you in our classes all these years? My skull is so solid to account for my *enormously* solid brain.'

Awe settled comfortably on his features. Anything but tight lines and hardened jaws should've seemed uncommon to her, but he was too tired to be angry, and she was too tired to care.

'Are you sure you still want to be here?' he asked.

'Why wouldn't I?'

'Because I'm not certain any more that Townsend is the

safest place for you to be. Few good things will ever come from associating with magic like mine. With witches like me. And after that letter . . .'

Aurelia nodded. She hadn't intended to leave, but she saw the way the empty threat of leaving weighed on him. 'If she found us once, she'll find us again. At this point, we're probably stronger together than we are separately.'

'To do what, exactly?'

Aurelia's brows furrowed hard. 'I don't know. Ask your friend at the bookstore. I don't have much experience with witch hunts aside from in theory, if you can believe it.'

'Well,' Ingram said. 'That makes two of us.'

Relief warmed through her. For better or worse, she was as stuck with the cottage as it was stuck with her. It was a sanctuary for them, and it was furtively becoming hers too. If she closed her eyes and listened hard, she heard the whistling of the grassy hilltop coursing through her veins – a harmony in the song of her witch's blood.

He said nothing else after that, welcoming the silence.

CHAPTER TWELVE

She started with the facts: she and Ingram had been at King's College on the night of an attack that left one witch dead and put a target on their backs. They had been outside the hall while this witch, their colleague, was pierced through the chest with a sword taken from the British Museum. They had seen nothing more than silver and crimson, and the wide-eyed, open-mouthed expression that lingered on the faces of the dead until someone else could close their eyelids for them. She couldn't tell Gemma why someone came to kill Margarita Palermo, or how she and Ingram inherited the witch hunter's wrath from her. Everything that came after that night at King's was an assumption. Maybe they were necessary. Maybe they were simply in the wrong place at the right time for Leona to pick up their scent on the wind and grow hungry.

Unfortunately, the looming threat that Ingram carried over to her house had become much more than an assumption. The most they could do was stare at all the disjointed pieces before them and pray it would start to look like something.

'Have you gathered anything from these?' asked Gemma. There wasn't much one could pull from the three gold tokens that didn't involve a range of dates or a regional classification.

Aurelia wiped the mirrored surface of the third one and held it to her eye. A record spun on the turntable nearby – a piano concerto that Gemma touted with pride. 'It's rare,' she'd said, 'that female pianists have their work recorded in such good quality.'

'I'm assuming that *this* symbol,' Aurelia said, gesturing then to the runic shape, 'is Yr and not Algiz. Only because I can't imagine someone with an ambitious chase like hers wants to hang the threat of life over our heads.'

'And this?' Gemma asked, pinching the first between her fingers. Aurelia hadn't spent much time in the basement since she arrived, but it appeared to be the most lived-in part of the already well-worn cottage aside from the kitchen. On the low, oblong coffee table, Louisa's chapter books and drawing utensils were a smattering of colour, bordered by some of Ingram's belongings.

'It's lavender. The imagery is straightforward enough, which makes me more hesitant about it. I don't think it was meant to be an objective representation, but I don't know what deeper meaning she'd want me to pull from it.'

'What makes you think otherwise?'

A sigh escaped from her lips. 'I'm honestly not sure. I wish I knew why, but for one reason or another, it doesn't seem like it should be this easy. Someone so dangerous should be smarter than that, don't you think? If she's the same person who Ingram believes made it into all these high-security institutions and managed to leave undetected, she would be smart enough to know the ins and outs of what she's taking. So why tokens? And how'd she manage to tailor them so specifically to us? His guess was that she took frivolously.'

'But that's not yours, is it?'

Aurelia pressed her mouth into a sharp line and shook her head. 'I don't think she would be that careless. I don't think she would put her hands on so many things and risk leaving all those prints. I think she took what she *needed*. Tokens of particular magic that she wants to possess. I think the etchings are a metaphor. I just don't know what for.'

Or *why* she would need them. Neither of them had landed on a motive in all their ineffective pontification. It was impossible to feel like they were getting any closer to an answer, or a personal sense of security, when all their conversations ended languishing in the basement throwing out half-baked, unproven theories as to what Leona would need them for. The threat seemed to ebb and flow in severity. The longer they went without knowing, the more dire it should have felt. Except, it didn't. Not always. Puzzling over who Leona was and what she wanted could assume, at times, an academic quality that instilled within Aurelia Schwartz a passion that had long since turned to thoughtless mundanity.

The faucet ran above their heads, sabotaging her trail of thought. Gemma angled onto her hip beside her, meeting Aurelia with a directness she couldn't comfortably return.

'The third still means nothing to me,' Aurelia continued nervously. She shifted in her seat, crossing her ankles neatly to prevent her leg from its restless tapping. She folded her hands in her lap and resisted the urge to chew on her nails again.

A cupboard shut hard in the kitchen. Gemma hissed between her teeth, 'Hell is he doing up there?'

'Breaking your things,' Aurelia muttered.

'God, I hope not.'

Aurelia flipped the mirrored token into the air like a coin, catching it in the negative space between her hands. It spun like a thaumatrope on invisible strings. She tugged and thought of bluebirds in cages, a bundle of flowers in a vase. A marriage of two images, suspended on a fine, golden thread . . .

Something in the mirror looked back at her.

Finally, Ingram started his slow descent into the basement, unsuccessfully securing several large mugs, Gemma's teapot, and his folded laptop in his arms. Aurelia rose from behind the coffee table to meet him by the stairs, snatching the token into her fist, but he urged her sharply, 'Sit, Schwartz. Don't even consider it.'

She collapsed back onto the couch with narrowed eyes. He handed the largest mug to Gemma.

Aurelia asked, 'Which one is mine?'

'You assume I brought you any?' Jeers aside, he handed her a mug adorned with multicoloured ladybugs, and said, 'Here. It's my favourite. Have I interrupted something?'

'Apparently I ask loaded questions,' said Gemma.

'She asked me about what I want to do after I get my PhD earlier,' Aurelia explained.

There was enough space between the two women for him to fit snugly, but he lowered himself to the rug beside Aurelia's knees with one leg extended in front of him, the other bent to support the lazy bow of his arm.

He tutted, brushing Aurelia's leg as he leaned back against the seat of the couch, 'Can't trust you to take care of my guest for a couple of minutes. You can't ask a medievalist something like that.' Then, focusing his widened, upturned gaze to Aurelia, he teased, 'She'll trap you here for ever if I don't stop her.'

The woman made a noise of protest as she sipped the tea. 'Oh, I like this one, darling.'

'You told me ginger cham was one of your favourites, Gem.'

Gemma leaned over the length of the couch and placed a kiss in his hair. 'I think I'm going to take this upstairs.' She smoothed an affectionate hand over it and left them to their devices.

'How d'you like it?' he asked Aurelia.

'It's sweet.'

'Is that good?'

So good. So was the thought of Ingram shuffling through Gemma Eakley's cabinet to select their teas that made Aurelia's chest swell with endearment.

She nodded, smiling into her cup as she sipped. The record drew to silence across the basement. Ingram shifted, but with a delicate hand on his shoulder, she held him down beside her knees and said, '*Sit*, Ingram.'

Two days ago, he'd shown her which of those records were Kenny's favourites, remarking with a faraway gaze that they would never really belong to him, but that he was still proud of how the collection had grown under his care. She rummaged for the one he'd lingered on earlier and heard his sigh resound behind her as she rested the needle on its edge.

'Bit hard to figure anything out without internet connection here,' he said. 'We ought to stop by the town tomorrow.'

'Perfect.' After seeing Marga's room trashed, she was itching for an opportunity to call Ryan and ask when they'd return. She couldn't do that from up here on the hill. 'You know, I didn't have that nightmare last night. I had a dream about those human thumbs from *Spy Kids* instead . . . Except they weren't totally thumbs. Some of them had faces of celebrities.'

Ingram's brow furrowed as she broke the connection of her hands to forge an image with them.

'You know what I mean? You've seen that movie, right?'

'It's been a while,' he replied, a bemused expression on his face.

'Right. So, there I was, surrounded by these movie star thumbs, crouched in my old garage while they chased me and my dog.'

'I didn't know you had a dog,' he said.

'I don't, but that's not the point. We're hiding from these thumbs, who are also movie stars and somehow also *highly* skilled in martial arts, and we're looking out from underneath the garage door when one of them grabs the edge of it and yanks it up. Now, we're staring into the face of this thumb celebrity whose name I can't remember in the dream, but I'm so terrified that I wake up immediately – just to realize I don't remember him in real life either. I know I've seen him, because he's fairly famous, but I still can't figure out who it was.'

'Why are you telling me this? Does this have anything to do with deciphering these?'

It started as a relevant story, but somewhere in her recollection of the dream, it stopped making sense to her too. 'Well,' said Aurelia, 'not really. I woke up terrified at around four in the morning, which, to be fair, was still much better than waking up from the King's College nightmare once I reminded myself that I wasn't currently being surrounded by flying ninja thumb celebrities. But I opened my phone while the last one's face was still fresh in my mind – to look him up, y'know. Obviously, I couldn't. I'm still a little pissed about it.'

Yes, that was the point, wasn't it?

Ingram sighed heavily, cocking his brow at her – poised, collected, and utterly infuriating.

'That was informative,' he said.

Aurelia frowned, returning to the couch. 'How is my celebrity thumb dream informative?'

'It's not. But your proclivity for oversharing is – your need to know, to have something to discover.'

'Is this the part where you try to school me in Jungian psychology?' she teased. 'I think Gemma might have already tried that.'

'You're ridiculous, Schwartz.'

'You're right. Freud's better for that. I think he's got a book called *The Interpretation of Thumb Dreams*.'

'I thought you were supposed to be a good student, and here you are ruminating on personified thumbs,' he lamented. 'Tell me what we know.'

'I hate to say it,' she remarked, resting her elbows on the tops of her thighs, 'but I think we're stuck at a threshold of information. We need something else.'

He glanced up at her curiously, and she had the contemptuous urge to ruin the tidiness of his hair. Ingram said, 'If you think we need some sign from the cosmos, Gem's got nothing for us. I've asked.'

She caught herself looking at his lips again – they were too red, too pretty – and it was all too easy to lose track of time doing so. Before she'd joined Gemma in the basement, the clock read half past twelve, and the sky outside their windows was white and blinding. She wouldn't be surprised if she walked up to the kitchen and found dusk on the other side of the sink.

He was closer now, but neither of them had moved.

Those red lips parted, saying softly, 'You have a question.'

'Countless,' she said.

'But something in particular is weighing on you.'

It disarmed her that he knew so easily. 'You don't . . . You don't practise common magic, do you?' she asked.

'*No* . . . I'm not well versed in it.'

'Then how do you release your magic?'

He blinked at her, dumbfounded, as if he'd never thought there was anything caged within him in the first place.

'I dunno,' Ingram admitted. 'Sometimes I think that it's *always* seeping out like sewage. Accumulation has never really been an issue for me. Is that a conscious decision you make to release it?'

'That's what I was taught to do.'

'Ah,' he said. 'But you were *taught*. I never had the luxury of a magical tutor.'

'I'm sure you had plenty of others though.'

'Are we back to this again?'

Aurelia bit her tongue, considering the defence that might have spewed from her mouth had she not. 'I'm sorry,' she said.

'I wasn't asking for an apology,' he said. She'd confused him more than appeased him. If those words had come from his mouth several days ago, she might have groaned and rolled her eyes at him, but all the malice in his words had since been eradicated.

'OK. I'm . . . Sure.'

She gazed at the token again, reforming the image of it spinning like the earth on its axis.

Something had seen her.

'What's your plan, then, Schwartz?' he asked, his voice low in the lull that fell between them. The pianist performing Rachmaninoff reached the height of her crescendo, spoiling their privacy.

'My plan? Honestly, Ingram, I'm about as lost as you are with all of these—'

'I meant for the rest of the day. I don't expect to stare at these any longer if there's nothing left for us to see.'

'Oh.' She wiped the sweat on her palms against her jeans. 'I don't have any plans.'

'Hmm. Hard to imagine you with nothing to do.'

'And how exactly did *you* plan on wasting the day away?'

Ingram's head lolled back against the seat, close to her thigh. 'I didn't. But I have a copy of *The Three Stigmata of Palmer Eldritch* waiting for me under that pillow you're leaning against. I'm perfectly content being a hermit.'

She bumped her knee against his shoulder in encouragement. 'We could do something, though. Something different.'

'I'm not having another bitter coffee at Petro's.'

'No. Anything but that,' she retorted. 'I have a proposition for you. Do you trust me?'

He gave an arrogant snort and pushed himself to his feet.

'Absolutely not. You'll be serving my head to Gem and Lou for dinner if I trust you.'

'I'm serious.'

She watched that facetious expression mould into something more sincere. After a moment of consideration, he nodded. 'Of course, I do. Though, it's completely against my better judgement.'

She lowered her gaze to the artefacts on the table to hide the redness of her face. Try as she might to capture it, his sincerity still caught her off guard. She found it in the softening of his shoulders while they walked or in the lines beside his mouth that formed when he smiled, but rarely was he outright with it, offering vulnerability that she didn't have to search for.

Amidst her silent contemplation, Ingram asked. 'What's going on in there, Schwartz?'

'What?'

'In your head. Have something else to overshare?'

She shook her head, dispelling those flowery thoughts for something more grounded in reality. 'Just meet me outside in ten minutes.'

'All right,' he called. 'You've coerced me out here in the cold. What's your plan?'

Aurelia grinned with a pivot on her heels, her sturdy Chelsea boots twisting into the softened dirt. She clapped her grimoire shut and extended it to him. He approached warily, eyeing it as if it were more than a collection of pages written hastily by an adolescent girl and her tutor; and the awareness thrilled her.

Aside from herself, the only person who had seen and understood the spectrum of gravity within those pages was Gabrielle. Opening it to him was like pulling him in front of a mirror beside her just to find herself at fifteen staring back at them.

Aurelia pushed the book into the rough wool of his coat, vibrating with excitement.

'Go on,' she said. 'You're too old to not know common magic.'

'You're serious?'

She nodded, stern-faced and focused. 'I couldn't be more serious,' she lied. Saying the words aloud let slip a grin from behind her militant facade.

Ingram opened her grimoire gently, with the reverence of an old manuscript. Under his breath, he muttered, 'You're trying to knock me down a peg, aren't you? Or are you trying to break my spirit?'

'That's noble of you,' she teased. 'Trying to save the integrity of your *wonderfully plucky* spirit. The point is that you're twenty-three years old. You should've learned these things a long time ago.'

He sighed. 'Fine. What do you want me to do?'

She'd anticipated a more frivolous argument from him, another clash of his stubbornness against hers. She'd almost hoped to quarrel with him.

He wasn't enthusiastic about the idea of learning common magic with her. Being taught anything by her was a humbling blow to his tight-laced ego, but there was a defensiveness in his posture too, his back too straight and his gaze acute. He turned the book in his hands and studied it.

She assured him, 'We can start with something simple like . . . like small object levitation.'

He made an effort to loosen his clenched jaw.

'We could light a candle instead,' Aurelia offered. 'Or turn off a faucet from afar.'

He gave an indecisive, half-hearted hum, resting his eyes on the frontispiece of the book. Aurelia's teenaged handwriting accompanied the illustration of an oak tree, spelling out her name with a poorly drawn flower at the end of it. She was never above drawing symbols after her name, like the barista at Petro's with her heart on his cup. Aurelia's marks were everywhere. Unlike his rather scholarly annotations, she'd been inclined to decorate in her margins. Ingram's fingertips slid down the page, lingering on her name. The shadow of a smile traipsed over his face as he flipped it.

'I could show you something instead,' she offered, although it came out like a plea. 'I could show you a magic trick.'

'Pulling a hare out of your hat?'

She shook her head. 'Don't worry. No more trees either.'

Turning another page, he said, 'If I think about it, Louisa would have liked having a tree in her yard.'

'Disappoint me enough and I'll conjure up another.' Aurelia stretched her hands and cracked her knuckles.

'Should I step back?' he asked.

'You can come closer if you'd like.' Aurelia held out her hands.

Ingram offered her the grimoire, but she said, 'Your hands.'

He tucked her grimoire beneath his arm and peeled the gloves from his fingers slowly, which she almost said wasn't necessary; but the new-found expanse of skin aroused a curiosity within her for what came next. He slipped his hands into hers with uncertainty, and she repositioned them gently beneath the hair at the top of her scalp.

'Ready?'

His Adam's apple moved underneath the high neck of his sweater before he spoke, 'If I have to be.'

Would it ever be easy to stand so close to him? To touch him?

She shook the thought from her mind and replaced it with another – an intention. She concentrated it into the follicles of her hair, the flurry of an enchantment flooding up to her scalp to the surface of his hands.

Colour rushed to her face too. She couldn't blame it wholly on the spell.

'Are those—'

A smile grew as she urged her head further into his hands. 'They're roots,' Aurelia said. 'It's cool, right? I'm basically a self-propagating life form.'

They were everywhere, tendrils of tree root protruding between thick strands of her hair. Ingram threaded one around his fingers, thoroughly engrossed. There was a repetition on his lips that he didn't voice: *roots* . . . He moved from one flimsy root to the next, wonder swimming in his eyes.

Aurelia knew magic as a secret hidden from her housemate and as a *given* with Gemma Eakley; but this was different. This wasn't a spurt of untamed magic like the tree. This was deliberate – a wilful discovery at the hands of someone less practised than herself. It had only taken Aurelia Schwartz several years to trust him with a secret like that. Even if he gaped at the roots in her hair or her muddied knees on the King's College greens with her fists full of dandelions, it was in awe, not abhorrence. As if she were something mythical and unreal that he wanted to believe in.

'I like to imagine that when I'm buried,' she began, 'the ground will swallow up my body and spit it back out as a bush or a tree.'

The crease in his brow returned, and he asked her softly, in the manner of secrecy, 'Does it comfort you to think about death like that?' He must have spent his entire life considering death for the question to come so easily. To be a child, perpetually mourning, was a burden impossible for her to fathom.

Suppressing the sudden pang of guilt, she answered, 'I'm not afraid of death – not really. Not if I can nourish a patch of fungi or something. It's customary for witch corpses to be cremated, but I want to rot. I'm not sure I believe in souls, but I think mine would be better off that way.'

'Does the resident medieval theologian think our souls *have* a choice like that?' Ingram's hand lingered in her hair, prodding at the roots. She imagined that he'd laugh if she broke one off and gave it to him, but that would've hardly been the strangest thing to occur between two people like them.

Aurelia told him, 'There's always a choice for souls to decide their resting place. It's a matter of following the gods or betraying them, revelling in sin, or repenting for them. *Caelum et infernum.*' She trailed off, acutely aware of the sensation of his fingertips beside her temple.

'But those are *souls,*' she continued. 'I'm talking about the vessel, the body. When you burn a witch, you make their magic untouchable. There aren't many witches who can say they'd rest easy in the ground, but when death finds me, I hope it lets me stay there. I hope it gives my magic one more chance.'

Ingram wound a curl around his fingers meditatively. She drew in a sharp breath, and he shifted away in recognition of himself.

She'd taken for granted how warm it was when he stood so close. Aurelia cleared her throat, tucked her hair behind her ears, and said, 'That's my party trick. Let's see yours.'

Ingram sobered to the occasion again. 'What do you want to see?'

Aurelia slid the heavy, leather-bound grimoire from underneath his arm and took several comically large steps backwards. 'Take this back from me – from where you're standing,' she said.

'Child's play,' he argued.

'Well, we need a starting point, and you told me you were shit at common magic.'

'I don't think I said that.'

'Prove it, then,' she said. 'I need to gauge where you're at.'

Even from afar, she sensed his reservation. 'You don't have to be nervous,' she assured him. 'It's just me.'

Ingram scoffed. 'Just you.'

He raised his hands in front of him and willed the intention through his loosely opened palms. She balanced the book in her outstretched hand to give him a target. His lips moved as he spoke the word aloud, and she sighed, relieved, unsure if he could be trusted to cast a spell wordlessly.

It was a different word, though. Was it *French?*

In five prolonged seconds, the book was weightless in her hands, floating toward the path of Ingram's pointed gaze. Puppeteering it through an invisible bond, he seemed to lose sight of everything else. He wore that expression when he read Margery Kempe too.

'You've got it,' she said. 'Can you bring it closer?'

In his focus, the grimoire rocketed toward his stomach and sent him reeling backwards with a pained, '*Fuck*.'

He clutched the book to his stomach, doubling over himself.

Aurelia's hands flew to her mouth, to the start of a laugh, until she saw loose pages spilling from between the covers of her childhood grimoire.

The wind picked up a folded signature, tossing it into the air. Morning's raindrops on the grass pulled the others down, blurring their ink and making them stick. 'Damn it, Ingram.'

'*Agh*,' he groaned. 'Bet you enjoy seeing me like this.'

She scowled, aggrieved that some of the papers had torn loose from the grimoire's binding. She collected them, signature by signature, as she walked to meet him.

'You were doing just fine, y'know.'

Ingram braced his hands on his knees, panting heavily, 'I think I'm going to be sick.'

She pressed down on his shoulder, urged him back, and told him, 'Sit down. And don't touch anything else.'

'You *do* enjoy this, don't you?'

'I'm overjoyed,' she deadpanned. He plucked a loose signature from the mulch and wiped it clean, but his hand left behind a smudge of red. 'Ingram, what did I *just* say?'

'What are these—'

Aurelia snatched another page from the grass and interjected. 'They're notes from my tutor.'

'But *this*—'

He gestured to the unfurled page in his hands. 'Words, Ingram – *use them.*'

'What did Leona say in that letter?' he asked. 'Her exact words: *I wear many faces.*'

Aurelia's eyes narrowed on the page, blinking through the blur of wet ink. 'You think our friend Leona is a *shapeshifter?*'

His eyes were blown wide, wild. She grabbed the page from him, narrowing into her own smudged words before turning inevitably toward her old tutor for guidance. There were traces of Gabrielle on every page: the scent of her herbs embedded in the paper, corrections and elaborations scribbled within margins at angles that didn't make sense. Magical entities from half-selves to demigods, wandering eyes to waning moon rituals . . .

Beneath their notes on shapeshifters, Gabrielle had drawn a kumiho and a nahual; and she had drawn them so badly that Aurelia could only remember their names from the way the illustrations had made her laugh. She remembered slurring her comment through a mouthful of brand-new braces, 'They look like they're slow dancing,' to which Gabrielle had pinned her with a stolid gaze and responded, 'They are fighting. Not dancing. There is nothing less trustworthy than a person that cannot look at you with their real face.'

It could've been one missing piece to a half-finished puzzle, but it was just enough for her to see a larger picture. If Leona was capable of changing her appearance at will, she could've easily walked into King's College as one person and left as another, undetected.

Aurelia's heart sped, her breath catching in her throat. Ingram scoured through the grass, finding the final, unsewn page to return to her.

'The dream,' she said, 'the *nightmare* I told you about . . . She was never the same person in any of them. I thought it was just my brain searching for a person to pin to the event, but maybe all those faces were hers.'

'Could you remember any of those faces now?' he asked.

She couldn't. They were intangible, born of the fickleness of thought. Gone before a feature could settle on the blank slate of her face for good. Even if Aurelia could remember, a lead based on appearance would be impossible to follow when it came to shapeshifters.

If anything, she and Ingram were further away from an answer than ever. Her stomach twisted again, and she searched through the grass instead of giving him a fear to find in her colour-drained face.

'Shapeshifting is a gift, isn't it?' asked Ingram.

'A useful one, yes,' she muttered.

'Is it *common* for witches to have more than one?'

'Not particularly. Married witches used to exchange their gifts, but it hasn't been common practice since the early eighteenth century—'

'So, it's probable our culprit is nothing more than a shapeshifter.' Ingram met her with a damning stare. 'And that dog whistle of hers was nothing more than a common spell.'

Aurelia's brow furrowed, lost in his logic. He gestured vaguely in the space between them, urging every piece into order. With a formative breath, he proceeded. 'I admit I'm not versed in common magic, so I assumed that whatever the witch at King's was casting was the result of a gift. It seemed too advanced – affecting three different witches in three completely different ways . . . But maybe I was wrong. What if it's common magic? A spell would be more practical than trying to sift through a sea of faces by hand.'

It could be. But knowing more than Ingram did didn't mean she knew everything. What if Leona followed those antiquated traditions? What if she wasn't even a shapeshifter?

What if? In the dark, every shape was hypothetical, and every morsel of hope was a clue. To throw themselves down any rabbit hole was a risk that could end up burying them.

'How would we know where to look?' Aurelia tucked all the loose signatures of her grimoire between the covers again. 'We would need a starting point. I can't cast something that stretches the entire country . . . Honestly, I don't even know if it's a spell I *could* cast – I've never seen anything like it before.'

'Could you try – if I told you where to look?'

The desperation in his voice addled her with grief. 'Y'know, Ingram, just because it's *unlikely* doesn't mean it's impossible for her to have more than one gift. See, with blood oaths, two gifted witches can—'

'I know what a blood oath can do,' he said. 'But our friend was *murdered* by the same witch who is using her magic to find us. I'm leaning on the possibility that Leona isn't multiply gifted and that we can find her before she finds us. For my family's sake, can we try?'

She thought he was reaching for her grimoire again, but he lifted her hand from it and squeezed it.

'Rory,' he said. 'Please. I can't do this myself.'

Rory.

She thought of Marga, of Ryan Jena – of her father and sister, who denied their power to live without the influence of witchcraft. Ingram was leaning on the slim possibility of their success the same way she leaned on all of them.

There was always Ryan, with their hand on her back while she folded weakly onto the bathroom tile. Marga cutting a knowing glance over the table at King's College. Her father allowing her to nurture her green magic despite his own aversion to it . . .

The same gravity tied her hand to Ingram's. Some bonds were forged through passion and fury, but theirs was born in the shadow of grief. It was quieter – less assuming. She needed a second to acclimate to the way his skin felt when it was firmly under her palm. It shouldn't have been so difficult for someone so versed in physical pleasure to touch something so warm.

An amalgamation of emotions washed over her, plainly writ in the curve of her brows and in the tightness of her face. Ingram saw it all, stopping short of another request. Perhaps he'd already known how closely death chased at their heels, breathing down their collars, ready to take hold of them in its final embrace. He'd had years to make death his friend, wielding the same fatal hand of acquisition like its errand boy.

It dawned on her in the isolation of Townsend Hill with

Ingram and his peculiar family that her father and sister might've been grieving her now. She might have left Ryan alone in that house to sift through her belongings and decide if her mark was worth saving.

The silence curled around her throat with a cold, skeletal hand. 'Let's be done for today,' she said.

'Let me try again.'

'It's OK, Ingram. We can just—'

'*Rory*,' he said again. Her name was a low, cautious utterance from his mouth, as if he thought forwardness would cause her to shatter like glass. 'Come here.'

He gripped her shoulders and eased her forward to his chest. Aurelia went rigid at first but sunk easily into his body. She circled her arms around his waist, her face pressed into the collar of his coat. She felt his jaw against her temple as he crooked his head to the side and made a space for her to rest beside his high collar. Her breath hitched. That familiar scent of his cologne teased her senses.

As if it hadn't been confusing enough, she began to cry. There was a threat against her life – *their* lives – that was closer and more fearsome than she'd ever dreamed imaginable; and it had finally taken colour. She had started to lose herself in the idyllic little town and the cottage at the top of the hill that she'd nearly forgotten why she was there. With him. They'd ended up in Townsend together, and that *arrogant prick* was holding her as if he was a shield – a reaper incapable of summoning a book without injury. And she wasn't just allowing it. She craved it. Not like a leap toward danger but a slow, tantalizing seduction toward some other monster she wasn't ready to face.

Aurelia merely whispered against the collar of his coat, 'I'm sorry.'

'Why are you sorry?' he asked.

'I don't know what to do. I feel like a blubbering idiot right now, and you're stuck with me.'

He tightened his arms around her shoulders, fitting together in perfect harmony. 'Or maybe you're stuck with *me*,' he said with a strain. 'What's worse?'

She laughed, tears welling in her eyes. 'You're right. I've got it worse.'

'That's the spirit. Remember how driven you were over spite for me, like, eighteen hours ago?'

Aurelia wiped her eyes, pulling her face from his body. 'I'm not mad at you, though. We're in this predicament together.'

He breathed deeply under the soft pressure of her hands. She couldn't remember slipping them beneath the opening of his coat; but if it was alarming to him, it didn't show.

'You and me?' he asked. 'Bloody mess.'

Her cheeks flushed bright at the mercy of his amusement. 'Yeah,' she replied. 'You and me. It's honestly a miracle I've lasted this long without tearing you to pieces in a fit of anger.'

He chuckled, detaching himself from her completely. 'God knows you're quick to it.'

'You make it easy,' she retorted, wiping her face with the heel of her hand. 'Especially when—'

He was looking at her again, not with passing curiosity but total rapture. She was more accustomed to the nuances of his expressions. His lips parted ever so slightly, and the gaze of his green eyes was absorbed by her. She fought the urge to smooth over the crease between his brows with her fingertips, let them drag down the bridge of his sharp nose, and rest them on his lips. He lifted his hand to her face, ghosting over her cheek with his palm while he slid his thumb over the last traitorous drop.

'When what?' he prodded. 'Don't you want to tell me how I get under your skin?'

'Why would you want me to do that?'

'Because I like it when you're mean. I think that's when I like you best.' Ingram smiled, halfway between diffident and bold. It surprised her how familiar he was in her arms. She half expected him to lose his shape, to undergo some bone-deep metamorphosis to become someone worth leaning on. The fact that she could still see the boy she'd fought with on the steps of King's College and avoided for years previously like a bear trap gave her the courage to step away, though she didn't want to. When they parted, she could feel something dislodging from her, letting in a draft of cold wind and loneliness.

'*Tomorrow*,' she said, finally. 'We try this again. With something less fragile.'

CHAPTER THIRTEEN

It began the same way – with darkness, incoherent muttering and then, at last, the sword. How was it that her fear was just as thick and palpable? At what point would she return to this moment with nothing more than acceptance of things yet to come?

Aurelia raced toward the end, but it was like wading through tar. She was bound to the timeline, forced to surrender to every beat of the all-too-familiar nightmare.

She should have awakened by now . . . Marga's death *always* marked the end of the nightmare, but the sword remained lodged in her chest, glimmering and new – untarnished even after centuries.

This was the point when she ought to find the solace of the moonlight waiting for her. But with the eyes of her dream-self still shut tight, Aurelia began to panic about what horrors lie on the other side of her lids.

She plummeted through a dark tunnel, lacking end or regard to gravity like Alice down the rabbit hole. She reached for the mud walls around her to dig her fingers into them, but they melted around her hands like nothing at all. With every second she endured the fall, the gaping divide in her ribs was sealing shut. She stared down in awe and watched the severed skin reconnect like a zipper beneath her fingertips.

Aurelia blinked the confusion from her face. Anything was possible here. This she knew – it was her *dream* . . . Only it had never gone this far, and the fear of what other brutality she might face hung like a grim mobile over her head while she slept.

She lurched toward the faint glow that materialized at the end of the darkness, making out the blurred, quivering edges of green and blue. Sunlight greeted her. Her skin grew warmer with every bit of distance she annihilated.

Within seconds, there were blades of grass between her fingers, snaking around her arms. Aurelia settled into them with ease. Here, her chest moved with breath and her heart beat more solidly.

Which made no sense, even in the realm of dreaming. In the throes of a dream, she never felt the real functions of her body. The way she moved when she slept and the way her subconscious puppeteered her were disjointed things.

Unless she'd dreamed this too, fabricating a sensation to supplement her curiosity. The buzz of the earth festered manically underneath her skin, stoking the concentration of magic in her palms.

She pushed herself upright, recognizing the hillside of Townsend's namesake peak, and the white flowers that ornamented the rustling green that marked the end of spring. The tall grass rose past her head as she scoured, and she found the cottage at the top of the hill blowing smoke out of its chimney.

When she turned, Ingram was there too, lying on his back beside her, his eyes shut peacefully, with a hand cradling the back of his head. She inched nearer to him. Was this a game? A test of some immeasurable criteria that would end with another witch living or dying?

Her fingers hovered, then fell.

'You're staring again,' he murmured lazily, opening one eye against the blinding white of the sun.

'I'm not,' Aurelia said. She smoothed a hand down her chest where the sword had once been sunk. 'Even if I was, what's stopping me? This is my dream, isn't it?'

He smiled. It was one of those rare, all-encompassing smiles that shifted the entire map of his face and made her own a mirror against her will.

Only because he wasn't there and couldn't hear, Aurelia told him, 'You're very pretty, you know that?'

'Hmm,' he said. 'Tell me again. While you still can.'

He propped himself onto his elbow. The feeling of his fingertips on her face was convincingly solid. So real that Aurelia shifted away and let her smile fade like an aroma on the wind. It was uncanny to watch him touch her, to play a part he didn't embody while she was awake, and look so frighteningly real. The olive tone of his eyes was too cool for the oncoming summer – he didn't belong here. Nor did he belong in her waking winter. He belonged in autumn, boots buried beneath shattered brown leaves and hair tousled by temperate winds.

He wore a heather-cream T-shirt that draped around his chest as he shifted toward her. She'd never seen him in anything other than black or grey, or the darkest navy blue that could be obtained before reaching either of those other colours; and somehow, despite knowing him strictly by the shades of a new bruise, he was so *real.*

But *real* was not Theodore Ingram inching closer, his fingers slipping past her jaw and around the back of her neck to leverage himself. She raised her hand to his chest, taken aback by the steady beating of his heart.

It couldn't have been her own. It was too quick for a resting heart rate, but she wanted to rationalize it somehow . . . She claimed a fistful of his shirt and tugged him closer, eager to discover how much of the sensation would translate.

Teddy's lips moved against hers, delicate and warm like the sun's own shimmer behind the thin layer of clouds above. She felt both things simultaneously, not having to think too hard about either.

All of it, she decided. Lips and teeth and the tickle of his narrow nose. He shifted onto his knees, urging her backward until she was lying flat in the curtain of grass, his hands on either side of her head to cage her in.

Real was not her compliance. It was pushing him away instead of studying the density of his tee. It was cursing him with a foul mouth and not parting her lips to let his tongue between them.

It shouldn't have felt so real . . . Especially when this was the furthest thing from reality she could have imagined.

She shouldn't have loved it so much when he bowed his head to kiss her neck with an open, hungry mouth. Yet she was arching her back, pressing upward into him, willing him for more.

His lips touched her collarbone above the hem of her loose, button-down blouse, and his words were a mere whisper against her skin.

'I still can't get over how it feels to kiss you, Schwartz.'

Aurelia's laugh was a little lighter. A small thing that the real Theodore Ingram hadn't yet heard.

'We've never done this before,' she told him.

'Haven't we?' he murmured. 'Maybe not in your dreams, but in mine.'

The friction of his hips between her legs translated even further. Through the barrier of this fantasy, she felt the familiar dull ache between her thighs.

Aurelia raked her fingers through his hair, acutely sensitive to the softness of it. 'I don't know what you dream of. You're not real, are you?'

He shook his head slowly, peering up at her through dark lashes. 'What do you want me to say? That I am a puppet of your own desire? Or that I am more liar than even you can comprehend?' He grinned, all teeth and mischief. 'Nothing will satisfy you.'

'I never asked you to say those things to me,' Aurelia whispered. The burn of her skin was vicious enough to break the boundary too.

'Tell me to stop, then.'

With nimble fingers, he slid the hem of her blouse up to reveal her stomach before kissing the newly exposed plane. Aurelia's breath hitched before she could say anything else . . .

The objection came to mind, but it was muffled by the breeze; she did not chase it.

He moved lower. She wanted him to disappear, to move faster, to be gone completely. She wanted him to carry on, to be rid of him, to be finished by him – all of it at once. Her intentions blurred together, aided by the grip of his hands on her stomach.

The taste of his lips lingered on her tongue, ruinous and divine like the forbidden fruit. Like everything else, it was a sensation so raw and tangible that she couldn't fathom it to be the mere conjuring of a dream, for even dreams had their limitations; and although this one had defied the laws of physicality, there would still be an end. There was *always* an end.

To everything. To dreams, to nightmares. She wasn't sure where this one fell. It was *good*, and that was *terrifying*. She heard him in her thoughts reciting poetry, drawing his words out the way he knew she couldn't resist.

Aurelia leaned back, impatient with longing as Ingram continued down the length of her body. She closed her eyes, moistening her lips, and ran her hand through his hair again, encouraging him further.

It was different with her eyes closed. She thought he might disappear if he wasn't in her sights, but the sensation narrowed further. Against her skin – a mouth that had never been good to her for anything but bitter words. Her hands knotted in his hair as if he had never been the cause of her grief. He tugged at the hem of her pants, and she threw her head back as his fingers teased the length of her folds.

Something was different about it. With *him*.

There was something stiff like branches between her fingers. When she opened her eyes, everything was dark again. Feathers fell in droves around her body.

'Teddy?' she whispered, jolting upward. A flutter of wings greeted her in response, but the boy had vanished.

Aurelia adjusted her clothing, bracing herself on a cold slab rather than soft grass. There was no late, glittering spring. No gold marking the lines in her hands. No twisted mouth drawing a pattern on her skin. There was only darkness. A dim orange light outlined a door in the blackness before her, taller and wider than herself. She was on the wrong side of it.

Something deep and monstrous answered from within the abyss, hoarse with age and deep with anger; but it had Ingram's accent and his lyrical tone of vindication.

'Heaven but the vision of fulfilled desire,' he sang, 'and hell the shadow from a soul on fire.'

'Not the right time,' she hissed, and darkness looked back.

The latch of the door unhooked from the outside. The hinges croaked, and a black, winged beast forced past her, shoving her to the ground again. Talons scraped her shoulder, leaving a gash. Rubbing her eyes with the back of her wrist, she searched for the beast and found only a bird.

Make sense, she pleaded. *Tell me what to do?*

From beneath the raven's wing, she formed an unfinished image of the person who granted her release. Black hair, greying skin. An emaciated woman with her ear to the surface of a door. Aurelia looked closer, weighing the odds of this woman's trustworthiness, but her features, which Aurelia tried to divine kinship from, shifted like sand in treacherous waters.

The woman tilted her head, moving with the deliberate slowness of submersion.

Aurelia kept her sleeve tight around the open wound on her shoulder and urged the grey, sullen woman forward. Sweet violets appeared at her back; and Aurelia felt a second of relief to see the planters in front of her house before she realized she was stuck inside the cupboard with her bins – and the bird that had died on her doorstep.

The grey woman reached for her with pale, slender fingers, pinching Aurelia's small form between two sharpened, black claws.

'Stop it,' Aurelia pleaded, bracing as the grey woman raised her to the light for inspection and squeezed her with the flat of her nails. Aurelia kicked against her hand. 'Don't touch me! Let me go!'

But the grey woman simply opened her mouth, placed the girl between her teeth, and devoured her whole.

Her eyes shot open to the blue shadow of Ingram's bedroom, her belly still housing that satiable ache. A medley of fear and arousal cycled endlessly through her as she came down from the vision, rubbing her eyes. She determined the actuality of her residence here.

Nothing. No one.

The ghost of Ingram's touch was just as present on her skin, steadfast with its grip as paranoia fell off her like loosened eyelashes. There was no sound of pacing in the room beneath her floorboards. No sign of life beyond her bed. Only the onslaught of frost at her window and the shiver it sent down her spine.

She glanced at the blinking zeroes on the nightstand, slipped her hand past the hem of her pyjama pants, and tried to forget that she was in his bed.

PART THREE

CHAPTER FOURTEEN

A wet ceramic dish slipped from Gemma's hands as she scrubbed it, fracturing around her feet.

Aurelia slid off her stool. 'I can get it.'

The woman waved her away, but Aurelia insisted. She swallowed down a thin slice of her apple and kneeled to collect the pieces of another bug-patterned bowl into a dustpan.

'Thank you, darling,' Gemma said.

'Any time.'

Ingram's voice spouted up the staircase, heralding his slow, red-eyed arrival. 'Putting her to work too? Christ, Gem, why do I trust you with my company?'

'She's insistent,' Gemma told him. Ingram seated himself on Aurelia's formerly occupied stool.

'I'm *nice,*' Aurelia said pointedly. 'I'm sorry I had to be the first person to demonstrate politeness for you.'

'Can you see all the way down from that high horse you're on, Schwartz?'

'Oh, stop it,' Gemma teased. 'Teddy, darling, you look tired.'

He nodded, shifting in his seat. 'I *am*. Hardly slept.'

'Too cold?'

Aurelia tilted the dustpan into the garbage bin. Ingram

frowned as the contents tumbled out and said, 'That's the best bowl she's painted so far. And no. Had an odd dream last night. Woke up once or twice. If it's twice, the second was hazy. I can't remember.'

Aurelia claimed the stool next to him, taking the bowl of sliced fruit she'd been picking from into her possession again.

Ingram cleared his throat and scraped his nails down his neck. 'Aren't you going to tell me about *your* dream?'

She prodded at a stiff piece of cantaloupe.

You're not real, are you?

'No,' she said plainly, though her heart skipped violently. 'Why do you ask?'

Ingram shrugged, resting his cheek in his hand. 'You seemed so eager to share those with me these past few days. Thought it might be a pattern.'

If he knew about her dream, he didn't care enough to test her, shirking off their conversation as he plucked a bitter strawberry from her bowl with his fingers. He thumbed the sheen of light pink juice from his lip.

'It wasn't very interesting,' Aurelia assured him.

'That's never stopped you before, has it? Nor have I.'

Regrettably, that was true.

Gemma's intervention kept Aurelia from fumbling over her words. 'Care to help me with breakfast?'

'Is this not breakfast?' Ingram asked.

'Course not,' said Gemma. 'This is hardly a meal for kings, and we dine like kings in this house. Teddy darling, cook a few eggs for me. I've not been keeping up with the hens.'

Gemma's hair wasn't fastened into her usual bun; the

brushed-out softness made her look younger, shielded the shadows from the creases in her face. Gemma Eakley couldn't have been much older than Aurelia when Kenny was born, she realized.

Ingram squeezed himself past them and into the kitchen.

'Are you going into town today?' Gemma asked. 'Al should be back.'

The two students exchanged a mutual look of exhaustion over the woman's head. Even his bedhead was perfectly tousled. The memory of it between Aurelia's fingers remained vivid into the morning. A discreet smile tugged lazily at the corners of his mouth. Which was *aggravating*.

'Why not?' said Ingram. 'Unless you'd rather do something else.'

Aurelia couldn't possibly suggest flipping through the pages of her grimoire with him today – her head was throbbing. After the teeth of the grey woman woke her, insomnia made her favour flipping through the separated signatures of her grimoire, stacking and restacking the pages in a way that she could sew them together again later.

She was also shamefully preoccupied with the way that Ingram's hands were moving as he situated his spices beside the pan and shuffled through the bowl of fresh brown eggs. Slender fingers hovered as he counted them out in his head.

The swift, effortless movement of breaking the shell, emptying its contents with one hand . . . She stared as he worked, committing the efficient delicateness to her memory. Those were practised motions. He moved like an artist.

Something was wrong with her.

She started calculating the last time she'd had sex. Surely, she could find an answer in that. If splitting shells over the frying pan caused her pulse to spike, seeing the flex of his fingers as he shoddily cast spells from her grimoire would decimate her already dwindling sense of dignity.

'You'd like Al,' Ingram said, pinching pepper over the pan. 'He's cool.'

That was as good as a knighthood to her – how many people did Theodore Ingram consider *cool*? Certainly not her, even if he did consider her to be *interesting company*.

'Everybody likes Al,' added Gemma wistfully.

'I wouldn't say *that*,' said Ingram.

'I would. Send him my love when you see him. He doesn't visit as much.'

'I imagine he's been busy again.' He slipped the spatula underneath the egg deftly, clinically. No yolks were ruptured. No edges spliced. Aurelia charted the map of veins on his hands, feeling like she'd lost her mind.

Gemma asked, 'Too busy for us, you think?'

Then, he looked right into Aurelia's eyes again as if to turn the question on her and smiled, catching that she was already looking at him. Looking at each other and seeing each other were two very different things. Be it her relief or her downfall, she and Ingram could do both.

She no longer knew which one this was.

Ingram crossed his arms over his chest, tilting himself against the door frame of the bathroom.

'I should have warned you – we don't do much for Christmas.'

Aurelia leaned over the sink to wipe the toothpaste from around her mouth before she turned to him and asked. 'Is that today?'

'No,' he said. 'But it's soon enough. I've got to pick up a gift for Gem while we're out.'

She passed a hand through her hair until it achieved the perfect balance of wildness and ease. A laundry day was long overdue, and she'd run out of her more practical garments the day before. Ingram took in the spirited ensemble with one fell swoop, etched with reluctant bemusement over the white, palm-sized stars scattered around her black leather miniskirt. She was wearing one of her nicer blouses on top, having exhausted her fill of jersey stretch long-sleeved tees for lounging around the basement or sifting through the dirt with Louisa.

Ingram seemed to forget the mirror in front of them, his gaze landing curiously on the top ridge of her spine where the buttons of the blouse's high neck remained unfastened.

With a hard blink, he added, 'I'm sorry if you expected something more.'

Holidays were trivial to her when they were preoccupied by the imminent threat of danger. Uncapping her lipstick, she told him, 'Trust me, I *didn't*. I don't do anything for Christmas.'

'Really?'

'Yep. Sometimes my dad and I get Chinese takeout from this place down in Portland. Same restaurant every year. It has this . . .' She trailed off, creating a wide gap with her hands in a demonstration. 'It has this person-sized painting of a chicken in the bathroom that used to scare me when I was younger.'

'That's sweet,' Ingram said.

Aurelia sighed, returning to the mirror to continue carving away at the uneven line of her lipstick with a blunt fingernail. Her reflection stared back, wide-eyed and void of warmth. She'd never thought of that ritual as *sweet* before, but in retrospect, it was priceless.

She would give anything to be there again.

'I should get them something,' she mused.

'You don't have to get them anything. I can cover—'

'Just because I'm not as *comfortable* as you are doesn't mean I can't afford something small.'

'That's not what I meant.'

Ingram's gaze dropped to his feet, wandering across the tiles as if he might find a proper response in the grout.

'Your friend that owns the bookshop . . . If he's there today, I'm sure I could find something. D'you think Louisa would like *The Little Prince*? I know it's a younger book, but . . .'

In the mirror's reflection, Ingram moved squarely behind her. She watched his hand brush against her shoulder and give it a squeeze; and following the uncanny images of him from the night before, that small, unassuming gesture happened in slow motion.

'That's *not* what I meant. I just . . .'

She turned halfway to face him, spiting the middleman of the mirror. His closeness alarmed her, and she caught the earthen scent of lemon and mint in his cologne with one small intake of breath. It reminded her of summers in Washington, of the sun-soaked vineyards she'd driven past with her father and sister.

'You know,' she started, 'I'm not offering because I feel *obligated*. I'm doing it because I *want* to. You're imagining that I feel some sort of pressure to buy them gifts for the holidays, but you have it all wrong. Besides, if I were back home, my father would have me celebrate Hanukkah with him.'

'I didn't realize—'

'You never asked.' Aurelia faced the mirror again. 'Will you fasten those?'

Hoisting up the ends of her short curls, she observed as his hands floated to the back of her neck where the three half-spherical buttons rested opposite their slightly-too-small loops.

She assured herself that, if he focused on those, he might stop tracing the curve of her lipstick, subsequently ignoring the blush that covered her face. Without the scrutiny of his gaze, she performed a study of her own.

Tell me again. While you still can.

'You *do* look pretty tired,' she told him instead.

He forced a smile, struggling to push the button through. 'You look the same as ever – which is to say just as tired. Maybe a bit jumpy too.'

'I'm not jumpy.'

He hummed to himself. She hypocritically followed the map of his lips as he coaxed the last button into place.

Peering through the street-facing window, the inside of the bookshop remained as dark as the first time they'd passed; but she must've missed something, because Ingram broke into a smile and muttered, '*Finally*.'

He twisted the knob of the unlocked door and ushered her inside. It was dark inside and noiseless. Dust lined the narrow rows of shelves. It smelled like every old bookshop Aurelia had ever been to – dry, musky, with a note of old vinegar and tea. It was a scent she'd wanted to bottle and carry in her toiletry bag ever since she could read. Leaning towers of books piled at the ends of every row, bowing slightly inward to greet whoever may pass through. Aurelia didn't want to file through them yet. The emptiness unnerved her, and something about being here without supervision reminded her of sifting through a person's private memories. The only source of light inside emanated through a basement doorway behind the wooden counter by the door, but even that light was unpromising.

'Al-*aaa*-ric,' Ingram sang, rapping his knuckles on the countertop.

'Are you sure he's—'

'I'm sure.'

A dog's collar jingled from the doorway of the lower level. The head of a thin, black hound appeared before making a hasty retreat to the place from which it had come.

The man Aurelia assumed was Alaric carved out a silhouette of his own in the soft light of the basement door. Black curls ornamented in silver poured onto his forehead, and his long face was held together by a proportionally long nose. Searching for the voice of his summoner, the eyes that met Aurelia's were the same shade of all-devouring brown as hers.

He smiled, baring his teeth. He looked similar in age to Gemma Eakley, but his soft voice lent him years he might not have had. 'You brought a friend,' he said, rounding the railing.

'Would have brought her sooner, but you weren't here,' Ingram said. 'What took you so long?'

'Her Majesty calls.' Alaric said it like a joke, but Aurelia suspected it wasn't.

'And your folks in Bath, I presume.' Ingram pulled the older man into an embrace. Alaric's calloused, scar-laden hand clapped down on the boy's back in a way that only men's hands did.

'I'm needed in many places,' Alaric whispered, though Aurelia heard it clearly. It had to be the town, she thought. It had its own gravity, pulling every whispered word and brush of hands straight to her, spilling their secrets to the wrong people. She couldn't even tell herself it was the result of cabin fever any more without thinking of Ingram's rebuttal.

You think that's what this is?

Every day, the puzzle beneath her shifted. She was stepping up a ladder only to slide back down the chute. Even the voice in her head recounting those words took on an unparalleled resemblance to the real thing; and more of Ingram was never a good thing to have.

'And *you*,' the pepper-haired man said. 'We haven't met before. You're a new face.'

It was a strange greeting, but it warranted a smile. If it was a new face, it ought to be her best one. She stretched out her hand and said, 'I'm Aurelia. *Schwartz*.'

Alaric held it with an unusually high grip. His fingers curled around her wrist, and he rotated it sharply, turning it upward. 'A simple verification,' he said, unfurling her palm.

'I – *what?*'

With the soft, inner flesh of her forearm in his grasp, she felt a jolt of energy shoot through it unprovoked.

'I'm vouching for her, Al. Take my word for it,' Ingram said. He disappeared down the nearest aisle, though, and his urgency left with him.

'Word for *what?*' she demanded.

'He's testing you for magic, Schwartz.'

She'd lived with hidden magic all her life, but these days, it seemed like everyone wanted to wake it up. Her fingers twitched on command – not *her* command, but Alaric's. A gold spark ignited around her fingers with a muted 'zap'. She jerked back, her politeness overridden by an undercurrent of fear.

The man nodded to himself, pushing up his square eyeglasses. 'Pardon my forwardness. It's a necessary precaution; this building has one face but many rooms.'

Without another word, the man lifted his hands like a conductor raising his orchestra, and the shop around her began to transform. The shelves expunged their covering of dust and the titles of every outward facing spine shimmered with an awakening. The ceiling rose, creating empty spaces on the walls for the gilded frames containing portraits of important-looking men and women that manifested themselves. A rickety wooden staircase began to form at the far end, slat by slat, with the rhythm of footsteps. Something new seemed to happen every time she blinked, so she stopped and stared, absorbing each metamorphosis as it happened. Gone was the claustrophobia – this room had become a cathedral.

Ingram reappeared from within the nearest aisle of bookcases, a book in his hand, unfazed. Then, a flash of recognition – this was all new for her. She was jealous again, that the incapable witch had *this* within his reach and still knew so little.

Alaric watched the transformation at her side patiently, until the awe subsided. Then, he pressed her with another statement. 'Your name – Aurelia. It comes from the Latin word for gold.'

Beaming, she replied, 'I know.'

He met her not with hospitality but a cold, interrogative stare. The smile fell slowly from her own face, settling back into an equally cold expression. She rubbed the wrist that Alaric had grabbed, smoothing over the memory of his touch and the electricity of his magic.

His steely consideration faltered, turning to a sheepish regret. 'It's good to meet you. I'm Alaric. *Friedman*.'

'And I'm looking for a Christmas gift for Gem,' Ingram said, turning over the book in his hand. 'Have anything in mind?'

'Did you forget again?' Alaric rounded the front counter, whose wood was now a deep cherry red in the warm light of new sconces.

'I never *forget*,' Ingram said. 'I've been busy.'

''S a bit late for remembrance, don't you think?'

Aurelia left the men in conversation, drawn through the elongated rows of shelves by her innate curiosity. Aurelia knew magical people, albeit few and far between, but she'd never known magical places like this. Was it a conscious decision that Gabrielle made not to teach her? She'd wanted to learn, and she only hoped it was by ignorance that the nature of it was omitted.

Behind her, Ingram and Alaric spoke in hushed tones.

'It's the V&A this time,' Alaric said.

'London again?'

Alaric gave no verbal response, but she imagined him nodding, black and silver curls grazing his forehead the way a rogue branch quivers in a breeze. Ingram sighed – she assumed it was him. For a student of early language and literature, his sighs said more than his words. She would pick them out during lectures over the scratch of pens and tapping of laptop keyboards, her lips twisting in disapproval while she busied her hands with her own form of notetaking.

'I called, you know,' Ingram said. 'Multiple times.'

'You're not the only witch who needs me right now, but you *are* the most demanding. I would have returned your call if I'd had something to report on—'

'So, you don't?'

Another silence. Too long. Aurelia slid a book from the shelf if only to make some noise.

'Nothing else,' Alaric said.

'Anything noteworthy about the V&A? What'd she take?'

'She?'

Aurelia's pulse hammered against her throat. She'd intended to ask, upon Alaric's return, what it meant to have this 'friend in high places'. The reasonable assumption was that the man always kept Ingram within arm's reach, and not the other way around; so, why should they know something he didn't? Alaric's stupefaction oozed from the lone word.

'Yes,' said Ingram. '*She*. Her name is Leona.'

'And she has a name . . . You discovered this *how*, exactly?'

Aurelia turned a page, reading none of it.

'She's after us, Al. She found us here. Martin intercepted

a letter she sent for us, but there was no address on it. Only her name signed at the bottom, which we saw after it was opened. I don't know how she found us. I don't know why she wants to.'

'And the name doesn't ring a bell to you?'

Ingram must have shaken his head.

'It might to me,' Alaric said. 'I'd like to take a look at that letter.'

'Later.'

Every bump on her skin rose. Slowly, she nestled the book into its former resting place, observing the gilded words on the narrow spine for the first time: *Profezie di Leonardo da Vinci.*

She took in the rest of the warm, yellow splendour, sensing that her time inside this strange edifice had come to its end. She touched the spine of bound prophecies, swearing to herself, 'I'll see *you* very soon.'

The promise hummed through the rows of towering wooden shelves as if it could feel her there, feel her wanting and curious. She turned to find Ingram silently rummaging through the shelf behind her.

'You need to wear a bell or something,' she said.

His features settled into a familiarly smug expression. 'Thought you knew I was there.'

She turned to pass him, but his arm barred her path as he pulled down another book from a shelf she couldn't reach. She braced herself against his chest. Like everything else in this room, he was warm, full of magic, a cage of hidden information. More than that – he was flesh and blood. And she was touching him again.

She'd done enough of that. Far more than what the situation warranted. She cleared her throat, averting her attention.

'I loved this one,' he said.

'Doesn't look like it belongs in this section.'

'Suppose you're right.' To Alaric, Ingram shouted, 'Will you see us out?'

Without another word, the warmth of the grand library began to dissipate. The shelves creaked as they shrunk, as the ceiling came down over their heads again. The grey and colourless interior of the shop reformed. When Aurelia first entered, it met her with a predictable charm, but it paled in the aftermath of the disappearance of Alaric's spellbound library, and the scent struck her as stale.

As the furnishings collapsed into place, Ingram pulled a smaller book from the shelf, wiping dust from its face. 'This one, I can take.'

It was shabbier, duller, brown in places it ought to be cream or beige. At some point, the title *Sir Gawain and the Green Knight* had been embossed in gold, but some of it had long since been scraped off.

He paid for it at the counter, and Aurelia found an illustrated copy of *The Little Prince* for Louisa. Alaric was quicker to offer a solution for Gemma's gift. Ingram took a round wooden box from Alaric's hands, tucking it easily into his coat pocket.

'Tea from a coven in Morocco,' the man explained. 'Have it together. Sign it from both of you.'

'She'll love this, Al.'

'Regrettably, I know she will. But I'll set aside my pride this time and let you have the honour.'

'I owe you one,' Ingram said. Alaric's eyes shut tightly behind his magnifying prescription.

'You owe me many,' the bookseller said. 'Take care of yourself. And you, too.'

He grinned warmly at Aurelia Schwartz, but she'd been listening to them speak behind the cover of dark wood and floating dust, and their conversation warranted no smile. The two men made an unusual pair. She was closer to cracking Theodore Ingram, but Alaric Friedman was a brand-new puzzle; and together they communicated using a language neither Aurelia nor the institution of academia could explain. Identical postures and unusual emphasis on their words . . . It was a language of subtlety – the kind that took a lifetime to master. And even then, it was limitless.

'I'll be back tonight, ' Ingram said.

'You know where I'll be.'

She stirred as both their gazes fell to her. One held a plea. A hopeful request. The other – a warning as sharp and precise as a needle.

CHAPTER FIFTEEN

'You didn't tell him about the artefacts.' His conversation with Alaric was replaying in her head without cease. 'Why not?'

He glanced around the vacant town. His wariness was different from when they were on the train and the mere utterance of *magic* was made. Was he more comfortable being a criminal than a witch?

'Didn't get around to it, I suppose,' he said.

'Haven't decided if you want to return them, you mean?' Ingram smiled and walked onward, without denying it.

She stuck close to his heels and asked, 'So, what are you thinking?'

'Regarding?' Ingram paused again at the closed door of the cafe.

Every day was a little colder than the last, but she didn't have to feel it until he left.

'We came for the internet, didn't we? There must be a reason.'

He lowered his voice to a tantalizing whisper. 'Is wanting to share bad coffee with you not a good enough reason?'

No. It wasn't. A traitorous smile was already tugging at the corners of her lips before the image of bright steel and the mouth of the grey woman returned to mind. She swallowed her ease, running her rough nails down her neck, recalling how long it had taken before the vision cut short.

The walls of the grey woman's throat pressing her from all sides. Poetry shouted back from within the abyss.

Aurelia's phone buzzed in her pocket. She tore it out, flashing Ingram an apologetic smile as her housemate's name flashed across her screen. He sighed in resignation, passing through the front door of Petro's while she accepted the call.

'Perfect timing,' she said into the phone. 'I've been meaning to—'

'*Fuck you* with your "perfect timing" nonsense. I've been trying to call you for days. Where the hell have you been? Why haven't you answered my texts?' It rushed out in a singular, shaky breath.

Removing the phone from her ear, Aurelia clicked through her messages, but nothing had come through.

'I'm sorry, Ry. I haven't had any service where I am, it's not—'

'And *where* is that? You couldn't have let me know? I came home to find all your shit gone from the bathroom and your room in a bigger mess than usual. When you didn't answer, I called Chloe, but she said she hadn't talked to you since the start of holiday. But she told me it was Marga – the girl who got the colleges shut down. She was in your programme, wasn't she? Were you close?'

'We probably weren't as close as I thought,' Aurelia admitted. 'Everything seems different in hindsight.'

'I'm sorry . . . I didn't know. I just assumed – Hey, where are you right now? I'm not going to forget that I asked.'

'I'm somewhere called Townsend. I didn't think you'd be back to Cam so soon, and—'

'That's not the point. I *worried* about you, Rory. I'm not totally convinced I shouldn't *still* be worried. What are you doing out there? Are you safe? Are you sick?'

There was no simple answer to that. 'I've been with Ingram.'

'Ingram . . .' Ryan repeated the name as if saying it aloud would jog some buried memory.

The person I told you I can't stand. The person whose presence I couldn't justify trying to enjoy. We're witches – not the kind you're thinking of – and there are others too.

All those things sounded more like lies than the half-truth she gave Ryan now. 'A friend. We're working on something.'

Ryan Jena went quiet. Aurelia waited, the line full of pops and creaks from the phone shifting in her housemate's hand, and she imagined the pieces sliding into place. The endless complaints. The feverish laughter of late-night gossip.

She watched Ingram move to a table on the other side of the glass, eyes darting along the walls of the cafe. It was starting to sprinkle outside. Aurelia huddled beneath the short canopy in anticipation of the downpour.

'You could have told me there was something going on with him, you know,' Ryan said.

'*God*, no. It's not like that. We're not—'

'So, you're just honeymooning with this guy you *totally* don't like and have *nothing* going on with? Have you been abducted? Have you gone mad?'

'It's complicated,' Aurelia said.

'Hmph.'

'Look, I'm sorry I didn't tell you. It was a last-minute situation, and I don't have any phone service at his place. I just . . . lost track of time.'

Ryan scoffed. 'So, you're staying at his place too. I find it hard to believe you're not keeping secrets from me.'

'I am not!' Aurelia insisted.

'Then you're there to break the poor boy's heart? You're strange. What a strange motive you have.'

She dragged her hand down her face and stifled a groan. 'Did you need something, Ry?'

'Oh yeah. I was half-tempted to file a missing person's report on you. Now, I think I'd rather let you go missing.'

'I love you too. I'll be back soon.'

'Whatever.'

Aurelia moved aside to open the door for a man lugging a cardboard box in his arms.

'How's the house?' she asked Ryan.

'Exactly where you left it. Smells a bit like something's died somewhere, but I haven't found anything yet.' Ryan's voice was small behind the noise of shuffling, words leaking with irritation. 'You're OK, aren't you? Your friend . . .'

Aurelia tripped on a response. 'Uh. Um, yeah. What was the—'

'Are you OK?'

The box slipped, the door closing back on the bell above it. The commotion called Ingram's eyes to the door, and with that look came a remembrance of everything that laid ahead of them. The phantom scar over her chest that held the sword between her ribs. There was too much uncertainty in her future to give her housemate any sound reassurance.

So, she gave another lie and twisted that blade in her chest. 'I'm all right. I promise. I haven't been axe-murdered or abducted.'

'And there's no gun to your head right now?'

She laughed, unnerved by how much she suddenly wanted to cry. 'No. I'm OK. But I have to go now. I'll call you soon.'

A strange, foreign sense of loss settled in her chest once Ryan Jena disconnected. Her housemate was safe in Cambridge, only a few hours away by train, but further away than ever. Dishonesty was a great divide that she couldn't always bridge. With every wondrous awakening and every new-found possibility of magic, the chasm expanded. Omission was always meant to protect her, but that didn't mean it didn't make a difference to Ryan Jena, did it?

As she took her seat, Ingram slid her a cup and saucer and asked, 'Your dad?'

'My housemate.'

'It's Ryan, right?'

She nodded, pleased that he would remember a detail like that. She brought the cup to her lips, blowing first, tasting blackcurrant after the heat had subsided. She nodded in approval.

'You can imagine how confused they were when I said I was with *you*,' she added, observing the discomforted shift in his posture. Sometimes, she thought he was past being wounded by her, but during instances like these, she wasn't so sure.

'Imagine that,' he murmured, gazing past her.

Behind them, the older male barista had begun rummaging through his delivery, arranging banded stacks of flyers and event promotion on the counter for closer inspection. He grumbled to himself at the soiled nature of the cardboard box, its printed contents blurring at the edges.

Ingram's chair scraped the wood as he rose abruptly. 'Anything from Cambridge?'

The man shook his head, his mouth twisting beneath his thick moustache.

'How about London?'

'I always ask for *something* from London,' said the barista, gesturing to a stack of promotional cards held together with loose rubber bands. 'It's a gamble whether they send anything. The larger proprietors rarely see the point in sending things our way. Are you waiting for anything specific?'

'This,' said Ingram, holding up an event catalogue. 'Thanks.'

Returning to the table, he dropped it in front of Aurelia, jabbing his finger into an open page.

Her face tightened in confusion. 'It's an art exhibit?'

'It's a gala, hosted by the Tate Modern at the end of every year. I'm surprised they haven't cancelled it in the light of the attacks.'

She frowned. He took note of the scepticism in her slow nod and told her, 'Spit it out, Schwartz.'

'I don't really see why Leona would be interested in the Tate. If our only factor is that these are all museums in the UK, then I see your concern, but she's only hit history museums – only taken artefacts from the Middle Ages or earlier. In that case, the Tate would have no reason to cancel anything.'

'As a precaution,' he offered; and she pinned him with an accusation, thinking of Gemma and the hairpin fastened above her daughter's ear.

'They're still bastardized, capitalist institutions. Cancelling something like a gala would require them to look past their opportunism. If they know they can rake in money from an event like this, why wouldn't they try? Besides, what use would Leona have for modern art?'

He exhaled, sinking in his seat with a defeat she hadn't anticipated.

'I don't mean to be cynical,' she started.

'I get it,' he said. 'I just hoped . . .'

Ingram trailed off into that uncomfortable, anticipatory silence again – the kind that swallowed and consumed what would have been their next words.

'My parents attend every year,' he said. 'Not that she would want them. They're . . . ordinary.'

'That's not possible,' Aurelia said. 'Magical children need at least one magical parent—'

'Well, mine didn't want me,' Ingram said, to which Aurelia paled. The oversight was careless, as if what he'd shared with her about his parents could be so easily forgotten.

'It's fine, Schwartz. We may not get along, but it doesn't mean I'm not afraid for them. As much as it pains me to admit it, I have a debt to them that I'll never outlive.' His eyes met hers across the table while his fingers danced along the edge of his cup. His parentage didn't look like a fresh wound, but there was no point in opening it up again. *Debt,* she reasoned, was a strange way to measure something that should have been love.

'And you want to go?' As unlikely as the idea of running into the shapeshifting witch sounded, Aurelia couldn't mask the unevenness in her voice.

With another deep breath, he answered, 'I do.'

'That's where you wanted to try a locator spell, isn't it?'

A nod.

'Can I think about it?'

He nodded again, finishing the last of whatever was in his cup. He'd ordered her a tea; bitter coffee be damned. She was thoroughly enjoying it, whatever it was. Something black, with an ample amount of milk and sugar.

'Too sweet?' he asked.

'It's perfect,' she said.

Ingram smiled, raising his eyebrows in question as he slid his fingers through the loop of her cup and tasted it, and given that she'd mostly drunk it all already, she told him to take the rest.

He swirled the last elusive drop gently, subduing another grin, and held the cup out for her to examine. 'Doesn't that look awfully phallic to you?'

The runoff of the tea bag that was plastered to the bottom did, in fact, look *awfully phallic.* She laughed, and it was a moment of carelessness in their too-careful and too-grave conversation. She laughed, and so did he, although he tried so hard to fight it. She laughed, and it hurt, because she couldn't remember a time she'd ever laughed so freely with him before.

He leaned back in his chair, as if it was a burdensome thing to be joyful.

And maybe it was. With every new day – every stolen grin – it made less sense to acknowledge the danger that followed at their heels.

At the start of the hill, Louisa waved a paper-wrapped baguette in her hand and raced to them from Martin's open door. The easy smile on Ingram's face wasn't as temporary as the other one he wore, nor as small. There were a hundred things on Aurelia's mind, but a large number of them were preoccupied with his strange contentment.

It was becoming familiar for her to climb up this hill, to step on the same cobblestones, to find a rhythm as her boots sunk into the dirt. There had already been a trodden path snaking through the grass, but it was starting to take the shape of her footprints too.

And *this*. Ingram smiling, his shoulder brushing against her puffer coat, her nickname in his mouth like the last bite of a thousand-dollar meal. She was getting used to it. It wasn't so foreign. She didn't know when it had changed, but she laughed when he hoisted Louisa onto his back, grateful that it had.

Sharp wind forced the rusty brown hair up from his forehead. He shook his head and tried to will it back into position without unhooking his arms from Louisa's knees. Stopping for Aurelia, he didn't have to ask her to push it back for him. He didn't hold his breath as she touched his face and tidied his hair – only after making it worse.

Louisa marked the way with her incessant giggling like a trail of breadcrumbs. Sighting a rustle in the undergrowth, the girl peeled an arm from his shoulders and pointed, 'Teddy, look! There's a goose!'

'Sure is.'

Then, Louisa asked, 'Am I heavy?'

'Lightest thing in the world.'

'Lighter than a feather?'

'Almost like nothing at all.'

The house materialized in the distance. It was warmer, stockpiled with crocheted blankets and a hundred multi-coloured candles, but looking at it now, Aurelia saw an end. A pattern that would always prevail. This moment of ease was a snagged thread from an otherwise even stitch.

But it didn't feel like she was back at the beginning. It was two steps forward, one step back – and not the other way around.

Louisa patted her companion's shoulders to be released and bounded through the grass ahead of them, sounding a piggish squeal. As he threw his broad shoulders back to stretch, Aurelia found herself watching with too much zeal. Observing him like he was art – a marble statue, draped in black and grey.

'Do you have something to say?' He hadn't looked at her, but had caught her staring nonetheless.

She shook her head, knowing that he would probably let her pull back those drapes and uncover him. Aurelia tightened her arms around her midsection and sealed the gaps of her jacket. 'Thinking about Louisa. About youth.'

'And what conclusion have you come to?'

'Sometimes I think I'll never be as happy as I was when I was Lou's age. I don't know what changed to make me so miserable, but I hope it never changes for her.'

'Are you not happy?' Ingram slowed to a standstill beside her, leaning into the breeze.

'Generally speaking?'

'Honestly speaking.'

She shivered as the cold crept underneath the high, puffy neck of the garment. Ryan once said that her bright orange coat could stop traffic, but Aurelia was discovering it did a terrible job at stopping a chill.

'I *am* happy,' she explained, uncertain. 'But sometimes, when I look at the numbers that Carney writes on my papers and everything that I've made for myself, I feel like I'm not allowed to be *un*happy.'

'That's—'

'Backwards, I know. *I know.* You don't have to remind me.'

'That wasn't my point,' he said. 'My point is that you're allowed to feel it all at once. To be dissatisfied and to want more, knowing you're in a good place already. There's how things *are,* how they should be, and what you want them to be. But those three factors are rarely all in alignment. If you waited until your emotions were pure to consider them with their due weight, you'd be waiting all your life. Your feelings will never be pure. They have never *been* pure. The only difference between us and *her?* It's . . . It's like holy water.'

'*Holy water?*' she asked incredulously.

'Surely, the best student theologian at Pembroke has heard of holy water. It can't be diluted. You can bless a drop or the whole basin, but you're always going to come out baptized. And you can feel the bitterness of being stuck in the same wheel, but it's still turning, you know? It's about asking yourself if you can pull happiness out of a fragment so small.'

He raised his head and gazed over the town beneath them. It could have ended there.

'You know, you always assumed I was out to *get you*, Schwartz. Like I could never be kind to you without an ulterior motive. That night I came to your flat, I know you didn't want to believe anything I had to say—'

'For more reasons than *that*,' she explained.

'I know. It's not like I wanted to believe the severity of it either. Still, I know how much you didn't want me to be right. You never do. You always wished I was worse than I am.'

Maybe you already think I'm a bad person, but I promise you I can be so much worse.

She hadn't believed him when he'd said it, but the actuality of it was a harsh buzz in her ear.

He *could* be worse. He didn't want to be.

'You don't have to deny it, Schwartz. You give away a lot more than you realize. It's not like I could remain oblivious to your distaste for me when you always looked at me like I was the bane of your existence. Maybe you've come to realize how little I enjoy reliving the past, but if it needs to be said: I don't. Gem thinks I run from it. I have no interest in knowing what *you* think of me, but I'll admit, it certainly doesn't feel like running. I'm getting ahead of myself, aren't I? What I . . . What I mean to say is that you . . .'

She didn't know which version of him she enjoyed more:

the frustratingly composed smart-ass or the windswept one turned pink by his own uncertainty. When had she decided to weigh them by *enjoyment* rather than *grievance?*

He cleared his throat and continued. 'I don't think I've ever seen you smile before. Not to me. Not genuinely. Sometimes, I'd see you smile at someone else in passing; but knowing I was there, it would vanish. Even now, it's rare, but I know that's *my* fault. If there's anything I can do to make it easier for you . . . I wouldn't know. I suppose I'm curious to know. Is it still me?'

'It's not,' she assured him, shaking her head. 'I let a petty grudge get too big, and it blinded me.'

'My question stands. If *I'm* not the pestilence in your mind, what is? Can't you tell me?'

She continued her path up the hill. 'Since when have you been so invested in my happiness?'

'Unfortunately, I'm beholden to your happiness.' He followed, waving his hand carelessly above his head. 'To all of it. Principally, your misery. I used to think it hovered like a dark cloud before I met you, but you hold it like an umbrella.'

'The hell is that supposed to mean?'

'Nothing.'

He backtracked, she realized. Which meant it was a mistake.

Her mouth curved devilishly. 'Are you trying to psychoanalyze me, Ingram?'

'I shouldn't have said anything,' he said.

That was the problem – not that he said it, but that he was no longer indifferent enough to her to tell her the truth. His honesty could only be delivered cruelly, sharp like a blade, hard and unforgiving as steel. When it counted, Ingram had softened to her, had come apart and lost his rigid structure, and she didn't know how to speak to him any more. Had she ever truly known how to speak to him? She had fallen into the rhythm of her vexation before they could ever establish something that rivalled friendship. To have it now—

Was that what he wanted? Friendship?

That word didn't quite fit. But the framework of friendship was all she had for reference. Friends said words like please, thank you, you're welcome, any time. Phrases she could weave into conversations with Ryan Jena with ease were self-inflicted marks of weakness when applied to Ingram.

They operated within a different set of boundaries. Ones where they rarely *asked* as much as they *told* – where she could fix the untidiness of his hair, and he would monologue about her smile, but he wouldn't be wholly truthful with her when she wanted him to be.

'Tell me what you were going to say.' She stepped in front of him and barred his way to the front door before he could enter. 'Before I rescind my words from the other day and push you down this hill.'

This must lie somewhere within those boundaries. Enough of the version of herself she knew would reach him, the demanding, overzealous girl he could spar with. The one she always wanted him to hate but wound up making him admire.

He advanced. She held steadfast until he was close enough that she could no longer be eye to eye with him without tilting her head. Testing her, he said, 'I know you *would*, but I suspect if you tried—'

'You think I wouldn't? Was it really so bad of a thought you'd risk a few foul bruises to keep it from me?'

'What are a *few foul bruises* if I can keep playing this silly little game with you?' He couldn't come closer without forcing her hand to his stomach to still him – forcing her to touch him again.

'I'm curious to know what kind of game you think this is, because I've never played it,' she said.

'Not this one?'

Breath caught in her throat as his fingers circled around her wrist, moving her hand upward, over the expanse of chest. It had become a game piece, she knew. Only she couldn't tell which of them it belonged to.

'This one, where you act like you still hate me, and I pretend I am not clutching at your mercies like I'm starved?'

Then, there was his heartbeat, fast but steady, underneath her hand. Her mouth was parched, words catching on the trip-wire of her teeth. 'That was never my—'

Behind her, Louisa wailed. Aurelia peeled herself away, shoved the door, and undid whatever moment she'd cultivated on the hillside.

She stepped aside to let Ingram pass and made herself alert to the source of the young girl's wail.

'Lou?' he called, bounding down the steps. 'Lou, what's happened?'

The girl's solitary voice wavered beneath the floorboard. Aurelia hastened down the hall, checking each room for a sign of Gemma's whereabouts, but the augur had left without trace. Aurelia joined Ingram and the crying girl moments later without Gemma in tow. In the centre of the basement, Louisa stood with her small fists clenched at her sides, quivering uneasily. Ingram fell to his knees in front of her and took her delicate, flushed face in his hands while she sobbed.

'Please, Lou, talk to me. Why are you crying?'

The girl choked on tears and mucous, hiccupping with every forced and incoherent response. She raised a shaky hand and gestured to the table behind her, where on it laid a sheet of paper.

Aurelia's skin went cold as she lifted it, before she could even read it, seeing the name signed at the bottom before the rest of its contents. 'Take it,' Aurelia said, pushing it into his hands as he rose. The sight of it was enough confirmation for him that Leona had been here.

Perhaps she'd overlooked the detail in which he could tell Gemma was gone from the house with only minutes of lingering silence.

In your absence, the diviner will do. But yours is the magic I covet. Please don't make me ask again.

Leona

Hoarsely, he said, 'I'm going back out. How long were we gone?'

'Wait—'

'They could still be here. She's a shapeshifter, not a bloody traveller. What if I can find her? I could find Gem. I could stop them.'

The girl sobbed, and Aurelia clutched Ingram's wrist before

he could be carried away by his manic determination – his ruthlessness. Before he could place himself in a situation that he would be too incapable of surviving and leave the last member of the Eakley family alone – *completely alone.*

The teeth of frenzy had already clamped around him. His pulse beneath the cuff of her hand beat fast and angry.

'Rory, let me go.'

'What if she isn't—'

'She has to be!'

Louisa sputtered what Aurelia could only assume was a nickname of Ingram's; her babbling had lost all coherence. Aurelia offered her hand, but the urgency only repelled the anxious girl.

'I *have* to find her,' Ingram declared, tearing his gaze away from Louisa. Had he waited with her any longer, his compulsion would wear to pity. He would have been the better comfort if he didn't think he had to be Gemma's saviour.

'Then I'll go with you.'

'Stay here.'

'*What?*' Her grip tightened around his wrist, making herself an anchor, a cage – an unyielding thing from which he could never detach. 'You can't leave me here, Ingram – you'll be compromised on your own.'

'Someone has to look after Lou,' he explained. 'I'll be damned if something happens to her too.'

'Then why can't that person be you? Think for a second. Neither of us knows what kind of monster we're dealing with here. We don't know what Leona is capable of, except that she's been completely untraceable so far. Do you really think you'd know what to do if you found her? Do you trust yourself enough to do the right thing if you found them *both?*'

Of all the low blows she had dealt him, this seemed the worst, invoking the crystallized memory of his best friend's untimely death. He paled and gritted his teeth as he tugged himself from her grasp. His true feelings had never been so plainly written on his face – he was *scared.* For Gemma and Louisa, but mostly for himself.

'*Think,*' Aurelia pleaded. 'You could hurt her too.'

She didn't truly know the extent of his magic, but she hoped that, coupled with his rage, the possibility of it going awry was enough to scare him. If cruelty was what it took to keep him here, she would deal as many harsh words as she needed – and without hesitation.

His eyes found Louisa, who was huddled behind Aurelia for safekeeping, and something in his mind fell into place.

'If not me, then who?' he asked. 'Because I would stop at nothing to find her. Nothing, including you. I can't let you stand between me and the people I love. I'm sorry.'

She braced for the emptiness that would come as he left, but there remained a heaviness in her heart. Louisa reached for him, and Aurelia thought if nothing else could convince him, the girl's slobbery, loud crying might.

He kissed her red face, turned it upward and said, 'I'll be back, Lou. I promise I'll be back.'

Guilt enveloped her. Aurelia followed him up the steps, leaving Louisa by herself in the basement. Ingram averted his gaze as he rummaged through his bag, so Aurelia waited until he had nothing else to look at but her.

'*Don't,*' he said softly.

And she didn't. She merely placed her hand on his shoulder to steady him, and it moved with his breath, forcing him to examine his eagerness and quell it.

He begged, even softer. '*Please. Don't.*'

She didn't understand why Ingram felt like he had to beg unless he thought she could *truly* keep him from chasing after Gemma. Maybe she could have. Aurelia ought to have set aside her pride and begged him not to be so careless, but in her heart, she knew there was no use begging. Someone would have to try.

She slid her hand to the side of his face, ran her thumb across his cheekbone, and whispered out of earshot from Louisa, 'Don't do anything stupid.'

He nodded and covered her hand with his but left it there on his cheek a moment longer. 'Be safe.'

CHAPTER SIXTEEN

Being above Townsend was starkly different from any other place he'd been – dim and vacant. Even Cambridge, which was analogue compared to London's vibrant, electric nightlife, seemed clear in the dark.

That was why they all hid here. They could easily disappear, be forgotten. The threat of the malicious and unjust humankind that Gemma so often spoke of would never find her.

To their downfall, Leona could disappear just as easily, if not better. Up here, the rain fell hard on him. Wind ripped through his black feathers and seared his skin. He remained alert to the mark of magic that he hoped would circle them.

They would be together when he found them. They *had* to be – he'd told Aurelia Schwartz the same thing, hoping it was the truth. If it turned out otherwise, it would be the end of many things. The infiniteness of his future, a family to lean on, a place to escape. And for Lou—

He didn't want to think about it. He narrowed in on the pain of his feathered body, the assault of the air through newly metamorphosized skin, and then – when he felt himself slipping on the wind – his breaths, counting them out while he scavenged for remnants of magic in the dark.

Soon enough, he spotted a gold glimmer of hope in the descending blue. Not Gemma, but Alaric Friedman and his frail, wiry hound. He dived for the ground, tucking his wings into his body, and came apart again beneath the tall grass.

The hound, Neil, sensed him first, bounding for Teddy's movement in the grass, but by now, the winged reaper had learned to revert to his human shape quicker than he could be caught. Once, in the beginning, he hadn't been quick enough. His shoulder was still marked by the wound of Neil's teeth. His wing faltered sometimes under the memory of jaws.

It was rare that he became the bird – this *thing* – because it hurt a little more every time. He'd never told Alaric before about how he feared the transformation would soon fail him, but the concern on the man's face as he drew back his dog was evidence enough that he knew something to be amiss.

For a moment, Alaric simply stared dumbstruck at the unnatural writhing of bones beneath skin, once displaced and now returning to their proper spaces. He knelt cautiously, extending his thin fingers toward the fabric stitching back together around Teddy Ingram's body, when the boy suddenly gasped to life again.

'It's Gemma,' rushed Teddy. 'She's missing. The shape-shifter was here.'

Alaric's mouth fell open, and he froze, curling his fingers around Neil's collar – not so much keeping the dog at bay but steadying himself on his haunches. Teddy hadn't yet risen from his crouch – the slits from which those feathered wings erupted weren't fully sealed. He gritted his teeth, coaching his breaths. The skin was still raw beneath his clothing. The garments could dissolve into his skin when he took this form, and it was hard to pull them from his body and make them separate again. Things stuck often and proved nightmarish to extract.

Alaric released Neil's collar, doling out a command for the dog in a language Teddy couldn't quite place, and it fled toward the shop. Pulling Teddy up by his elbows, he murmured, 'What the hell have you got yourself into?'

'I didn't mean to,' he said. 'But Gemma – she was here when we left to see you and gone when we came back.'

'When?'

'I don't know.'

'How do you know the other witch was here?'

A cough sputtered from Teddy's throat as he recounted the contents of Leona's letter. He was hardly a person when in the aftermath of a transformation, which never failed to remind him of how inhuman he was. His body ached. His bones clicked into place. There had always been room for error, especially under the command of an incapable witch like himself, but he pressed forwards, nonetheless.

For Gemma – who had always been more of a mother to him than his own blood.

For Lou – who had already been deprived of a brother as the result of Teddy's own naivete.

'God. What's happening to you?' Alaric said.

'*Forget about me*, Al. I have to find her. She's in danger.'

'The others . . . Lou and your—'

'Fine. Please, let's go.'

The disappointment on Aurelia's face had shaken him, but Teddy thought of her too. Pitifully, he thought, if she'd been there with him, Leona wouldn't have made it past the bottom of the hill.

She always knew what to do – had always been better than him in that sense. And she'd looked at him with such despondency that he vowed to prove her wrong.

He would find Gemma. If not now, *soon*.

He found his footing with Alaric's arm around his back, and they started across town together, hell-bent and ravenous. Quietly they moved, through the narrow roads of Townsend and then into the vastness of the city.

Nothing. And no one.

By the time they were desperate enough to believe that Gemma might have disappeared by train, it was already too late. The last train departed the station. Teddy could feel his eyelids slipping, his pulse thundering in his ears, over Alaric's begrudging suggestions for the boy to relent.

If it had been Teddy alone, he would have followed the promise of gold dust to the ends of the earth – past the human realm.

But night soon blanketed the town in shadow. The black sky wept and soaked through their clothing within minutes. Teddy drove on with Alaric at his side, pillaging through silence, propelled by a small, dwindling hope that there would shine a familiar light ahead. That they would see Gemma, idling in the street, still shivering in her warmest coat.

Instead, Teddy returned to the house defeated, with Alaric at his side, missing pieces of himself that resembled the shape of his youth.

CHAPTER SEVENTEEN

It had taken hours for Aurelia to assuage the girl's weeping. Hours of *almost* falling asleep, then being thrust back into the throes of her terror. Louisa's breathing had finally steadied. Her hair insisted on pasting itself to her face, and Aurelia busied herself with peeling it away while the girl slept.

She wanted to rest. She always wanted to rest, but never could. Already, she wondered if the nightmares would be different. Would they take the shape of Leona's letters? Would they fill in the blanks of whatever seemingly unimaginable torture might be happening to Gemma while she waited standing impatiently still?

She'd never felt so useless. Her anger grew with every passing hour wherein he didn't return, and she held fast to his promise even if doubt coloured her mind.

I'll be back. I promise I'll be back.

She never thought she'd be relieved to hear the sound of his voice, joined by another she quickly recognized as Alaric.

After the initial relief came the remorse. Only two men walking alone, without Gemma.

She'd suspected that Ingram's attempts would prove fruitless, but it left her with a cold, desolate reality: Leona wanted them enough to follow them here, craved them enough to steal the only part of them she could find – Gemma Eakley.

This was hopeless.

All her life, Aurelia yearned to keep the witch within her awake and involved, but the problems that came with her witchcraft were more destructive than anything she had imagined.

Louisa stirred. Ingram and Alaric had spoken too loudly.

Aurelia tiptoed to the ground floor after pulling a blanket over the child. She saw them through the thin curtains, obscured by the black of night. Her coat wouldn't be warm enough for her to linger very long, and she hovered in the doorway, waiting for them to come inside. She held herself tight, nursing her shiver as she eventually closed the front door behind her, creating a barrier between the sound of their voices and Louisa.

Somehow, they hadn't seen her. With his back still toward her, Alaric gestured to something in front of him, something she couldn't see: the wards.

'Could she have found us if they were completely closed?' Ingram asked.

'No,' Alaric responded, grim. 'No one could find her. Which is why she wanted to keep them open.'

'Damn it, Gem. She never listened to me. She was never careful enough.'

'As if you could have known. She wasn't clueless, Teddy, she was lonely. Would you not have done the same in her shoes? She needed someone to know she was there. You couldn't have been there for her all that time, you know. No one could have predicted that having a selective ward for witches would be so disastrous.'

'Why are you talking about her like that?'

'Like what?'

'Like she's already dead,' Ingram hissed.

Alaric Friedman gnawed at his bottom lip, sparing the boy a harsher reply. 'We'd be fools to rule it out,' he said, his voice low – but not low enough.

'*Quiet! Both of you!*' Aurelia whispered from near the door.

Alaric was the one to be relieved by her presence – she only found shame in Ingram's face. Of what? She couldn't tell. Of everything, maybe. Even the smallest of his motions were hindered under its improbable weight.

'It took hours for Louisa to stop crying,' she said. 'The last thing I need is for her to overhear the two of you and start all over again. We'll have more than enough to deal with in the morning.'

Ingram's head fell as if the promise of tomorrow was too painful to think about, and then he conceded, leaving Alaric in the grass to meet her in the doorway. He stopped beside her and asked, 'How is she?' His voice was small. Aurelia harboured enough anger over him to know that whatever crept through was *not* that. Pity, perhaps. The anger dissipated as he met her gaze, hopeful for resolution. Something promising. If she could be anything for him, it would be a resting point.

'Down in the basement. She never stopped crying.'

He reached for her arm, then paused. She knew she could be an anchor for him too – if that was what he needed. But they'd never been defined in certain terms, always nebulous ones, and something about his touching her now seemed so *certain*.

'I wouldn't wake her up if I were you,' she whispered. 'Did you find anything?'

He shook his head. 'Nothing.'

She knew better than to ask for anything more. 'Rory, I'm . . . Thank you. I shouldn't have—'

He stopped himself short. Neither of them expected an apology – the other would hate to relinquish one. That much had always been true between them.

She captured his attention with a pointed gaze and so much to say, but all that came was, 'Don't try that shit with me again.'

He nodded and slid past her, treading down to the basement.

Alaric Friedman's line of sight was somewhere in the grass, and without looking at her, he lifted his hand and beckoned her closer.

'It upsets me that we had to meet on these terms,' he said. 'Did Teddy tell you about the wards?'

'A little. How much do you know?'

'Everything,' he said. 'I built them for her. I need to re-establish them.'

'So, you knew her before she came.' It wasn't a question, but she waited patiently for his answer.

'You could say that.'

'Is there a debate?'

'I loved her,' Alaric said. 'The whole reason she ever moved to Townsend was because of my request. For a time, I thought I knew her better than I knew myself.'

He surveyed the brush around him, and Aurelia realized he was searching for the existing ward. Was it gone? Could he not see it?

Alaric shook his head and plunged his hand beneath the brush, trailing his fingertips along the ground to outline a new ward. Gold dusted from his fingertips, illuminating the path behind him. As the distance grew between them, she followed it, keeping to one side of the line.

Curious, she asked, 'What happened, then – to change that?'

Alaric sighed, permitting the dark curls to fall over his forehead while he drew. 'When Kenny died, I knew a part of her went with him. It wasn't that I loved her any less after that. I wanted to . . . She became someone else. Grief altered the motivation behind everything she did, and a person can only change so much before they must kill the former version of themselves. I saw it take hold of her. I felt myself becoming a stranger.'

She nodded wordlessly as they closed the circle around the cottage. Alaric rose from his crouch, massaging his shoulder, and he adjusted his glasses. They fogged, but he moved on quickly.

'Have you cast a ward before?'

Warming her hands, she replied, 'Once, but I know I can do it again.'

The man grinned back at her, drawing more lines in his face. She found the deep ones that hid behind his greying scruff. 'Good. Take that side. We raise it on my count.'

He began to walk, and the weight on Aurelia's shoulders dissolved slowly. She wanted to be useful. Lately, she'd felt exactly the opposite.

Before Alaric could fall away into the dark, she sent a final question through to him. 'When did you meet *Teddy?*'

Alaric took another step before he offered an answer. 'When I helped him bury Gemma's son.'

Losing the inclination to speak again, he nodded in question. *Are you ready?*

Her palms opened forward by her sides, touched by the dewy blades of grass. *I am.*

In unison, they summoned the circle of gold from where it rested in the dirt. It inched upward in tendrils, like rain on tempered glass. Aurelia observed the motion of Ingram's body behind a window. He looked small through it, and Louisa – even smaller in his arms. The girl's forearms hung loose over his shoulders as he ascended the steps of the basement, half-obscured by the solid windowpane and transparent curtains. Aurelia caught the slightest trace of his hand rubbing circles into her small back, comforting her.

As gold edged upward in her periphery, she thought of Gemma Eakley placing the pin in Louisa's hair, a twisted knot between them that Gemma refused to cut. A mere sliver of bronze fastened into her mushroom-brown curls . . .

The ward rose, swirling in the periphery of her vision, and Ingram disappeared behind it like a mirage.

Louisa and her home disappeared with it.

CHAPTER EIGHTEEN

The sharp white light of Aurelia's phone pierced her eyes in the darkness, displaying half past three. Her body quivered beneath the pulled-taut sheets, a sheen of sweat marking the residue of her nightmare. Outside her window, snowflakes flurried downward to dust the tall grass in dew.

It hadn't been Gemma. Again, the impermanent face of the shapeshifting witch followed her into her subconscious, feeding from her fear.

It was unbearable. Waking up to a violent shiver was only icing on the cake.

She sacrificed what little heat the duvet provided and swung her legs off the edge of the bed to source a central heating system or her orange puffer coat – whichever came first.

The door squeaked as it opened, but if Louisa was awake, Aurelia could be assured the girl was safe. Slowly, she twisted the knob, peering through the crack to find the young girl buried beneath a heap of blankets, fast asleep.

The parted blinds on Louisa's window revealed a small crack down the centre of the glass. The thought of stealing one of her blankets was tempting, but it seemed unfair to her that the child should have to sleep in a room with a cracked window in a place as cold as this.

What mattered, she thought, was that Louisa was OK. Beneath that pile of blankets, the girl was asleep, unharmed, *not crying.*

Aurelia closed the door behind her, resolving to fix her issue some other way. She hadn't expected to find a thermostat, but its absence disappointed her, nonetheless. Encircling her arms around herself, she trotted to the coffee table in the front room where her jacket hung on the back of a wooden chair.

'Cold?'

She gasped, startled by the dark, hovering shape of Theodore Ingram behind the kitchen counter. He held a mug between his hands, covering as much of it as possible with his palms to absorb its warmth.

Though barely visible, she was taken aback by the difference in his posture. Uncertainty was crushing him. She still wasn't used to seeing his neck. Or his arms. He covered himself up with long-sleeved turtleneck sweaters so often that seeing any inch of skin that wasn't his face came as a surprise. He was pale and lean, and something about the flesh of his inner forearms seemed particularly inviting.

'Freezing,' she said. 'I couldn't sleep through it.' Pulling the sleeves over her arms, she granted him another look and observed him with less tenacity. He stared back as if he could tell that her answer was only half true. 'What are *you* up for?'

He shrugged, raising his mug. 'Bit sore. Just felt like a cup of tea.'

So, they were both liars. She couldn't blame him for finding solace in the omission of Gemma's name, though.

'Is the kettle still hot?' she asked.

Ingram shook his head with a sniff, avoidant of her. He sipped from his cup before extending it to her with a slight tilt. 'Take the rest.'

'Oh . . . Thanks.'

It was lukewarm by then, hardly warm enough to give her any comfort in that sense, but it was easier to hide the quivering in her hands with her fingers curled around the mug.

'You should head back to bed,' he murmured softly. 'I'll bring you another blanket.'

'I'll be fine with my jacket. It should suffice.' It was well padded and covered her torso, but Ingram wasn't convinced.

He offered her a weak, near invisible smile. 'I doubt it'll be comfortable to sleep in with all those silly, marshmallowy puffs. And it probably needs a wash. Can't have you spoiling my sheets with your filthy outerwear.'

Aurelia's nose wrinkled. His hand slid to her shoulder, moving her gently from the kitchen's entry to pass her. For a moment, it lingered, and she was exhausted enough to imagine what a good idea it might be to reach for his hand and hold it in place against her.

Down it glided, hissing against the fabric as it left her just a little colder.

'I'll bring one up,' he said. 'Just in case.'

Aurelia nodded, frozen in position while her head tilted to find his eyes. He couldn't refuse her – when she wordlessly posed a question, he had to answer. But she hated that *this* was where she found power over him – in a ring of red around his eyes, the glassiness that birthed stars in the pool of his muted whites. Throughout her brief adulthood, she had catalogued men by the way they looked at her. She had filed away all their lingering stares into a locked drawer in her mind. Sometimes she'd resurrect them, but most went there to die. To be forgotten. It was always *one look*, something just long enough for her to understand how she could become what they wanted.

This was another look that she would undoubtedly keep. She would remember it clearly, because he would likely never be this vulnerable with her again.

Those warm green eyes were a weakness. And he turned away, too little, too late, thinking he could still keep it from her.

She tucked herself in, breathing as silently as she could to listen for the sound of him downstairs. He hadn't come up yet. Aurelia thought he had changed his mind and decided on her own that she would be better in that bulky jacket. Time passed, and she wasn't keeping track – more than enough to have located an extra blanket and brought it up. Maybe even enough time for her to have drifted back to sleep . . . Exhaustion settled in, relaxing her muscles, and slowing her breaths.

She had almost been thrusted back into her nightmare again when Ingram rapped at her bedroom door, pushing it open. In his hands was an afghan identical to the one she knew he slept in.

'Still awake?'

'Barely,' she slurred, pulling the duvet to her chin. He swung the door behind him but left it unclosed. Her heart sank. She wasn't coherent enough to fathom why.

'I didn't think you were coming,' she said.

'Was nursing a bad ache,' he replied with an apologetic tilt of his head.

The blanket unfolded over her. She struggled to keep her eyes open, watching as Ingram leaned over to spread the blanket over the compact furl of her body.

He bewildered her sometimes. Aurelia moved to assure herself that she was not already asleep . . . If this was a dream, how long had it been since she came into it? She suspected, at any moment, the cawing of birds would wake her to an empty room in which she had no reason to call him in and be kind to her.

That might have made more sense than whatever was occurring now, in which he covered her thoughtfully, leaving no limb without an extra layer of warmth.

After pulling the edge of the blanket to her chin, he squeezed her shoulder. 'Good?'

'This is yours, isn't it? What will you sleep with?'

Unconvincingly, he answered, 'I have a spare.'

Her hand slipped out from underneath her cocoon and fell on top of his with caution. 'You could stay here, y'know. If you want.'

'I'll be all right, Schwartz. Don't worry about me.'

Had she been any more alert, she would have let the issue die there, but she was just as stubborn half-asleep as she was while fully awake.

Besides, it didn't have to be about him. Aurelia could

pretend she'd never noticed the redness of his eyes or the quiver in his voice. She didn't mind risking the illusion of being vulnerable if it meant it would ease his worry.

It wasn't real anyway – at least, it didn't *have to be.*

His thumb caressed her knuckles. Her hand curled around his.

'I might be warmer having you here too,' she said. 'Body heat, y'know? It's not a big deal though. This is already . . .'

A yawn broke apart her sentence. She could hardly hold onto her words, and the sentiment fell away like kicked bedsheets.

'You're asking me to?'

'I'm *offering,*' Aurelia corrected, nuzzling against her pillow. Donning a lazy mimic of his voice, she added, 'Against my better judgement.'

'I'll never understand how you find the energy to mock me when you're asking for my help,' Ingram whispered, seating himself on the edge of the bed. 'Move over.'

He lifted the blanket, undoing the neat tuck, and slid beneath it. The few seconds of exposure sent a violent shiver down her back that then subsided with his touch. His arm snaked around her shoulders and urged her closer.

The contact woke her slightly, but she held still as his arm fell to the dip of her waist, fearful that inviting him in would cross a line for what he deemed too close. Her hands wriggled upward between their chests, meant to maintain an inch of distance between them, but her fingers curled instinctively around the fabric of his shirt.

It was automatic, she reasoned, a gesture her body wasn't

*un*familiar with, even if it felt new and tentative with him. Aurelia had never believed herself capable of holding him close or wanting him nearby, but time and time again, he proved her wrong.

Warmth radiated from the skin beneath his shirt, and despite the depth and evenness of his breath, his heartbeat was wild and heavy against her hands.

'For body heat,' he whispered, inching closer to her.

Yes, for that.

That was his new line, drawn in the sand far past where the first one was. It instilled in her enough courage to close that pitiful distance and allow him to ease an arm beneath her head, effectively enveloping her. She knew then that she could drown in his comfort, breathing in the scent of freshly broken soil and citrus that wafted from his skin. He adjusted the covers over them before tethering her to his body with a delicate, bare arm.

'You all right, Schwartz?'

She nodded, brushing the cold tip of her nose against his collarbone. 'I think so.'

'And are you—'

'Warmer now. Better.'

His fingers threaded through her curls, untangling a strand from itself, and he whispered, 'Good.'

It was an uneven line, roughed over by lapping waters.

'Where does it hurt?' she asked. 'That ache.'

Ingram was silent long enough that she nearly lost the question in her fatigue, tucking herself even closer to his chest. His eventual answer came through a laboured breath: 'Everywhere.'

He didn't wake her up. Instead, he served his half-true

purpose, and his fingers lulled her to sleep. He whispered something against her hair, but it was hazy, and her face – already too slackened to ask what it was.

Seconds passed before sleep devoured her again.

She didn't tell him when she slipped out of his bed. She had always considered sleep to be more intimate than sex. She could think of nothing more intimate than lying her head on someone else's pillow and letting them see her without her guards.

Especially *his* pillow. She had to remind herself that all of this was his: his life, his family, his home. Already, she was too close, woven into the fabric of his routines. She needed to be cut loose.

There was something off about him in the mornings. To start, he was glowing. It was clearer now as he slept, under her scrutiny, that Ingram wore his magic like a garment. When he didn't mask it beneath a focused expression or his black and coal grey clothing, it shimmered. He was radiant and *sort of* beautiful, adorned in that gold mark of magic like Apollo himself.

Sometimes it slipped past her mind that he could be as soft and warm-hearted as herself. The role he played had always been structural and apathetic – so displeased by everything that life had to offer him . . . She could forget that his skin was not hardened like stone. He didn't look like the kind of witch that knew where all living beings went to die, but that was the nature of witches like him – harbingers of death. Perhaps it was a miracle she could even wake up when all that power seeped from him unknown.

He was more vulnerable now than ever. Maybe he didn't understand how much she could hurt him when he was like this, but she would never let that thought cross his mind. There were more important matters to attend to.

The door to Louisa's bedroom sat ajar. Between finding the room empty and spotting Louisa down the hall, sitting at the kitchen counter, a pang of fear crept up Aurelia's throat. Just as quickly, it subsided. Louisa's eyes found hers, and the girl sniffled.

'Need a tissue?' Aurelia asked her.

Louisa shook her head, but Aurelia knew better. Children, for better or worse, wanted to be tougher than they really were. Aurelia spooled an excessive amount of toilet paper onto her hand as she passed the bathroom and brought it with her.

Louisa's nose was practically dribbling when Aurelia neared.

'How'd you sleep?

'I dunno,' the girl said. 'I can't remember.'

Which was *better*, Aurelia thought. Better than being awake with those thoughts, remembering those nightmares. Most nights, Leona's mutable face haunted Aurelia, and she was forced to remember it in sickening clarity.

'How about some breakfast?'

Louisa shrugged.

'Cereal?'

'We don't have cereal,' the girl said.

'Tea, then?' Aurelia offered, desperate. She didn't even know if children drank tea – was it like coffee? Should it be kept in cupboards higher than Louisa could reach?

For all her knowledge, there were plenty of simple things Aurelia didn't know. She shook her head, rounding the counter to boil some water for her own cup of tea.

'I'll have some,' said Ingram. He wasn't nearly as dishevelled as his small surrogate sister, but it was clear that he'd seen better days. He rested his elbows on the counter, sliding into the seat beside Louisa. His hand fell to her shoulder and gave it a squeeze. Aurelia tried not to listen as he whispered, 'You all right, darling?'

The girl sniffled in response and reached for the wad of toilet paper that Aurelia had left on the countertop.

The water hadn't reached its boiling point before Louisa retreated to the bathroom and shut herself inside. The remaining two continued silently, Aurelia pouring two cups of tea and Ingram watching her, but not really paying attention. They listened for Louisa, for a cry that didn't come. Aurelia slid a cup toward him.

Hushed, he began, 'Suppose you'd like to get back now – to Cambridge.'

She kept her eyes on the grooves of the counter, waiting for her drink to cool. He sounded reluctant to speak and voiced the option to her so she would have something to reject. 'It's probably the smarter thing to do, given that we can't hide from her out here,' he continued. 'Even if the wards keep anyone else from finding us, I doubt she'll believe that a house managed to disappear into thin air.'

Aurelia nodded, raising the cup to her lips, although it was still too hot for her.

Once it was clear he had nothing more to say, perhaps

because digging too far in one direction would only make it seem like he truly wanted her gone, Aurelia lowered her voice in return and said, 'She never wanted Gemma. She wanted *us*.'

'Is that supposed to comfort me?' asked Ingram.

'Don't you think that's worth examining? That *ours is the magic she covets*.'

'What is there to examine, Schwartz? Isn't this reason enough to toss ourselves in separate directions? If, for some reason, the coexistence of our magic paints a brighter target on our backs, wouldn't it be best to just . . . I don't know.'

He couldn't voice it. Putting the option before her would give her the opportunity to choose it; she could tell he didn't truly believe that separation would save them, or that, if he *did*, he certainly didn't want her to agree with him.

Thankfully, she rarely ever agreed with him. That seemed to placate one of his fears and rouse up another.

Leaning closer, with her elbows against her side of the counter, she muttered, 'Desire is a dangerous motive. And she *wants* us, or what we have, because she doesn't already have it. Think of how much power threads between the two of us alone. Even with whatever . . . *issue* I have going on right now, I'm capable. When I'm *not* faltering, my gift is cultivated. When I *am*, I'm still a damn good spellcaster. And you—'

She'd leaned a little too close, she realized.

'You're practically leaking raw power. Which isn't a good thing, by the way. You should really fix that.'

Ingram scratched his neck nervously, as if she had instead commented on the way he smelled or something in his teeth.

'If that was the case, she would have thought twice about

coming after us, but she didn't. It didn't stop her from taking Gemma, and I'll be damned if I let her get hold of Louisa.' Quickly, he added, 'Or you, for that matter.'

She had never felt so relieved to be an afterthought to him. She couldn't break his heart even if she tried to. Even if she wanted to.

'I'm not leaving,' she told him, downing her tea. 'Unless this is your way of kicking me out for the holidays, in which case, you'll have given me a valid excuse to hate you again.'

'You know, you really are a pain in my arse sometimes, Schwartz.'

'It's not hard to be. You are exceptionally frustrating.'

Halfway down the hall, Louisa Eakley crossed from the bathroom to her bedroom where she kept her head down and the door slammed shut behind her. Ingram slid off his stool but didn't move much farther. He simply watched the door close from the counter where he stood, and his posture fell, defeated once more.

Aurelia filled his cup again and slid it back to him. 'I want to go to the Tate,' she said.

'I . . . I don't know.'

'It was *your* idea, Ingram, and now, I want to go.'

'At one point it was, but things have changed. If anything happened to me when Gem was still here, Lou's world would keep moving, undeterred. I can't risk doing anything reckless now. Like you said yesterday—'

'What if I told you Leona would be there?'

He paused, mouth ajar with an unfinished sentence. 'How?'

'That token,' she began. 'I think it's a "wandering eye".

There's a page in my grimoire on wandering eyes that I didn't remember until the other day, but Gemma's been using them too. That hairpin she makes Louisa wear – it does more than track her. It listens. It *sees*. They were popular tools for espionage during the Wars of the Roses, made primarily out of reforged helmet metal. Supposedly, you could look into the surface of the metal and key into the whereabouts of whoever had its sister piece. They could be made out of anything. Armour. Coins. *Mirrors*. The right spell can transform anything into an invaluable tool.'

Or a weapon, she thought.

'You think that's what the tokens are? *Eyes* following us?'

'Just the third one,' she said. 'I'm not banking on the first two to mean anything at this point, not if the third token gets us what we need. They're more like addresses – to *us*. One for me, one for you, and one for her eye, fixed to our every move.'

Ingram buried his face into his hands and released a small groan. Aurelia stirred her cup of tea with her spoon until he looked at her again. Some conversations couldn't be made through a wall of fingers.

'If we can somehow *agitate* it,' she whispered, leaning over the counter, 'Leona might come. I doubt she'll have any use for modern art, but London has to be a hub of places she could potentially take from. If she's already looking for us, she'll have another reason to follow us there.'

He looked at her briefly, his face full of angles and tautness.

'Better in London than out here. And this time, you'll have me there,' she told him. 'If we find Leona together, I don't think she'll stand a chance.'

He lowered his gaze back to his cup, rotating it against the counter. It shifted on the granite with an irritating squeak. 'Do you really believe that?'

Slowly, Aurelia nodded, tracing the crease between his eyebrows, down the slope of his nose. Marked by the words of his last argument to her, that familiar expression became one of immeasurable sadness.

'And if we find her?' he asked.

Her fingers curled around the edge of the counter. In her mind, it was simple: become something so fearsome that Leona would have no choice but to reveal what had happened to Gemma Eakley. It couldn't be hard when her companion was capable of such dark magic. She and Ingram could figure out the details another time – they were as inconsequential to her as her next meal or the colour of his T-shirt.

'What do you want?' she whispered. 'What would you do?'

'I don't want to be a murderer,' he stated. Aurelia couldn't tell if that was where his sentence ended. Everyone had a limit to kindness before they would snap. In his shoes, Aurelia would have snapped already.

Even now, whatever willingness she possessed to make peace with Leona had disintegrated, with only an inch left to her candle's wick before it soon burned to nothing at all.

She held out her hand, touched his back with delicate, chewed-up fingertips, and turned him to face her.

'You see how much Louisa loves you, don't you? Losing you wouldn't have been easier for her if Gemma was still around.'

'I shouldn't have said anything.'

'But you meant it,' she said. 'I'd do it, y'know. I'd kill her if I could. If I had the chance, I'm not sure I'd turn it down.'

'You shouldn't,' he said. 'We don't have to do any of this, Schwartz. We could *hide*.'

'Is that what you want? Haven't you all hidden long enough?'

Ingram's hand rose to her face, and it touched her in another new, unexplored way. 'It could be different this time. We would make it work – she'd never find us.'

'We?' She stuttered on the lone syllable. Then, it was his turn to bait her with silence, drawing her closer, as if his hand didn't already find a home beside her jaw. She felt his thumb barely an inch from the corner of her mouth. The urge to tilt her head and press her lips to his flesh was indomitable.

'Whatever that means to you,' he answered.

Her hand came up over his, removing it from her cheek. 'It *means* that you'll follow me to the Tate when I decide to chase her. As long as Leona is out there, hunting other witches for sport, none of us are safe.'

'But are you willing to be the one to . . .' He had the words, but they strangled him. He stared, sucking his gums in consideration.

'Yes,' she answered. 'If that's what it comes to, I'll do it.'

The words were not a weight off either of their shoulders. It sunk between them and made the house seem several times smaller. She released his hand, having almost forgotten it was still melded to hers; and by then, her fingers had waffled together with some of his. Ingram could have embraced her if he didn't look so demoralized, as crazy as it seemed to her. He talked about hiding as if doing so made it easier to remove themselves from the timeline in which they still hated each other.

As if they could start anew.

She thought of his lips against her hair and his arm over the curve of her waist as she slept. Vaguely, she recalled those arms pulling her closer as her nightmare jolted her awake, but she didn't trust that it was real.

Real was the threat that found them in Townsend. Ingram had his family and his home, a great collection of reasons that he should want to see the shapeshifting witch dead, but Aurelia would have to wring her dry for nothing. Self-preservation had driven her for years; and if her life depended on it, it would lead her all the way to murder.

She would have done it for herself alone had he not been masochistic enough to invite her to stay, to share with her every wonderful thing that Gemma and Louisa created for themselves. She would have done it for herself if she didn't love them so much.

Her ambition was cruel, but she was made of more than just ambition; and all those things working in tandem made her *unstoppable.* What was a goal without motive – and what greater motive was there than loss?

Aurelia Schwartz would do it for them too. And when she did, she would not fail.

CHAPTER NINETEEN

The holidays came and went silently. Frost dusted in the night and warmed to dew by morning. Louisa cried most mornings, and her tears gave way to anger by midday. Ingram spent their final days at the cottage following her, bending to the young girl's every whim, soothing all the outbursts that arose in her grief.

Aurelia stayed out of their way. Ironically, it's what she should have done from the very start – but by now, she wasn't following the same set of loose rules that were set when she first arrived. The tides had changed, throwing her life off-kilter, punching holes in her boat, and they had found several ways to sneak inside. She kept herself at arm's length, closing up the wound she'd let them open up inside her and take root in.

What they needed now was objectivity, and no one could draw further from the situation than she could.

She shut herself in the bedroom on the first morning, legs tucked beneath her while she slouched over her grimoire. She and Gabrielle had been thorough when they compiled it, even if the signatures were now disorganized in the aftermath of Ingram's hiccup; but there wasn't enough. The spell that Leona had cast during the event at King's College remained an enigma to her, and Aurelia still wasn't convinced that it didn't come from some kind of gift.

Wandering eyes were less enigmatic, but more finicky than she'd anticipated. From the wrong end of one, there wasn't much she could piece together.

She let the piece of gold spin over her palm as she read, like a coin tossed for ever that'd leave a tie unbroken.

It was clear that she would need more than whatever answers her tutor had already given her. Gemma was bound to have kept at least one grimoire in the house, but every room was cluttered, belongings strewn wildly over one another in a way that only Gemma could have truly known how to navigate. If Louisa could make sense of the colourful disorganization, she would ask; but she had a feeling that the girl wouldn't be much help behind her blurry eyes and snotty nose. Ingram might tuck her behind him like a thin-legged fawn and make her unquestionable.

'She's fragile,' he had said the previous night, curled over his knees on the edge of the basement couch.

Aurelia had given him a glass of water, which he drank like he was drowning, and she asked, 'What are you going to do?'

He shook his head, bumping that now-emptied glass against his knee rhythmically. 'I don't know. I wish I could tell her that her mother will come back if she waits, but I don't even know if she's still—'

'She's *alive*, Ingram,' Aurelia spat. He reached around her legs to place his glass on the coffee table behind her, stealing a glance at her from where he sat below; and a glimmer of hope flashed in his eyes that made her realize she was too close, too embedded in their family's well-being. She saw the war behind his eyes fought between the desire to believe, to make her words into a faith he'd follow to the end of the world, and the knowledge that it would make him just as gullible and naive as Louisa. Aurelia's words were no fuller than his, as empty of a promise as saying she would return soon.

Wishful thinking could get them far enough, but it wouldn't bring Gemma Eakley back. All it did was shatter the last formidable leg of their delicate unit.

By the afternoon, she decided to weather the walk to Alaric's bookshop again.

Aurelia caught Ingram halfway down the staircase as she left. He opened his mouth and promptly closed it, having exhausted himself of anything he felt worth saying.

'I need to see if Alaric has any resources on locator spells,' she explained, unprompted. 'I remembered seeing a few older spell books on his shelves while I was there. If I can find anything, I'll find it there . . . I just need something else.'

She wasn't sure why it sounded like justification coming out of her mouth. Years of yelling at one another from the opposite ends of a cavernous divide made her incapable of believing he would accept anything less, that he would need another reason or more volume to hear her.

He nodded, understanding her perfectly. He held up his finger for her to allow him a moment to disappear, and when he returned from the basement, he held a folded envelope containing Leona's letter. Before she left, he gave her hand a gentle squeeze, gazing up at her from his lower step with those same red-ringed eyes. While Louisa's grief was loud and fiery, Ingram's was much quieter. Aurelia never saw him cry, but the evidence was there every morning, staining his pale face in red, hollowing out his cheeks. Guilt for her own lack of visible remorse consumed her, but she didn't think she was permitted to feel the same kind of grief that Louisa and Ingram felt. What power could answer that, she didn't know. Things like this made gods seem more than ever like wishful thinking.

He murmured, 'Be safe.' An unnecessary warning, but it served as a reminder of everything else that could be lost if they didn't succeed.

She held up her pinkie, and Ingram almost smiled as he hooked his own around it.

The rain crashed unrelentingly as she wandered down the hill, and she kept the letter pressed between the inside of her jacket and her body.

Alaric gathered her from the downpour, saying little as he offered her a towel with which to dry her hair. There was only so much of the rain she could handle being drenched in, and she wrung it from her curls neatly.

The man waited for her impatiently, wiping the fog from his glasses on the hem of his shirt. Aurelia wondered if she was inconveniencing him with her arrival. The bookshop looked empty, but maybe the other *rooms* were not.

'I'm sorry I couldn't call,' she started, unzipping her jacket to grab the envelope. It was damp, mostly from sweat, but she could faintly see the unblemished ink of Leona's letter through the layer of paper.

He said nothing as he let loose the folded contents, turning toward the front counter to examine them. Upon dissecting them, Aurelia noticed a new page in Alaric's hand.

'Do sit down while I have a look at these. You'll have to forgive me for being quiet today. Been a long week.'

She glanced around the shop, finding nowhere to sit. Sensing her confusion, he made an inexact gesture with his free hand, and the room began to transform again. Something beneath her feet rumbled. The old portraits manifested themselves on the elongated walls, telling her she would soon be back in the grand library, in which case she was taking up space that should have been home to a short table.

Aurelia stepped back, and the table in question sprouted before her feet.

'The furnishings will usually wait, but not always. Best to get acquainted with the layout.'

'I don't know if I have enough time for that,' she said, forcing a laugh. 'I need to get home sooner or later.'

He raised an eyebrow, pushing a dark curl from his face with the blunt edge of a paper fold.

'Cambridge, I mean.'

'I assumed as much. You carry yourself like an academic.'

She didn't know whether it was meant to be a mere observation or an insult, but his unfeeling response gave her reason to believe it wasn't a compliment.

'The last time I was here, you told me "this place has many rooms." How many are there?'

He sighed, distracted from the task at hand. 'In total, I'd say fifty, but my access changes so frequently that I can't be certain.'

'Access,' she repeated under her breath. 'They aren't all yours?'

'They're portals. More or less. This room is mine, but I am allowed passage through the others. It's a perk of the job.'

'I guess you're not really a bookseller, then,' she said with a slight laugh.

'Oh, I *am.*' Gesturing with his hand full of papers, he explained, '*This* doesn't make me any money. Although, I admit it's far more tasking than stocking shelves and taking inventory. Running my shop is a labour of love.'

'And what is it you actually do?'

Aurelia began to search the shelf nearest the front door, wondering how long it would take her to find what she needed amongst all the cluttered rows.

Alaric paused, biting on his fingernail in a way that closely mirrored how she bit hers. 'Ah, I suppose you Americans have a much different culture regarding the distribution of magical knowledge. There aren't many rooms that lead to the States. I am a bookkeeper on all fronts, but here, I am also a caretaker. We caretakers bear the responsibility of maintaining and protecting a collection of important magical artefacts.'

Her eyes brightened. 'So, somewhere in the world, there are fifty other rooms that look just like this? And you can just come and go at will?'

He shrugged. There was obviously more to the rooms than what she had reduced it to, but Alaric had lost the interest – or patience – to explain it any further.

'Shit,' she whispered.

'Yeah. Shit.'

Her eyes followed the tower of shelves up to the top. Alaric's library alone brimmed with the kind of knowledge she'd only ever dreamed of.

'So, you must have something on locator spells here.'

He considered it, then disappeared into an aisle of the grand library and unearthed something for her to take back to the cottage.

As he covered it neatly in anticipation of the rain, he added, 'It's almost impossible to find a person, unless you are gifted. Trust me, I have another caretaker on the council searching for her already.'

'Almost?'

If there was a sliver of a chance to find Leona – to find *Gemma* – Aurelia would take it. She would curl her fingers around it and fuse to it like they were two halves of a whole.

'A person is a much harder thing to track than an object. If you possess the proper knowledge as well as an object of reference – an anchor . . . It's advanced magic, but it's manageable.'

'And if you *are* gifted?'

He pushed up his glasses, accosting her with his gaze. He hadn't realized they were talking about someone other than Gemma until now.

Warily he said. 'Then, you can find anything. Have you searched the house for missing things?'

'I haven't. I wouldn't know what to look for. Ingram has his hands full with Louisa, so I don't expect he's done anything like that either. Besides, he's not the most well versed in the principles of magic.'

'Yes,' Alaric murmured. 'He's rather hopeless.'

'If you don't mind me asking, do you really think Leona would have taken something other than Gemma?'

His fingers rapped against the wooden counter. 'Not Leona. *Gemma.*'

A dull ache grew in the hollow of her stomach, branching outward with tenacity. 'You think she knew?'

'Of course,' he said, as if there was no other plausible answer than that. 'She was a diviner, and a paranoid one. If anything were to threaten her peace up here, she'd know. Hell, she probably knew it before your shapeshifter did.'

Aurelia shuddered, reaching for her coat again to steady herself. 'Does *he* know?'

Alaric sighed, circling the counter. 'If he hasn't figured it out by now, the time has passed to tell him. He needs to clear his head. And *you* ought to be distancing yourself from this as much as possible.'

'He should know,' Aurelia said. 'What if it helps him find her?'

'What do you think will happen to him if he discovers that Gemma left without warning him? It's not like this was a bloody sacrifice. She had a child. And now, that child is without her mother. If he finds out that Gemma offered herself up to the wolves and left *him* to pick up the pieces, it will destroy him. Frankly, I don't want to be the one to tell him that. It's not my responsibility. It will do nothing to bring Gemma back. Honestly,' he continued, 'I'm not even sure if he would believe me. He loves her too much. In his eyes, she can do no wrong.'

Slowly, Aurelia lifted the soggy coat to her stomach and gripped it for comfort. She'd realized the extent of her lies to her human best friend, but she'd never lied to Ingram before, as a human or witch. That's how it always was, as certain and true as magic in their blood. They were honest, even if it was cruel and irreversible. When he kept things from her, she'd learned exactly how to extract them and open him up again.

Surely, he could do the same to her. Not that he had ever tried. She had never given him a reason to.

'If you must tell him, let it be from your own mouth. I'll do what I can to find Gem, but I will not hurt him any more than he is already hurting. God forbid that he decides he doesn't want to be a part of Lou's life any more.'

'He wouldn't,' Aurelia said. 'She's everything to him.'

'I thought he and Louisa were everything to *Gem*.' It was quiet, careful. She hadn't realized how silent the room was until he left her with Gemma's name and a confession. 'Up until now, I had enough faith in Gemma to believe that she would grace us with a warning, were anything like this to happen. Some kind of sign.'

Aurelia pulled the wet garment over her arms again, hiding the shiver that came from it.

'We're going after Leona. I'll . . . I'll keep that in mind.'

His lips narrowed into a straight line – the way that Ingram's often did. In her mind, the expression belonged to Ingram, and it was similar to witnessing him in someone else's body.

The mirrored piece of gold turned in her mind. The coin flipping endlessly.

She gripped the doorknob, freezing in place. 'Thanks for the book.' She secured it beneath her jacket, wondering if the caretaker would try to stop her. Someone had to try. Who better than the one who was easiest forgotten? The one who had spent her whole life in pursuit of the perfect camouflage.

All Alaric said was, 'Careful out there,' before she left again, feeling closer to an answer but further from the truth than ever before.

She had an excuse to be in Gemma's room, but it certainly didn't help her find what she was looking for. It was a harder task to find something that was missing than something that had appeared without reason, and that was only if she knew what she was looking for.

To make matters worse, Aurelia realized upon stepping into Gemma's room that she had never actually *been* in Gemma's room until now. So, not worse. Impossible.

She had to tell him. Another day had passed since she visited Alaric Friedman's bookshop, and the guilt had admonished her more than she could successfully handle.

Ingram knocked on the door, and it creaked open, having been left open to give them both an air of transparency. Aurelia glanced at him from Gemma's open wardrobe, fingers hooked around a coat that wouldn't fit her.

'Find anything?' he asked.

She shook her head. He meant the clothes, a *dress*. Something nicer than what she had packed in her bag for a lazy holiday with someone she didn't truly care to impress – but still, she thought of the other way she could answer that question.

She would find Leona, and they would bring Gemma back before she ever brought the truth to his attention. As much as it pained her to admit, Alaric Friedman was right. Knowing Gemma's involvement in her own disappearance would only weaken an already fragile person.

And he was *fragile.* It became increasingly obvious to her how easily he could break, and she found herself holding her breath whenever Louisa would defy him. It wasn't anger that she feared – it was withdrawal. He remained so attuned to the inner workings of Louisa Eakley's tender heart that the weight of her sorrow fell on his shoulders too; and it was crushing him, burying him in rubble. Soon, he might be impossible to reach.

'Any requests?' Aurelia asked. Her voice was too rough to be light-hearted – her thirst unrelenting. She kept herself busy to write over the racing thoughts in her mind, but Ryan wasn't there now to remind her to slow down and have a drink, even if that drink was something alcoholic and fruity.

Ingram sat lightly on the edge of Gemma's bed, as if creating creases in her duvet was a punishable crime. 'Odd thing to ask of me. I don't really want to think of you in her dresses.'

She sighed. 'If I had anything else—'

'I didn't mean it like that. Sorry, I'm not . . .'

He didn't have to finish. His head fell into his hands, and then his hands slid to the back of his neck to cradle it.

Aurelia pulled the smallest dress she could find, still too wide for her but doable with a belt. Even on her, it would look like Gemma's dress. Blue, covered in a minimalistic floral pattern. She held it to her body and turned to him.

'Passable?'

He hummed, perching his chin on his folded knuckles. 'Sure.'

Aurelia smiled. He didn't seem to see it, and she crossed to the bed where he sat, laying the dress neatly beside him.

'You know that dress I wore to King's College?'

'I vaguely remember it.'

She bit her lip, knowing it was a lie. She caught a hint of pink collecting around the shell of his ear.

'I've worn that one to about ten different events. It's the only one I have for formals. Took me months of saving my wages before I felt like I could buy it, and now I can't even look at it without wishing I had something else to wear.'

Her fingers traced the pearlescent white buttons that lined the bodice of the dress. Ingram followed the small movement with curiosity. He scrutinized her often, but this was different – he was too tired, too unconcerned to probe her. Less of a study than a retreat.

I am a resting point, she thought again.

She could be that for him.

'I told Ryan it was because I felt like I was stuck with it. Objectively, I know it's a good dress. I bought it from an antique store, so I'm sure it spent a while collecting dust too, but what mattered was that it was new to me. It was *me* wanting to feel new for a change, rather than something tired and overused. And I did, for a while, but after showing up to every event in the same thing, I wanted the option of not defaulting to it. I didn't want it to become something I depended on. I wanted to be able to choose it.'

Ingram's hand slid to the fabric, touching it softly. Aurelia felt his gaze as surely as if he'd touched her hand instead – his sight being such a tangible thing to her.

'You don't have to look at me wearing this dress tonight and think of it as an extension of *her.* Pretend that I'm wearing it because it makes me feel *new* and not for some other convoluted reason. Soon enough, I'll be out of it, and you'll never have to see me in it again.'

The line of his jaw softened as he looked up at her, eyes wide and exposed. She raised her hand and coaxed the ruddy brown hair from his forehead, leaving the glassiness in his eyes on full display for her to see.

'In my mind,' he murmured, 'you're always wearing that green dress.'

Aurelia removed her hand from his hair and placed it on his shoulder.

The last time she'd worn it, he'd made a point of dissuading her from the idea that he thought of her at all. The realization of it made the colour rush into her face. She swallowed the word: *Liar.*

'I should get changed.'

He nodded, sobering a little. 'Right.'

'I'll be out in a few.'

'Sure.'

Ingram shut the door behind him, and Aurelia collapsed onto Gemma Eakley's bed. She, too, had been fighting exhaustion, and it circled her like a predator waiting to pounce.

The time ticked by slowly, the terror of their errand gnawing like decay inside her body. She closed her eyes, pressing her palms to her eyes until she could see white.

Take the train. Find the witch. Survive the night.

She lifted her head and opened her eyes, but their quest still felt far away, like a dream.

The ward sealed shut behind Louisa. She frowned, unable to see the cottage. Ingram held out his hand, and the young girl took it.

Aurelia walked ahead of them, subjecting her fingers to the bite of the air in order to draw up the hem of Gemma's dress in her fists. Her boots would be muddy, but the cleaner she seemed, the more she might look like she belonged at a gala. That was if everyone looked past the fact that this dress was made of spring and frolicking in fields rather than sophistication and allure.

All she had to do was disappear, and she didn't entirely trust that was possible.

Louisa's voice was small behind her, and Ingram's voice so low that it might have been a whisper, but she could hear it all. The fear behind her question: 'You're coming back, aren't you?'

The uncertainty in his response: 'Of course, I am. I wouldn't leave you for ever.'

Aurelia wanted to hunt down the shapeshifter and tear her limb from limb, but in that moment, she prayed that they would not find her in London – that her gut instinct about modern art holding no interest to her would be proven correct. Anything to convince herself that she would bring him back in one piece.

Then, maybe she would consider the rest of what Alaric said and return to Cambridge on her own. She had no part in whatever came next for them, even if they had already made a new chamber for themselves in her heart.

It wasn't her problem. Nor was she theirs.

She was at Alaric's door again, knocking on it. Through the windows, she could see that the library was already erected as they entered. She didn't fully understand how the shop and the library could exist simultaneously, except for magic – which, in her book, was as good a reason as any.

Alaric hurried them inside as if they'd interrupted some time-sensitive task. 'Quickly,' he whispered and locked the door behind them.

They would be swift to leave once Lou was in his care, but he couldn't risk being overheard. He asked in a hushed tone, 'When will you be back?'

'Tonight,' Ingram said. 'Can't say when.'

The caretaker stroked his scruff considerately. 'A word, please.' He slid his arm around the younger man and pulled him farther into a deep aisle.

Louisa leaned against Aurelia's hip in a way she'd done with her mother once before. It made Aurelia terribly uncomfortable. Still, she let her hand fall to Louisa's short, thin braid and twirled it around with her finger.

'You're coming back too, right?' Louisa whispered.

Aurelia nodded and forced a smile.

'Can I tell you something?'

'Sure.'

Louisa sighed. Her voice dropped even lower, and she said, 'I think you're *really* cool. I wish we could be friends.'

'Why can't we?'

'Because I don't like tea. Teddy lets me have some of his and I hate it. It tastes like grass.'

'I wouldn't make you drink tea, Lou. I wouldn't make you do anything you don't want to do. I'd be a bad friend if that were the case.'

'Oh.' Louisa considered it thoughtfully. 'I guess we can be friends then.'

Aurelia smiled. From down the aisle, Ingram turned toward where she and Louisa stood. Alaric was whispering something into his ear, the man's hand holding him in place by the nape of his neck. Ingram nodded at something said, still watching her.

Why was he looking at her like that – like she was a hunted creature in their crosshairs? She couldn't hear them, no matter how closely she tuned in. Seconds later, as she occupied herself with the braid between Louisa's shoulders, he sidled up to her, void of such wariness, wearing only the intensity she'd already been acquainted with.

'Ready?' asked Ingram. He brushed his palms down the front of his coat, ridding himself of the conversation like lint. 'Have fun while we're gone, darling. Be good.'

Be good. Be safe.

Ingram kissed the part in Lou's hair before his hand curled around Aurelia's shoulder.

'Ready?' he asked again.

Alaric was still watching her, puzzling over her. She tore her eyes away and turned squarely to Ingram, nodding.

'We have a train to catch.'

CHAPTER TWENTY

Londoners buzzed around her as she and Ingram boarded the Circle Line toward Blackfriars. Through the skylight at Liverpool Street Station, Aurelia saw daylight. It hadn't taken them long to reach Townsend from Cambridge, but the climate was slightly warmer. She felt the difference between her fingers, on her exposed cheeks, and caught the familiar sense of normalcy that she had been missing amongst the crowd of city folk.

Cambridge was starkly different from London, at least to her foreign sensibilities, but it was easier to disappear here. Everyone had something to do – a friend to text or a song to plug into. She stepped into the packed carriage of the London Underground, nestling between melded bodies and leather bags to follow her companion, who moved with startling ease for someone so tall and rigid. His hand found a vacant space around the yellow bar above their heads, and he grasped it as the tube gave a quick lurch and snaked away. She steadied herself against him as she searched for a handle of her own, and after a few seconds, his hand came around the back of her waist as if to say: 'Use me instead.'

That was the only comfort he could provide. His gaze

flickered nervously over the heads of the crowd. Aurelia listened. She couldn't see much in the close proximity of it all, and she forced an evener breath, feeling mildly claustrophobic.

She heard little over the shrill whine of the tube along its tracks, whirring beneath the streets of London, rocking her like an inconsolable baby. The clamour of metal and squeaking shoes was its own kind of symphony, from an orchestra of people dressed just like Theodore Ingram. She had been to London several times with Ryan, but she hadn't been so observant then – at least, not of the people. She had stared up at skyscrapers, along the grooves of the walls of historic buildings, inhaling the scent of Indian food and peri-peri chicken. The people were a blur for her then, but now, she saw them a little more clearly. With Ingram's arm around her, she had a reference point.

She thought he might have had a place among the gorgeous aesthetes of Pembroke, but it was a janky fit compared to the one he occupied here.

Soon the doors slid open, and the voice of London instructed: 'Mind the gap.'

'I thought you said we were getting off at Blackfriars,' she said.

'Not yet.'

She assimilated haphazardly into the stream of bodies that flooded from the station. The wind whipped her hair over her face, stinging her skin. The pockets of her borrowed blue coat were compromised, baring her fingers to the frigid winds through thin, moth-eaten fabric. Ingram ushered her along as he seized a lull in traffic to cross the street, and the cold kiss of the air skated beneath the hem of her dress. Aurelia shivered, grumbling to herself.

With a grimace, Ingram demanded, 'Where are your gloves?'

'I couldn't find them.'

'Did you even look?'

'*Yes,*' she said. 'Matter of fact, I did. Not that pointing it out to me *now* would make me any less cold.'

'Hmm.'

She struggled to keep up with his pace, but it was the pace of everyone around her too, and she felt one step away from drowning in it.

'Where are we going?'

'Killing some time. Gala doesn't start for a couple of hours.'

Her arm flew out to slow him, and he came to a halt at her touch, stepping aside until they were both leaning against a cream-coloured stone wall. Only inches from the steady stream of people, they were somehow completely isolated, like being in the silent eye of a storm. Never had Aurelia been somewhere where privacy was so *loud*. She reasoned it was easy to keep secrets living here. Everyone moved too rapidly to catch more than a few words in whatever they had to say to each other.

'Well?' she asked.

He shrugged, tucking his hands into his pocket. 'I need a little distraction, all right? Need to find things to do. Places to go. If I think too hard about what comes next, I'm afraid I'll turn around and run.'

'You're *afraid* . . .' She trailed off, unsure of why she felt the need to repeat it in the first place. It benefited neither of them to send that word into the ether. And though it was barely a whisper beneath the cacophony of cars and countless accented conversations, he caught it.

His lips twisted in dismay. 'Aren't *you?*'

'Sure,' she admitted, compliant as he pulled her back into line. 'I'm just not sure where we're going right now.'

He gave a mirthless little laugh. 'You'd be upset with me if I told you.'

'Now I *need* to know.'

Ingram was already turning her again through the cracked-open door of a small store. A bell above the doorway called the attention of two white-haired men to her – whose width took up most of the narrow passage.

'Is that one of ours?' one man asked, hopeful. Ingram brushed his hands down his coat lapels and nodded.

'Good eye.'

Frighteningly good, she thought. The man who had spoken – the bonier, dark-skinned man – was referring to Ingram's black wool coat, which Aurelia thought looked the same as every other expensive black wool coat she'd seen in her lifetime.

'What brings you in today?' asked the other man gruffly.

Aurelia had only started scouring the shelves of stacked tartan and lush knits when Ingram replied, 'Just these.'

She spun to the counter again and caught him pushing a pair of gloves toward the thin man.

'*No.*'

'Ignore her.'

'"Ignore her," my ass,' she muttered. 'Here, can I?'

The man behind the counter gave a knowing look to Ingram, and her face went hot with shame.

The cost was more than she'd ever paid for a pair of gloves – she caught the handwritten digits on the tag before the man had even relinquished them. Too much. She knew she couldn't afford them, not with all the other things she vowed to pay Ingram back for, and it *stung*. How a number like that could weigh so heavily on her chest was inconceivable, but it didn't stop the compression of her lungs from bearing down on her.

Saying nothing, she moved past him, back through the door where her reason to need a proper pair of gloves was there to embrace her and force its frozen arm down her tightening throat. She tucked her hands beneath her arms and managed a deep, meditative breath.

The things that had wrung the tension between them over the years were always so small. Hundreds of words in clipped tones and cast glances of bitterness stretching her thinner and thinner. The irony of being thrust back into that scornful place by something as small as a price tag filled her with loathing. Such a *small thing* that might have looked like kindness to him that endowed her with the unbearable urge to cry.

The bell jingled behind her only a minute later, a sigh amidst the urban chatter. With her back turned to the door, she sniffled. It was the only indicator that she might have actually started to cry if he had not been close enough to hear it.

His hand grazed her shoulder as he greeted her again, not cheerily but without any note of concern: 'Hey.'

She shrugged it off lightly. 'Don't.'

'It was nothing, Schwartz,' he said.

'That's why it bothers me, Ingram. It was nothing to *you.* Just like it was nothing to buy me coffee, or a train ticket to Townsend. Or the round-trip ticket for both of us to come *here.* I haven't even questioned how much it cost to get into this gala, but the fact that you bought our entry for that too is just as concerning. It's not like I'll ever be able to unlearn the fact that you're loaded beyond belief, but it would be . . .'

She swallowed her next words, knowing they would emerge uneven and weak. Not something she wanted to be – with him, with *anyone.* He stared down at her with that familiar knit in his brow like he was anticipating volatility.

Reason assured her it wasn't volatility waiting at the threshold of her unfinished sentence, rather a naive embarrassment.

She met his gaze. 'It would be nice not to be reminded of what I can't provide for myself all the time. It's nothing to you, but it's an IOU for me. I don't need expensive gloves. Just something cheap to last me until I get back to my flat. Every time you give me an option that's out of reach for me, it feels like charity.'

Ingram's stare left hers, and he gave a plain nod. 'Is there anything I can do to convince you that I don't see you as charity?'

Meekly she shrugged. 'I should probably tell myself that you don't like me enough to do nice things for me – even out of charity.'

He rolled his eyes. 'That's a start.'

'Can we go now?'

'After you put these on.' Ingram carefully unfurled the gloves in question, removing the pin with the tag before it could be read again. 'It's not charity by the way. But it *is* several days too late. Happy Hanukkah.'

She bit down on her bottom lip. Despite the knot of shame that bounced around in her chest, she couldn't have been angry with him – not *truly* angry. At this point, her anger was just another garment to wear, to change at will with little consequence. Underneath all that, she was somewhere between willing and fond when it came to Theodore Ingram.

That she resented his cavalier use of his finances and that he somehow knew precisely what colours of yarn she'd want around her hands . . . Those ideas coexisted in her mind surprisingly well.

She sniffled again, gathering her composure.

'Do you like them, at least? It's all right if you don't.'

He sounded so cautious that it almost made her break again.

'I love them.'

A blithe smile wound up the corners of his lips. It felt like the easiest thing in the world to build one up for him too.

'Let's keep moving then,' he said. 'Wherever you want to go – I'll take you.'

Eventually, he took her to the edge of the Thames, near Blackfriars station. By then, everything had darkened enough to trigger the streetlamps and neon shop signs. Aurelia sipped the paper cup of tea in her hand and offered it to Ingram. Wordless, he took it, leaning over the wall of the bridge to watch the ripples of colour dance along the river.

'We're close,' he said. 'It's just there.'

'Maybe we should turn around, then.'

'I want to show you something first.'

There was something vaguely intimate about that phrase. He'd stopped hiding from her, but willingly sharing things with her didn't have to be the thing that came after. Aurelia only expected progress to be made to a certain degree.

She wondered if he felt the need to make amends, to say goodbye. Her hands found the shape of the eye at the bottom of her pocket, and she ran her thumb over it absent-mindedly.

He gestured to something on the other side of the river and said, 'You see that building with all the white lights? With the purple light at the top?'

There were plenty of colours across the river to discern from, and they all seemed to meld together against the vibrant shade of deep blue. He moved from the edge to let her see it from his point of view.

'That one there. That's where my parents live.'

'You say that like you've only ever seen it from this side of the Thames.'

He smiled faintly. 'I've never been. It's not where I grew up. I'd rather show you that place, but I'm afraid we don't have enough time today.'

'Some other time, then.'

He nodded, possibly without understanding the implications of her words. 'Some other time.'

To talk about other times at all seemed hopeful. Alaric's words were an echo in her mind as she idled with the paper cup in her hand. His warning that Ingram's duty to the family might not permit him a return to the life of academia they'd been so devoted to.

Aurelia had thought little about how much of Lou's life depended on his until now. Without Gemma, they had no one but each other. Where he would go, so would Louisa; that was the optimistic outcome. The more likely one was that he would go wherever Louisa needed to be, which was not Cambridge.

The mere thought of his absence at the Pembroke College pub filled her with dread.

'You know, Schwartz, I let you carve me like a ham to find my deliciously tormented past, and yet I know so little about yours. Tell me, did you fight with your sister a lot? Or go to summer camps? I swear, you've been ripping me open for details and deflecting from all of your own.'

'I don't think I asked you to show me where your parents live. And I'm pretty sure I've told you things before.'

'I know I had to extend into the boundaries of your religion to keep your fingers from getting frostbitten, but other than that . . . Tell me again. My memory's shit.'

She tucked herself close beside him. 'Doesn't sound like a very good ham.'

'Try me.'

'You do realize you can give a person a gift apart from on celebrated holidays, right?'

'The barbarity,' he deadpanned.

She sighed despondently. 'Besides, it's my dad that's Jewish, but I've never – I'm not exactly . . .'

She didn't know where to begin. Judaism was matrilineal, and even though Aurelia had no relationship with her mother, she'd learned enough to know that her mother was not Jewish. Her father had lapsed often in his faith and never took his girls to worship. She couldn't speak the necessary language to recite verses from the Siddur. The majority of her experience with the Torah came from Cambridge. In all senses, she had ostracized herself from the identity of her family; and she had let her father's faith become another piece of curriculum. Another tear in a weave that seemed too extensive to stitch back up.

Ingram started, 'You aren't . . .?'

'My family and I have never quite matched, but I've always been the oddest one out. There were things I believed in that made belief in anything else unfathomable. But we carried out most things differently, not just faith. Dad's comfortable where he is, always has been. He avoids new things. He's had the same job for twenty years, eats the same four meals on rotation. My sister and I grew up dreaming of big things and bright fantasies; and that might have made us closer if those things weren't in opposite directions. She's chasing a North Star and I'm chasing the history of medieval religions.'

'Is that not important?'

'To me?' She raised an eyebrow. 'Absolutely. I love what I do. It makes me feel capable. I couldn't imagine deciding to pursue another subject. You know, this is Ryan's third degree change?'

'Can't say I did,' he answered, mirroring her lean against the wall.

'They've already switched subjects twice. They wanted to be an animator. Got accepted to an art college in Manchester before they decided to try their hand at illustration. Now they're here . . .'

She lowered her voice, mockingly. 'Studying *art history*. It's hard to watch them talk about it sometimes – I know they don't love it. They told me that something about illustration wasn't clicking for them, and I always thought they were being too hard on themselves, because they're *fantastic*. Just – look.'

She fished her phone out of her bag and found the last illustration that Ryan sent through text: a cosy, green gouache piece of Aurelia in their kitchen. As he looked, she thought it would have been better to scroll farther up and show him something that wasn't her. Was it vain? Would he even know it was her if he saw her through Ryan's eyes – easy and domestic, with her hair a little messier than usual?

'It's stunning,' he said.

'I know,' she replied. 'I wish they knew it too.'

She wiped the eager smile from her face and tucked her phone away.

'So, what *do* you believe in?'

'That's a little heavy, don't you think?'

'For a student of religion? I would have thought the opposite. Where does this chase bring you?'

She turned back to the river, letting her sigh roll down into the lapping water. The mirror image within it looked oddly still. She thought of home, the cool rain, and all the streams she'd dip her shoes into when they camped. Cambridge was easy to immerse herself in because of the odd similarities she discovered, but even the lush greens and historic buildings could not give her the same rose-coloured memory. But desire and single-mindedness brought her here. She never expected it to be the same. Only expected it to be beautiful – and it *was*. Undeniably beautiful.

Now what? Finish her degree and do *what*? She laughed whenever someone asked her that question, but it haunted her in private.

'I'm a witch,' she began. 'Like both my parents before me. I never knew my mother, but my dad always said I was just like her.' Sometimes that was a good thing, but most of the time, it was distress that marked her father's features. Like she and her mother weren't comparable in eye colour or dialect but by sharpened teeth and bloodlust. 'That kind of thing is hard to hear when the person in question abandoned you. But when I was younger, I used to pray to *her*. Not that she was dead or anything, but neither was God. To me, they were both the same kind of unperceivable deity. I thought that if a god could hear me, maybe she would too. I'd ask her to come back. And I thought, maybe then, I could finally meet the woman who left me with this' – her hands eased through her hair – 'this uneven curl pattern and half-chewed perception of love.'

Ingram's brow furrowed. An admission like that should have been heavier, but Aurelia had stopped deifying her mother years ago. Now it felt like less of a loss than when she'd had her wisdom teeth removed, and God was only a thing she studied in school.

She'd done fine without her mother. She'd done well on her own, for herself and no one else. For all that she had accomplished, she held the idea of her mother at bay, so as not to fall into the trap of appealing to ghosts and shadows.

'That's not entirely fair,' said Ingram. 'Calling love half-chewed.'

'It's not like I said it was indigestible,' Aurelia told him. 'I have plenty of it for my friends. Just not a lot for anyone else.'

'Is that what happened to Lawrence?' He said it so abruptly that Aurelia wondered if she'd heard him correctly.

'*Nothing* happened with Lawrence,' she told him, shoulders sagging. 'I don't know why everyone thinks that.'

'Because he did,' Ingram replied. 'He talked about you often. Not to me, of course. I'm sure you told him how insufferable I was before I could ask him to stop. Still, I heard . . . He made no effort to hide how much he fancied you.'

She'd left many burnt bridges behind her, but she made a point never to look back at them, because she thought it would hurt – like a wound beneath stitches, still tender and raw. Like Orpheus damning Eurydice with his affection.

It *did*.

'He wanted things I couldn't give him.'

Incredulously, Ingram asked, 'Like sex?'

'Like *love*. I'm a big fan of the one-night stand, y'know? But I hated the part where I had to wake up next to someone in the morning, or when they'd ask me, "When can I see you again?" Having to tell someone who thought it could be something more, that it was just a fling. I try to make it clear, but no one likes to be told they aren't desirable another time over again.'

He avoided her inspection, ashamed of this dead and buried resentment for her that he'd dragged back to his surface. Was he jealous? She didn't think she had anything that Ingram would covet. She had always assumed he and Lawrence were close (and maybe they were), but some intimacies belonged to lovers that friends would never know. She'd been wrong about his connection to Marga. What if she was wrong about Lawrence, too?

Who was she to think she knew what Ingram wanted?

'I get it,' he said placidly. 'It's a perilous descent.'

'Mhmm.' She pressed her lips together, feeling the reminder settle like an aftertaste on her tongue. 'Affection isn't something I enjoy giving up.'

'Does it always feel like giving up? Giving something away?'

Of course it did. Even saying it aloud to him was enough to make her uneasy.

Before she could respond, Ingram said, 'I don't think it should feel that way.'

'We don't think about love the same way. Honestly, I don't think we agree on most things.'

He grinned. 'Fair.'

The curve of his lips did little to quell the quick rhythm of her heartbeat. Her history of romantic aversion and her festering affection for him were somehow *also* coexisting inside her.

It was a lot of feeling, too much, even. And for someone who always needed an answer – a solution – there was nothing she could do to appease it.

A steady breeze pushed through her hair, and it would have been so *easy* to follow it into him. She knew it was wrong to detail all the ways she couldn't be steady for him and then ask him to keep her warm, but she glimpsed the sight of her own gloved hands folded on the wall and thought, *Aren't you doing that already?*

It was getting darker with each minute. The city lights across the river had made the fact less obvious to her until now, when she found herself looking for a distraction from him. She traced the skyline once. Then again.

'And your friend Ryan?' he asked. 'You're close?'

The attempt was pointless. Ingram wanted to be looked at. He had a face *made* to be looked at.

'Closer than anyone, probably. Why? What about them?' she asked.

'What would they think about how you love?'

'That's different. It's a different kind of love. I wouldn't subject them to any of the other.'

Not that she hadn't thought about it. She held it all at a distance, but deeper wants still crossed her mind. She wanted to be held, touched, admired. They were the only person she trusted not to take her heart and wrench it in half. To others, she had become nothing more than sex, and that wasn't exactly the kindest thought to mull over in her mind, but it was the sensible one. The one she made herself default to, knowing she would never win her race against time. A promise to herself as much as it was a limit.

'You say that like your affection is a rotten thing,' he said.

Aurelia shrugged. 'Because it *is*. Mine is. Like you said, it's all diluted.'

And it's just you I'm rotten with.

'Suppose I did say that.'

'It's muddy in there,' she said. 'It's more grime than tenderness. Nobody wants that.'

Ingram's coat brushed her hip. She didn't see him move

closer, so she assumed she'd been wandering, but she examined him from this angle nonetheless. His dark lashes and warm eyes – always kind when the rest of him was so cruel. His face went pink and splotchy at the mercy of the wind, marking out the spots she would have wanted to kiss if she wasn't so keen on digging herself into a grave.

''S pretty dark out now,' he said.

The museum loomed nearby, illuminated in vibrant neon. Those that walked the path behind them were dressed to the nines, neatly coiffed and elegant. Listening hard, Aurelia heard music too, the strumming of a guitar by the entrance of the Tate Modern. A man was singing, tearing apart a Tracy Chapman song while another man dropped a note in his guitar case. A group of friends staggered along the pathway behind them, coats of tassels and fringe slung over their shoulders and a smattering of bright glitter on their cheeks. They laughed over a shared phone screen, holding each other up between uneven steps.

No one could have known what she and Ingram were there for, that they were both searching for danger and dreading it. No one was there to fear an ambush. She wished she could have witnessed that night through their veil of optimism too.

At that moment, with the river lapping quietly beneath them and dusk fast approaching, Aurelia could pretend that nothing would hurt her. She wanted to live in those hours for an eternity – close to him, somewhere new, in another dress. Maybe in that version of history, she would kiss him. Maybe he would let her.

'I guess we should go inside,' Aurelia said.

'Guess so.'

Neither of them moved from the wall. She thought of curling her hands over the edge, until someone would have to pull her away or scrape her off like a piece of dried gum.

But they had an objective, a mission, and dire consequences awaiting them. Nothing about tonight would be more important than what happened in the Tate.

'Are you scared?' he asked.

'Didn't I already tell you?'

He nodded, clearing his throat. 'I thought you might have been saying that for my sake. To ease my thoughts.'

'Did it work?' Worrying about him might have been the only thing that kept her from running too. She slid her hand beneath his coat and touched his stomach. 'Can I . . .?'

'Please.'

With his permission, she let her arm circle the rest of his waist then, too. Her grip tightened until she could bury her cheek against the knit of his black sweater, where his shoulder began to curve into his chest. She wanted to be tucked under his coat and kept hidden like one of his thousand secrets.

'You're breathing hard,' he murmured, his breath tickling her scalp.

'So are you.'

'I don't know what comes next.'

'I do,' she said. 'We go back to Townsend. I leave for Cambridge, and you come with me. We fight again. You act like I'm the worst thing that's ever happened to you, and I confirm to my housemate that I hate you profoundly. And everyone you love is OK.'

His hand came beneath her borrowed coat, his fingers moving in slow circles against her back.

'That's beginning to sound more like wishful thinking every day.'

She nodded, detaching herself. 'It'll be the truth.'

It had to be.

CHAPTER TWENTY-ONE

In the lower atrium stood hundreds of people in their best attire, laughing with drinks in hand, scattered about the floor. 'You're Celia's boy?' asked the attendant at the museum's entry. Ingram nodded, unenthused, and they passed without a ticket check.

'Is this a good time to ask what your parents do?'

He huffed. 'My father's a doctor. Mother's head curator here.'

'Here?'

'Yes,' he said curtly. '*Here,* Schwartz.'

From the main level, where the majority of the people gathered, one could look upward past several stories of art galleries to the glass ceiling and into the night. Aurelia didn't make it that far. She caught sight of those on the upper levels with their arms hanging over the glass barriers, looking down at them and the jazz quartet that played in the centre of the room.

Most of them were older. She gathered from the tight bouffants and well-pressed suit jackets that they were all some degree more comfortable financially than her family had ever been, and the reminder was getting old.

Ingram fit in like a lost tooth. Within seconds, he had drawn the attention of another older man with crisp white hair and a lintless coat. Ingram whispered something too quickly, too quietly for Aurelia to catch it before the man was within earshot, and then he pulled away promptly.

'It's been a while!' said the man.

Ingram nodded, baring a cleanly fabricated smile. He held out his hand, and the two men shook. Aurelia tried not to care that he didn't greet her – she wasn't here to socialize. She let her gaze wander as the others fell into a cordial reintroduction. The man reminded him of his name, Clem Bradford, but it was obvious to her, from only the lilt in his voice, that Ingram had no recollection of him even as he lied and said *he did.*

He lied so masterfully. His comfortable stance and poised responses crafted a disguise of complete knowing. He looked too much like the version of him she knew in Cambridge – dazzling and proud, disgustingly perfect. She hated the sight of it but couldn't help admiring his false composure. Only when Clem Bradford mentioned the fabled Celia Ingram did her counterpart address her. 'Rory darling, this is a friend of my mother's.'

She shook Bradford's hand, made herself alert to the conversation at hand, all while running the word *darling* over in her mind. Running it into the ground until it was bloody, reduced to pulp. 'Hi there.'

'Evening,' said Bradford. 'How's the museum been treating you so far?'

'We haven't been introduced yet,' she answered.

'Ah, first time. Have you been to London before?'

'Aurelia studies with me in Cambridge,' Ingram explained.

'Our tastes are somewhere within antiquated and archaic. I've never been keen on modern art, but I thought I could weather one night out here if I had another medievalist with me.'

Bradford raised both unruly white brows. Suggestively, he said, 'So, you're classmates?'

'Colleagues,' Aurelia said, barely noting the quirk at the corner of Ingram's mouth. His hand slid around her lower back and tugged her closer. It seemed Ingram had no intention of playing along with her charade. To Bradford, it probably looked like she was leaning into him.

The man chuckled like he was in on a joke they didn't intend to make. 'Maybe you'd like a tour of the museum, then?'

She looked up at Ingram, his face too close for comfort. He met her gaze and smiled.

'I'll be sure to show her the new Maciá room,' he said, delegating himself the task.

'Of course,' said Bradford. 'It's actually moving to a new home soon. "Taking Flight". It's a good thing you're here to catch it before it leaves.'

'Why don't we head upstairs, then?' Ingram asked her. As if she could say no. As if she thought that anything about this conversation was preferable to her.

'I'm game. It was great to meet you,' she said to Clem Bradford, as if she'd retained anything he said to Ingram while she was scouring for exits.

'Pleasure's mine.'

Had they been inside the museum more than five minutes before Clem Bradford approached them? She had underestimated just how much Ingram had a presence here. Though her classmate hadn't remembered him, he left enough of a mark of his own to be identified so easily. Bradford certainly wouldn't be the last. Ingram had a magnetism that pulled separately from the reputation of his mother. Even with her last name, he was an island.

A woman who looked to be close in age offered them champagne from a platter. Aurelia couldn't recall an event where she had ever been offered something this way. 'Cheers,' Ingram said and tapped their glasses together. It was strange being reacquainted with this version of him – having his hand on her back like they weren't just parallel lines but twisted together as one. Watching him lie without being on the opposing side to him.

'Do you lie that easily to me?' she asked softly.

He swallowed and replied, 'I don't lie to you. Not any more.'

Her thoughts reconvened at the spot where they were still attached to one another. 'I don't think we convinced him that we're just *colleagues*.'

That seemed to remind him of it too. Deterring him was something else, though – not something she particularly wanted to do.

Ingram's voice fell low and smooth against her ear. 'Well, while Bradford was boring you half to death, someone else was ogling you like their next meal. That man over there.'

'Maybe it's our shapeshifter,' she whispered, amused only to hide her true discontent. 'Maybe I *am* a meal.'

'If it's her, then she harbours more lust than bloodlust.'

The humour in his voice was spiteful. Sure, he was still holding her, but he wasn't looking at her. His gaze was somewhere in the crowd, lost with the man in question.

Carefully, she asked, 'Is there a reason your hand is still there?'

He tilted his head down to look at her, his eyes half-covered by lowered lids and dark lashes. 'Should I move it?

'I'm not exactly aggrieved by it. Just alert to its presence.'

His fingers shifted further around her waist, curling into the fabric of her dress. 'Because I like touching you, Schwartz. You ground me. And,' he whispered, 'if we have the misfortune of running into my parents tonight, you're my *girlfriend*. Not my bloody colleague.'

'Why?'

'Because I'm dashing, of course. And you like the way I smell.'

'That's not what I meant,' argued Aurelia.

He was right, though. She'd found that scent to be most potent in the crook of his neck, first on the hillside, then in his bed. Aurelia would never admit to him that she'd followed that earthen, citrusy sensation like her own North Star ever since.

'I made myself look like an idiot in front of Bradford for nothing, then,' she grumbled, taking a larger gulp from her glass. The band went quiet as a tall woman took to the stage and introduced herself in a welcoming speech.

'It was an afterthought,' Ingram whispered. 'But if you need a *thanks* for that – thanks for that.'

The woman's voice bounded off the concrete walls. Aside from the floral centrepieces that marked tables on the perimeter of the main floor, the Tate was an industrial, lifeless construction. It posed an issue for her, surmounting her aesthetic preferences. If she called for natural intervention within the limits of her gift here, it would not come. At least one concrete wall stood between her and anything rooted in soil, though she knew green magic would hardly be useful to her if they came face to face with Leona. Aurelia had her fingers crossed that Ingram could point himself in the right direction if—

No.

What they needed was to find the shapeshifter alive. For their own benefit, it wouldn't come to a point where Ingram's gift was necessary.

She leaned into him. To the room, they didn't look like two desperate witches chasing carnage but lovers, and it was easy to play that part with him. It was easier to fixate on that ploy than what would come next – that she would place her hand into her pocket where the wandering eye lay and charm it to *open*.

When she looked toward the centre of the room, she could see Marga, sword-impaled and seeping with blood, imprinted on the backs of her eyelids like a trick of the light.

'Maybe you should give me a rundown of what you expect to happen tonight.'

'Hopefully, nothing.'

'With your *parents*, Ingram.'

He sighed, having understood her the first time. The crowd around them applauded at something the tall woman said, granting him cover to speak clearly.

'All my life,' he whispered, 'I've been inadequate to them, except for the times when I was nothing at all. And every time I'm here, I do my best to assure them that I'm more than what they think of me. Prove I'm successful . . . In at least one aspect of my life, I'd like them to see that.'

He left that statement with room to fill. The hand on her waist suddenly felt hollow.

'That's stupid,' she said, which made him frown. 'You have top marks at one of the most rigorous academic institutions in the world.'

'Second to you,' he said.

'Stop that,' she pleaded, and the tension in his jaw softened. 'You know you're doing better than almost anyone else in our programme. I don't understand how they could see you as anything *but* successful.'

With another sigh, he answered, 'I've been wondering that for years, Schwartz. Beats me.'

The crowd erupted into applause again before dispersing. He kept himself alert, although Aurelia couldn't tell if he was looking for Leona or his parents. As it thinned, she became more conscious of the level of formality that everyone seemed to carry – and how she didn't have it.

'Honestly,' she muttered, 'I don't know if *this* is how you spell out success.'

'Might not be up to dress code, but it's entirely you.'

In another version of history that might have been an insult, but the way he looked at her dictated the opposite. He'd said one thing, but the sincerity in his eyes left her with an addendum.

It's entirely you. And I like you, Schwartz.

And then came that smile. A truly devious curve of his red lips that sunk a final blow into her chest.

Bastard.

'You said there was a new exhibit?'

'I guess it isn't new,' he said. 'But it is my favourite. They should have it open tonight.'

'Take me, then. I should see it before we leave.' Before they could encounter something grim. The finality of it fell silent between them.

He led her upstairs, and Aurelia traced the sea of faces for a mark of gold as she went, glass in hand. The second floor was far less busy than the first, and the third even less so. This was where they stopped – Aurelia leaned over the glass barrier to peer back down as she had watched others do to her. Ingram paced down the dim corridor and back as her gaze roved through the ground-floor crowd again.

'She could be any one of them,' he said.

'Or none of them. I wish I found that comforting.'

'I wish we knew what we were looking for,' he replied.

Aurelia's fingers curled around her flute of champagne, holding it to her chest as an excuse to measure the heaviness of her heartbeat. Taking in the enormity of the event, the scope of their uncertainty, panic rose in her chest.

'All right?' he asked.

She nodded, coming to realize how tight her grip was. Ingram donned his usual mask of reservedness, leaning beside her. With the flute in a more delicate hold, she tossed the last of her champagne back before placing it on a marble bench beside the barrier. Again, Ingram frowned.

'What?'

'That's a sculpture, Schwartz.'

'You're joking, right?'

He remained firmly in place, his features unmoving. Aurelia felt the colour drain from her face, and she swiftly retrieved her glass before one of the few event goers around them could spot it.

'Modern art is a sham,' she muttered underneath her breath. 'It looks like a bench.'

Ingram's face contorted in an attempt to hide his amusement. 'It *is*. I'm messing with you.'

'Dick.'

He gave a lazy chuckle.

'You're not supposed to have a sense of humour.'

His hand flew to his heart, feigning hurt by her words. 'Why ever not?'

Because she couldn't deny how handsome he was when he laughed, and if he caught her off guard, she might not say the right thing. She might divulge too much or make him a promise she couldn't keep. The lines beside the corners of his mouth deepened into the hollows of his cheeks when he smiled, the crease in his brow smoothed away again . . . His laughter was an elusive sound, which made it so much more valuable to her.

More dangerous, too.

Slowly, he asked, 'Would it be wrong to assume that our friend can't change her clothing when she transforms?'

She couldn't answer. It was possible that the same gifts could vary between different witches. There were few laws of magic that could be written in stone. Few that wouldn't yield. Aurelia knew enough to control the magic that darkened her blood, but Gabrielle warned that she would never fully realize it. No one could . . .

Which meant that Leona could thwart their expectations entirely. Maybe Leona's clothing kept its form while she changed her skin. Maybe it would change its form when she did, and they ought to have kept their eyes peeled for a boy wearing the uniform of a server instead.

Maybe she could disappear, transparent as night itself.

Aurelia didn't respond immediately, until she remembered that, whatever she *did* know, it was likely that Ingram knew even less . . .

'What do you know about shapeshifters?' Aurelia asked him.

'I have . . . A narrow view of them,' he said. 'The things I know won't help us find Leona.'

The answer gave her no comfort. Shapeshifting, like all other forms of witchcraft, was a malleable gift whose terms could evolve with time. Gabrielle, who had been thorough and scrupulous with Aurelia's instruction, could not have taught her anything past the principles of transformation.

Aurelia could do nothing more than nod in acceptance. 'I was told that I should never trust a shapeshifter if I had the chance to meet one.'

'Who told you that?'

'My tutor. I see what she means now, but it always felt like such a narrow mindset. I can't help wondering why Leona would divulge to us that she's a shapeshifter. I mean, I wouldn't tell anyone . . . I wouldn't give anyone a reason to doubt me. No one should have to ask themselves if the person in front of them is who they claim to be.'

'You'd make a compelling politician, Schwartz.'

She bumped her shoe against his and said, 'But I'd be a terrible spy. Maybe you're a better fit for the job. "God hath given you one face, and you make yourselves another."'

A grin formed on his face that she struggled to ignore. 'Could that be the prince of Denmark?'

'You remembered,' she murmured.

'You say that like it wasn't meant for me.'

Their catalogue of inside jokes would reach a quicker end if he stayed in Townsend. It was hopeful enough to imagine that they would return to Cambridge and complete their respective programmes together – that Ingram wouldn't inevitably lose sight of his academic career to keep Louisa afloat.

She swirled her empty flute over the edge of the barrier. 'I don't know where to put this.'

He shrugged. 'Find something else that looks like furniture and try again.'

She didn't have the heart to pretend to be cross with him. She wanted him to wear that dazzling smile all evening without having to worry about who else might catch it.

'Here,' he said, taking the glass from her hand. With it, he gestured to a yellow light that poured from a doorway at the end of the corridor. 'That's the Maciá room. I'll meet you there.'

Aurelia eyed his half-empty glass with a silent question, and he downed the rest in answer.

'Be quick,' she said, hoping he'd understand that she really meant 'be safe'.

When he replied, 'Stay put,' it meant the same thing. She lost him to the crowd, and the whispers of birdsong beckoned her inside.

She took a seat in the centre of the bench that hugged a wide wall. Before her was a strange map, with bells and names she didn't recognize drawn on the wall parallel to where she sat. Whistles came from her left, chirps from her right. An installation from Oswaldo Maciá, read the plaque.

Aurelia thought she understood the pattern of birdsong, but it couldn't be that easy. They were jumbled and irregular, as nature intended, a response to a call.

All of it untrue. Maybe Ingram enjoyed the symphony of birds, but Aurelia had to shed the bitterness from her mind. If siren songs were not beautiful, men wouldn't have sailed to their deaths to chase them. She couldn't wield her magic in a place like this. This was not natural. With so much at stake, a place like this could be a prison. Every bit of distance she'd placed between herself and Ingram was a heartbeat skipped.

But if she closed her eyes . . .

She shut them and pretended there was no concrete barrier between her and the person she had to bring home. She was on the hillside in her mind, in that late spring dream again. She found Gemma Eakley in every call. A saint whose recognition was long overdue.

She learned that, *perhaps*, birds would always make her think of Gemma.

'Do you like it?'

Ingram joined her but didn't sit, offering his hand to pull her up again. Their palms slid together, his fingers cold to the touch. 'It's a little on the nose, don't you think?'

'How so?'

'The birds,' she said. 'And your augur.'

'Ah. Of course.' As if he'd forgotten what they were searching for all this time.

Aurelia let him help her to her feet, even let him tug her close to his body and fold his hands over the sides of her face. Her breath stalled in her throat.

'It's lovely here, isn't it?'

She'd wager that there was never a time in her life that she'd been as red as then, but his slender palms hid her embarrassment from view. Slowly, she nodded.

'Are you about to kiss me, Ingram?'

His fingers slipped further back and into her curls, and his eyes crinkled with the making of a new, secret smile. She let him do all of that, wondering if she could rationalize letting him go even further. If she gave him permission, how much would he take? Could she forgive herself for the question if it resulted in another burnt bridge? There was no time for her to decide otherwise as Ingram bowed his head and pressed his lips to one flushed cheek.

'Do you want me to?'

She decided nothing and kissed him herself. Her lips were hard and hungry against his, her hands falling beneath his coat to encircle his waist. He swallowed up the noise that slipped from her mouth, and the hands which had felt so hollow moments ago solidified against her skin, discovering places on her body that she had only imagined in her most harrowing dreams. Treacherous scenes of entangled limbs and feverish flesh. Things she wouldn't divulge for the sake of her own dignity.

'We could leave,' he managed to say, moving his lips to her jaw. 'You and me. We could turn around and go home.'

'We could,' she said, keen on pretending they had a place where *home* was something they shared. Birdsong would make her think of Gemma, but lies jogged the thought of Theodore Ingram. She was always pretending with him – to hate him, to love him, to feel assured. Maybe that's why this room was his favourite.

He kissed her again. She wound her arms around his shoulders and pulled him flush against her body. His lips trailed to the tender place beneath her ear, and he whispered, 'Can I show you something else?'

Aurelia nodded, breathless as he released her. His hands fell to her hips, his grip loosening slightly.

She mouthed, 'OK,' unable to say much more. Her mind was reeling. He took her hand, and she marvelled at how they fitted with such precision.

He whisked her down the steps from which they'd previously come. Aurelia tried to say something funny about stairs and steps, and though the meaning was lost in her incoherent babbling, he laughed anyway. It was an easy laugh, loud and brash, one she'd never heard.

Outside the installation, once the birdsong had fallen away, she heard the sound of his footsteps again too, like the beat of a song she'd heard thousands of times before. She knew the sound of his walk, the way he scribbled in the margins of his books, the ball of worry that was permanently embedded in his chest even as he boasted ease and nonchalance.

This wasn't him. His steps were too even.

By the time she realized it, his grip was fastened around her wrist. They were snaking through the crowd with frightening immediacy.

There were few things that she and Ingram had gathered about Leona, but one thing Aurelia was almost certain of was her penchant for witch's blood. It was precious and invaluable. Something you only relinquished in an act of desperation – to a witch you could trust. It carried their magic, their livelihoods. Their gifts and their identities . . . It could make a green witch into a reaper, if asked to. It could make a girl into a monster.

At the first clearing, she tried to jerk her hand back. Nails dug into her arm – ones that Ingram didn't have. She had stared at those pale, slender hands long enough to know that his nails were always filed short.

She surrendered to Leona's pull, afraid that resistance would only give her what she wanted – easy flesh to break, blood to spill.

'Cause a scene,' Leona said. 'I dare you.'

'That's your game, causing scenes,' Aurelia spat.

'You have me all wrong,' the shapeshifter whispered, smooth as Ingram's voice would ever be. 'I thought you wanted to see me. I thought you wanted me to come.'

'Go fuck yourself.'

The threat was hollow. Still wearing Ingram's face, Leona pulled her into a dark, concrete hall, isolated from the main event by a large, solid door. The humans behind her disappeared from view. The cold edge of a blade dug into Aurelia's side, Ingram's hand gripping the handle.

'Try anything funny and I draw blood,' she said in his voice.

'Isn't that what you want? Is that why you murdered my friend? Why you took Gemma?'

'Not like this. And not like *that.*'

Leona eased her through a final doorway into darkness, and if the place was ever soulless and vacant before, this room was beyond nature – beyond life.

CHAPTER TWENTY-TWO

'Hands behind your back.'

Trouble would come quicker if Aurelia resisted. Darkness engulfed her. Leona snapped her fingers, producing a weak flicker in the palm of her hand as she stepped away. Trading one spell for another, the facade of Ingram's body fell off her like snakeskin. The woman looked perhaps a few years older than Aurelia but aged with greyness, a translucence, that made Aurelia think of long-dead corpses.

'Clasp them,' Leona demanded.

Again, Aurelia complied, gritting her teeth as she unwillingly barred herself to the possibility of summoning a spell through her own palms. Her pulse quickened at the glint of the knife in Leona's other hand. It was a weak shine – from a weak flame. To produce a bright flame should have been one of the easiest common spells to master, but it faltered, an ebbing shadow obscuring her true face.

'Oh, this?' Leona gave the knife a wiggle. 'I don't have to be the one to hold it, if that's what scares you.'

'Go to hell.'

'Why did you come if you weren't going to be reasonable? This' – Leona gestured about the empty room like a circus ringleader, a maestro, pacing backwards into nothingness – 'is important to me. This should be important to you if you have any wits about you. You're a scholar, aren't you? Or were you at King's College on a whim that night? I could smell you from a mile away.'

Leona sheathed the knife in the band of her denim pants. 'I know you have questions, and I have answers. But I have questions too. Ask me something.'

To this, Aurelia's lips stilled. Every question seemed vital now that she'd lost the luxury of time.

'Where is he?' It was the first of many. The one which all others hinged on. If she could know nothing else before she left, he would help her to unravel the rest.

Leona clicked her tongue. 'I hoped you would know. I wanted him too. He leaves a strong trail in his wake, but I must have lost it.'

'Why are you—'

'My turn,' Leona interjected. Aurelia gritted her teeth and pressed her fingers into her knuckles behind her back. 'What injuries can you heal?'

'Excuse me?'

Across the hall, Leona huffed. 'Don't be coy. I know what you are, healer. Magic has a scent, the same way it has a colour and a sound. I know your gift. Bestowed by Raphael himself.'

The etching of lavender on the first token's surface was vivid in her mind's eye. It was a calling card, not for green magic but of an archangel. She had puzzled over it for days, yearning for another discovery to redeem her efforts, but the issue remained unresolved. The healer Leona needed was not her.

'I'm a green witch. You don't want me.'

'Maybe you found comfort in using your magic to heal the living body of the earth, but you aren't a green witch. These days, I am unsure of many things, but my born gift never fails me. I know what you are. I know what the boy is. And you both have something I want.'

'Is that why you killed my friend? For her gift?' Her words echoed, but so did the silence that followed. It was heavier, graver than the question itself.

The flame danced from one opened palm to the other, tossed easily like a toy.

'I wanted something of hers too. And she let me have it. She made me a promise and swore it to me. Then, she broke it. Oaths written in witch's blood cannot be broken.'

That was how magic, born of blood and intention, could be extracted. Offered by a witch from one slitted palm to another's – a willing transference of magical blood – it gave them new language to enact their gods-given intentions. The vocabulary of someone else's gifts.

'She wasn't killed by the terms of a broken blood oath, and you know it,' Aurelia said. She had to shout for the words to leave her mouth, but her apprehension seeped through effortlessly. 'No blood oath involves a sword. No blood oath involves stolen artefacts and burglary. You murdered her in a room full of people, and you would have murdered us too. Why should I trust you?'

'That's another question.'

'Answer it, or I give you nothing. You want a chance to win my obedience? This is it.'

Leona advanced, stalking like a cat toward its prey. As she neared, Aurelia traced the sharp outline of the woman's features, her dark, narrowed eyes and chapped lips. Her skin was pale and sheer like tissue, her features melting into her jowls like wet clay.

Behind her back, Aurelia's hands unfurled slowly, loosening around each other as Leona came close enough to touch.

'I know what you are, the way I knew what she was. And we *deserve* to be known. To be cherished. And yet, we live in fear of a lesser creature. I'm really tired of hiding.'

'Humans are not lesser,' Aurelia said.

'Aren't they? Have they not hunted us out of fear – that we are stronger and more capable than they are? What is this fear that witches will make the world a worse place when they have brought about disaster themselves? Consider it. We have the gifts of gods in our hands, and we are forced to carry on in these silly routines like humans do. To agree to their stasis and avoid making rifts.'

'I think . . .' Aurelia trained her gaze on Leona's cracked porcelain face. 'You owe me a question.'

The shapeshifter grimaced. 'The world could be a beautiful place with us at its helm, but they must prefer it spoiled. If they won't let us help, we must take it for ourselves.'

Aurelia leaned away. 'What do you want? Freedom or domination?'

'The one where you and I do not have to fear the pyres of humankind. Where we can be limitless.'

There would always be pyres. And if there were none now, then the scars of pyres built and burned long ago remained.

Memory prevailed where the present could not. They couldn't escape it. To believe that they could was heresy in itself.

'What you do is a beautiful thing, healer. I want you with me. With you by my side, we could be indestructible.'

'I am not a healer,' Aurelia insisted.

'You are not mature,' Leona said. 'You haven't come into your magic yet, but it yearns to break free. I could help you. We could help each other.'

By now, Ingram must have realized she was missing. She wondered if he would find her before she became the next nameless body in a building. Another witch, covered up without reverence. Had they buried those bodies? Or burned them to rid themselves of the essence of witchcraft? Had those witches been prodded for harvesting and ravaged like rats for testing?

'That is a beautiful dream, Leona.' Knowing that Marga's magic had been torn from her body before her death made Aurelia's lie burn all the way up.

'It is,' Leona answered. 'The fruits of my labour would be so sweet if I could only taste them. I'm afraid the time for us was ripe for years and now it has begun to rot.'

'And when I come with you,' Aurelia said, placing the promise of *when* within that hypothetical, 'do we eat together? Or do you wield me like a tool to dispose of once you've tired of me?'

Like my friend, she thought, who had done nothing wrong besides leave her trust in the wrong witch. It should have been Aurelia who she confided in. Aurelia, who Marga Palermo came to with her dilemmas. When the promise of an answer wound up at your door, it was easier to ignore the trouble that followed than to shut it in its face.

She should have been there instead.

'Humans keep so many gods. What difference would a few more make? It doesn't take much to be holy these days, it seems. Call your lover, and he will come too. There is room enough for all of us.'

The words rang hollow, laden with deceit. Leona didn't want a healer for the good of the earth – certainly not for humankind. She wanted a fail-safe to pillage and conquer as she pleased. She wanted armour while she fought to be all-powerful.

'He won't come,' Aurelia said. 'You ruined your chance when you followed him home.'

'But he would hear you if you called. He would run to you if I made you scream. An empath as strong as him could feel your agony from above your grave.'

Empath.

Healer.

Lover.

Leona was wrong. All of it was wrong, and yet, Aurelia couldn't shake the misgivings from the forefront of her mind. 'He is *not* my lover. And he won't come.'

Then, he was there again, standing in Leona's place. Aurelia had merely blinked, and the witch was gone. It was Ingram's hand rising to her face. Aurelia had nowhere left to retreat except into the wall.

His voice was a whisper, and his shape covered in black as the flame within Leona's hand flickered out, relinquishing one spell for another.

His lyrical voice teased against her ear. 'Your tongue said *otherwise.*'

His slender nose dipped to Aurelia's neck and inhaled. Aurelia drove her foot into Leona's shin. Hands fully unclasped, she sunk her fingers into the other witch's flesh, dragging the shapeshifter to the ground with all her might.

Leona fell, bracing herself for the concrete first. Reaching for the knife at her hip second.

Aurelia sent another kick to Leona's gut. The knife clattered to the cold floor, dislodged from her grip. Just as swiftly, Leona summoned it back to her hand.

'To hell with you,' Leona said. 'All I need is your blood.'

Did she not know? That blood without intention was nothing. 'You're wrong about that too,' she said, a glow igniting in her palm. Even the most incapable witches like Ingram knew that a transference of gifts could not be established without consent.

Leona sent the blade flying toward her. Small object levitation – simple enough for the newest witch to learn, but in the hands of one as cruel as Leona, it was fatal. Aurelia moved, willing the blade herself, but its path redirected late, slicing through the sleeve of her borrowed dress. A chill swept through a tear in the fabric – or her flesh. She couldn't stop now to check. She'd made her choice, and she wouldn't dig her own grave.

She summoned the knife herself, secured it in her hand, and swung it toward the woman, striking her with her fist instead. The handle writhed within her hand, unable to wiggle loose and return to its master.

'You want to kill me?' Leona spat. 'You think it will bring your friend back?'

'No,' Aurelia said, void of doubt. The shapeshifter staggered back like a shaking dog. 'But I'm tired of your bullshit.'

'And when the cameras catch you covered in my blood, what will the humans believe? Can you protect yourself from them alone? You'll wish you had my safety. You'll wish you had my gifts.'

'I don't want to be a god, Leona. And I want *nothing* to do with you.'

Leona struck fast like a viper, crashing into the younger woman in a desperate attempt to keep from being caged. Leona discovered the wound she'd made with her knife seconds previously and sunk her sharpened, shifted claws into it.

She caught it and held on for her life.

Aurelia screamed as Leona forced her nails into the gash. Leona's grip wrenched around Aurelia's hand, pinning it to the ground. Crimson tinged the woman's sharp nails as she brought them to her chest and wiped them on her jacket.

'I feel him,' Leona hissed. 'I told you he would come.'

A sliver of light fell into the hall, but it didn't touch them. 'Stay where you are,' Leona commanded. For better or for worse, Theodore Ingram did not move a muscle.

Aurelia turned her head and breathed his name before Leona's hand came down against her throat and pinned it to the concrete.

'I feel sorry for you, boy,' Leona said. 'You could have been a killer, but you yearned for a moral compass. You should embrace your nature. Someone has to.'

He gave the slightest shake of his head, opening his mouth just to say nothing at all.

'You have options, reaper,' Leona said. 'You could watch me

slit her throat and take her gift, and you *might* have the chance to find me again. Both of you could relinquish your gifts to me and walk out alive, with my word of allegiance in your pocket. Or you give me your gift like the shirt off your back. And if you're nice enough, I won't use it on her. I see only one option that benefits us all.'

Ingram shook his head. Prying the knife from Aurelia's limp hand, she persisted, 'What will it be, reaper? Your—'

Aurelia jerked upwards in a last-ditch attempt to throw the shapeshifter off. *Nothing.* Leona had bound her to the concrete as if it were the soil she'd hoped to sprout from in death.

This wasn't how she wanted to die.

Ingram held out his hands, not as a spellcaster but in surrender. Aurelia didn't trust Leona, but if she was true enough in her promise that Ingram could return to Townsend in one piece, was that worth giving her his gift of destruction? He hadn't been able to hide from Leona's pursuit before. Would there be any place that saved them – saved *Louisa* – from Leona's inevitable retribution?

'Anything,' he said. 'Just let her go.'

The last thing Aurelia Schwartz wanted was for Leona to wield the hand of death. She'd needed less to kill Marga, less to keep the country in terror. A smile stretched over Leona's face as she jerked her chin to welcome him closer. He moved with caution, his eyes trained on the hand held to Aurelia's throat.

'Tell me something,' he said.

She should have known it wasn't him in the Maciá room. He never asked. He posed his questions like commands: *Tell me. Let me.*

Can I show you something else?

'For your sacrifice, I will,' said Leona.

If Aurelia had to die, it would be with the knowledge that she hadn't known Ingram well enough.

'What have you done with Gemma Eakley?'

When Leona stared blankly at him, he slid to his knees, hands still bared for her to see. 'Please,' he begged.

The woman couldn't answer. Gemma had *known*. Gemma had known, and she left them believing she'd been taken.

Aurelia gasped out something like a warning. Leona tightened her grip, reducing her words to nothing. She couldn't speak. Couldn't breathe.

'I don't know who you're talking about.'

Ingram's face fell, brow knitted over his eyes.

'If I may,' said Leona, 'I've answered your question truthfully. You owe me something. Or *anything*, if we're being specific.'

He was so smart, Aurelia thought, and mostly more composed than she was, but this was a new type of recklessness and oversight she didn't anticipate from him.

'Your hands,' Leona said, with hers still fastened tight around Aurelia's throat. 'I'm not cutting them off, reaper. I just need your blood.'

Aurelia hissed, 'Don't—'

'*Quiet.*'

A different kind of blackness overtook Aurelia's vision. The one that dragged her, sick and frail, up the steps of her house on the arm of her best friend. One that teased the edges of her vision as the tree took root on the slope of Townsend Hill.

'Here's how it works,' Leona said. 'You stand on the far side of the tank. I slide you the knife and let you draw blood yourself.'

'She leaves first,' Ingram insisted. 'Let her go, and I'll comply with any of your terms.'

'Non-negotiable. I need to ensure you finish the task. And I need her docile.'

Ingram measured the distance between himself and Leona, then Leona and Aurelia. There was a calculation occurring in his mind, which reassured Aurelia slightly of his capacity for rationale; but she also caught the moment wherein he found a solution, and he seemed displeased with it.

'Do as I say, and she walks out of here alive.'

'Unharmed?'

'Alive.'

She stuck her nails in the gash of Aurelia's shoulder.

'I'm going to start walking,' Ingram rushed, then rose, his hands still open for Leona to see. She could see no circling of gold around his fingertips, nor a flicker of light in his heart lines. He was entirely compliant.

Aurelia's vision grew darker, breaths gasping out. *Please, have a plan.*

Leona kicked the knife across the room, and it slid with a high-pitched shriek against the cold floor. 'Try anything, and you carry her out dead.' She hoisted Aurelia in front of her as a shield, digging an arm into her neck instead.

'I won't,' he assured.

Aurelia threw her head back against Leona's jaw, to no avail. Instead, the hold around her neck tightened. Leona seethed into her curls. 'Here I was admiring how well you were behaving.'

'Fuck. You.'

'I'm sorry we met on such poor terms. I like you very much. Thankfully, he does too, or else I'd be depriving the world of a very good kisser.'

A quiet hiss echoed across the hall as Ingram made the incision into his palm. Leona's head perked up, predator sensing prey, and she inhaled deeply, savouring a delectable aroma that Aurelia could not smell herself. Her eyes darkened, irises wide and black like lakes in the night. 'I'm doing good in the world,' Leona whispered. 'I wish you'd see that.'

'Killing witches seems – *agh* – counter-intuitive.'

'Not all of them are as nice as you. I need to source my gifts somehow.'

'Has anyone been willing?'

Leona laughed to herself. 'One witch. Soon to be two. I hoped it'd be three, but I suppose, his gift is the one I wanted most. I won't have to worry about ones like you that fight.'

Aurelia dared not tell her that the oath would not work without complete consent. To have tried before and failed, to live with all that magic in constant resistance to her body . . . Aurelia couldn't imagine her surviving it much longer.

'You have time to change your mind, healer,' Leona whispered.

Healer. Perhaps the only gift Leona could source that would truly save her. But it was wrong. All wrong.

'What next?' Ingram's voice carried through the hall.

'You already know what comes next. Put the knife on the

ground and swear your magic to me.' Then, to Aurelia, 'Who was it before you? The one who made him an empath, gave him a soul?'

Ingram strode forward, his incised hand held outward in anticipation.

'I don't . . . know,' Aurelia breathed.

Had he truly done this before? Did he mean to complete the vow? Maybe he knew how easily he could thwart the efficacy of it, which would have been a brilliant plan if he was less efficient.

'Sweet boy,' said Leona. 'You're doing a good thing.'

'If I thought this was a good thing, I wouldn't be doing it.'

'But for your lover, you would. I used to know how that felt.'

'Did you extract their magic too?' Ingram looked at Aurelia in a way that often came before he'd touched her, but his hand remained poised to take Leona's. 'Did they beg you to stop?'

The shapeshifting witch grimaced. 'He's alive. He wants me dead. None of that matters now. Take my arm, reaper.'

The arm she put forth was wrapped in bandages. 'Open it. It's an old incision.'

The wound beneath the dirty gauze was black and spread like branches, extending from her wrist to her elbow. It wasn't an incision anyone would make on themselves; it was a wound inflicted to kill. Aurelia felt like she might be sick. How hard had *Marga* fought? Her magic was still inside of Leona, fighting even after her death.

'So sweet that you'd do this,' Leona repeated. 'My last tried to gut me with my own knife. Do you feel the way it burns?'

'Yes,' Ingram said.

Aurelia dug her fingers into Leona's arm, wishing she could take it into her mouth and bite it. It wouldn't kill her the way the wound on her other arm eventually would, but it would buy her time. Just once, time could be the thing that saved her.

Leona's arm tightened more, and Aurelia vision faltered further. 'Do you feel the way she breathes with my arm around her neck?'

Ingram might have nodded. Everything was hazy. And slow.

'You feel all of it, don't you? How devastating. Grab my arm,' Leona instructed. 'Let's finish this.'

Two silhouettes moved toward each other. Aurelia saw the gold shimmer of a transference enacted, an oath sworn. She went limp, her knees giving out beneath her. Leona strained beneath her weight. 'Get up. Get up, *now*—'

But she couldn't, even if she'd wanted to. The room's blackness grew even blacker, and suddenly there was no arm around her neck but solid ground under her body. She felt the ache under her ribs late, the temperature of concrete most unbearable against her skin.

Aurelia didn't see it happen. Shock bore over her as breath filled her lungs. The arm around her neck had vanished, unable to sustain her weight. But Leona was screaming. And Ingram—

She couldn't find him anywhere.

Ignite. Aurelia pleaded, *Ignite,* attempting to conjure a flame in her shaking hands from where she laid limp. Nothing came except weak sparks. The intention was soft behind the gong of her pulse.

Leona's skeletal hand circled her throat again, and Aurelia swung her arm blindly for the knife she knew in her heart would be much further from where she fell. She summoned it weakly, the scrape of metal on concrete sounding somewhere far away and unreachable.

'Where is he?' Leona hissed. 'Where the fuck did he go?'

'I don't . . .'

Breath was a heavy thing made impossible by Leona's hand. A puddle of blood oozed from the hand that wasn't choking her. Where was it coming from? Aurelia lifted shaking fingertips and found the source.

Leona's blackened forearm was missing, severed at the place where Ingram had grabbed it. The shapeshifter flickered out of clarity as she released a grisly scream.

'Fix it,' Leona seethed. 'You have to heal it.'

'Can't,' Aurelia breathed.

'You useless witch. I'll cut it out of you myself if I have to.' Leona rose to her feet, shoving Aurelia's cheek to the ground in release. Leona stumbled to the place where the knife had clattered minutes previously and fell to her knees to search for it.

Aurelia didn't see it happening – not clearly. A voice whispered through Aurelia Schwartz's mind, made of sand and smoke. It sounded almost like Ingram, but she couldn't see him. She saw nothing. Nothing at all. She reached toward the sound in the dark.

'*Don't move.*' Another hand made of rigid, inhuman material came around her wrist and pinned it back to her chest.

'Let me go.'

Leona was still searching, still cursing to herself, and the figure before Aurelia hadn't silenced her yet. Her bonds unfurled like talons. They *were* talons. She grasped onto the figure above her and the hard ground beneath her, feeling feathers everywhere.

The knife scraped the floor somewhere in the distance, and Leona sputtered an exacting threat. 'You're finished, healer. You're *fucking done.*'

That voice and that feathered body was Ingram's, and that was all Aurelia needed to know to trust him. 'Close your eyes. Keep them closed.'

She whispered another response as a blanket of feathers fell over her body and gathered her into an even smaller shape like stones beside a riverbed. Warmth surrounded her where seconds ago there had been ice and terror. Wings encircled her – enfolded her – while she brought her knees to her chest and bit back a sob.

Beneath feathers, she felt the puzzle of his bones coming together and tearing apart. Why didn't it stop? The skin underneath his feathers burned unnaturally hot. None of it seemed finished, as if the creature, cursed by something, was forbidden to take its true form.

'Are they closed?' he whispered, and she obeyed without question.

Whatever worked, she thought. Whatever kept them alive.

With her eyes shut tight, behind the veil of feathers, she didn't see how Leona Sum died. Only that the view behind her eyelids was bright red, and the sudden blaze of light that filled the room might've burned her if there weren't wings folded around her, shielding her from the inferno. There was a shrill cry. Then, a curse from the version of Theodore Ingram that felt more animal than witch. But she kept her eyes closed because he was there. Because she trusted him. He'd tell her when to open them, and she would do it, and face the beast of his change. So, she did nothing but *trust* and wait for the sound to fade and for the light of this heavenly fire to extinguish.

Until red faded back to black once more.

Aurelia lifted a hand to the strange body around her just as it fled from her touch. The knife clattered nearer. The sound was heavy around her.

Ingram shouted out in agony. His talons scraped the concrete before his hands could become hands again, slapping against the ground far from her again.

Where was he? Where are you going?

The towering walls of concrete lurched at once. Out of all the things she'd misinterpreted in her stupor, she wanted to believe the shift was the result of her own imbalance. Except the door on the other side of the hall collapsed under the weight of a compressing door-frame and swung off its hinges, the frame no longer viable.

Aurelia didn't see the fire or the murder, but she saw the beast for a fragment of a second, like in a flicker of candlelight. It passed over the iridescent feathers of his wings and the sharp, tarnished blade at his side before everything went black again.

Leona had struck through his wings. Wings that were folded around Aurelia's body. Wings that would soon melt into the human shape of Teddy Ingram. And there was blood all around him.

The hall started to crumble.

CHAPTER TWENTY-THREE

Dazed, she staggered to her feet. Some light persisted through the doorway as the walls around it began to crack, dismounting themselves from each other; but it was still too dark to see clearly.

Ingram uttered a low, breathy whine. Aurelia threw her hands out, still wavering, reaching for him. She touched the familiar fabric of his coat with quivering hands and panted, 'Teddy, the walls.'

He said nothing, recoiling at her touch. She couldn't tell if he had been knocked unconscious; she slid her hands against the wool, finding the solidness of his body, and pressed down harder to wake him.

His subsequent scream broke the cloud of haze that was muddying up her senses. She drew back with damp hands, acutely aware of just how much blood soaked his clothing.

As the cracks around the door expanded, they produced a deafening echo within the hall.

'Teddy, are you with me? I need you to move.'

'It *hurts*,' he gasped out. Aurelia finished circling his body with her arm, wriggling it beneath him as he shuddered in pain.

'Can you feel your legs? Please, I need you to stand.'

He slurred something indecipherable.

'For fuck's sake, Ingram, *move!*'

Beneath his back, her fingers brushed through spare feathers, and he screamed again as she discovered the open wound beneath his clothes.

Where there were once large, beautiful wings now stretched two parallel pathways of marred skin that she felt beneath his soaked sweater.

His hand shot to her arm with a bruising grip. If he couldn't stand by himself, she'd need to help him to his feet, but she was still so weak. So unsure.

Ingram bent his legs with some effort, and she nodded in the dark. 'Come on,' she muttered. 'A little more.'

The other door swung open, its frame decimated. Light poured in, revealing the horrific scene in totality. There was his blood seeping from his shoulder blades into the small puddle around him. In that puddle were soggy black feathers that had been detached from him in his raven form; and beside him, just out of reach, was the other body. With her hands on Aurelia's neck, Leona had seemed so solid. Even now, after Teddy's spell had all but mangled her into a carcass rather than left her a corpse, there was something impermanent and transparent about her. As if she was more ghost than person. An illusion.

With both doors off their hinges, Aurelia heard the conglomeration of guests shouting outside. Some were orderly enough to dole out commands to file toward the front exit, but mostly there was terror. Enough incoherent blabbering to slip right into unnoticed if she could get him out of this room.

Ingram forced himself upright, his head lolling forward against her shoulder.

'A little more,' she repeated.

'I don't think I can.'

'I'll carry you.'

He racked out a small sob. 'You can't carry me.'

'Let me try.'

Once he was on his knees, she pulled him up the rest of the way. She bowed under his weight, and he struggled to find the balancing point that made it easiest for her to urge him forth. Teddy was right. He was taller, more muscular, and *solid*, which had always made him seem unbreakable; but he was crumbling now, one misstep from folding into himself like delicate origami, and she could hardly stand him upright. She kept her arm low around his back and ignored the moisture seeping down from his wounds.

By the time they'd neared the crowd and someone realized that there was an injured man in their midst, Aurelia could pretend they'd been there the whole time. Glass was shattering above their heads. Someone else had already been sliced by a small splinter of it and clutched their arm, bleeding themselves. Someone in a server's uniform caught sight of Teddy's weight overtaking Aurelia's small frame and hurried toward them.

Teddy gritted something out that sounded like, '*Don't touch me*,' but he was hardly able to dictate to either the employee or Aurelia in this state; and the boy managed to weasel under Teddy's opposite arm to carry him.

Outside, the crowd gathered by the river and stared, clutching their garments in shock as the Tate's formidable structure disintegrated. Few noticed that injured people were being coaxed onto the ground around them. Those who did were already on their phones, dialling 999.

Aurelia collapsed under the weight of her companion as he toppled ungracefully beside her. The awful retch that emitted from him brought some attention, and someone shouted, 'Is there a doctor?'

Just as it dawned on her, it seemed to dawn on Teddy too.

'No,' he said pre-emptively.

'You need help,' she said. 'If it's anyone, it should be—'

'*Don't call him.*'

She didn't, only because somebody else had already done it. In a few short moments, Teddy Ingram's father emerged in a well-pressed suit, guided by the same employee that had helped carry the two of them out. It took seconds as the man kneeled down beside Teddy to discover that it was his son. Aurelia slunk back onto her heels, catching her breath.

From behind Teddy's father came a woman's gravelly voice demanding, 'What in God's name are you doing here?'

Aurelia assumed this was Celia Ingram. Her tight, blonde knot of hair had barely come loose in the calamity, as did her expression; she was shockingly unfazed or exceptionally talented at masking her true concern.

'Theo,' whispered his father. 'What happened?' His hand slipped beneath the collar of Teddy's coat, attempting to push it off his shoulders. His voice was so careful and doting that Aurelia couldn't recall why Teddy resented his parents. Teddy opened his mouth to speak but a guttural cry rushed out instead.

His father ceased, turning to Aurelia instead. '*You,*' he said. 'Do you know anything?'

She, too, opened her mouth, but Teddy cut her off. 'No. I left her upstairs for a minute, and then—'

He groaned again. Aurelia nodded in agreement. Teddy's hand wound into the pooling fabric of her dress for comfort, and that was enough context for his father to stop asking about the specifics.

Gravely, the man with prematurely greying hair and olive-green eyes looked at Aurelia. 'Can you take him to the hospital?'

'Back to the house,' interjected Celia. 'He should be looked at there.'

'*No,*' spat Teddy.

His father looked at him solemnly. 'It's that or the hospital, Theo. At least there, I can look at you myself.'

'I need to get back,' Teddy said.

'Where? Are you in town for the night?'

Teddy held in his response. Mr and Mrs Ingram gave each other a despairing look that Aurelia knew could only mean they were aware of his other life in Townsend.

The building seemed to lurch behind them. The hand on Aurelia's dress brushed her knee lightly, and Teddy stared at her with some cocktail of emotions he would have never verbalized if he'd been in his right mind.

She took his hand. The gesture didn't go unnoticed by either of his parents, which might have been killing two birds with one stone if she hadn't forgotten about that first bird.

'Please,' she mouthed. 'We should go with them.'

'Let's get him to the car,' said Celia. 'Out of here.'

Aurelia watched Ingram's father in her periphery running his fingers through his son's hair. Before they could prop up Teddy's body and haul him away, she heard him whisper, 'It's going to be OK. I'll meet you at home soon.'

With his father's arm around him, Teddy wobbled forward with the smallest addition of ease, begrudgingly compliant until they could nestle him firmly in the back seat of a polished black Mercedes. His father left him with a warm but cautious brush upon the cheek before stepping aside to let Aurelia pile in after.

'You're not coming?' Celia Ingram's lip twisted sharply.

'Soon. Let me check on the others.' He passed his hand over his son's hair again, as if he couldn't bear to let him out of his sight after so much time, and gave him a short smile. He seemed noble in Aurelia's mind, and for a moment, Teddy looked back at his father with something that looked like affection, or at least appreciation.

Then, the door shut behind them. The way Teddy looked at his mother was excruciatingly colder.

'My building is a fucking disaster.' Celia gripped the wheel until her pale hands turned an unnatural shade of white.

Teddy leaned forward onto his knees to prevent his back from touching the seat, but the violent manner in which Celia laid her foot to the pedal made him jolt.

''S not my fault.'

Technically, it was. But Aurelia could see the cold stare of his mother through the reflection of the rear-view mirror as she sped through the streets of London and knew that interjecting would bring neither of them any good. Aurelia sat distant from Teddy Ingram, but her thoughts were wound around him in a way that she acknowledged was *protective.*

Which was how Teddy's mother probably *should* have been feeling. Instead, Aurelia had a niggling suspicion that Celia Ingram felt nothing at all; and that was indescribably distressing.

'Am I supposed to believe that you show up after years of unanswered calls, to the place where I work, on the same night that it collapses – that you have nothing to do with it? Try me.'

Teddy huffed in response, hiding his face in his hands.

'What about you?' the woman hissed.

'What about me?' asked Aurelia.

'You must know something. Silence won't help you. There's going to be an investigation, you know. If you're not going to tell me you were at the right place at the right time, I'll have no choice but to think otherwise.'

'I don't know,' Aurelia lied. 'Everything changed so fast. He went to get me a new drink while I was with the crowd downstairs—'

'*Upstairs,* Schwartz,' he mumbled.

Aurelia stopped short to hiss, 'Stop. Talking.'

Celia had already heard her slip up. 'Who do you think you're doing favours for right now? I see no point to your lying unless you had something to do with it; in which case, you've ruined my career along with your lives. You understand that I'll be sacked for this if it comes back to you, yes, Theo?'

Aurelia scoffed. '*That's* what you're worried about? Your fucking *job?* Can't you see your son is bleeding out?'

'If you knew him half as well as you think you do, you'd know he's not my son. Right now, he doesn't even want to be his father's patient. Harry'll come home, patch him up, load his pockets with money and send him on his way like he always does. And what else will Theo do except take advantage of that? Blow it all on that dingy little shack in the middle of nowhere, right? To be with his *better* family?'

At the marginal mention of Gemma, Teddy's breath grew more strained.

'Who am I badgering,' his mother mused. 'He's a hard person to love. Believe me, I want to, but he makes it so bloody impossible. He uses everyone. He's probably using you as a scapegoat now – the ungrateful thing. You defend him tonight, but he'll throw you to the wolves the second that the chance arises.'

'At least he never told me you were a total cunt.'

Mrs Ingram scowled in the mirror's reflection. 'I know what I am talking about.'

Aurelia stifled an uglier rebuttal. When Teddy spoke, his voice came perilously close to pitiful. 'I'm not going back to the house.'

'You most definitely are,' said his mother.

'No,' he said. 'I'm not.'

Aurelia curled her hand around his elbow and whispered, 'It's your best option. *Our* best option.'

'But we have others.'

'I'm serious,' she whispered.

He shot her a look that said 'only one of us is mutilated, and it's not you', which was a compelling enough unspoken argument to give her pause.

'Don't be daft,' came his mother. 'You should listen to her.'

Aurelia didn't want to agree with her, but it was the truth, so she stifled a counter-remark.

Celia continued, 'Your friend can go if she pleases, but you need to be tidied up.'

'I'll be fine.'

The woman scowled again as if the permanent state of her face was ice-clad and full of resentment. 'In any case, you'll rouse suspicion walking anywhere all bloody and limp.'

Aurelia didn't bother saying that Celia was right. It was already bad enough that they agreed upon anything, but to voice it to him aloud seemed like just another twist in the wound.

'You're recognizable, Theo,' said Celia Ingram.

'I'm sorry I soil your reputation, Mother. I, too, wish you had a better son.'

She made a disagreeable humming noise that sounded regrettably familiar.

'Take me to Liverpool Street station.'

'*Teddy*,' Aurelia hissed.

'I'll be fine.'

'You're being stubborn.'

'Call it even, then.'

'Slow down and consider it,' she pleaded. 'You're injured. You're not thinking clearly.'

'I'm clear, completely transparent. Invisible, even. We are not staying.'

Celia's eyes flashed bright and crystalline in the mirror. 'Is that what you want?'

Aurelia half expected a bitter and sarcastic response regarding the quantity of his requests and the validity of them. She half expected him to rise up in his seat, straighten his back proudly, and tell her she was foolish for being so worried.

Unfortunately, Teddy Ingram knew how to get what he wanted – his cold, unfeeling mother included. His eyes, warm and enticing as ever, if a little tormented too, met his mother's in the reflection again and held her gaze for as long as she could keep her eyes off the road. 'Yes, Mother.'

This was helplessness, Aurelia knew. Nothing she said would deter him.

Celia grew stony again, which was when Aurelia realized that she'd been momentarily softened. 'We're not far.'

'Thanks.'

He didn't look at Aurelia. To be fair, she thought that if he simply glanced at her or touched her hand, she might break down in tears. No one ever enjoyed being helpless. She couldn't stand to face him. She *despised* him, for better reasons than before. For being so reckless and brash. For always getting what he wanted even if it might kill him. She despised him for being unable to swallow his pride to insist on leaving; and most of all, she despised his mother for letting him leave.

There was little affection behind Celia Ingram's eyes, if there had been any to begin with.

When they reached the station, she let Aurelia coax her son out by herself, bearing all his weight on her smaller frame. She let Aurelia fish into his pockets while supporting him to retrieve their tickets; meanwhile she stood with crossed arms on the other side, displeased.

It was apparent even in the rough way she grabbed Teddy's chin and turned it up toward hers. Her eyes narrowed – the look could petrify.

'Expect a visit,' she said.

Teddy Ingram gathered all his strength and stood just to spite her.

PART FOUR

CHAPTER TWENTY-FOUR

Their negative space was cold and unforgiving. Miles lay between them in their train carriage as it whisked the solitary passengers to Townsend's nearest station. Rage teemed beneath her surface, anguish under his. Teddy looked more boy than man, wearing his dread like a crown. But they would be back soon. They would be back, and she would ensure that the tracts of blood on his back were finished weeping, and that Louisa would not lose another family member before she had even turned ten.

Teddy met her with a blank stare sitting opposite from her seat.

Less than a half-hour left to endure the rocking train. Little time for him to be jostled and stretched against his will as he tried to keep himself as still as possible. He was trying to close his eyes, either chasing sleep or avoiding Aurelia, but neither was possible as long as the motion of the train kept agitating his wounds.

Of course, coupled with Aurelia's anticipation was frustration. She looked back at him, observing the discomforted position he sat in with his shoulder in the spot where his back should have been and knew that it could have been avoided. It shouldn't have happened at all.

'Don't look at me like that,' he muttered.

Her face hardened, an astounding effort to make while she was so tired. 'It was one night, Teddy.'

'I'm *fine.*'

'Bullshit,' she hissed. 'Was it really too much of an injury to your pride to let them take you back? To let them stop your bleeding and take care of you?'

'Christ, you're such a hypocrite. *You're* the one who's pissed off at me for intervening when you had hands wrapped around your fucking throat! I saved your life. The least you could do is give me some credit since you're not going to be grateful.'

Grimacing, she said, 'None of this would have happened if you hadn't intervened and nearly got yourself killed. You can't do that, Teddy. We agreed you wouldn't have to – that you would leave Leona to me – and now look where we are. Your clothes are covered in blood, and I have to lug you up a hill by myself in the freezing *fucking* cold just to clean you up myself.'

'Then don't,' he grumbled. 'No one ever said you had to.'

'You're being obtuse.'

'I was trying to help you.' His eyes were alight with rage. 'Because I know that narrowly avoiding death and meeting it when you're twenty-three are completely different things. I'll handle this one if it means you survive. If I've given you another day, and you want to put yourself back into the path of danger, then by all means, go ahead. You have a chance to do that now. Throw your life away.'

Teddy shut his eyes, his fists clenched around the fabric of his coat as he gritted his teeth through another lurch of the train.

That's the point, she thought. Not that she wanted to gamble away everything that she had worked for, but because there was less to lose if she failed. Ryan would mourn her. Her father would mourn her most of all, but she knew he would lower his head and work through his grief the same way that he did everything else. Did the willingness to offer herself up like a sacrificial lamb make her callous or noble? The weight of a lifetime wasn't something one enjoyed measuring, but she thought she had left a dark enough mark over anyone that mattered – savouring the days like a fine wine and not the promise of rain on her tongue. It was a fickle thing, never certain, always seized.

But Louisa was only seven years old, already vulnerable and riddled with the fear of her mother's sudden disappearance – a fear which Aurelia still struggled in silence to live with. Aurelia's life was her own to ruin, but Ingram's was *not*. There was a weight to it that hers did not bow under.

She pulled herself up and crossed to his side, propping herself up by her uninjured shoulder. Teddy sighed, and she watched that breath shake through him with a force that could level mountains.

Gravely, she whispered, 'You could have died. And if you went . . .'

Teddy shook his head, turning it away. She eased back the piece of hair that fell limp over his forehead and cleared the path for him to look at her – and truly *see* what she meant.

She wouldn't let him become a martyr if he could just become a shield.

'If something had happened to you, Louisa would have wound up alone. You know better than anyone how hard it would be to recover from that. You should have let me take it.

You risk a lot more than yourself. For fuck's sake, you brought down half a museum—'

'And I would have brought down all of bloody London for you if I had to. I don't care if that makes me irretrievably selfish. I wasn't going to stand by and let someone touch you. Let someone *hurt* you.'

Teddy's shoulder knocked hard against the seat as the train rounded a wide curve. She forced his guttural noise from her mind, the memory of his scream in the dark.

'In my pocket,' he said. 'Grab my phone and call Alaric.'

She braced herself against the back of the seat beside his head and slipped her hand into his coat pocket. Another lurch and she could crash into him, hurt him a little more. She couldn't help hoping. She wanted to be the thing that made him squirm.

Being this close, feeling him embedded in her history, reminded her she'd had her tongue in a mouth that looked just like his only hours ago. How eagerly she had agreed when he had suggested that they run.

She should have listened the first time. In Gemma's kitchen, still dizzy from the warmth of his body, he'd told her they could hide instead. He'd followed when she asked, held her when she doubted, and tucked her beneath his coat – and his *wings* – as if she was the one in need of consoling.

It would have been simpler to stay angry than let regret consume her; but as she dialled Alaric's number and followed the path of Ingram's eyes to the gloves hanging from her pocket, she let both burning ends of her rage meet and dissolve into smoke.

*

With Teddy's other arm slung around Alaric's shoulder, they decided against climbing the hill. Alaric pushed the shop door open with his foot, muttered something beneath his breath, and the transformation commenced.

'Where is she?' asked Teddy.

'Asleep,' Alaric answered, walking them both through aisles of books and toward a part of the grand library that Aurelia hadn't made it to last time. She'd seen the spiral staircase, because it crept up past the height of the shelves, but she hadn't walked up it. She hadn't imagined that her first time would be spent staggering under the weight of another person. Certainly not one drenched in rain that smelled like iron.

'Check on her,' Teddy said. Alaric nodded, not contesting the demand.

Alaric gestured to a couch nearby, shifting some of Teddy Ingram's weight back onto Aurelia's shoulder before he retreated toward the upper level.

Teddy fell ungracefully onto the burgundy upholstery, biting his tongue to withhold an ungodly sound. Aurelia was distantly aware of his stained grip on the loose fabric of her dress, the way he leaned into her even when he wasn't touching her.

Her own hands were bathed in an even darker shade. Carefully, she sat beside him, placing them high on the shoulders of his coat, clear of the wounds.

'I need to take this off you.'

'Can it wait?' he asked.

'No.'

She coaxed the collar of his coat up from around his shoulders, maintaining a steady hand. At some point, she would have to disregard every hitched breath that escaped from behind his clenched teeth and finish it. *Be ruthless*, she thought, feeling his hand against her thigh. *Pretend that you like it.*

She discarded the soggy garment and touched her fingers to his back. The knit of his sweater was stretched and mangled by the moisture, made blacker by his blood. Aurelia could see the grooves in his skin through it. The fabric caught in his wounds. She would need to rid him of his shirt too, but that would be a far more gruesome task.

'It's stuck,' she whispered aloud. He shut his eyes, bowing his head. 'We might need to cut it off.'

'Must you?'

He seemed to know the answer already. His hands braced on his knees, and he huffed out a breath. Above their heads a door shut, and within seconds, Alaric was beside them again with a towel in one hand and a large basin of water balanced underneath his arm.

'Is it—'

'Ugly,' she said. 'I think some of his sweater is stuck in the wound.'

'Bloody hell.'

Teddy moved to untuck the sweater from under his belt, every move a flinch. 'Make it quick.'

Quietly, Aurelia said, 'I don't think you're in any state to give demands.'

For the first time in hours, Teddy broke into a smile and

laughed, wild and rough, too deep in his exhaustion to pretend to be mad. 'Shut up, Schwartz.'

The compression in her chest eased then, as if with one strained laugh, she could fashion a warm shelter to rest in. Something like hope bloomed in her gut and made her feel a little less cold.

She focused on the rise and fall of his back, thankful enough that they were still breathing.

Her fingers hooked around the lower edge of his sweater, and she began to roll it up his torso. 'Are you ready?' she asked them.

Alaric nodded first, then Teddy. He gripped Alaric's hand as she lifted it. She favoured a languid, tender motion over one that would hurt him swiftly, but breaths still seethed through his teeth.

'It's all right,' Alaric Friedman whispered to him. 'Almost done.'

The force of Teddy's hands turned Alaric's knuckles white. For someone so hard to love, it seemed an awfully great profession of love to let Teddy Ingram hold on to him past the point of bruising.

Another sound ripped through him as the sweater tore out of his rough skin, and Aurelia swallowed her disgust at the sight of his mangled back.

'Shit.'

'Don't say that,' he breathed.

Alaric peered at the parallel slats on Teddy's shoulder blades and shut his eyes to it, quickly.

'It's ugly,' Alaric confirmed. 'But I'm sure you already knew that.'

Teddy gave another grim huff that might have been a laugh if he could manage it.

'Your arms,' Aurelia said. Teddy raised them with difficulty, and she finished removing the garment. After all of that, she thought it stranger to *not* touch him than to touch him unclothed. She'd seen him shirtless before – not that it mattered, but they'd maintained their distance then. They'd lacked the lingering stares and shared bed-sheets that twisted them together now.

'How did this happen?' Alaric asked them both.

'He became this . . . this *bird,*' Aurelia said. 'I'd never seen anything like it before.'

For a moment, Teddy Ingram had been more beast than human. A thing of nightmares.

'Because it pains me,' said Ingram. 'It leaves my skin raw and my bones unfixed; and it makes me monstrous.'

The small motion of Alaric's thumb over Teddy's wrist ensnared her. It must have grazed an inch or two, but the tenderness of it could have swallowed her whole. No monster could be touched so sweetly. No person unworthy of love could be cared for so wholly.

'Leona clipped his wings while he was like that,' Aurelia added.

'I must have absorbed some of my clothing during the transformation.'

The caretaker dipped a corner of the towel in the basin and pressed it lightly against the top of one gash.

Little by little, Aurelia watched the cream-coloured towel turn pink, then red. By the end, Teddy Ingram had grown numb to the sensation. Exhaustion crept in as his body fought to reject every bit of pressure over the raw skin, and his grip vanished from her dress. She smoothed the creases down her knees, noticing spots of his blood where none had been present before.

Alaric and Aurelia continued cleaning his wound, saying nothing to one another aloud, and Teddy drifted into sleep, half-propped, half-entwined with her, slurring something lazily that she didn't bother interpreting.

She slouched into the back of Alaric's couch, still clothed in her torn, dampened dress, Teddy's head at home in the bend of her stomach.

'You can stay, of course,' Alaric whispered over the body of the sleeping boy.

Aurelia considered it. She had no other clothes here or a bed, but there was a large leather chair beside the unmade fireplace that she could probably curl up in. She wasn't opposed to the idea of sharing the couch with Teddy Ingram, but there was simply inadequate space for two. Once he configured his long legs and sensitive torso, he might find there to be inadequate space for *one*.

'Your arm,' Alaric said. 'What happened there?'

'She grazed me with her knife.'

'Looks like more than a graze.'

'It was a graze,' she said. 'Leona knew I was bleeding before I did. I don't know how – I couldn't see. But once she had caught my scent, she grew nails and tore the incision open completely.'

'How deep does it go?'

Aurelia shrugged. Teddy shifted in her lap, wincing but not

waking. 'I haven't been able to check it yet. It's hardly the worst thing that happened tonight.'

Alaric's lips pulled tight over his face, etching those lines deeper beside his mouth. He rubbed his eyes beneath his glasses and rose to his feet.

'Nevertheless, you should clean up,' he said. 'Clear your head. I'll grab you something for tonight, and you can shower upstairs . . . Make yourself at home.'

Home.

Her head grew heavier with the thought of it. The echo of Teddy's voice was another disloyal birdsong.

We could turn around and go home.

She had to remind herself that it wasn't him. And as much as Townsend began to feel more like home than anywhere she'd lived in a long time, those weren't his words. This wasn't her place. She had found herself a home on an unsteady foundation, built her nest on a worm-eaten branch.

She knew Cambridge couldn't welcome her back with open arms either after bearing witness to Marga Palermo's murder. She couldn't clear the thought of Marga's lifeless body from the dining halls of the colleges. It followed her to Townsend, to London, and into her dreams . . .

Home had always been a thing out of her grasp.

'Alaric,' she murmured, 'thank you for this.'

He looked down at the murky basin and towel in his hands, as if understanding for the first time how much his hands could heal. 'Of course. It had to be done. We're all we've got.'

*

She mulled his words over while she washed under the water. By then, the witching hour had come and gone. The voice in her mind spoke slowly, thoughts slurred and soldered together. Her limbs weighed a hundred pounds each.

In the foggy bathroom mirror, Aurelia examined her shoulder. Her vision was still hazy and made hazier by the steam of the shower. The clean edge left by the knife had been sabotaged by Leona's claws.

Now that the shapeshifter had a face, Aurelia wondered if the face in her nightmares would take shape too. The gash on her arm glared back at her. Sluggish, Aurelia brought her hand over the wound, obscuring it from view.

I know what you are, Leona had said.

Healer.

I'm tired of hiding. Aren't you?

Aurelia took a deep breath and repeated a word in her mind, casting off her trepidation. Just for a moment. *Heal. Heal.*

Her fingers lit a gold spark, and the severed skin grew taut, but didn't seal.

Maybe it wasn't the right word, but she'd commanded something she'd been unaware existed until now. Excitement swelled in her stomach. Her laugh came out nearly as a sob, alone in the bathroom with her reflection, still naked from her shower.

Come on, you son of a bitch. Heal already.

Both sides of the gash tugged toward one another, tendrils of skin outstretched like fingers seeking to entwine. She held her breath and watched it connect.

Her mind raced with a dozen other synonyms for the word until she was certain that it was real.

Leona's cruel, silver tongue spoke again in her mind. *I am never wrong.*

A rough scar outlined the place where her flesh was just exposed, still raw to the touch. Even when the redness subsided, it would be unignorable. She would have to answer questions about it when she wore that green dress or joined Ryan and their friends at the beach; but if that was all she had to worry about, she would manage fine. Better than fine.

All that mattered tonight was that they'd come back alive.

The sight of Alaric Friedman met her at the bottom of the stairs after she'd changed into a borrowed pair of sweatpants and a T-shirt. He should have been asleep by now, but he idled in front of the now-burning fireplace that flickered beside Teddy's sleeping form, alert as ever.

He turned slowly, observing as she placed Gemma's soiled dress and coat on the floor beside the table.

'You're still up,' she mused aloud.

'Yes.'

The walls were littered with a strange amalgamation of landscape paintings and old music posters, but no clock. When Alaric didn't move, Aurelia cleared her throat. 'Did you need something? I mean, I know you live here. I'm not trying to make you leave.'

Alaric raised one peppered brow at her. 'Does this not keep you up at night?'

'Well, yeah,' she said sheepishly. 'And no. I don't know. I get the striking feeling that you don't like me very much, Alaric.'

'I'm . . . sorry. Fatigue is eating me. You might not believe this, but at one point in my life, I was a creature solely of the night. A dirty, rotten punk with too much time on his hands. By the time mornings came, and I'd start to think of sleep, I'd be six or seven bottles deep. I had things to do then. Dreams to chase, shows to see . . . I don't often get the chance to experience late nights like this any more. The fire's warm. It's impossible not to feel my age these days, but it's nice to remember what it was like back then. My problems were a lot different back when I was your age, but they felt monumental.'

She wasn't convinced that he was being honest about liking her. At most, he seemed indifferent, and she didn't know why it maddened her that he wasn't more than that. Her feet throbbed as she stood, serenaded by the crackling of flames before them, but she was numb to pain at this point, mildly delirious.

Alaric spoke next, filling the emptiness between them. 'I want to know how it happened. All of it.'

She raised her eyebrows. 'Is there a reason you want it from my mouth when it already came from his?'

'He's said everything he intends to say. I won't get any more from him.'

Aurelia folded her arms over her chest and began, 'Well . . . It was about six when we walked in. Everyone had shown up by then, and it was crowded, so I knew it would be hard to spot her. Of course, we didn't know what we were looking for, so it was damn near impossible. We went upstairs after that, and we talked for a while. We were both drinking, and when I finished my drink, he offered to take the glass downstairs for me. Leona must have been watching us the whole time, because she knew how long to wait before she came to me. And she came to me looking like him. Wearing his face and his clothes, and I wasn't thinking straight.'

'Where was he?'

'I don't know, actually.'

Alaric discarded a second question and instead encouraged her for more. 'What then?'

'She cornered me,' Aurelia said. It wasn't a lie, nor was it the full truth. He didn't need to know about what happened in the Maciá room. 'I should have figured out earlier that it wasn't him, but she was convincing enough that I didn't give it a second thought. I know I should have, but . . . I just . . .'

'Did it take long to realize?'

'Longer than necessary. She took me somewhere secluded, and I couldn't risk the chance of letting my magic slip free in front of all those people, so I let her. I knew I'd only endanger myself if I fought back.'

Because she knew in her heart that there was a fragment of truth in Leona's words, and that terrified her.

I'm tired of hiding. Aren't you?

Aurelia had been more afraid of what could befall her at the hands of humans than Leona's personal brand of torture. Maybe that was wrong. Maybe that was the sickest, cruellest part of it all. She had seen the blade driven through the heart of her friend, and yet no threat could be worse than that of the unknown. When stories framed humans lighting the pyre beneath her feet, the glint of a sword seemed the easy way out. The better of two evils.

'Could you have run?' Alaric asked.

'I don't run,' she said, too quickly to be convincing. There was a question behind Alaric's eyes, but she couldn't read it – and blamed it on his glasses. 'We were alone then. She wanted him to come, and so she made me collateral. She said—'

That even in death, he would feel me.

Alaric waited for her to finish, but that was a different conversation – one to have with the boy who slept behind them. For all the unspoken truths between them, she needed only to ask, and they'd be offered up of his own accord. They were done tiptoeing around each other.

Confessing to empathy couldn't have been worse than confessing to being a reaper.

Clearing her throat, she pressed on. 'Leona took a knife to my shoulder and tried to strangle me. She wanted our magic. She would have bled us for it without knowing that she needed more. She looked weak from failed attempts.'

'She was taking magic?'

Aurelia nodded. 'She didn't know that the transference wouldn't work without consent. She thought she could rip it out of me like a bone, that it wouldn't fight back once it was inside her. If Teddy hadn't stepped in . . . He thought . . . I don't know. Maybe I *did* need help.'

'There is no shame in that.'

'We *killed* someone, Alaric.'

Saying it aloud was violent enough to make her cover her mouth with her palm. Was she shaking? She couldn't tell. She'd been so numb by the time they exited the station that she'd put off feeling all the guilt until now.

All she'd known about Leona Sum from beneath Ingram's

black wings was that she needed magic. But like her and Teddy Ingram, Leona had also wanted to live.

'I've known monsters like her,' Alaric said. 'I've met them before. I've had to hunt them myself. They've been around since the dawn of our kind, and for as long as witches walk the earth, they will be here. It needed to be done.'

Aurelia chewed the fingernails nervously as she nodded.

Alaric shifted his weight onto one leg. 'I like you, Aurelia – trust me, I do. You frighten me, though. I know the kinds of treacherous minds that are birthed from academia. I see who wields the power, and it's always the same. For humans and creatures alike. It's earned by those with drive but seized by those without shame or mercy. You're bound for something great, but will you take it with snapping jaws? Without remorse? I'd admire your drive if I knew that you wanted the right things.'

'How could you possibly know what I want?'

Teddy stirred at the sound of her voice – she had broken her whisper. Alaric stared down at her, unflinching.

Lowering her voice again, she admitted for the first time, 'Sometimes I don't even know what I want.'

There had always been conflict within her mind, but she kept it hidden behind a curtain of feigned confidence. No one else had to know that she was following motions as long as she kept moving. As long as it took her where she needed to be.

'Then you walk blindly.' Alaric stated. 'Is that any better?'

'It can't be any worse,' she told him.

'I hope not. I want to trust you, Aurelia. Teddy certainly does, and I'd like to trust in his decisions too, even if it's only to ensure that he can take care of himself once I'm gone.'

'Gone?'

It'd been a slip of the tongue, not something he'd meant to share. 'I suppose . . . This will arouse some attention. I asked a colleague of mine – another caretaker – to help me look into Leona Sum just after you delivered her letter. She had friends. Loved ones. The last records I can find of them are a bit dated, but I suspect that Leona wasn't working alone. And if she has allies, they'll seek vengeance. I can only hope that they're easier to reach than she was. I'll have to—'

He cleared his throat, quieting his voice even more.

'I'll have to clean this up. Half my job is to ensure that witches aren't at the crux of humanity's problems. I'll go where I am needed. Wherever that is.'

Aurelia's lips thinned in dissatisfaction. 'Sounds a bit like walking blindly to me.'

He smiled back. 'I know where this chapter takes me. I know what the end holds for me. The beats of my life are knotted on a string of fate, and I've seen where it gets cut. Gemma told me once when we were younger what I'd be and where I'd go. I've made peace with it.'

At some point, the voices and words became a blur. Leona, Alaric, Teddy, and now Gemma. Hers was the clearest – melodic like church bells. If Gemma's was the birdsong that sang her to sleep, Aurelia would savour every note.

Alaric turned to leave, and then he remembered the end – or lack thereof – of her recount of the long and gruesome night. 'I'm assuming that was when his wings failed.'

She nodded, swallowing hard as if she'd been force-fed honey. 'When he found me, Leona had her hands around my neck. He said he'd do anything . . . I didn't think he meant it, but I might have needed saving. I guess we got off *easy*, but I'm terrified of what comes next. The Tate's in shambles. News will spread by morning if it hasn't already – that this attack was the most catastrophic yet. If anyone's looking hard enough, they'll place us at the Tate Modern *and* King's College. I . . . I don't want to think about what happens if we're caught.'

Alaric squeezed her shoulder gently. 'We have a lot to clean up. I can take care of that first.'

She smiled weakly. It was her turn to succumb to the gravity of exhaustion.

'You should sleep, Al. It'll be morning soon.'

'Will you?'

She shrugged and folded her arms over her chest. 'Maybe.' She thought she might actually be exhausted enough to escape the inevitable nightmares. Knowing her luck, sleep would show her no mercies either.

'Alaric,' she said. 'What else was in the envelope?'

He looked to the couch where Teddy Ingram lay, then to her. 'His bank account information . . . For the off chance that he didn't come back. He takes care of them, you know. Always has.'

As Alaric left her by the fireplace, Aurelia moved to the leather chair nearby, curling around her knees like an owl in its nest, and watched him disappear into the shadows upstairs. Only when the sound of Alaric's footsteps became too distant to hear did she unfold the blanket that hung on the back of the chair and lay it over herself. So close to the heat of the flame, she really didn't need it. The hearth burned bright, casting figures on even the furthest walls of the grand library. She angled herself so that its light wouldn't bore through her closed eyelids.

Two things came together in her mind then as she slipped into unconsciousness. The first, that she might be somewhere else in the world right now and simultaneously in Townsend, given the impermanent nature of this room, and she had no idea where she was – like Schrödinger's cat, neither alive nor dead. Here nor there – at least, until she opened the front door.

The next, which was somehow both more *and* less consequential than the first, was that Alaric's books were in the proximity of a raging fireplace. They were far enough away that they might not catch flame, but surely, they would be damaged by smoke if the nights were always this cold . . . It seemed strange to her that with a role as important as preserving magical texts, Alaric would be careless enough to light a fire in their presence.

Maybe he expected her to snuff it out before she went to sleep, but the leather chair was a lover's embrace after months away at sea, and she didn't intend to break it. Here, she was warm. She was safe. She found that she didn't really care much about whether or not the flame crept out of its hearth and swallowed her whole. She was tired of being cold. Tired of being in the rain. Tired of living unembraced.

I'm tired of hiding. Aren't you?

But that, like all her other burgeoning questions, was something to answer another time, when she was more rested and less dizzy, when the dark and soiled promise of glory wasn't ripe in her mind, and Alaric's words hadn't practically lobotomized her.

Aurelia Schwartz pulled the blanket to her chest and slept. She let time pass without her.

CHAPTER TWENTY-FIVE

Aurelia clambered off the chair at the sound of a sharp groan, eyes darting to the boy on Alaric's couch. She rubbed her eyes and clutched the blanket to her chest, worried that the world was being swept out from beneath her. Light poured in from a tall skylight over the sitting area – *morning* – and it hurt, being so bright so suddenly.

But Teddy was fine. He squirmed, made a significantly quieter grunting noise while he propped himself up, and caught sight of her too. A shadow of an apology crossed over his face for the startling efficiency with which he had woken her.

'My back,' he explained. 'It's . . . *Fuck*, it's killing me.'

Aurelia gathered the blanket she'd kicked to the floor and reached for her phone on the table.

'It's not even nine yet,' she said. 'I was sleeping so well.'

Teddy huffed. 'Lucky you. I assume this is only the first time I've woken you. You, on the other hand, woke me up more than once last night. You and your little snores.'

'I don't snore.' She did.

'You absolutely do,' Teddy insisted, shifting onto his stomach again. 'It's small. A bit like how cats snore.'

His eyes closed, and he tucked his cheek into the pillow to

rest. Despite the discomfort, he flashed an absent-minded grin that was only partially visible against the cushion. With his eyes shut, he didn't notice her smile back at him. Perhaps that was for the better.

'Guess I should find your date from the pub and tell her I was mistaken.'

'Hmm,' he said. 'Oh, yes. You ought to. I'm feeling terribly put out by my injury and would like someone to dote on me.'

'So *I'm* definitely out of the question.'

He shifted again, groaning into the pillow. Alaric's library was warmer than the cottage, but Teddy had slept without his shirt to let the gashes on his shoulder blades breathe. The chill was finally catching up to him.

'This is horrid,' he said. 'How's your shoulder?'

'My—'

Clean. Aurelia's fingers were already stroking the pulled skin on her shoulder. Scarred over but healed.

She'd almost forgotten about it. Some part of her had been clinging to the belief that the previous night was only a bad dream.

'Nothing to worry about,' she said.

Leona's voice welcomed her into the new day, a righteous whisper in her ear: *Healer. Empath.*

Aurelia permitted herself to think of the other word too – *lover* – but quickly expelled it from her mind. Ingram was shirtless. And that hadn't mattered to her last night while she was sanitizing his gashes, but beneath that severed skin was smooth, lean muscle. Lower around his tapered waist were countless pale freckles. She saw them clearly under the morning light. They were delicate and pink, most prominent on his shoulders above the gashes, but they were strewn about the rest of his torso too.

'Need something, Schwartz?'

It came slightly out of breath, as if the shift to and from his elbows (and then onto his side to face her) had expended all his energy for the day.

'Are you looking at my arse?'

'*What?* No – I'm looking at your *back*. Because you are insufferably reckless, and I'm still upset with you.'

She was only a little upset with him, all things considered. The relief of having him safe and capable enough to make assumptions about her line of sight far outweighed the displeasure. He smiled again, his hair tousled over the pillow in a way that made her blush even more.

'I've been told it's quite nice,' he replied, 'so I wouldn't hold it against you.'

'I think I prefer you when you're grovelling.'

'Good,' he concluded. 'I expect to grovel all day. Possibly all week.'

Aurelia's smile diminished. Her phone had also read the second of January, which meant several things to her. First, that she'd overlooked New Year's Day and another customary call to her family back in Vancouver. The second, that Lent term at Pembroke would be starting in a few days. Which brought about the third thing: that she'd have to go back. She had meetings to set with Dr Carney, a new schedule to craft and to compare with Ryan Jena's, and a new *job* to find . . .

With Leona gone, what purpose did Aurelia have to stay?

'I don't have all week,' she told him.

Teddy sighed, understanding. He'd probably been more aware of its looming than she'd been – it spelled out a change that he didn't want to accept. Change that could only be reversed with Gemma's return, if and hopefully *when* it happened.

And if it didn't, Aurelia wouldn't see him any more. She wouldn't be running into him at Tesco any time soon with her housemate on her arm or in the court while she was rushing to finish a sandwich from Cafe Pembroke . . . She'd known it was a possibility. She'd been right in her assumption; and normally Aurelia would have taken pride at knowing something before he did, but now it felt like a hard kick to her diaphragm.

'Pity, isn't it?' he whispered.

'What is?'

'All of it. And to think, Gemma's still out there somewhere. I don't know where to look. But I need to find her.'

They hadn't spoken about it aloud, but Aurelia had always known the cost of returning without Gemma. They'd quelled the threat of Leona, but it hadn't brought back the augur of Townsend Hill. Louisa was still without her mother. Teddy without an answer. If she'd left, why didn't she warn them? Why had she chosen deliberately to lead them off her scent like she was fleeing the scene of her own crime?

'I don't understand how she could have left without telling me anything,' he said.

'Worse,' Aurelia said unhelpfully. 'She'd rather you go looking for her in the wrong directions.'

An idea flared to life behind his eyes, then quelled itself almost instantly without the energy to keep raging on. 'Who says it was the wrong direction? We did what we had to do, didn't we? Maybe it's just a matter of waiting. I wish she wasn't so bloody cagey about everything.'

Waiting. Wasn't it always a matter of waiting? No matter how proactive she tried to be in taking her life's goals by the leash, she was always at the mercy of someone else's decisions. Their schedule. Their secrecy.

'You're not coming back to Cambridge, then, are you?' Aurelia asked.

That, too, was an answer she'd already foreseen. 'One day, I'll be able to take Louisa away from this place, but it'll have to be somewhere new. Somewhere the people don't recognize me. It's astounding how easily word gets back to my parents from Cambridge. I try to keep my head down, stay out of trouble . . . I let Louisa and Gem stay with me *once* when Lou was younger, and after Celia found out, I didn't hear the end of it. I was getting messages for days about familial loyalties and threats of evicting me from the Cambridge house for allowing "squatters". It's never been easy with Gemma, but it was always worth it. They were always worth it.' His voice fell to a murmur. Aurelia had to strain to hear him over the quiet hiss of his dishevelled hair against the upholstery fabric.

'I'm going to find Gemma and bring her home, no matter where it takes me. As much as I hope it eventually leads me back to Cambridge, there's no telling what comes next. Or how long I'll have to wait. I must be missing something. Some sort of . . . *sign*.'

'I had a hunch,' Aurelia said softly, digging at her cuticles.

Teddy gave her a weary smile. 'Oh, Schwartz, will you miss me?'

Aurelia couldn't answer. She didn't have the proper filters in line to prevent herself from saying something she'd regret, like the truth. She rose from her chair, which no longer felt like the most luxurious thing on the planet after being curled up for so long in it. Her shoulders were tight, her spine stretching out like an accordion as she brought her arms over her head and twisted. Forcing her curls down, she crossed to the couch and perched beside Ingram's legs.

'You know, Leona told me something last night – about my magic. I didn't really believe her, given that she was trying to drain me of all my blood . . . but my shoulder – it's totally . . . I mean, look at this.'

He pushed himself up beside her and bit back more foul language. Rather than bunch the elbow-length short sleeves up, Aurelia brought the neckline of Alaric's massive T-shirt down. It was large enough and *loose* enough on her to accomplish it this way, but it gave him a full view of that tender crook where her neck met her shoulder and yearned to be touched. She brushed her hair behind her neck, tidying the stray curls. He eyed her scar with curiosity. This close to his face, she had to refrain from looking at his lips again. It'd be more noticeable, and undeniably more foolish.

'She called me *healer*. She insisted that I hadn't come into my magic. I hadn't healed anything in my life before this, besides the occasional dead plant, and that's probably why the scar's rough around the edges . . . But, Teddy, I fixed it. She was right.'

As he looked on, lifting his fingers to the mark, something resembling awe and regret flickered across his face, but it wasn't enough of either for her to truly discern what he was thinking.

Frankly, Aurelia couldn't rationalize what *she* was thinking either.

His fingers were light on her skin, like English rain or fluttering leaves. She wanted him to lean forward and touch his lips there too.

Objectively, it made little sense. There were too many complications that arose from kissing Teddy Ingram. His name was synonymous with 'arrogant', 'spoiled' and 'reprehensibly dishonest'. Hers was, for the most part, unsullied in the eyes of anyone whose opinion really mattered to her. More than a handful of people knew that her name and his would never belong together, except for on a class ranking list; and that had to mean something. More likely, she'd find their names together in a news article as persons of interest, two individuals caught in attendance of more than one of Leona's public attacks.

And somehow, Aurelia had ignored the twisted bramble of complications until it sprouted thorns. What she'd done the previous night with his false image was something she could write off as a mistake. Being with him now, close enough to thread her arms around his waist, surrounded by the conservation of a magic that rivalled myth, was less complicated in her mind than it should have been, but it was a restart. A second chance to do things the right way. To be another person whose eyes she covered with an empty promise.

She rested her palms on his sides and urged him to turn away.

'I think I could heal these. They'll leave nasty scars, but I could try to seal the wound.'

Teddy raised the eyebrow visible to her from the angle of his profile. Nine was too early for him to look at her like that.

'Think you can—' Teddy stopped short and shook his head. 'Why am I even asking you that . . .'

'You're right to ask. Do your due diligence and whatnot. If I closed them, you wouldn't have to worry about catching an infection or getting sweater fibres stuck in them.'

He exhaled deeply, draping his elbows over the arm of the couch. Aurelia tucked her feet underneath herself and hovered her hands over the tops of the gashes.

'You'll feel a pull,' she told him. 'Mine wasn't bad, but it wasn't comfortable either.'

He curled his fingers into the armrest pre-emptively and said, 'Maybe you should give me something to bite on, too.'

She swallowed hard. 'Ready?'

'If I have to be, yes. I trust you, Schwartz.'

Aurelia froze, hands suspended inches from his skin as she gathered her thoughts. She'd been compelled to open her mouth and say it back, but she was unable to say it with the plainness of a returned 'good morning' to an acquaintance.

'I really hope you don't regret that.'

Her fingers twitched with the coming of a spell, the incantation bold and bright in her mind. Its grasp was stronger than green magic, and she swore she could see the current of energy flowing toward her hands in the shape of veins, barely visible at her elbows but set ablaze around her fingers.

The gold, shimmery essence of it shot forth, unlike when

she'd summoned it for herself last night. She'd slept since then. It had more of her energy to siphon from – and siphon it did.

'*Fucking hell,*' he seethed.

'Hold still.'

'I am.'

The deep incisions in his back sealed shut from top to bottom as she lowered her hands, ending on his ribcage.

Through her mind sang the word, *healer, healer, healer.* She'd done this last night, albeit on a smaller scale, but this was a confirmation as opaque and binding as ink.

It was also terribly draining.

Gasps shuddered through them as she released him from that magical tether. Teddy's shoulders slouched forward, uninhibited by the pain he'd spent the night with. Aurelia leaned back into her heels and against the back of the couch. Her head throbbed lightly, blue and white light pulsating behind her eyelids.

Teddy lifted his arm to brush his fingers along the top edge of a gash. 'You . . . you did it.'

'You're welcome,' she said plainly.

'And you're utterly brilliant, Schwartz.' He twisted to both sides, testing the parameters of his new-found mobility. He stretched his arms first, then clasped his hands above his heads and stretched upwards, elongating his torso in a particularly delicious, solid way. She fixated on the scars, trying to find something hideous about him.

Those pink freckles stared back at her, thwarting her efforts. 'How's it look? Bad?'

'Not the worst,' she answered. 'I'm sure it'll fade with age, though.'

He turned on his knees, wove his arms beneath hers, and lifted her to his chest. She held her breath as he buried his face in the side of her neck, the warmth of his skin seeping through her borrowed pyjamas.

'You're wonderful,' he whispered. 'You probably already know that, but you *are*.'

Her lips parted in shock against his hair, the promise of honest words wilting on the tip of her tongue. What could she say? She clutched him tightly, conscious of his sensitive new scar, hoping it would say more than what she felt brave enough – and stupid enough – to admit to him aloud.

A door creaked open above their heads, and the sound of an array of footsteps followed. First, it was Neil, Alaric Friedman's wiry hound that bore an uncanny resemblance to his owner, silver peppered curls included. Then came Louisa. Her face peeked out from between the slats of the banister. At first sight of her, Teddy's face illuminated with a grin.

'You're here!' she shouted.

'My darling,' he said. 'I'm so happy to see you.'

Bounding down the steps toward him, she sang back, 'Good moooorrning!'

Hurriedly, Alaric followed with an armful of folded clothing. 'Thought I heard voices,' he said, tossing a clean shirt over the banister for Teddy to cover himself. Teddy kept the sight of his back from Louisa until he could shrug the black, long-sleeved shirt over his head.

The girl threw her arms around Teddy's hips, nose dribbling from a fresh cry. 'I didn't know if you were coming back,' she told him, and he replied easily, 'Of course I would. I always do.'

Within seconds, he had her in his arms. He muttered a string of delicate reassurances to her that Aurelia couldn't bear to hear. Alaric seemed equally as antsy, and they found each other on the outside of it, mere bystanders to something precious.

'Sleep all right?' he asked.

Aurelia shrugged, and the man responded likewise. He offered her Gemma's dress and coat from the previous night, freshly dried and scented of lavender detergent instead of iron. She muttered a quiet *thank you* before departing silently toward the upstairs bathroom to change.

The tear on the shoulder of the dress gaped at her knowingly. The scar peeking through it in a taunt. She'd have to fix it when she returned to the cottage. She'd rifle through the pages of her grimoire for the right command and use common magic – over and done within seconds. More time had passed than Aurelia could account for. It had turned a corner and run from her; reality had outrun her completely. Within days, she'd be back in Cambridge for the first time since the colleges shut their doors, and things wouldn't be different at all. Her life had been rattled and thrown off-axis, but she would have to confine it to this moment – everything between her arrival in Townsend and her departure. She would have to pretend it never happened, that she hadn't loved and lost and *killed* for something as beautiful as this place. For everyone's sake.

Everyone's sake, except Marga's.

It was both a blessing and a curse, to leave Townsend exactly where it was. To harbour it in memory would only open the wounds again.

This wound was too visible through the torn sleeve. Aurelia threw Gemma's coat on next, gathering the clothes she'd borrowed from Alaric. She crept downstairs, alerting no one except the bookseller's dog.

'Thank you,' she whispered, standing at the caretaker's side. 'For the clothes. For everything, really.'

'It was nothing,' he said.

'I would love to come back here someday, if that's all right.'

Alaric's lips pursed under his overgrown, flecked stubble. 'I'm sure he'd like that. I would too.'

'Speaking honestly, do you think there's a chance he'll come back to Cambridge?'

'Speaking honestly – no. He does nothing without his full heart in it. He commits to things with every fibre of his being. Sometimes too eagerly. And if Lou is his decision – as she ought to be – he will stop at nothing to make sure she's provided for.'

Then, as if to assure them both, Alaric added, 'That's a good thing. This is a lot of change for her at once. She needs something consistent. He can be that in a way that I can't.'

'You'll look for Gemma, won't you?'

'Of course.'

She swallowed, drained and dehydrated. 'Do you think she'll come back?'

'She should have been back already,' he said stiffly. 'She should have never left.'

Aurelia watched Louisa and Teddy from where she stood, her fingernail wedged between her teeth. It was easy for them to lose sight of anything that wasn't each other. Louisa found a bruise on Teddy's arm, and he effortlessly fabricated a story behind it. He antagonized the two thin braids that fell down her shoulders, and she insisted they were *fine, just fine.* Aurelia had no place between them. She could see the cracks in Ingram's exterior, just large enough to let her hope slip through if she wasn't careful. But she didn't want that. She didn't think she could live with herself for trying to fit into a space that was never meant to house her.

Alaric's voice interrupted her voyeurism. 'How long do you intend to stay?'

She sighed again. 'I should leave as soon as possible. Term starts in four days, and I have things to take care of before it does.'

'Will you visit before you leave? I'll be sure to stay in town.'

She smiled feebly. 'Why not?' If he was fond enough of her to promise that much, Aurelia couldn't say no. Between Alaric's request and Teddy's fawning over Louisa Eakley, Aurelia was brimming with a pitiful kind of lovesickness. It squeezed her chest and warmed her skin. If she allowed it, this wanton hopelessness would bury her.

She leaned into Alaric's arm, a little unbalanced, but brushed it off as affection. 'I should go. My things are at the cottage, and I need to pack.'

'Wait a minute,' he insisted. 'You look a bit—'

She knew that Teddy's eyes had found the concern in Alaric's face, and she smiled brighter to assure him all was well.

'I'm perfectly fine. Can you show me out?'

*

She began composing a schedule on the floating grid in her mind, covering its lines in potential tasks. She sorted through formal events, knowing she rarely went to them. Ryan's name was listed every Sunday, because that was when they took care of laundry – Aurelia did hers on Wednesdays. She made room for a job, not that she knew where she would be working yet; only that she would have to work if tutoring got slow.

All the words were written in her handwriting, in black ink. It was refreshing to think in something other than gold, which was a feeling she'd never wanted to endure before.

But she needed a distraction, from Townsend and Teddy Ingram. From magic and new discoveries.

She also hoped her head would stop throbbing.

Unfortunately, the sky above Townsend was blindingly bright. The charm of the small town remained steadfast under the hazy grey of winter, but so did the headache. Aurelia wrapped the coat around her stomach and walked toward the green slope with her head downcast to the stones. She tucked her hands into her coat pockets, overcome by the absence inside them. The wandering eye slid neatly between her fingers, but her gloves . . . Had she left them in the library? On the train?

'Where do you think you're going?'

Aurelia frowned. Her hair blew unkempt around her face when she turned to face Teddy Ingram, and she eased it behind her ears.

'Needed some air,' she said. 'Where's Lou?'

'Alaric is taking her to breakfast.'

'You should go with them. Catch up with me later.' Aurelia

continued toward the hill, her footsteps harder and angrier than usual. She'd spent weeks learning to feel, at most, content with his company, and all she wanted now was to be rid of him again. Could she not smear over those rose-coloured thoughts of him in peace?

He jogged up beside her, more agile than she'd anticipated after her spell. That, too, was magic unfamiliar to her. Could she learn it like green magic without something to heal? Was it a gift she couldn't harness without a person in need of it?

'Rory, you're tired.'

'Yes, because you woke me up.'

'You were teetering back there. I don't want you collapsing on your way up the hill.'

She grumbled her response, avoiding the pull of his warm eyes.

'You know, if you collapsed up here, I might have difficulty finding you.'

'Teddy, I'm fine. Leave it alone.'

The universe had other plans for her. Her foot caught on a cluster of uprooted grass, and she stumbled. It was merely a loose step, but his hand slid around her elbow protectively.

'Look at you,' he muttered. 'You're *still* teetering.'

'It was the grass,' she said.

'God, you're stubborn. Come here.'

She didn't know what to expect as she faced him, but it certainly wasn't that he'd testify to the efficiency of her healing spell by lifting her off the ground.

'The hell are you doing?'

He secured her quickly. She was *not* wrapping her arms

around his neck for any reason other than imbalance, she reasoned. This was, in fact, much worse than being a little dizzy. He'd accomplished nothing more than another disservice to her equilibrium. The swaying would give her motion sickness.

'Repaying a favour,' he answered. 'I seem to recall you making a comment about the difficulty of hauling me up a hill in the rain.'

She grimaced and shifted a little. 'It's not raining. And we didn't carry you up.'

He narrowed his green eyes at her. She had no choice but to look at them now.

'Then I suppose I still owe you one.'

Any protest she made was wasted and lost to the ether. Besides, she was nothing if not forgiving to him. If he was so insistent on carrying her, what kind of person would she be to deny him that?

Realistically, every reference he made to debts made her feel terribly guilty. She toyed with the lapel of his olive green coat, wondering if it belonged to the caretaker; it fitted Teddy Ingram so well, so different from his usual wool.

'You don't owe me anything, y'know. I'm sorry about what I said last night. I was terrified. And angry.'

'You saved my life, Schwartz,' he said, simple and with total conviction, like the time of day. 'I'll always owe you something.'

'You saved mine too.'

He tilted his head toward her, features soft and adoring. In her mind, she cursed herself for all those years wasted on pushing him away.

'We could call it even,' he said. 'In the spirit of honesty, I'll admit I had ulterior motives for following you out here, and things I had to say that would be easier delivered knowing you couldn't run away.'

'My interest is piqued. Do tell.'

He gave her a squeeze. 'An apology.'

For what?

'For Cambridge,' said Teddy, as if she'd spoken those words to him directly. 'For being proud as always, instead of admitting I was wrong and clearing the air. What I said about you . . . How I behaved toward you . . . I reviled you so much that it was so easy to make conflict our resting state. For so long, I thought it was a game to you. It took the King's social for me to understand how much I'd hurt you. It shouldn't have taken that long. And I'm sorry.'

While he walked, the cold wind blew the front piece of his hair out of place. She smoothed it back, a little more dazed than before, and without an adequate response. She'd forgiven him already. When exactly, she wasn't sure; but it hardly mattered.

'Can you be honest with me a little longer?' Her hand lingered in the loose bit of dark auburn hair.

'If you insist.'

'What did Leona mean about your moral compass?'

'Are you confirming that I have one?'

'No, but I'm sure whatever you say'll answer that too.'

'I have one,' Teddy assured her. 'Although, at the time, it probably wasn't pointing true north.'

'That's not what she meant, was it?'

'Suppose not.' He sucked his gums, considering.

'She called you "empath". Just like she called me "healer". Which I didn't think anything of until I fixed the gash on my shoulder last night. She was right, at least, about one thing.'

'Hmm.'

'You've done it before, haven't you? You made a blood oath.'

'Yes,' he said. 'Kenny was the empath. Always feeling, sometimes too much. He was the good one, whereas all I seemed to do was ruin things. I assumed he must have known what it felt like to live with the magic I had. He could feel it in me. So, he must have known what he was getting himself into. If you knew how close we were, you'd understand why we thought it was a good idea, but maybe I'm wrong. How far into the future can you really see at fifteen? Maybe it makes no sense at all. Maybe I'm still blind to the way I loved him.'

'I'm sure it makes some sense,' she assured him. 'You're fairly intelligent.'

Teddy scoffed. 'Fairly.'

He stopped walking. His gaze was distant, past the wards of the cottage. A gust of wind tousled his hair again, and she pushed it back. This was a better game. The stakes were comfortingly low – his hair always fell back in the same shape.

'It was *you* she really wanted, y'know. She wanted me to hurt so you'd feel it and come running. Did you?'

His fingers curled around the crook of her knees. As he walked on, Aurelia thought she'd pressed on too far – asked for too much.

He added in his own time, 'When Kenny died, I was in London on holiday with my parents. He and Gemma lived about an hour away from where I was at the time. I felt him though. Cities apart, I felt him stop breathing, and it was like the breath had been stolen from my lungs too. When someone is that integral to you, losing them feels like . . . Nothing you'd ever imagine. That's what it felt like with you. One minute I was walking back to you, and the next I was doubled over on the staircase, suffocating, and everything was darker. I thought . . . I thought you might already be dead by the time I found you. I thought, *How could I have been so stupid to leave?* So, when I saw you alive and breathing, I hesitated. If I lost you—'

The clean Townsend air never felt so hard to breathe. He was so close and yet so unattainable at the same time. Her arm around his neck felt limp and useless.

He cracked a smile. 'Who else would criticize my taste in music if you disappeared?'

A bitter laugh racked through her body. 'And your startling lack of hobbies.'

'I do have hobbies, you know.'

'Like what? Meddling in the affairs of Great Britain's magical evil masterminds?'

'Aside from that, plenty. Like watching you flirt with barmen for drinks and being oblivious to modern art.'

'You're really hung up about that night at the pub, aren't you?'

Teddy's lips quirked, and that fluttering bird in her ribcage was singing again. 'Just a bit.'

Aurelia's hand dropped to the collar of Teddy's jacket again. 'Maybe you should go back. See if people still like you when you're not faking insobriety.'

'I'll consider it.'

Her fingers found the opening of the coat and splayed over his heart. 'Do you feel it when you kill?'

'So much that I think I kill a part of myself, too. Death shouldn't be such a light thing in my hands. It shouldn't be easy. It's not something I should have ever shared. If I thought my magic was a curse when I was younger, losing Kenny showed me that it would have to be a burden I bore alone.'

She tucked herself closer to him, thinking of Gabrielle, thinking of home. The sway didn't disorient her as much as it lulled her into a deep relaxation. She couldn't remember the last time anyone had been this careful with her or touched her this gently.

'You're good too, y'know. You're not monstrous.'

His heartbeat leapt under her palm; and she was Icarus, unwinding as he held her to his chest. How far would she go before it was too late? Before enough of her had melted off that she could no longer be reshaped.

'Your compliments unsettle me,' he replied.

'Be unsettled, then. It's the truth.'

Had it not been for the skip of his pulse, she could have pretended the sun was still light years away. It was not a love story after all – between Icarus and the sun – but an obsession, a chase. She had always found a method of getting what she wanted. It was a shame she wanted Teddy Ingram. His heart was there, already in her hands. Never before had it felt so easy to break.

'I'm beginning to think I left the real Aurelia Schwartz back in London,' he said.

'You're questioning my merit?'

'I have to. You're being kind to me. Looking suspiciously prettier than I remember.'

Just burn me, she thought. *Let both our wings be damaged.*

Teddy added, 'Heavier too. Lean on me if you have to, but I need to put you down now.'

Quickly, she was grounded again, familiar soft earth beneath her feet. They remained in each other's orbit, but a galaxy had formed between them. A moment of stillness – ruptured. For now, Icarus drew a new path of flight, his wings still intact.

'Was I heavier than death?' she asked, swaying slightly.

'Marginally lighter. All right?' He held out his arm for her to take, but she declined them.

'Just tired.' *And cold.*

'Pack later, then.' Teddy walked forward, his gait irregular.

The ward shimmered in front of them. She half expected to see Gemma Eakley waiting for them, calling them home like soldiers at the end of war. It'd be easier to return to Cambridge, she thought, where she would have someone waiting for her. She didn't want to walk any more. Moving forward no longer seemed like the best option. She wished she could steal all those moments back from the universe and wait. Just wait.

She felt lightheaded with Gemma's absence, spent by her beginner's expulsion of healing magic, leaning against the door frame as he ushered her inside.

'I'm OK,' she said, pre-emptively, even if her world grew hazy and the loss unbearable. She clutched the sleeve of Teddy's jacket, less for security than for comfort.

'I need to talk to Al about the eye. Will you be OK?'

'Of course,' she said. Another lie. An instinct. She would busy herself with packing, find a piece of common magic in her grimoire that could stitch the gash in Gemma's dress, and try to forget the way it felt to be so integral to someone before she would have to release them.

Rivalry, like love, required some measure of possession. As long as Gemma was absent, Ingram could be nothing to her, and that was worse than having him come back and revile her.

He watched her ease the jacket from her shoulders, piecing together the incorrectness of her answer. She'd wanted him to stay. To rest with her in the certainty that Leona wouldn't be chasing them. But that was to deny the other uncertainties looming overhead. 'Can you stick around until I fall asleep?' she asked.

It wouldn't be long. Her magic tugged at her insides trying to replenish itself, and her thoughts moved slower than usual. Gold fading to sand. Colour to black.

Before long, she was gone again, folded into another dream that the illusion of Theodore Ingram couldn't reach.

CHAPTER TWENTY-SIX

He couldn't bring himself to leave just yet. Schwartz's fingers curled lightly into his sleeve while he worked a pillow beneath her head. She protested softly to the movement, but her words were incoherent. He knelt beside her and lifted her hair from her face. Her fingers twitched to keep him in her grasp.

Her hands were heavy with regret. Even in sleep.

The world was not fair enough that it would let the guilt die with Leona. It'd bestow guilt upon him without reprieve, fastening it to his back like the heavens onto Atlas.

Schwartz was *alive*. That was enough for him now. As fully as he felt the sum of their guilt, he had to feel his longing too, and that ardent protectiveness that kept him at her side. Their desires were intertwined, his and hers and his again by means of his empathy; but when Teddy was left alone in the rare quietness of her mind, he had only himself to blame for being so enraptured by her. There was no use skirting around it any more – after all they'd done together, he would have given her anything she asked for. A clear answer. A promise. A moment at her bedside before he was inevitably pulled back to the issue at hand.

His longing was entirely his own, and it gnawed at his chest hungrily.

Her fingers tucked themselves under the sleeve of his coat as she slept, and the uninhibited softness of it reduced him to a trembling mess. His eyes welled. He blinked it away, bit hard on his lip to think of anything else. Gone was the deafening white noise of her inundated, hyperactive brain that had often plagued him back at university. She had made herself a reflection of everything she *did,* and there was always so much to do that no one ever questioned if it was real; but when she'd curled her arms around his waist or asked him into her bed, she'd offered him a glimpse of that gentleness that lurked below.

And Teddy was in love with her. That, too, was an emotion he felt threefold.

She stirred again, her dark brows knitting together as she succumbed to her exhaustion. Once it won, Teddy would have to find Alaric. If anyone knew how to make sense of the wandering eye, it was him.

You have to get rid of it, he thought. *This time, you cannot hesitate.*

He managed to remove her coat and tugged off her boots with some difficulty. For all the solid fronts she constructed, she didn't need him to be another ravaging force that made things break. She needed to be held, to be treated gently. She whispered something unintelligibly as he pulled the duvet over her chin. It sounded like a question, so Teddy took her hand in answer and brought it to his lips. 'It's still me.' She hummed again as if she'd heard, but Teddy knew she was elsewhere. She was dreaming. Dreaming of mundane things like the cluttered desk in her bedroom but also of him. Of nonsensical shapes that danced across a carnivalesque stage. He squeezed her hand

and kissed it, whispering words into her palm for her to hold like a secret. 'I'm here. I promise.'

He could steal a few more minutes with her like this, slipping his boots from his feet and the jacket from his back to slide into the bed beside her.

'It's just me, Schwartz,' he whispered. 'I'm right here.'

In the library, Teddy studied the token again. 'You knew?'

'I had my suspicions,' the caretaker answered.

'You should have told me.'

He passed his thumb over the mirrored surface, wiping away his prints. Alaric joined him at the table again, delivering a short glass of water. Teddy sipped from it slowly, eyeing the caretaker from where he sat in the leather chair. Both letters they'd received at the cottage lay open-faced on the table in front of them. Alaric had pointed out the differing swoop of the g to him, the tail Gemma would give her *o* that led into the following letters. Tendencies assumed through cursive. If only Teddy hadn't been so quick to leave after he'd read the second one. He should have seen it. He should have known these letters weren't penned by the same hand.

'I don't pretend to know Gemma's motives,' Alaric said. 'But you've expected so much from me that I didn't want to promise you an answer I knew I wouldn't have. She has always been vague. And I thought . . .'

Teddy leaned forward, replacing his emptied glass on the table with a hard thud.

'I thought she would have a plan. I still hope that she does.'

'Would she have seen it all?' asked Teddy. 'Would she know that she could come back?'

Alaric shrugged, tense as Teddy ruminated on the possibility of Gemma Eakley seeing him turn. That magic killed her son. Would she know how it consumed him? Would she forgive him for his desperation?

He didn't bother with God. Forgiveness from someone he loved was worth more than from someone he feared.

'I don't have an answer for you,' Alaric said. 'Not for her. The eye, however, can be dealt with in a number of ways. I suggest we destroy it.'

'Someone has already used it,' Teddy remarked. 'I can't ensure that Lou is safe with someone like *that* knowing where we are. Leona said she had a lover. I can't give them the space to avenge her. I have to make sure Lou is untouchable.'

Then we can destroy it.

Dread grew on Alaric's face, tugging at the creases in his skin. 'There is another option.'

'None that will put me at ease, I'm sure,' said Teddy. Part of himself was present in the conversation, but the other part was preoccupied by Aurelia, resting in the cottage while the two men spoke in private. Teddy didn't know why Alaric wanted to discuss this in the library, but the fear of leaving the cottage without supervision made his skin crawl.

Alaric's foot began to tap restlessly. His mind had gone cloudy with the white noise that Teddy was used to with Aurelia Schwartz. Townsend was a place he went to escape it, but something equivalent followed him.

'Tell me,' Teddy said.

Alaric's mouth twisted in consideration. 'We move it.'

'And *where* do you suggest we move it?'

The caretaker summoned the piece from Teddy's hand, smothering it in his grip. If there was something on the other side, it couldn't hear them. It became a coin between couch cushions, something left in a pocket and put through the rinse cycle.

'Somewhere far, somewhere desolate. If we destroy it here and now, we leave open the possibility that we stayed here; but if we were to take it elsewhere, let it sit for a while, and destroy it in . . . let's say, half a year . . . It would appear to the person with the other piece that you'd left Townsend. That you had resettled.'

Teddy scratched his neck and weighed the caretaker's recommendation.

'Do you think it'll work?'

'It's worth a shot, isn't it? Isn't it wiser to try?'

Trying gave him no peace of mind. They'd been discovered somehow, prior to the eye, and that was enough to instil fear in him.

He asked Alaric Friedman, 'Do you have a place in mind?'

'Several,' Alaric answered. 'But I'll leave that choice with you.'

The caretaker took the third token back and wound it in a heavy piece of cloth, smothering it while they spoke in their hushed tones. He offered Teddy options slowly, as if he thought the boy could be spared from being overwhelmed, but the damage was done. Teddy's mind was in several places at once: in Alaric's Luxembourg library, his bedroom at the top of

Townsend Hill, in his parents' car in London . . . How far could he stretch it? Was it not enough to leave it here? Was it not enough to destroy the eye?

'Do you need a moment?' asked Alaric, perched on the table in front of him.

He shook his head then, wiping the indecision from his features. 'It'll be traceable?'

Alaric nodded. 'That's the point, isn't it? To lead them off your scent?'

Because they had been hunted. For no reason other than that they were gifted. To be hunted by those who were meant to be their allies. To be abandoned by the one woman who could have helped them run . . .

His eyes were burning, turned raw and red from days of feeling that grief, and betrayal made them sting even worse. If he thought he felt too much before, his empathy led his heart into unreachable depths. Alaric rested his large, calloused hand on Teddy's shoulder and squeezed it, undoing his restraint. 'Tell me what you need, Teddy. We'll make it work somehow. There is nothing I wouldn't do for you. You know that.'

'For her, you mean?'

'For you,' Alaric said. 'And for Louisa. Gemma made her decision. Right or wrong, we need to find out what that was and bring her home.'

The helplessness of not knowing was the sharpest nail in the coffin.

Teddy chose where to deliver the token, a snow-covered city in South Korea called Namwon where it would remain in the possession of another trusted caretaker. It was eight in the morning in Namwon, and Alaric assured the boy that the eye would be delivered promptly as he showed him out of the library, through the shop, and onto the pavement.

They lingered by the streetlamp, a flurry of snowfall descending to their feet. 'I would take you with me, if it eased your conscience.'

Teddy had never crossed with Alaric into another one of his rooms – he'd been told it wasn't permitted without justifiable cause. To his knowledge, Schwartz was still soundly asleep. Maybe, if he was quick . . . Maybe, if he did not still feel the phantom clutch of her fingers around his hands.

'I would go if it were not so far,' Teddy told him. 'Goodnight, Al.'

CHAPTER TWENTY-SEVEN

Her recollection of the passing day came in fragments.

Midday light, streaming through the slats of the window, guarded from her eyes by the pillow against her face.

Teddy Ingram's fingers in her hair, lulling her to sleep.

The latch of the front door as he left and the cold that overcame her shortly after.

Her tongue was dry with an insatiable thirst. The waxing moon gave her a sidelong look from where it hovered. She flexed her toes and stretched her legs. She hadn't meant to sleep so long, had only meant to take some comfort in the few minutes of unadulterated closeness she had left with Teddy Ingram. She'd underestimated how much energy her untapped magic would steal from her. A whole day – precious and valuable time – lost at her back.

At least she'd been spared nightmares this time. Though the late hour was disorienting and her stomach aching, Aurelia felt surprisingly alert. She couldn't remember the last time she'd had a dreamless, undisturbed sleep. Which was a *damn shame,* because half her life had been wasted trying to chase a moment of solitude like this. Trying to shut down. Trying to keep her eyes shut. Nurturing her worries until it was impossible to do either.

She'd lost a day of packing. She could start now – her belongings were few, and the cottage was only so big – but there was more to leaving than packing alone. There were conclusions, loose ends to be tied. There was savouring to be done, memory to be indexed for some other time in the future when she would need to revisit peace.

When she thought of home and where that was, this place might come to mind. Leaving didn't have to mean 'goodbye for ever'. Sometimes it meant 'until next time'. And whether or not that was the truth this time around, it hurt less and lacked the finality that Aurelia had grown so accustomed to.

She hated goodbyes. So, she wouldn't say them.

She changed into pyjamas for the remaining hours of the night and scrubbed soap against her cheeks in the bathroom quietly. Aurelia hadn't heard Louisa return, but she was asleep in her bedroom now, buried under her heap of blankets. In the spare room, Aurelia collected those few items of clothing from the edge of the bed and folded them neatly in meditation.

Working in the quiet of night allowed for a careful consideration that daytime couldn't squeeze in. She laid her clothes beside each other and made a space for her grimoire in the centre of it all like a bed to tuck it into, to lay her magic to rest for the journey back to Cambridge.

Her fingers traced the etches in the leather, making a study.

She missed Gemma Eakley. Without Louisa and Teddy there to remind her of the distance that kept her apart from her grief, Aurelia missed her fully. How many years would pass before Aurelia Schwartz found another person to talk about her magic with so freely? She would leave for Cambridge, and

Townsend would exist in her memory as a distant, foggy thing to be absorbed by the rest of her life.

Being here, in this hidden realm of magic, she'd learned how much she *didn't* know. The fault lines in her magical knowledge had been covered up until now, and she wouldn't have time to fill them in before she left.

So many things to learn – about witchcraft, about herself... Not enough time.

So many things she'd leave unsaid, too.

Gemma, come back. Wherever you are, come home.

She set aside her task, left the grimoire on her bed, and crept into the hallway. Aurelia slowly eased the door of Louisa's room closed, a slat of light seeping through to remind them both that someone was there on the other side if needed.

Aurelia Schwartz couldn't remember anything about her mother except the few things her father had let slip, but Louisa was old enough to remember hers . . . Gemma knew it. Teddy knew it too. Louisa would have to live with the fact that her mother had abandoned her for some reason unbeknownst to them. And they could only hope that Gemma would return, with an explanation as to why she felt it appropriate to vanish. Why she thought she could retreat like the sun behind clouds and take with her all the joy and vivacity that this house had to its name—

And leave her kid.

It had to be a *good* fucking reason.

She pulled a glass from the kitchen cabinets, startled by the moving shape of a spider behind the cupboard.

Aurelia wasn't afraid of spiders. They were fascinating

creatures in theory, but unnerving nonetheless, especially when they were situated beside the bowl of fresh fruits on the countertop and a whole kitchen's worth of shadowy corners.

This one was bathing in moonlight, wanting nothing to do with the witch. It was making its house in a corner of the floating window in front of the sink. Aurelia watched it spool its thread and spin its web in reverie, thinking of how nice it must be to make a home wherever she went.

She was thinking of Gemma again – or was rather unable to stop thinking of her – wondering if home was a person, wondering what happened when that person disappeared.

The front door unlatched behind her. She spun to face Teddy Ingram as he entered, shaking the moisture from his clothing and hair.

He stared, questioning for a moment. She went to ask instead if he was the true Teddy Ingram, seeing her in pyjama shorts and a marching band T-shirt from high school, defenceless in the empty kitchen.

Before she could speak, he asked, 'Cold again?'

He'd probably give her the jacket off his back this time if she said yes. She shook her head. 'Can't believe I slept so long.'

'Seemed like you needed it. Are you sure you'll be fine going back to Cam?' Teddy removed his shoes and came behind her warily, resting his hand on the countertop where they'd shared breakfast in the mornings. His eyes never strayed from hers, colourless and deep in the blue.

'I miss my bed,' she told him. 'And Ryan.'

Teddy sucked his gums again, his head cocking to the side in consideration.

'Not that this place wasn't lovely, it's just—'

'I know,' he said. 'I've never wanted to leave so badly.'

She saw the possibility being beaten to death in his mind. The missed lectures, the withdrawal. The dissatisfaction of knowing he could not shove another awarded grant in her face. He could make it work with Lou at his side, couldn't he?

He sighed and ran a hand through his hair, casting it into disarray. Aurelia returned to the spider. It was perfectly centred over the waxing moon, resting in its bow.

'You talked to Alaric?' Aurelia asked.

'And made some arrangements. Dealt with the eye. Your train ticket for tomorrow is paid for, and you're not allowed to pay me back.'

She smiled to herself. 'You're so eager for me to leave.'

He knocked his wrist against the tile. 'You know me. How long have you been up?'

'Not long. I've been watching this spider on the sill. He's making a web now.'

'Ah.'

'I sort of admire them. Spiders. How they can pick up and move, and home goes with them.'

'I imagine their standards for home are much different from ours,' said Teddy.

'It works for them, though. It traps their food. It's mobile. In America, academics are meant to be able to move at the beck and call of their institutions. Maybe it's different here, but that aspect always seemed daunting to me. It takes so long to make a place your home, that the only way to keep doing it is to have no home at all. A spider'd have no problem with that.'

'Do you know a lot of spiders with PhDs?'

'If it's a deathly fear of spiders that makes you unappreciative of them, you can tell me. I won't laugh.'

'They're *fine*,' he said, stepping beside her to enjoy the view. 'I can appreciate them. Not sure if I'm sold on living in something that comes out of your arse.'

His eyes were on the spider, his hip against the edge of the counter, but that quirk of his lips was just for her.

'I didn't think a person that held the hand of death would be afraid of something as trivial as spiders,' she told him.

'You'd be surprised by all the things that scare me.'

Aurelia raised her brows and turned to him, realizing exactly how close he was and how much she didn't mind it.

'Like what?'

'You,' said Teddy, peering down at her. 'You terrify me. And torture me a bit too.'

All things considered, he had the upper hand. How unfair was it that he could know what she felt and take all the time in the world to figure out the things she would want to hear? He always knew the right thing to say. And when she thought he hated her, it was because he knew the wrong thing to say too.

'Sometimes I think you can read my mind,' Aurelia muttered.

'I don't know that I'd enjoy being in your head more than I already have to be.'

'Is there a difference if you can already pick up on what I'm feeling?'

'There's quite a bit of nuance that gets lost between feeling and intention. Feeling you, hearing what you say, and *knowing* you are things in frequent conflict. You say plenty of things that hardly align with what you feel. Bit of a toss-up if I'm honest. You might be the messiest person I've ever met.'

Aurelia bowed her head, hiding a smile. He smiled back, less keen on hiding his.

'For the most part, you're like white noise in my head,' he said. 'But sometimes, I get a word or two.'

'Like a spirit box,' Aurelia mused.

'What?'

She waved it away. 'Never mind. Continue.'

Rolling his eyes, he did just that. 'Mostly, it's the insults. I know you've called me *bastard* more than a few times. Odd timing too, like in class when I was focused on my work.'

'Does it distract you?'

'All the time. I suspect I only hear it because you direct it at me. Or maybe it's because you put your whole heart behind it and give me no choice. You're undeniably loud. I used to swat at the sound like a gnat before I figured out where it was coming from.'

She let a laugh loose in spite of herself. 'I used to say it more often before, though.'

'I know,' said Teddy wistfully. 'I hear it less. Now, there's a sense of relief with it . . . Like you're glad I haven't changed.'

The spider fell, capturing her attention once more.

Something *had* changed, though. All this time she'd sought to find the change in him, but he was steady as always. He was possibly one of the only things she could rely on to hold fast and stay true. That, at one time, was a burden to her, but now she saw him as a fixed variable. As something to cling to while the rest of her life was uprooted and stomped on.

The iron fortress of his was unyielding. She had made a home in it.

So, it must have been her. It became increasingly harder to map this change when she wasn't exactly sure where she'd started, only that she knew where she wanted to end up – and knew with plenty of bitterness in her heart that she *couldn't.*

Too many seconds passed in silence. Aurelia became transfixed again in the spider's web and the rapid twisting movement of its legs; and they'd both seemingly lost track of whose turn it was to speak.

His hand moved aside a strand of hair from the back of her neck, but she only felt the tickle of her curls and gave a small shudder. His other hand rested firmly on the counter beside hers.

'Your guards come down at night,' said Teddy, close enough she felt the brush of his breath against her skin. Still, he wasn't close enough. She didn't think he could ever be close enough. 'I don't think you realize how much you repress your emotions, but I do. Because when you sleep, that white noise disappears. Things come through clearer. Your thoughts run quiet . . . That's when I start to see things.'

Her breath stilled. 'Like my dreams?'

Like your dreams. He didn't have to answer it aloud – she found an answer in the subtle arch of a brow. If he could feel her tense, could he also feel the way she refrained? Was it worth *trying*, or was the refrain a sensation equally as telling as the red on her face?

She couldn't help it. Ease be damned.

'Lou dreams of dragons,' Teddy offered, sensing her hesitation.

'Little ones mostly. They follow her around like familiars while she does whatever the hell she wants. They're there with her most nights. Always the same.'

The hand formerly tasked with arranging her curls slid around her waist, his arm hovering above the surface of her back. If it was meant to be comforting, it achieved the opposite effect.

The spider, she thought.

The spider was crawling back to its web. Relentlessly.

'They fascinated me, of course,' he said. 'I'd reckon every medievalist has a buried obsession with dragons. The ones Lou thinks up have the texture of cockroach shells – a bit unnerving.'

'The dreams are that vivid for you? You feel them?'

'I feel everything,' answered Teddy, as if that didn't cause her heart to spike again. 'Can't do much to stop it. I'm resigned to watch at the mercy of them. Can be a bit of a nightmare sometimes, even when it isn't.'

'I bet.'

His thumb had slipped beneath the hem of her shirt at some point. It drew lazy circles into her skin above the waistband of her shorts.

The spider was in its web again, hard at work.

The casual touch – the ease of his body behind hers – was humiliating. She couldn't be more antithetical to it, made of rigidity and angles and tension. She was staring at the web, the moon behind it, listening for an owl's song. Anything to not think of how warm he was, and how cold she was everywhere they didn't touch. She counted her breaths, trying to replace him with something else.

'Gem is always a bluebird in hers,' Teddy went on. 'She doesn't have to be caged to this town in her dreams, so she travels. She's hardly familiar with the world outside of Townsend and Liverpool, so she builds this imaginary topography.'

'That's—'

Where were the words . . . In the web, maybe.

'Sad, I know,' Teddy finished. 'She has always stayed for Lou, I suppose. Or out of fear. I imagine she'd be disappointed with how the real world compares to what she comes up with. It's beautiful when she dreams of them, these cities brimming with magic. I get to be a bird when I'm with her, without the consequences of changing.'

'Does she know you're there?'

'She shouldn't be able to,' said Teddy, his gaze beyond the walls of the kitchen. 'But when I'm with her there, up on the wind, she'll turn her head to where I am; and I swear she sees me.'

He didn't say much after that. What was more maddening: to talk about what he'd seen – him kissing her on the hillside in late spring – or to pretend it never happened? To ignore that she thought of him more often than not, with the memory of two traitorous versions of him that would never be the real thing?

It was just late enough, or early enough, for her to risk asking. Something about conversations past eleven p.m. made her fearless. Maybe even a little stupid. Ignorant of repercussions. After all, how much time did she have left to figure it out for herself?

Aurelia tilted her face up toward his, prepared to ask. He

gazed back, mere inches from her face, with such an intensity that the will abandoned her.

'It's all right, Schwartz. Ask me.'

She swallowed, and it hurt. 'I think I know the answer already.'

His hand settled flat against her waist, mostly on skin.

'Ask me something else, then.'

Aurelia had no fucking clue what that spider on the sill was doing. That hand on her waist became the epicentre of all the warmth in her body.

'Is it ever hard to tell apart your feelings and someone else's?

'Once, it was.'

Which she took to mean 'not any more'.

She nodded, tearing her eyes away. A spider. A web.

'I know what I feel,' he whispered.

That heat blazed a trail to her lower belly, followed slowly by his hand. He pulled her closer, brought the hand that gripped the counter over hers, and wove them together.

'And me?' she asked. 'How do I feel?'

Wax wings. A perilous ascent.

Her eyes closed, memorizing the sensation of his fingers between her own, the cold tip of his nose on that uncovered plane of her neck.

'Like heaven, Schwartz. You feel like heaven.'

Aurelia curled her fingers with his. Teddy's lips parted against the side of her throat, and he drew a kiss down to that corner she'd dreamed of him touching earlier that day. Her breath came short, his name on the tip of her tongue.

Beneath her shirt, Teddy's other hand crept upward, feather

light and warm, scaling over her ribs like the spines of a book. 'Sometimes you feel like the only thing that's right in my world.'

I am Icarus, she thought. Caught in the heat of the sun. Aurelia Schwartz was igniting beneath his lips, burning, her body diminished to pure sensation. She reached up and ran her blunt fingernails along the nape of his neck, into his hair. She arched into his touch, and he responded in like by tightening his arm around her.

'Touch me. *Please,*' she whispered.

'Show me where.'

Where to begin when she wanted him *everywhere.*

His hand slid delicately over her breast, coaxing up the fabric of her bra. 'Here?'

She nodded furiously, clutching his other hand to guide him lower.

She fumbled with the drawstring of her shorts and felt him hard against her backside. The evidence of his desire drew an unbidden moan from her mouth. She ground into it, needing more, *more.* His fingers slipped past her underwear, and she gasped, curling her fist into his hair.

'You drive me mad, Schwartz.'

She turned her chin over her shoulder and pulled him by his hair to kiss him, panting as he teased his fingers between her legs. With his arms still firm around her body, she was rooted in him. If she were to descend from the heavens, void of wings, she would take him down too in a plummet toward her demise—

And she thought she could be OK with it, as long as he was

there too. Touching her, wanting her. Those long, perfect fingers against – *inside* – her body.

Her other hand tugged his hips against hers, nestling his erection between her thighs. Teddy muffled his sigh against her shoulder, eyes shut tight.

'I want you,' he whispered. 'Tell me you want this too.'

She forced her words out from a mouth half-covered by his. 'Teddy. *Please.*'

'God, I love it when you say my name,' he said. 'Every part of it.'

Their mouths met in a disjointed, feverish collision. She should have known kissing him would be imperfect. She should have known they would clash and tangle, and that it would not be as simple as what she'd done in the Tate Modern. She couldn't have known, though, how desperate he was to kiss her, how ruinous it would be to give in. How *awful* it'd feel to slow down, to pull away.

No, she wouldn't have dared.

The sharp whistle of the kettle jolted them apart. Teddy staggered back, fumbling for one of Gemma's potholders before he could remove the kettle from the flame. It shrieked as it cooled. Aurelia covered her mouth with her hand, her skin bright with shame. She nursed her breaths back to a steady pace, turning from the counter and the spider, to face him with the fullness of her embarrassment.

From Louisa's room came a small thud. Teddy shook his head as if to wake himself from a stupor and left the kitchen with a silent, '*Jesus.*'

And Aurelia was alone again, standing in the kitchen with

rumpled pyjamas and a heart heavy with self-loathing. Tea, she remembered. She pivoted toward the kettle and grabbed the handle without thinking to cover it with a dish towel. Heat flared against her palm. What the hell was she doing? Kissing him had made her senseless. The regret was making her rash and clumsy. She had set *rules* for herself to make the leaving less painful – rules to leave as little of a stain on her lovers as possible.

She didn't know what Teddy Ingram was to her any more. Not a lover. Not an enemy. She'd become too enmeshed for leaving to be anything other than brutal.

When he returned, his head was tucked sheepishly.

'Lou's fine,' he whispered. 'I'm sorry. That was—'

'We shouldn't have done that,' Aurelia muttered. 'I don't know what I was thinking. This was a mistake.'

He pressed the heel of his palm against the counter. 'That wasn't exactly what I meant to say.'

It wasn't what she *wanted,* but she'd meant it. Maybe it was a good thing her mouth had let it slip before she could doubt herself, otherwise she might have found herself asking him into bed again, with less clothing and more poorly chosen words.

Where she was going, he wouldn't stay. This place had a gravity that would drag him back no matter how much she pulled.

Teddy couldn't properly train his features as he asked, 'You don't . . . really believe that, do you?'

Proud as he was, they were entwined with one another, and she risked breaking him by separating so quickly. 'You're not coming back to Cambridge with me, Ingram. If this goes any further, it'll only hurt us both.'

'I thought this was what you wanted,' said Teddy. 'One night, and nothing more.'

'Is that what *you* want?'

He scratched his wrist, discomforted, before busying himself with pouring a cup of tea, leaving her without answer. Without reassurance. Not that he could have said anything that made Aurelia Schwartz feel less like crying.

'No,' he finally admitted. 'I don't . . . I don't know. I thought—'

'You thought it'd be easy.'

Because that's your way out, she thought. *You, who has always run, don't have to be the one to run this time.*

At the very least, she'd laid out the path for him and washed his hands of the blame. She had planted that poisonous seed of information in his head, and somehow expected it to flower into something beautiful.

'I should go,' she whispered.

'Let me make you some tea,' he said.

'I don't want any.'

'Rory darling, please—'

His fingers were light, his grip pliant and open, but she stopped as if she'd been tied to the earth. Teddy cupped her face, tilting it to meet his gaze, which felt warmer and more encapsulating than before.

He touched his lips to her forehead, and for each second that passed, Aurelia thought she heard her heart split all over again. She had wanted this. For days, maybe weeks – she couldn't recall the moment it had changed – she had wanted him to take her heart into his hands and be gentle with it.

'I just want to make you some tea,' he said.

Her eyes welled, and she kept her gaze beyond the floorboards so he couldn't see it. It would always be her secret. He could assume whatever he wanted from her feelings, but she would not let him see her cry again.

She cleared her throat, curling her fists into his sweater. 'I know you have to take care of her. You said it yourself: I can't get in the way of your family.'

He tucked his face into her shoulder and replied, 'I'm eating my words now, and they taste like utter shit.'

'But it's true, isn't it? Your life is here. Mine isn't.'

'It could be,' he said. 'There's room for you here too.'

'*Teddy*,' she scolded.

He exhaled deeply, defeat washing through him. 'I know,' he whispered. 'I know.'

For several seconds that seemed both too long and too short, Aurelia stood with him in the kitchen, her hands in his shirt and his braced on the counter beside her. Neither moved, as if time was a predator that they could elude by simply standing still.

CHAPTER TWENTY-EIGHT

Aurelia stared at the bag hanging on Ingram's shoulder with disdain. He had brought many things with him to Townsend, but he was leaving without much at all. The duffle bag was light, made to be filled with his belongings from Cambridge and promptly returned here.

He kept his hand around the strap the entire time Aurelia spoke to Alaric.

Alaric took that cue to embrace her. His cheek pressed into her curls, his arms folding around hers in a crushing display of affection. He hugged her the way that her father did – and it *hurt*. Thinking of this place, of its people. How home could be a person, and how she'd tried not to find it with anyone . . .

But here they were. Teddy, Louisa, Gemma and Alaric. Leaving was as good a reason as any to never let this happen again; and before she could feel the emptiness they'd leave within her, she first had to be carved away.

'Thank you,' she whispered.

'For what?' Alaric asked.

'Everything. I'm going to miss you almost as much as I'll miss your library.'

His chest moved with a silent laugh. 'You can come any

time. There's a place for you here. With us. This room will always be open.'

They had all made space for her, and she couldn't help feeling guilty for leaving it unfilled.

He loosened his hold around her shoulders but kept his face close, his breath tickling her ear as he spoke. 'A word of warning, my friend. Your magic is still blooming. Don't let it consume you.'

'I won't.'

'That's easier said than done,' he said, pulling away to look at her. 'But maybe your studies will have you before your magic will.'

'Maybe,' she said.

'We should hurry, Schwartz,' said Teddy. Louisa ran forward and threw her arms around Alaric Friedman's legs.

'Silly bug,' Alaric told Louisa. 'You've got so tall. When you come back, you'll be the size of the hill.'

'I'll be even bigger,' Louisa said, the air huffing out of her like a squeezed balloon.

'Take care of Teddy for me.'

'I know.'

'Bring me back a souvenir.'

'I will.'

'And *behave*. Don't let any spells slip through the cracks. It's crowded where you're going.'

It was *control* that Alaric spoke of. Control was what Aurelia Schwartz knew best – what she'd once wanted so badly to return to.

Now, she wasn't so sure.

*

Only when Louisa Eakley fell asleep with her small, drooling face smashed against Aurelia's sweatshirt did the older witch realize that this was the girl's first time out of Townsend and its neighbouring city. Louisa boarded the train with wide, glittering eyes and a wondrous smile, expending her energy on the first hour of their ride back to Cambridge.

Sitting across from her, Teddy Ingram was ever so obviously itching to speak to her, even if he could barely look at her. With all the open ends they'd left unaccounted for, he would have plenty of topics to choose from: his withdrawal from Pembroke, Gemma's disappearance—

Whatever the hell happened last night.

She'd spent hours thinking of his words and his mouth, hoping she'd done the right thing by keeping him at a distance, but there was a dissonance between them she hadn't seen before. He knew her so well, but it was all wrong. She'd become disposed to short-term flings and one-night stands out of necessity, making it easier for herself to leave unscathed.

Aurelia's fingers traipsed through the young girl's hair, down her rosy, freckled cheeks. Several minutes passed before Teddy finally spoke. 'The dragon is bigger this time. They're fighting a monster.'

Aurelia nodded plainly, not looking at him.

'I'm sorry about last night.'

'For what? Kissing me?'

'No,' he said. 'Although I do wish I'd gone about that differently. But for whatever reason, you decided that I was worth a little more than one night, and I'd assumed . . . Well, you'll have to forgive me for not *immediately* jumping to that conclusion.'

'I thought I was readable,' she said.

'Yes, but I can't read your mind, Schwartz. I know you want to kiss me. You've wanted to kiss me for a while. But you, who is so unafraid of anything, never did. I assumed it was because you didn't want to risk the regret of waking up next to someone in the morning.'

Next to me. The intention ghosted through in his words.

Aurelia's fingers rose to her mouth. She didn't realize there were nails in her teeth until she bit too hard and hurt them. How often had she rehearsed all the ways to say 'it's not you, it's me' without using those words before she arrived at this point where it wasn't her at all? She had wanted time with him, more than one night and all the mornings that came after too; but time wouldn't wait for her. Time had a cruel hand that gripped without restraint. It only gave a little before it'd seize her harder. Who could stop it? Human or witch, she was no god; and master of death, he should have known by now the mortality that all things faced.

'You think I am unafraid?' she asked.

'Yes,' he insisted. 'I think you are unbreakable.'

He couldn't have been more wrong. Maybe he couldn't see it, him being the thing that made her cave. Standing too close, he wouldn't see the cracks in her glass, but if he stepped back and went away to Townsend again, he would see that pieces of her were missing. They'd fallen somewhere on the hillside, soon to be buried by rain and mulch. She was one hard breeze from shattering, her residue carrying away like the mangled tree.

'You'll move on,' she offered.

'Maybe it's news to you, but that isn't exactly an option for me. Not while Gemma is still gone. Everything's tangled.'

Of course, it wasn't news. But she didn't expect to be the thing at the forefront of his mind as he picked up the mess that Gemma Eakley left in Townsend.

Even with the wandering eye taken care of, one witch had already discovered them; and the idea of someone else coming to finish what Leona had started was more than enough to make him pack his things and take Lou elsewhere.

For what twisted goal, Aurelia still didn't know. Had that dream of security not been birthed from the mind of someone as terrible as Leona Sum, Aurelia might've crawled for it too. For a future where she would never have to hide, where Louisa wouldn't be bound by her mother's fears of humankind.

When she thought of Teddy, she understood why it would never come to fruition. His gift was a weapon – one that *he* was reluctant to wield but others would surely vie for.

He'd probably spend the rest of his life hiding, too.

'I know,' she said. 'You underestimate how much I've considered it.'

'I never underestimate you. If anyone knows how much is happening in your head, it's me.'

That wasn't news to her either, but it stung, nonetheless.

'Rory.' He leaned into the vacant space between them, eyes on hers with such intensity that it felt like staring directly into the sun. '*Darling.*'

That word fastened her to him in a way she would have been ashamed of had she not been so tired.

'I don't know what comes next,' he said. 'To be fair, I've

never been more afraid of what will happen once it's just the two of us up there. I messed up once, and I'll carry that guilt with me for the rest of my life. But I couldn't mess up in Cambridge. Not when all I had to worry about was my work. I invested everything I had into making sure it was perfect, and the only thing that could interfere with that—'

'Was me,' Aurelia said.

Teddy dragged his fingers through his hair, scratching his scalp.

'I'm terrified that I'll end up stuck like Gem. That I'll lose sight of everything that isn't Lou, until all I have left is this place. With nothing to show for myself.'

'That's not going to happen.'

He shook his head. 'It's simpler than you think to disappear. It takes effort to be remembered, more effort than being forgotten.'

Louisa stirred in Aurelia's lap but didn't wake. Teddy sighed, resting his lips against his knuckles.

'I can't fault you for wanting to forget what happened here. Some mornings I wake up thinking it's just another stage of that dreaded nightmare. But seeing you there . . . seeing *her* there . . . that's how I know where I am. I remember that I'm safe. If *forgetting* is what you want,' he continued, 'I can pretend for your sake that we don't have feelings for each other, but we both know that isn't the truth. There are plenty of things that happened between us that are worth forgetting. But if I'm allowed to curl my fingers around those good moments, I'm not going to let them go. And if that isn't what you want . . . I suppose I'll just have to live with it, won't I?'

CHAPTER TWENTY-NINE

Coming back to Cambridge should have felt like a homecoming. It wasn't as if she'd been gone for years or fled to a different country, but it felt nearly as monumental. To come back to Cambridge was to return to a world where her magic was stifled, confined to secret, stolen moments and dark corners; and she had been comfortable with that before, but now she wasn't sure.

Coming back was like losing something – wonder or hope. Finding out that her things were all exactly where she'd left them.

Aurelia lugged her duffle bag up the stairs toward her bedroom, finding even more of her belongings unmoved. She didn't know what she'd expected, didn't know why it came as a shock to her that nothing had disappeared.

Townsend had changed her. Physically, she was no different than when she'd first left Cambridge, save for half an inch of growth at the root of her dark hair, but her eyes held a new sparkle, brought to the surface of her dark irises by the stimulation of magic in her blood. A small change she could only see in the divide between *before* and *after*. It surrounded the rest of her in an almost imperceptible glow.

She knew it was because of Townsend, but it was far more specific than that.

She had a clearer definition between the parts of her life that came *before magic* and *after magic*. Magic in theory and in practice had startling effects on her physical well-being. Despite the unfortunate circumstances that spurned it, she liked this version of herself better. She wished it could stay.

A leaf crunched under her toes. The plants that cluttered her bedroom made it a relic of what her magic was before, when she had no one to share it with. She kicked them into a pile as she glanced around her mustard yellow walls silhouetting her numerous hanging plants and art prints, of which the sizes varied uncontrollably. Most had been gifted by Ryan. Almost none of them were remnants of the place from which she last came; and if things carried memory, she'd chosen to leave them behind in favour of something new.

What was left of her last harvest lay dry, scattered in broken pieces across her floor. She needed to dispose of the mess. She chucked her bag onto her bed to be dealt with later, seized a broom from the cupboard, and began to sweep.

A clatter of silverware rang from the kitchen. Aurelia paused. Ryan had to be back in Cambridge by now, but she hadn't seen them . . . She called down the steps, but Ryan didn't answer. Aurelia walked silently down the staircase again and peered around the door-frame of the kitchen, and she saw her housemate at the sink with their enormous pair of headphones on, tapping their leg to something Aurelia could hear from where she stood.

At the sight of them, a hearty grin swept over her face. 'Fuck, I missed you.'

She sped into the narrow kitchen and threw her arms around Ryan Jena's waist.

Ryan yelped, fumbling with the knife and sponge in their hands.

It all happened before Aurelia could understand what she was doing – a flash of metal, her best friend's sharp intake of breath, and a trail of blood running down the drain. Ryan stumbling backward. '*Fucking hell!*' They clutched their thumb, and blood seeped from the crevices in their fingers. '*My fucking thumb!*'

'Oh my—'

'*Why would you sneak up on me like that?*'

Aurelia staggered back, almost to the doorway again. 'I didn't! I thought you heard me – I said something!'

'*Aaaaghhh!*'

She unwound an excessive number of paper towels, knocking down a pepper shaker in the process, before forcing Ryan onto a nearby chair to cover the incision.

Which wasn't an incision at all. Ryan Jena had sliced the tip of their thumb clean off.

As they drew away their other hand to let their friend wrap it, Ryan lamented again. 'I don't have time to go to the bloody doctor today.'

'I'm so sorry, Ry. I swear, I thought you saw me.'

'*Gaahhh!*'

'I'm so sorry,' she said. 'I'm so, *so* sorry.'

'When did you even get in?'

'Just a few minutes ago. Damn, that looks . . .'

'I don't want to look at it. *Jesus*. Do you think you could call a taxi for me? See if the other piece fell into the sink?'

She'd healed the deep lacerations in Teddy Ingram's back, but Aurelia thought she might vomit looking at Ryan's decapitated thumb. She nodded and searched the sink for it.

'Number's on the side of the fridge,' Ryan said. 'Just there.'

It was written hastily on a scrap of grid paper attached to the fridge by a frowning dog magnet. Aurelia stared at it, unmoving. The tip of Ryan's thumb was lost somewhere beneath the floor of dirty dishes in the sink, leaving them minimal hope of ever having two near-symmetrical thumbs again.

'For God's sake, I'm bleeding out here, Rory. Could you hurry up?'

She swallowed, disoriented. Ryan hissed out another sharp breath as they applied more pressure to their wad of paper towels.

'I'm not taking you to the doctor.'

'Like hell you are!'

Aurelia kneeled in front of Ryan's chair, eyes on the spots of blood that seeped through the wad. Slowly, she unfurled her friend's hand and held the thumb upright in a cocoon of hands and paper. 'I need you to trust me.'

'On *what?*'

'I promise I'll explain it. I'm going to fix your thumb, and I need you to stay calm.'

'I don't like this,' Ryan muttered, sniffing their glasses up. 'Can't you just call a taxi for me?'

Aurelia pushed her hair out of her face and met Ryan's eyes firmly. Ryan Jena begrudgingly assented. They surrendered their hand to her and squinted, wanting to know and not wanting to see.

Aurelia moved her hands around the injury without touching it. 'You have to say you trust me first.'

'What's the matter with you?'

'Say that you trust me.'

'Fine, all right, I trust you. My thumb is literally oozing.'

Ryan cut themselves off with a howl as Aurelia closed her hands around Ryan's thumb and disregarded the rule she'd lived her entire life by: humans must remain ignorant to magic.

And while the intention of healing turned over in her mind a hundred times in less than a minute, she was also thinking, *I love you, Ry. You love me. Please don't forget that.*

Ryan's arm shot back. They gathered up the wad used to encircle their thumb, drawing short as they discovered fresh, sensitive skin where there should have been blood.

Aurelia saw a lifetime of secrecy disintegrating in the widening of her housemate's eyes.

'How did you—'

'Please don't be angry with me.'

'*It was a bloody mess!* It was *gone!*'

'Everything's OK,' Aurelia insisted. 'Just calm down and listen to me, and I swear I'll tell you.'

Ryan flexed their hand once, then again, checked the other hand to make sure they hadn't been confused enough to mix them up, and finally they dissented.

'It's . . . It's OK? I think,' Ryan said, trailing off. 'Have I gone completely mental?'

Aurelia shook her head, tears already welling in her eyes. 'No, Ry. You're completely, perfectly sane.'

'Right.'

'And given that you're perfectly sane, you probably won't believe what I'm about to tell you; but I need you to stay with me here, OK?'

Her friend nodded, some of the shock dissipating from their face. The anger that Aurelia thought she'd find in Ryan was merely a thing of her imagination, and she braced herself as she spoke for something else to move in and take its place.

It never came. So, she told them everything.

She spent an ample amount of time beating around the bush, proposing examples like collecting leaves and infrequent, unexplainable illnesses that tormented her without ever getting to the purpose. By then, she'd collected herself enough to look her best friend in the face again. They looked back, thoughtful and awestruck as ever, which made the consequent tears spout viciously.

And from there, she admitted truths from which she could never return. Truths about magic, about her childhood, about truth itself, and how much of it she'd been keeping from them. How she'd pushed her friend away because she didn't have an answer at the time for why her health was in such rapid decline; but now she had one. It was the same answer to reverse her downward pitch as it was to repair her housemate's thumb.

She laid her head in Ryan's lap, and Ryan ran their fingers over her cheeks to comfort her. Against the steadiness of their hand, the racking sobs that shook through Aurelia's body were evidently more jarring.

'I'm sorry,' she said. 'I'm sorry I never told you. I'm sorry I kept anything from you, Ry. I hated it. I wish I could have told you everything, but I'm not supposed to. And you're supposed to hate me. I didn't want you to hate me.'

'I *don't* hate you,' Ryan added.

'Why not?'

Ryan laughed, folding over in their chair to circle Aurelia's shoulders with their arms. 'I do feel a bit mad, but you've always been odd. Always had unusual habits and lukewarm excuses to cover them up. And we've always known each other far too intimately. You could never lie to me, Rory, but that doesn't mean you can't still puzzle me.'

'I never wanted to lie to you. But after twenty *plus* years of being half myself, sometimes it felt like that was all I was . . . And that I wasn't lying at all.'

'You were scared.'

Aurelia sniffed back another sob. 'Nothing scared me more than losing you,' she said. 'You're my best friend. When I was at my lowest, you were my *only* friend. And it's likely that I'll never tell another living soul about what I am besides you.'

'The dead ones, then,' said Ryan.

'Yes,' Aurelia mumbled. 'The dead ones.'

'Do my ancestors know about this already? Were you waiting for me to join them before you told me?'

'Don't joke about that. You aren't going anywhere.'

Ryan clicked their tongue, and Aurelia tightened her hold around her friend's lap. They'd both lost Marga, but Ryan didn't know how close Aurelia had been to losing someone else: Teddy Ingram, be it a friend or not.

'OK,' Ryan said. 'I won't.'

'Good.'

'Are you OK?'

Aurelia shook her head again but eased her chin onto Ryan's lap with some semblance of dignity. 'Of course not. I've had my whole life to collect guilt over this, and now there's just an empty space. I didn't think I'd ever have to share this. I thought I'd have to be OK with this for the rest of my life. But that place . . .'

She hadn't told Ryan about Teddy's magic. Only that Townsend was a safe place, that it felt more like a homecoming to her than dangerous and unexplored territory. 'It's strange. So much has changed since I was here last with you; and to continue on as if everything is *normal* – as if *I'm* normal – feels like a disservice to everyone.'

'I wish I knew what to say.'

'It's OK. *I'm* OK. I promise.'

'Do you mean it this time?' Ryan held up their pinkie and hooked it around hers.

'I always mean it,' she said. 'I'm just not always right.'

'No. You can be a real idiot sometimes for someone so smart.'

Aurelia wiped her nose with the long sleeve of her shirt. 'I'm so happy to see you, Ry.'

Their face lit up, and Aurelia realized how devastating it was that Ryan didn't smile more often. They were a lodestar of joy, a beacon of hope. If everyone smiled like Ryan Jena did, witches would have revealed themselves decades ago.

'I'm happy to see *you,*' Ryan said.

'I'm happy I didn't fuck up your thumb.'

'I'm bloody thrilled about that.'

Aurelia laughed, rising up to meet her housemate, rickety on her own two legs. Ryan caught her and gathered her into a proper embrace.

She wiped her face against Ryan's hoodie. 'I want to tell you everything.'

'I want to hear it. It's not every day your cool best friend tells you they're a witch.'

'Where I'm from, it is. Just not the kind of witch you're thinking of.'

'Do you think,' began Ryan, sheepishly, 'if it's not too much to ask, you could make some tea for us? I don't want to be in this kitchen right now. Too many sharp objects, so soon.'

'I really am sorry for that.'

'I'll live. Suppose I would have lived regardless.'

The questions were endless. They persisted through tea, over lunch, sporadically into the evening as Aurelia unpacked her duffle bag – they met her with a hundred instances of 'just one more question'.

By the time the lampposts flickered on outside her window, both Aurelia and Ryan lay reclined toward each other in her bed. Mentally, Aurelia was drained, but her body was alert and eager to move. Still, she slid in beside her housemate when they asked, afraid that with enough distance between them, the cloud of amazement would clear from Ryan's view and show them just how horrifying the reality was.

So, she stayed close. It eased her fraught mind to know that Ryan Jena wasn't going anywhere.

'That's mad,' Ryan said. 'Wow.'

Ryan said that a lot too: *Wow.* Their face was alight with innocent wonder, and so Aurelia spared them the more gruesome aspects of what happened while she was away. To someone else, magic could still be a beautiful thing, one that healed without the capability of ruining. To Ryan, it could be anything Aurelia wanted it to be, even if the truth was long overdue.

She omitted the details of her run-in with Leona but told them it had happened. That she got to see London again, and it was bustling and fragrant as always. That she wasn't in danger. She spent a lot of time assuring Ryan Jena that everything was OK; and only after the fifth reassurance did Ryan understand it was because something was ever wrong.

Ryan's fingers interlocked with hers on the pillow between them, agitating her hand distractedly. It took hours before Aurelia felt like talking about Teddy Ingram any more than she already had.

Because behind her, there were over twenty years of discoveries for Ryan to make, and outside the scope of Aurelia's life, there was an entire race of witches that lived unbeknownst to humans like them. Leona Sum and Teddy Ingram were at the forefront of her mind, but they didn't have to matter more than that to her housemate.

'Am I allowed to say I'm jealous of you?'

'No,' Aurelia said with a faint smile. She confiscated the knitted hat from Ryan's head and tossed it off the bed. 'It's complicated.'

'*Complicated,*' Ryan drawled, mimicking her accent. 'It's fucking cool.'

She sighed. 'Sometimes. We'll always have a house full of healthy plants. And I doubt you'll be losing any appendages from here on out.'

'Do you think another version of me will grow out of my severed thumb?'

Aurelia smiled as Ryan tapped the tip of their thumb against her nose.

'What if you can't tell us apart?' they asked.

'I already know two of you,' said Aurelia. 'The *you* that's for me and the *you* that's for everyone else.'

'So, everyone else just shoves off, then?'

'Exactly.'

Aurelia's phone buzzed angrily against her desk. Her eyes flickered downward, and she released a piteous breath. Ryan blinked back at her, expectant.

'Going to answer that?'

'I don't know. It's probably him.'

'Then you should *probably* answer that.'

'And say what?' Aurelia tucked her knees into her chest, easing the throw over her shivering ankles. 'There's a clear outcome if I ignore it, but I'm not sure what happens if I pick it up. I don't know that finding out is worth it.'

'Maybe start with "hello". Like a normal person.'

Because that's what I am. Normal. The phone buzzed intermittently. Ryan peered over her shoulder to confirm the name that flashed across her screen before it disappeared, and they were left in the permeating silence.

'No one ever calls to say hello. It's always "hello, how are you?" Or "hi, can we talk about something?". "Hello" is the easy part of a conversation. I don't want to deal with everything that comes after.'

'But he does,' added Ryan.

'He doesn't. There's no *after* at the end of this. He'll leave, and I'll be here getting on with my life. I can't tell him that after spending so much time nursing my wounded ego, I wish he would stay here. Don't you see how crazy that sounds?'

Ryan shrugged. 'People justify a lot of crazy things with being in love.'

Her body froze. The overbearing, aching reality of it seized her all at once, even while she tried to tell herself, *That isn't what I am.*

She couldn't expect that from him either. Not now. Not ever.

Ryan inched even closer, breath tickling her face. 'What scares you about answering it? You like him, Rory – and don't try to deny it. I didn't believe you for a second when I called the other day.'

'I was telling the truth, Ry. It was all so sudden.'

Less than two hours later, she thought, he brought her hand to his chest, and she would have let him kiss her.

'But between then and now, there's something you think could get ruined by answering the phone. Let's say you're being honest with me for once . . . What's stopping you from letting it happen?'

Aurelia couldn't answer and picked at a loose thread on her pillowcase instead.

Ryan caught her hand swiftly. 'Was I right in thinking you'd break his heart? Did you cut him loose like everyone else when they wanted more?'

'No.'

'Did he break yours? In that case, I'll phone him myself and tell him to bugger off.'

She tucked her face into the pillow and huffed. 'Don't be silly. No one ever breaks my heart.'

'Then you're just moping,' said Ryan. 'I thought you were above moping.'

'I'm above nothing. Despite how much I want to be.'

'Do you love him?'

She failed to draw her next breath.

'He's so like me sometimes it's almost narcissistic; but I *like* him. I like him more than I've liked anyone else before, and that's already more than I can stand.'

Ryan raised their eyebrows.

'Do you think it's possible to know someone too well?' Aurelia asked.

'It depends. Can you accept the other parts of someone that they want you to know too?'

She'd never had to ask herself. But she'd done it faithfully, easily. Giving them back wasn't even an option she would consider.

'You can tell me if you love him, Rory. I'll try not to be too jealous.'

'Jealous,' she murmured. 'Of what? I'll always love you, Ry. That will never change.'

'Swear it on your life?'

She tapped her thumb to Ryan's nose in an identical manner and whispered, 'Yes. Always.'

CHAPTER THIRTY

She ran errands around her college the next morning and ignored the phone in her pocket. It might've been ten years since the last time she considered herself adjacent to boy-crazy. Ryan joined her for lunch, eyes peeled for something Aurelia had no clue of. When she asked her housemate, they'd said, 'Being out with you now feels a bit like hiding contraband.'

Aurelia laughed. They were huddled close for warmth, catching powdery white snowflakes on their tongues as they meandered toward their flat.

'I'm still me,' she said. 'Always the same.'

'That's not true. You're hardly the same person day to day. I can't keep up with you sometimes.' Ryan stamped their feet on the doorstep before unlocking the front door. 'I realized something this morning.'

'Oh yeah?'

They nodded, pulling the black gloves from their fingers. Holding up both thumbs beside each other, Ryan said, 'It's shorter now.'

'You're never going to let this go, are you?'

'Well, it was yesterday. So, *no*.'

'I'm freezing. Let me in.'

'That was my texting thumb. My *drawing* thumb.'

'I'm losing toes here, Ry.'

Aurelia's housemate stretched their arms over the width of the cracked door and lamented, 'That thumb was my livelihood.'

'Let me inside.'

Ryan held their wrist to their forehead like a near-fainted Regency mother. 'Enter if you must, but grieve for my loss.'

Aurelia slid past them, stealing the keys from their hand, and depositing them into a bowl beside the door.

She checked her phone again for a text that hadn't come yet before hastily returning it to her pocket. After Ryan had fallen asleep the previous night, Teddy Ingram sent her a message inviting her to dinner.

An olive branch, she'd told herself. *Nothing more.*

'When was the last time you were on a date, Ry?'

'Officially? Haven't the faintest.'

'Do you remember if you called it a date?'

'Probably not. Labels these days feel archaic.'

Aurelia rolled her eyes. In her back pocket, her phone began to buzz.

'Speak of the devil,' said Ryan.

'Speaks for himself. *Ingram?*'

She heard a faint chuckle on the other end of the call. '*So* stern.'

Ryan pulled a grave expression and mouthed those two words back in jest. Shaking her head, Aurelia resumed the call in the privacy of her bedroom, feeling thirteen and defensive over her unscathed heart. That buried adolescent yearning pulled at her proverbial heartstrings as she sifted through her wardrobe, pretending that her pulse didn't race at the thought of having one last moment with him – and where they might finish it.

Ten years was nothing, it seemed. Her skin reddened with the same cues, heart aflutter as Teddy Ingram's laugh came through the phone. *Nothing.* A virulent seed planted in her newly tender self, that she would test the invisible boundaries of time if it meant she had calls like this to look forward to. In it, there was the promise of more to come.

Five thirty, he'd said. 'I'm glad you're coming.'

'So am I.'

After it ended, Ryan helped her choose something to wear. When the time for dinner came, she stuffed herself and the orange puffs of her coat into his car.

'Do hurry. I've left a seven-year-old alone in my flat with a very expensive meal.'

Aurelia shut it behind her, her unwound umbrella stuffed by her boots. She tucked her hair behind her ears, the action being both a vessel for her anxiety and a calculated trick – he was looking at her lipstick. She'd worn another shade. In her peripheral vision, his eyes traced the edges.

'I figured *you'd* be cooking,' she said.

'I did, yes. But I'm particular with my materials.'

'Silver spoons?'

He hid a smile, adjusting his grip on the wheel. 'Fresh ingredients. You know, good cheese. Fine wine.'

'Wine,' she echoed.

'To pair with whatever heinous programme Lou's picked out for us to watch.'

She edged toward him over the console, her nose wrinkled. 'Should we pretend to be drunk?'

She thought he might kiss her then, and recalled that the first time they'd *actually* kissed, they'd been twisted uncomfortably against a hard kitchen counter. Being so close to him now, harbouring that memory, made her pale with embarrassment.

He smiled, bright red with it all, and answered, 'Totally sloshed.'

Louisa had acquired several new chapter books, and Teddy some storage tubs.

'Don't mind those,' he muttered, ushering them aside with his leg. He hadn't started packing yet, but he would soon. The contents of his drawers and cabinets lay scattered around their rooms, prepared for wrapping.

Aurelia shrugged out of her coat and threw it over the back of a wooden chair. Louisa recounted her day in the city with an unspoiled innocence. He'd taken her to Heffers Bookshop, the greens of the college where they studied, the spoils of Market Hill food vendors. He'd bought her a box of candies to help her bide her time until they returned to Townsend.

Teddy called Aurelia into the kitchen, raising a wooden spoon to her lips.

'It's warm,' he said before pressing the edge to her lip.

'Tastes expensive.'

'Good. We'll eat downstairs.'

His walls were mostly bare, painted a deep grey that seemed both elegant and lonely. The neat piles on his coffee table and the edges of his bookshelves made it evident that he'd cleaned before she arrived, but those piles were made of work and study. It took a comfortable sum of wealth to make a place look fashionably empty. Loneliness, though, required some degree of clutter. A pile of work wasn't the mark of leisure that Aurelia knew from her father's hoard of television remotes or the box of pre-rolled joints her sister kept on her table.

Downstairs in the basement, he'd made a marginally cosier space for himself with a small love seat, low table and television configuration that reminded Aurelia a bit of Gemma's cottage. As Teddy placed plates in front of her and Louisa on the table, he made note of his other shelves to her. 'I keep my favourites on this one. I've got a few from Al's shop down here.'

He wiped his hands on the front of his sweater and pulled a marbled leather copy of *The Rubáiyát*, ornamented with gold foil, and slid it into Aurelia's hands.

He went upstairs to retrieve his own dish, and Aurelia skimmed through the pages, tracing her fingers down his annotated margins. Some had pages embossed through by the scratch of his dying blue pens. Some annotations overtook the text completely, until the book was more his work than anyone else's. To love something was to deface it – to give it a mark and change its identity for ever. Beneath her thumb, every word felt like a divulgence.

They gathered around the low table, ravenous for a home-cooked meal. Teddy poured her a glass of wine, and then another; he downed two of his own consecutively. He told Louisa not to pick at her food with her fingers, and she argued they were recently washed – 'so it didn't matter'. A dash of pasta sauce lingered at the corner of the young girl's mouth. Teddy thumbed it off her face with a comical groan.

Aurelia had been ambivalent about the idea of domesticity thus far, but the scene in Teddy's flat was nothing short of blissful. A glimmer of magic in the mundane. Louisa picked an animated movie for them to watch on Teddy's small television set. She'd sprawled out on the love seat without regard for the two larger bodies sitting at the base of it, picking from a bowl of clementine slices that sat between them. Teddy had his arm along the couch's seat, ghosting around Aurelia's back. Their knees pointed toward each other, their bodies curved around the small bowl of fruit like handles.

Aurelia turned and found the young girl snoring half an hour into the film, her freckled face smashed against a matching pillow and her arm hung limply off the edge.

'Was it good?' Teddy whispered.

The food, he meant.

'I'm thoroughly impressed.'

By all of it. You especially.

Teddy's hand crossed over her side of the fruit bowl and touched her knee, which was close enough that it nearly touched his. There was a snag in her tights beneath his fingertips that he found quickly.

'You'll tear it.'

'It's already torn.'

You don't understand, she thought. *I want you to. I want you to unravel me completely, starting with my tights.*

Hours ago, she'd held the dress to her body in front of her mirror, worried that he'd see it for the cheap thing it was, but he didn't seem to care – or even notice. He'd stopped reading the film's subtitles minutes ago in favour of it, tracking the scatter of light in the weave in her tights, and the way it disappeared completely at the hem of her skirt.

His fingers slid around the back of her knee, and he touched the hem there too.

Louisa stirred once behind them, muffling something into her pillow. Teddy's hand could have rested in the crook of Aurelia's knee untouched, but she wrapped her fingers around it, pretending she didn't feel the raise of a scar on his palm, and lifted it away.

Some moments you destroy because you love.

He gathered their dishes in his arms and took them to the kitchen.

Aurelia leaned down and touched her lips to the young girl's forehead, leaving all that blooming affection in the moment, the softness of her kiss. She didn't know if she was allowed to love Louisa Eakley – if she could ever be a part of her life the way she'd needed someone to be there for her, but she ran her fingers through Louisa's silken, ash brown hair and imbued it with an intention.

Be safe. If she could weave magic into those words and make them a spell, she'd have cast it already. No spell could fully encompass what those two words meant to Aurelia Schwartz. It meant, *I hope that magic will always be good to you. I hope you will never have to harden your heart the way I do. I hope that when our paths cross again, your smile won't have faded.*

In none of those intentions was a goodbye. 'Goodbye' was too honest, too true even though she didn't want it to be. Sometimes, truth drew blood. Sometimes, truth was a monster under your bed that you would have to face with age. She'd known too many of those to become one – to be a ghost in Louisa's life.

Aurelia rose quietly and crept up toward the ground floor. Teddy shut off the kitchen sink and twisted to face her. There was a flicker of ease on his face that fell knowingly when he looked at her for longer than a second. She tried not to let it reach past her exterior, but he'd found a way through the labyrinth of her heart somehow. When he left, she knew there would remain a gaping chasm in his wake.

He opened his mouth to speak, drying his hands on a dish rag, before he closed it again.

'I should head home,' she said. Teddy gave a wordless nod. 'Thank you for this. I'm glad you asked me to come.'

He smiled back, realizing how little she called him by his last name any more. It was fitting now that they'd ended up here again. She was still grappling with the idea that stony Cambridge medievalist 'Ingram' and the boy who thought he needed to run away to Townsend Hill could be the same person.

'Yeah,' he said. 'Any time.'

They idled in the front hallway, waiting for the other person to break. She opened her arms. He pulled her firmly to his body, his waist to hers, her face tucked neatly into the soft curve of his neck.

'I have to go,' she whispered.

'Who says? You say that like it has to end.'

It was delusional to think otherwise. His knowing somehow

made it worse. Part of her wanted him to fight for her, to be irrational and unrealistic. To argue just for old times' sake.

'Doesn't it? What happens come Sunday, when you and Lou head back to Townsend and Gemma isn't back? You've made it clear to me that your life isn't in Cambridge any more, but mine *is*. Besides, there's nothing for us to end. You've never been my friend. Have I ever been yours?'

'Yes,' he said. '"How could you so long have failed to recognize me?"'

Another inside joke, one they'd probably never make again. He'd been her ire, her equal, her shameful secret. So many things to her that she'd lost track of counting. But tonight, he was her Tristan, her lovelorn knight, and Aurelia his untouchable Iseult. They were a story with endless potential. A myth she could always rewrite.

'I don't want this to be the end, Schwartz. You're the cleverest person I know. If anyone could make this work, it's you. It's *us*.'

'I don't know what choice I have.'

'You could stay,' he whispered, winding one of her curls around his fingers. 'That's a choice. Unless *this* is what you want – to be over and done with me.'

She had plenty of reasons, not just to avoid kissing him but to leave now and never look back. Frankly, all of them were smothered in the back of her mind, drowned out by the desire that lurched within her gut. She disregarded all of them, lifted her hand, and laid it against his chest over his heartbeat – the small mercy he'd asked for once on the hillside.

'If you knew how I felt, why didn't you ask me before?'

Tucking that curl behind her ear, he asked, 'Have I not made it clear how much you afflict me? Aren't I asking you to stay?'

'You're *offering*,' Aurelia added pitifully. 'There's a difference. We've spent so long hiding behind our indifference that I'm not even sure I know how it feels to say yes to you.'

She slid her hands up his shoulders, behind his neck and into his hair, where she'd seen his own hands so many times and always longed to touch.

'The last time you held me like this, I ended up with a knife to my throat,' Aurelia whispered. Teddy blinked, uncertain. 'We've done this before – in the Maciá room. You should have been there. It was magical.'

'And you let me?'

'Of course I did. And now I'm worried you might do something worse like break my heart. So, *ask* me,' Aurelia whispered. 'Ask me to stay.'

A mark of insecurity flashed across his features and softened his expression. Gone was the crease in his brow and the tension in his jaw, and she yearned to touch her fingertips to the subtle part of his lips and prove her willingness to answer him. To say yes.

Several things occurred before his mouth touched hers: a union of the wall and her back, the arching motion that aligned her hips against his, and his hands . . . His hands were on her face, then her hips, threading all the space between with a loose running stitch. Teddy drew her close and kissed her slowly, learning the extent of Aurelia's willingness through the graze of teeth. Her fingers raked through his hair. Teddy *asked* with a despondent groan, and she answered, swallowing it up.

'God, Schwartz. Am I too late? Did I wait too long?'

She looked indecent, even by her own standards. Her eyes were wide, pupils probably dilated past the biological limit. She kissed him once, quick and breathless in the dark, and assured him, 'It's OK. I waited too.' Only because it was easier than saying, *Yes, you are. Yes, we did.*

'Will you stay with me?' he whispered. 'I don't care if it's sex or sleep, I just want to . . . to be with you while I still can. To be on the same page for once.'

She nodded, her resounding 'yes' a mere gasp against his lips. Her chest heaved, every inch of her skin surely flushed. She knew desire, but *longing* was a wicked new sensation made of patience and impermanence – two things she'd never cared for.

'If you want to head into the bedroom, I'll be right in. Through the door to the right at the end of the hall.'

'Can I borrow some clothes for the night?'

'If you insist. Could wear me, if you'd like.'

'You're *hilarious*, Ingram.'

As Aurelia stepped toward the hallway, Teddy caught her hand and brought its open palm to his lips. 'Kissing you makes me a bit of a mess. "A good fool at no loss for words."'

Her fingers flexed, held close to her chest. Who was a greater fool than Aurelia Schwartz who could get so visibly flushed by the bastardization of Joseph Bédier being whispered into her hands?

'Be up soon,' she told him plainly. 'Kiss me again.'

CHAPTER THIRTY-ONE

It happened slowly. Inevitably.

Teddy kissed her first, but Aurelia kissed him harder, pressing her unabashedly eager body flush with his. He locked the bedroom door behind him with a fumbling hand. She curled her arms around his shoulders, her legs around his hips. He touched her in a rush, as if he had only moments to discover this underlying facet of her. There wasn't a spot on her body that she didn't want him to know, his fingers engraving his signature in gold like the spells written in the dark of her skull. What was a kiss without hands but a letter left unsigned – intentions only halfway delivered?

He pulled away briefly to make space for his hands between them. She sat herself on the side of his bed, and he cursed softly, attempting to unzip the back of her dress when the zipper caught. She tugged the bodice downward, baring the soft expanse of skin to his gaze and to the cold. Something softened in his face that was almost indistinguishable within the shadow of his room. Then he eased her back with a weighted palm to her sternum and covered her in his warmth.

His lips trailed down the shallow valley between her breasts. Every inch of her skin roused with his rapt attention. She wanted him lower, to make right on her unfinished dream, but he paused beneath her ribs, braced by hands against the mattress. Several torturous seconds passed wondering whose turn it was to speak, until at last, Teddy Ingram admitted, 'You're so pretty, Schwartz. It makes me sick sometimes.'

She knew that sickness, the ache in her gut, the fever between her thighs. An absence she could not sate herself. Aurelia reached for his waist and pulled his hips into hers by the belt loops of his trousers.

'I wore this for you, y'know. I wanted you to take it off.'

'You're so good to me,' he said. 'I don't deserve you.'

Aurelia slid the dress over her head, and Teddy rolled her tights down her thighs. His palms slid around her legs. She propped herself upright by her elbows, naked and cold, while he kissed a path along her inner thigh.

She wanted to see him. To know what he looked like at her mercy. She'd never seen someone so beautiful. His green eyes were grey and gentle in the dark. She pushed her blunt fingernails through his hair again and grabbed, desperation in her every move. If she could keep nothing else for herself, she would have his look of unparalleled reverence branded into her mind. She wanted to be drunk on him too, and this feeling—

This feeling.

His red cheeks and wide pupils had her yearning for the feeling of something more inside her – tongue, fingers, *anything.*

His mouth moulded to the centre between her thighs, already slick from wanting. 'Right there,' she whispered. 'Just – like that.'

He hummed, and she unravelled against the soft vibration

of his mouth, relishing in the knowledge that he was *hers*. At least, for one short-lived, exquisite moment in time. He thought she was pretty, thought she was smart and capable, but above all, he knew that she possessed the kind of magic that made monsters out of people. He wanted more. To be everywhere on her at once – touching, tasting, savouring her whispered encouragements like a precious wine.

He dragged her to the brink of finishing, then fell back, flushed with heat and arousal.

'Your desire,' he murmured, 'is so dizzying.'

He pressed his face to the soft flesh of her inner thigh and kissed that too. The tip of his nose was comfortingly cold against her skin, like the first snowflakes of winter. He crawled over her, pinning her beneath a cage of limbs.

'Seems unfair that you're still fully clothed,' she said, trying not to squirm beneath his gaze; but he looked at her with an intensity that was impossible to ignore. She hooked her index finger around his high collar and muttered, 'It's so *cold*.'

'My body is hardly a sight at this point. Before, maybe. You should've seen me without my wings.'

Did he believe the familiarity with which she gazed at him might make him less enticing to her? Or that the way she might remember his mangled, bloody wings when she touched his scars would make her feel repulsed? She tugged the hem of his sweater loose from his trousers defiantly. He couldn't have been more wrong. That version of her was not real and had never been real. She had always known him too well, too much for her own good, and she'd be damned now to give someone else the courtesy of knowing him best.

'We're not pretending now, are we?' she asked as Teddy shucked his sweater off and tossed it aside.

'I'm nothing any more if not real for you,' he said.

She reached for his belt and made haste to unfasten it. She should have been good at this. She didn't know why her hands fumbled as she worked to free him from his trousers. His finger slipped beneath her chin, and he tilted up her face to meet his. The rest of his hand followed, sliding around the back of her neck and into her hair. She kissed the light dusting of pink freckles on his abdomen. He bristled against her unrepentant tenderness, and she did it again, abundant in her affection.

'I want this to be real,' Aurelia said. 'Us. And *you*. You think I'm unafraid, but I've never been seen so clearly before; and that terrifies me.'

Out of all the short ends and scattered lovers she'd had, he was the only one who'd known of her magic. To know magic as they did was to know its horrors, the greed that could consume a witch and drive them mad for more. But they knew magic as they knew each other, like another line on their palms or a word with the right intention. Although it wasn't a facet of herself that came up in bed, it was too significant a part of her to overlook. If sex was a carnal act so far, it was only because she'd never been known so plainly.

Aurelia brushed her thumb across his bottom lip. Ingram took the tip of it between his teeth and bit it. She ventured further into his mouth and pressed it to his tongue.

Everything was quiet. The walls were thin, but the feeling was large, and every whispered sentiment shook her with a brazen heaviness.

'You're so beautiful,' she told him.

'Sometimes I think I was made for you,' he said. 'To be yours. To touch you like this.'

He let Aurelia part his lips with her tongue even if the taste of her was still present on his mouth. She met him with kisses that'd bruise, kisses that were more teeth and hunger than self-awareness. Reaching for his nightstand, he unwrapped a condom and slid it over himself, a question laid in the ellipsis between one kiss and another: *Yes*, she nodded. *Yes*.

With his tip pressed against her entrance, he eased into her, clutching her hand, kissing her neck. She wound her other arm over his shoulders and pulled him against her, full and hard, hiding her gasp in that serene fragrance in the crook of his neck. Her knees hugged his sides, drawing him in, keeping him there while she adjusted to his size.

'I love the way you smell,' she confessed.

His laugh was severed by the heaviness of his breath. 'I know you do, Rory. I wear this stupid thing for you.'

'Do you?'

The way he imbued her name with devotion was a sorcery of its own merit. He made it a spell to add to his repertoire. He nodded, hiding his face against her neck. 'Mhmm. It's one of the only things you ever liked about me. I couldn't very well do without it.'

He moved then, pushing deeper until he reached that threshold of pleasure and pain.

'Is this OK?' he asked. 'Are you OK?'

Those words wound around something soft and delicate inside her she didn't know was still there. She shut her eyes as he tipped his forehead against hers, knowing if she granted him that intimacy, she would never get it back.

'If it hurts, tell me to stop, and I'll stop—'

'Don't,' she said. 'Keep going, just like that. You feel—'

'So good, Rory,' he answered, pushing his full length inside of her. '*Fuck*, you feel so good. We should have been doing this ages ago.'

She wanted to disagree. To say that they were never in a position to have each other like this, but that wasn't the truth. In the kitchen with his hand up her shirt, she would have killed to touch him this way. 'After that dream – in your bed.' Her words were fragmented by his movements and his infrequent kisses. She whispered it in his ear, nails dragging down his scalp. 'I was thinking of you. I wanted you.'

'I thought of you too.'

Aurelia froze as the tips of her fingers grazed the scars on his shoulder blades. He breathed his sharp consent. 'It doesn't hurt. Touch me, Rory. I want you – to touch me.'

Something about that broken request shattered her. She touched him everywhere, tugged his hair, and dug possessive fingers into his hips. He slid his arm beneath her waist and pulled them together, burying himself to the hilt. He hitched her legs around his waist, moving them together, and with another sharp thrust, she reached that blistering orgasm with her palms pressed into the uneven scars on Teddy Ingram's back. Her body arched in the heat of her pleasure. He bit down on her shoulder and silenced a strangled noise of his own.

Her ears rang, but her mind was still. It was rarely ever that still. Her mind hadn't been so quiet in years. Aurelia clung to him, wanting to preserve it.

He slid to his elbows moments after, spent and slicked with sweat, and he kissed her forehead where his own had last laid. His lips mouthed the words 'ages ago', but made no sound. He shut his eyes and trained his breath, and he kept her silence perfectly intact. As if he knew already.

He always seemed to know.

A T-shirt flew toward her face, and she caught it clumsily. 'Don't think I'm not absolutely pleased by having you naked in my bed, but I knew a girl who liked to remind me of how warm I was.' Teddy smiled to himself, adjusting his black briefs around his waist.

'Damn her,' Aurelia muttered. 'She's missing out now.'

The grey fabric smelled of his usual scent of earth and citrus as she pulled it over her body. She breathed in a second longer than usual, committing it to memory, pinning down every point thus far in which she'd allowed it to penetrate her lungs.

'Can I keep this?'

Afront his dresser, Teddy turned to face her, luminescent under the moonlight and still unclothed save for his briefs. He leaned forward, kissed her gently and answered, 'It's yours. I'll be back in a second.'

Aurelia burrowed into his duvet, wearing nothing but her underwear and his shirt, and she watched closely as he disappeared into his bathroom. He started the sink, scrubbed his face, and all the while she was left to imagine what it looked like as he stood before the mirror and carried out his nightly routine behind the half-shut door.

Out of all the things they'd shared, the mundanity of his life was something she didn't completely understand. When the whisper of running water died, she thought he might be playing with his hair or tugging at his cheeks until his eyes grew uncommonly long and sad. Perhaps he was eyeing an inconsistency in the mirror, or a mark that didn't please him – one that was easier to see than the lashes on his back but impossible to find by anyone else.

Most insecurities were palimpsests, scars long since grown over but still feared. People like them had been the bearers of far too many not to spend a handful of minutes searching for them in the mirror.

Maybe, though, he was smoothing lotion over his arms, lathering it over every knuckle on his hands to keep them soft and unburdened. That was a comforting thought. A lasting ritual.

Aurelia debated on a shower herself. It wasn't *that* late – her phone read ten o'clock exactly, as well as showing a few text messages from Ryan. She typed a quick response for each and added simply, *Staying the night. I'll text you tomorrow xx*. Then, she replaced her phone on Teddy's nightstand, on which sat a cylindrical lamp and a short stack of books. At the top rested his copy of *Sir Gawain and the Green Knight.*

She slid closer to his nightstand and opened to the first page. The familiar blue scrawl of his handwriting littered the margins of the first fit. Aurelia traced her fingers over them as she examined both sets of text.

She would miss his cleverness. It came through in every needless scratch of ink. He'd read it before – they'd had to analyse it in their first year as medieval history students, when they'd first discovered just how threatening the other could be. As much as his presence antagonized her, Aurelia didn't know if there was ever a time since meeting him that she thought they'd be apart. If there was any other researcher whose work she'd want to dissect . . . another face to scowl at during a quiet lull in her lectures.

It'd be boring without him there. Maybe boring was exactly what she needed now.

Teddy reappeared, a shoulder propped against the doorframe. He was wearing a T-shirt, even though she hadn't seen him leave with one. His hair remained unkempt from her hands and his face held some of the redness from the steam of hot water. He flashed a reserved grin, folding his arms over the faded image on his shirt.

Aurelia leaned forward, clasped his warm, damp face between her hands and brought their lips together.

The only way she wanted to kiss him was deeply.

Slowly, he crawled into the side of the bed she'd left most open. Her hands found the edge of his shirt as he moved, and she pulled away to say, 'Let me see. I can't see it in the dark.'

'Must you need to know everything?' he drawled.

'Yes,' she replied. 'Is it more French new wave? German techno?'

'No. I learned my lesson on making mention of that with you.'

He obliged her as she pulled the hem of his shirt down and

leaned back to take in the image. 'Fontaines D.C.'; it sounded vaguely familiar.

Teddy plucked her hands away easily and slid his long legs under the covers.

They configured together in a confident reiteration of the first time she'd asked him to come to bed with her – one of his arms beneath her head, the other around her back, her arms between them. But there had been fewer words then with respect to all their dread, so she'd tucked her head beneath his chin and slept. This time, she wanted him to look at her, to fall asleep looking at him until the *next thing* came and she wouldn't be allowed to any more.

The hand that wasn't currently trapped beneath her rose up to Aurelia's cheek and adored it.

'Hi,' Teddy said.

'Hey.'

His eyes scanned over every feature of her face, blue scrawl written beside the image of her he kept in his mind. She yearned to know what it read. She had the distinct feeling that Teddy Ingram wouldn't be thinking of her in that green dress any more, but rather like this, in his bed, cheeks flushed in a way that only happened after good sex.

'I think I had something important to say, but you look so unreasonably sexy in my clothes now that I can't seem to think of anything else.'

'As opposed to?' she asked.

'Ghastly,' he told her. 'A creature of Lovecraftian proportions.'

Her nose crinkled again, which he noticed even in the dark.

'You know,' he started, 'there was a moment when we were at the Tate where I was looking at you – and we were talking about shapeshifters – and I wondered if something terribly wrong was happening to me. Because things were so fucked, and I was so bloody tired that I would have fallen asleep on the tube if we hadn't been made to stand. But there you were . . . I'd never looked at you for that long, with that feeling, so I wondered if it wasn't even *you* standing next to me. In which case, I was done for.'

In his pause, Aurelia asked, 'What feeling would that be?'

Teddy began the impossible task of separating each of her curls with delicate fingers.

'Helplessness,' he admitted. 'You looked so beautiful. And I'd had my arm around you that night as if that was something I already knew, but I'd been refusing to believe it up until then. It felt like everything I'd believed about you and myself and our *magic* had been dismantled and rearranged against my will; and I didn't really know what to do any more except that I wanted to go home and take you with me. More than anything, I wanted to run. It wouldn't have solved anything, and Leona would have had another day to wreak her havoc, but I wish we could have left that night unruined. I think I would have mustered up the courage to kiss you by then. And now I'm stuck with the disgustingly unfair knowledge that you would have let me.'

Teddy smoothed a strand of hair behind her ear and added, 'That's something I'll never get back.'

His fingers travelled down the length of her short hair to her shoulder, where the scar lay hidden by the borrowed shirt.

Goosebumps raised under the path of his touch, up from her elbow to the shoulder beneath the sleeve.

'You wrinkled your nose at me once while we were upstairs,' Teddy said. 'That's how I knew it was real. That you were still with me. If I had to be there with anyone, it was you.'

'I knew you by your walk,' Aurelia rushed. 'It's a little uneven.'

'Didn't think anyone noticed that. It's . . . such a *small* thing.' Teddy smiled, and then he leaned forward and pressed that smile against the scar on her shoulder. 'Sometimes I think you are the only one who sees me.'

'And you're going away,' she whispered.

'As you so love to remind me.'

'That's not true.' Aurelia perched onto her elbow until they were face to face once more, a mirror and its subject, two selves trying to find something they didn't recognize. 'I hate it.'

He tore his gaze away. 'So do I. I'm tired of all this. The running, the hiding, the *danger*. I know I'll miss Cambridge once I'm gone, but I never thought I'd have to miss you like this.'

'Maybe it's better if we just . . .'

'Maybe.' Teddy leaned back against his pillow and lost himself in a thought, his eyes on the edges of his books. 'What do you think I'll do once I leave?'

'Move on, probably.'

'Hmm.'

Aurelia didn't know if she wanted him to argue with her on it. Couldn't decide what choice she'd make, knowing that she might make one tonight and regret it tomorrow, repeating the cycle until her indecision ruined her once more.

'Do you want me to?' he asked.

In a motion almost indiscernible, she shook her head, saying nothing. Voicing it would make it too real.

'OK. Come here.' His hand scaled through her hair again, knotting into it as she bent forward to kiss him. She wanted to pry apart his ribs and crawl between them. How long could he hold her there in his chest? How long could they carry onward in this delicate state?

Not long, she decided. *Not long at all.*

She nipped his bottom lip and pressed herself harder into him as if he might absorb her. It'd be nice, for a change, to not worry about all the things she worried about – to not hear all that noise. Her knee slid over his hip. His erection pulsed beneath her. It would have been effortless to slip her underwear to the side and let him take her again.

'We don't have to,' he whispered. 'I know you're tired.'

She lied, 'I'm not tired,' and hitched forward against his pelvis, drawing up a soft groan from deep within his lungs. 'We could have each other all night. Unless you don't—'

He shook his head, already firm beneath her. 'Quite the opposite.' Aurelia reached for the nightstand herself, tearing open another wrapper with a patient drag. His fingers grazed her thighs, drawing up goosebumps and soft hairs. They slid over her calves, down to her ankles, up to the place where her borrowed shirt pooled around her.

She sat up and slid his briefs down, widened her knees, and eased him inside of her again, already pliant and slick.

From here, she noticed how he held his breath, the places he'd touch with his palms instead of his fingers. He loved the bend in her hips and the hollow at the bottom of her ribs. Those soft hands which now only bore the blemish of Leona's knife fitted her hips in rhythm around his.

She was a text to read twice, three times over. One whose margins he'd imbue with his own words and fingerprints. He sat up underneath her, tipped her chin back with a hooked finger and learned the colour of her neck after he'd tainted it with his mouth, so carefully that Aurelia almost forgot it had Leona's bruises on it first. Then, Teddy arched her back to discover that the colour was the same when he tainted her breasts and her sternum.

She wanted to tell him. *I love you, I love you, I love you so much that I cannot think about what comes next.*

But saying those three words aloud would make it too real. Make it hurt more. If love was a defacement for him, she would let him write over the memory of the knife and sharp teeth. She whispered his name as she canted her hips against his, pretending it meant the same thing. How she loved him whenever she'd ruined his hair. How she loved him as her fingers grazed the lashes in his back. She held his shirt within her fists and tugged it off him again, if only to experience his fullness again before it disappeared. The skin, the scars, the memory of feathers and talons . . .

They stayed up late and pretended they had time. They pretended they weren't tired, even as their movements became languid and clumsy. And when, at last, she succumbed to sleep with Teddy's face tucked into her shoulder, she pretended that this was a beginning instead of an end.

It was blissfully quiet in her mind.

CHAPTER THIRTY-TWO

It wasn't like mornings she'd had before. Rather than hurried *goodbyes*, she met the beams of light cast by Teddy's window with toleration. She had fallen asleep twice, the first time interrupted by the visceral memory of Leona's claws around her throat, at which point Teddy pulled her back against his chest and kissed her hair. 'I'm here, Schwartz. Right here.'

'It's so real,' she'd whispered. 'Every time I see her – every time I *feel* her.'

'*I'm* real,' he said, 'and I've got you.'

He placed another kiss in the shadow behind her ear. With that promise, sleep consumed her again. When she woke, it felt as if no time had passed at all.

This is how it should be, she thought. Like homecoming. Like relief.

The sound of steel utensils and Louisa's mousy voice wafted up through the cracked door. Teddy was asking if Louisa wanted to go to the market a few streets away, and she agreed emphatically. In the previous night's clothing, Aurelia crept down the hallway. A hardwired instinct in her brain commanded her to be as unassuming as possible, to escape without drawing attention, avoiding a need for *goodbyes.* Except she wasn't going anywhere this time. Not yet.

Teddy was attentive toward the eggs in his skillet, seasoning them. The toaster perked up with perfectly browned slices behind him, which he plated and slid to Louisa for buttering.

The young girl spotted Aurelia in the doorway and swarmed her. 'Aurelia, will you come with us to the market?'

Over her head, Teddy mouthed, 'You don't have to.'

'Do you want me to?' she asked Louisa.

'Yes, please!'

Aurelia tugged Louisa's crinkly pigtails and nodded. 'Sounds like a plan, then.'

Teddy smiled, sliding two cooked eggs onto a plate. 'Brush your teeth, you little heathen. So we can leave sooner.'

Aurelia crossed to him once the girl left and threaded her arms around his waist, sinking her cheek into his shoulder blades. Through the fabric of his T-shirt, she felt the beginning of the line of roughened skin and kissed it. It wasn't an intention or the darkness of her blood that gave it power, but the sweet, unencumbered affection. His mother said he was a hard person to love, but Aurelia couldn't imagine anything easier.

He peered at her over his shoulder, one eyebrow cocked. 'Thought you might want some space.'

Her voice was muffled against his shirt. 'You're *so* wrong.'

'Hmm.' Teddy craned an arm around her and pulled her to his side. 'That's better. You all right, Schwartz?'

'Great. Just hungry.'

He pointed to the two recently plated eggs with his spatula, whispering words into her hair. 'Those are yours. Eat.'

Ingram brushed his lips against the parting of her hair. The sweetest kinds of spells were the ones whispered for her ears alone.

She watched him dress after breakfast, from the bed to keep warm. He brushed his teeth, then kissed her, stealing each moment of closeness he could find. The actuality of their future might not relent, but they could forge something secret, full of lingering touches and wishful thoughts, and then stow it away.

She kissed him hard, without any of the hesitation that often came with *morning afters*, because who knew when or if they'd have another? Time could not touch them in the alcove of her memory. It couldn't undo what tenderness he'd already imbued into her lips or what affection she'd given up to him; nor would it fill the gaps that Townsend left in her edifice. They'd remain just as he did, an empty house of ache and longing.

He chose a wrinkled collared shirt instead of his usual turtleneck, and wound a scarf around himself that she'd never seen but *knew* had to have come from Gemma. While he gazed into the mirror, torturing his hair into perfection, Aurelia curled her fingers into the knit and adjusted it over a spot on his neck she'd marked with her lips the night before. That scarf was the only bit of colour in his uniform of black and grey, but the earth tones drew out the pink in his cheeks and the olive green from his eyes in a work of wonder – as if such colours were never fully realized until they were adorned on him.

She glimpsed the quirk of his mouth in the mirror's reflection as she rose onto her toes and bit his cheek. The bitten skin turned from pink to red with his fluster.

At the market, he pulled Louisa onto his shoulders so she could see the vastness of it, his small corner of an endless world that she had yet to explore. The girl giggled, ruining the tidiness of his hair, then urged him into shop after shop. Aurelia bought her housemate a new plant – a promise that she'd spend the rest of her life tending.

Late afternoon descended over Cambridge, and with new blues and a sweep of orange came the moment where she should have said goodbye. To Lou, she offered a firm embrace that swept the young girl off her feet once more, and a 'see you soon'.

For Teddy, she had even fewer words. She'd already said everything worth saying that wasn't 'goodbye'.

Lingering by her door as he dropped her off, Teddy Ingram took her into his arms and kissed her again with tongue, teeth and hunger. Hands that promised nights and mornings and all the time between that. He kissed her cheeks, until that torturous, longing ache became a bubbling giddiness.

He rested the back of his knuckles on her forehead. 'You're warm,' he said.

'Feverish again?'

He kissed her another time, his grin sealed on her lips. 'No. Just flushed.'

He moved that kiss to the place on her forehead left cold by the ghost of his hand. His thumbs glided across her cheekbones, fingers curving around the back of her neck. They wove through her curls, beneath the collar of her jacket, fisting into the fabric of her dress as if he could sew himself into it.

She should have been embarrassed of how he touched her

simply for the sake of touching her; but she'd been no better, braving the cold outside her door to keep kissing him.

She knew he had to go home. To pack his things and pull himself out of her orbit.

'Take care of Lou.' It came out of her mouth like a question, and the familiar crease between his eyebrows reappeared. She rested her own against it. 'Don't let magic become something she fears. Or you for that matter. I like you so much better as a witch.'

'I won't,' he assured her, too firmly for a person who had seemingly rejected magic all his life. She pushed her nails through his hair and tugged, wanting to believe him. Wondering if, after all this, believing Theodore Ingram was the right thing to do.

When he left, she resigned herself to doing what she knew best, and missed everything terribly.

EPILOGUE

No one in their homes could recall the movement or the sound, but they discovered, at some point, that some of the walls of the Tate Modern had folded in on themselves, and learned that the epicentre of an earthquake had struck London days before . . . They wondered, watching the story break on their screens. Collectors came for their pieces, only to find glamoured curators and directors with canned apologies on the tips of their tongues.

In London, something happened at the Tate Modern that could only be described as a hiccup in time.

In Cambridge, Aurelia Schwartz unearthed the book that Teddy Ingram had slipped into her bag, finding her name at the top of that page of blue ink – his at the end. She read his letter in her bedroom, then tucked it back inside *Sir Gawain and the Green Knight*, missing him profoundly, missing Townsend.

In Namwon, South Korea, a caretaker named Ji Hye-Jin awoke to the sound of shuffling in her library. She muttered beneath her breath, ignited the lamp beside her low bed, and heaved herself down the steps toward her collection.

'Hye-Jin,' she heard a man whisper. 'Did I wake you?'

She confirmed it with a grumble. 'It's late. You come unannounced.'

'Because it is important.'

Alaric Friedman. He always came with important tasks, though his visits had become less frequent throughout the past year. A threat had arisen in his country and kept his attention, to both the relief and trouble of the other caretakers. If he had returned to his usual practice of turning up in places without forewarning, that threat was either quelled or more dire than before.

She found him by the vault, where she kept the vast majority of her collection under enchanted locks. He looked tired, although it must have been daytime in England, where she knew he spent most of his time. Hye-Jin couldn't be sure. Her eyes strained under the dim, red light as she pulled her robe tightly around her body.

'Have you brought me more trouble, Friedman? It's been a long time since you bothered *my* collection.'

He did not deny it, nor did he say much else. Alaric Friedman merely slipped a small, locked box from his spacious coat pocket and held it out to her. 'I need you to store something for me. Can you do that?'

'Does it belong in my vault?'

Every caretaker was tasked with a different thing to care for. Within the vault in Namwon, Ji Hye-Jin kept potions – ones that surpassed the calibre of human-made concoctions. There were poisons for masses, elixirs of eternal life, with powers that only she and the other caretakers could harness, for they were the only ones who knew to what extent magic could transform.

'No,' Alaric answered. 'But I've been asked to take this far from England.'

'Oh, Alaric,' said Hye-Jin. 'What do you get yourself into?'

'Hopefully, nothing,' he said. 'Inside this box is a wandering eye. I've taken to covering it, but should it need to be removed, let no one else see it. It's been formed from a very valuable artefact that should not have fallen into private hands.'

'This *is* trouble,' Hye-Jin whispered.

'I will take care of it. Give me a few months for the dust to settle. Until then, I need it gone from my library – and my shop.'

Ji Hye-Jin accepted the small box, examining the wood for no reason other than to distract herself from his curiosity.

'Can you do that?' Alaric asked again.

'Yes,' she told him. 'But this is a wandering eye, you say?'

'It is.'

'Who is on the other end?'

He pushed his glasses up his long nose and crossed his arms over his chest. 'There *was* a shapeshifter. One with bad intentions. Someone that needed to be taken care of.'

'And now?'

Alaric cleared his throat in that irritating manner he sometimes used to change the subject. 'I'm figuring that out.'

'Does it need to be brought forth to the council?'

Alaric shook his head. He was a sore thumb on the hand of the council, but Hye-Jin was told that he had been better than his father, and that had to count for something.

She escorted him to a door that, when opened, showed the warmth of his library in Luxembourg. He hovered in the doorway, and she offered him a slow, conciliatory smile as she secured the box beneath her arm.

'Thank you,' he said. 'It's been too long.'

'Next time, do not wake me,' she said. 'I was having the most wonderful dream.'

Schwartz—

There's a line in this translation by Marie Borroff that made me think of you. 'On the inner part of his shield her image portrayed, That when his look on it lighted, he never lost heart.' In Tolkien's translation, it goes, 'that when he cast his eyes thither his courage never failed.' It comes early, but there's something so poignant about devotion that drives men to impossible deeds.

A lot of what I do at Pembroke is read translations. I read six of Sir Gawain and the Green Knight last Lent term, and each one was like a layer unpeeled from the same epic romance – a petal unfolded. A new orator in my ear shedding light on a dark corner that I overlooked in my quest to understand.

I used to think I understood you. Still, sometimes I do, but under a much softer light. I know fairness is subjective, but I can't imagine anyone finds it more unfair than me that there was ever a time I didn't adore you. You were cruel. Stubborn. Horribly evasive. Quick to tell me I was wrong. And none of that has changed throughout our time here, but I know now that your stubbornness makes you an achiever. I know that it was my fault you felt the need to be cruel.

I'll even admit that a fifth of the times you told me I was wrong, you were right. But you'll get nowhere trying to fight those odds, Schwartz. You are brilliant enough as it is to get a fifth when no one else gets me at all.

Mostly, I've stopped thinking of you as a bad inevitability like London traffic and more like the silver linings around dark clouds. I started hoping you would find me at the top of Gemma's stairs or outside by her chickens just to strike up a chat with me. The inevitable nature of you became something I loved. For once, I hoped we could be inevitable too.

Maybe you were in the process of rewriting everything I thought I knew about you. Maybe I just knew you at your first translation. I prefer the latter, simply so you can't have the second fifth of telling me I was ever wrong. You and I have always understood each other perfectly – just in fragments. Through lenses I never thought I'd want to switch out so badly.

I'd like to think I'm unbiased enough to translate something in different ways. That I could make Sir Gawain take another six forms, and I could unravel every new piece of you that I managed to get my hands on. Figure out the best way to make you tea. What kind of books I'd have to keep on my shelf to make you come around? I like you, Schwartz. Sometimes I think I wanted you even when I wanted to hate you too.

I wish we had more time. Maybe, sometime in the future, we will. I know you well enough to know you never leave a task unfinished, and I'll bet anything there's more to us than what we got. Inevitability was never meant to be finite, and I'm hoping that, out of everything I've said to you, I can still be right about that.

So, consider me stirred by this development. This is my favourite translation.

Yours,

Teddy

ACKNOWLEDGEMENTS

Modern Divination was self-published in January 2023 with its own set of acknowledgements. Since then, I've been so fortunate to work with a handful of editors, authors and publishing professionals at Pan Macmillan to bring this book to a wider range of readers.

Brace yourselves, reader. I have a lot of love and gratitude to share from both iterations of *Modern Divination.*

Thank you to my first editor, Marina Green; my original cover illustrator, Nastya Litepla; my interior artist, Kirsten Valerie Driggers. Without your invaluable work and insight, which undoubtedly earned the self-published version of *Modern Divination* much of its notoriety, this version of the book might not exist. It is because you gave this indie author a chance that they were able to finagle their way to the big leagues. I adore you all.

To my superstar of an agent, Sheyla Knigge: you complete me. I am eternally grateful that the universe brought us together when it did. Your unwavering faith in me and fierce advocacy is more than I could have ever asked for. It overwhelms me sometimes, how much you believe in me. You make me believe that my ambitions might *actually* be within reach; that's simultaneously terrifying and freeing. You are magical. Let's write so many weird books together.

Thank you to Gillian Green at Tor/Pan Macmillan for seeing the promise in that book. I will always feel proud of what that book was before, but I could work on this book for ever and find new things to change every day. I was so damn thrilled to be able to return to it with new edits and fresh eyes. I'm so honoured to have the opportunity to do that with you. To the editorial team at Pan Macmillan, including Kate Tolley and Judith Leask: thank you for being so patient with me during a tumultuous debut experience. I worked with you while grieving a loss and moving across the country, and you made everything so much easier to manage.

To all the artists and designers who have, in any capacity, contributed to *Modern Divination*'s success, including my enormously skilled jacket illustrator Em Allen and the utterly impressive Little Chmura. I love you. I treasure you. I am so honoured to have made the inspiration behind such beautiful bookish art. To every fan artist who has ever drawn Teddy and Rory, you are the passion that compels me to create.

Even before my book deal, I was surrounded by other authors. *Modern Divination* would not exist if not for my love of their stories. I'm blessed to be able to call some of these authors my friends now. Thank you to every author who was generous enough to provide a blurb: Ava Reid, Allison Saft, Lyndall Clipstone, Skyla Arndt, Hannah Whitten and Olivie Blake.

Special thanks to Sarah Underwood, who was my first writing friend back when Camp NaNoWriMo still had cabins, and to Sophia Slade, with whom I often lost my mind. You ground me. I ride for you for ever.

Thank you to all the readers and booksellers who supported me in my author infancy. To Kassie Weeks and Eden Hakimzadeh for uplifting me and cheering me on when I was too insecure to think my book was worth even a humble signing event. I miss you guys all the time. You deserve the world. To the baristas who let me sit in their coffee shops too long, and to the crew at Coastal Film Lab who distracted me from my work all the time by being so damn funny. To the folks who always interact with my Instagram stories when I'm nervous about sharing excerpts: thank you for taking a chance on me. You didn't have to do it, but I'm so happy you did.

Thank you to my parents, who support me from both coasts, over countless phone calls and barrage of animal photos. To my partner, who supports me in person, enables me in bookstores and feeds my *X-Files* obsession. I think, should any of you read my books in totality, I would want to pitch myself into the sea. Luckily, I don't think you will, but you love me all the same.

To my most beloved friends who might *actually* read this: Andrea Cayasso, Gabrielle Marchicelli and Grace Alberti; and to my roommate, Maeghan Morrow, who makes writing roommates such a blast that they all seem unrealistic. I'm kissing you all on the mouth through this page. Kiss kiss.

Lastly, I want to thank my cat, Mosse, who cannot read but deserves the thanks anyway. You got me out of some rough times, buddy. Here's to many more evening writing sprints with you curled up on my lap, keeping me warm, even when it hindered my word count. We got the job done, anyhow.

ABOUT THE AUTHOR

Isa Agajanian (they/them) is a writer and illustrator living in the United States. Raised in California and spirited away to Florida, then Oregon, Isa is never writing in one place for too long. They are joined in their pursuit of good stories by a hefty grey cat named Mosse and at least one roommate at a time. *Modern Divination* is their first published novel.